AF574390

WHAT READERS ARE SAYING:

It's a story of love, a story of hate; a story of joy, a story of pain; a story of fear, and a story of power. And it is not the power of white male supremacy that endures here, but rather the quiet, gentle knowingness of her own identity that Kate is able to claim once she recognizes the totality of her being . . . and nobody can take that away from her. The story touched me deeply. The journey through it was intense. It stirred up anger and hopelessness, then a deep sense of sadness -- a sadness felt over the reality of the oppression that has indeed existed. Yet, I did not put the manuscript down with hopelessness and sadness, but with a renewed sense of my own power as a woman. Pat Kemerer: psychologist

I'm not sure I can put into words the depth of my reaction to your book. My 'womanness' responded with no conscious effort on my part. That's the very special part of **The Fourth Woman** to me: the continuity of 'women'. Oppression will not continue to work. I hope your book is extremely successful; it is beautiful. And it brings a real message of strength and hope. Thank you for the pain, the courage, and the spirit of womanness that produced it. Now I have a clear knowledge of the dues you paid to be a woman - For us all! Pat Sexton: teacher

I had just finished the first section when my husband came home. I was crying. He said, "You've been reading Audrey's book, haven't you?" Joan Morris: cooking instructor

I loved your book. I bathed myself in your words. You painted an incredible picture for me.. When I finished I was sorry. Stephanie Kendall: businesswoman

I found the plot very intriguing and each individual woman developed with layers of emotional character. I felt each of those women's lives deeply. It brought up fear, anger and resentment at how women have taken the brunt of men's sexual desires and abuses for centuries...centuries. Sherri Southard: artist, teacher

Audrey, you have written a lovely and important book, one that was an absolute joy to read. It involved me deeply and affected me deeply. It was so real and so mystical all at once. What was most powerful for me was how the book, the ideas, and especially the women all stayed with me afterwards, lingering, settling, becoming a part of my conscious and subconscious. Their effect on me was so powerful. It is a book I will remember always. Marika Blades: actress

THE FOURTH WOMAN

AUDREY SAVAGE

Word WeaverPublishing Co.
Indianapolis

THE FOURTH WOMAN
by
Audrey Savage

Published by:

Word Weaver Publishing Co.
Post Office Box 30072
Indianapolis, Indiana 46230

Printed in the United States of America

printing number
1 2 3 4 5 6 7 8 9 10

ISBN 0-929698-00-2 Softcover

This book is dedicated to four women:

Jenny - my grandmother, who gave me my soul.

Kate - who gave me more than she knows.

Lena - who gave me her greatest gift when she gave me her trust.

Lee - who has loved me through it all.

Can you hear it? This powerful
yet gentle wind that moves
through the centuries?
That touches us all - that inspires
by its sound and its touch -
that moves us, that pushes us . . .
away from stolidity. away from
immobility - toward our goals and
destinies.

It whispers to us about the greatness
and beauty we possess -
It compells us to fulfill the plan
for us all
It argues against the oppression
that has slowed us in our process

It caresses to rebuild our faith
and self-confidence and over-
come our fears
It calls - each time more insis-
tentently - for us to be all that
we are and have always been.
It asks that we answer and add
our own whisper or cry or shout

to this moving force
to be heard and felt through
eternity
It beckons:
Come . . . *Be . . .*
be strong and powerful
be loving and nurturing
be sensual and beautiful
It demands:
Come . . .
Be . . .
Woman . . .

. . . by Pat Sexton

TABLE OF CONTENTS

Acknowledgments VIII

Beginning 1

The First Woman - Duanna (1503 - 1524) 22

The Second Woman - Sabia (1762 - 1783) 105

The Third Woman - Amanda Rochelle (1883 - 1912) 193

The Fourth Woman - Kate (1931 -). 303

About the Author 423

Order Blank 425

Acknowledgments:

In making these acknowledgments, I need to thank the people (and there were many) who told me no, as well as those who told me yes. It is, perhaps, true that those who said no, no matter how insensitively, taught me more than those who encouraged and helped me. First, I want to acknowledge the myriad of publishers who sent me enough rejection slips to paper not only my bathroom, but my living room (some were large slips - letters, even). Then, I want to acknowledge four 'no saying' literary agents who strongly influenced the style of my writing and my self-confidence. Mary Yost asked to see the manuscript when it was still mostly an outline in my head. Her rudeness in the way she returned it, after a year of writing, made a marked impression on me. Elizabeth Pamada encouraged me to rewrite . . . then she rejected it. Lisa Collier Cool thought it would be hard to sell to publishers. Vickie Bijur essentially said the same thing, but said it in such a way that I was validated as a writer. Each of these women gave me a new piece of determination. Mary caused me to question my writing ability to the point where I was willing to rewrite and rewrite until I and my readers were totally satisfied. Elizabeth gave me a piece of encouragement at a time when I was about to give up. Lisa, inadvertently, told me that publishers would **not** buy my book, but not because it was a bad book. Vickie praised both the writing and the story in such a way that I became convinced that even though publishers would be unlikely to buy my manuscript, it **had** to be published. I owe all of these women a great debt of gratitude.

Two events influenced my pursuing this project when a more sensible woman would have given up. The judges of an international writer's contest sponsored by *Manuscripts* awarded my book Honorable Mention out of a field of 5,300 writers. They said things like "dynamic, unforgettable story", "Caused a bit of a stir", "Job well done," and other good words designed to give me confidence in my book. They suggested an editor to clean it up a bit. I chose Nan Dibble of Writer's Digest Editing Service. Her words will be forever etched in my brain. "You don't need me: you need a publisher!" I couldn't give up after words like that.

Well, it did need an editor . . . and it did need a lot of cleaning up. For cleaning it up . . . time after time after time . . . I want to thank Pat Sexton, a writer in her own right. You will remember her name from the front of this book. Once, after typing late into the night to get it ready for one publisher or another, she was inspired to write the beautiful words of the poem with which I have opened this book. Her eloquence in writing the poem, her knowledge in correcting the mess of my punctuation, spelling, and wording, and her friendship and encouragement throughout this long ordeal have been invaluable.

For editing, Kate Struck deserves top billing. Early in my writing, during my first inadequate steps, she pushed and prodded, cajoled and argued and essentially expressed her undiluted feelings about what I was saying. Some of it was great fun, some of it was not fun at all, but it was **all** unsurpassed in its usefulness. Sarah Blandina tried very hard to make a smooth writer out of a turnip. Sometimes she succeeded and sometimes I remained a turnip. Charlotte Wright took the manuscript in its final stages and got rid of (most) of the rough edges. I reserved the right to keep **some** of my rough edges through eternity. What I know is that each of these women should be writing their own books, not editing mine. I hope, when that time comes, I can be as useful to them as they were to me.

Paula Frantz painted this incredible cover. When she unveiled it to me, I couldn't believe my eyes. I was pulled into the picture, as much as I had been pulled into the four lives that have taken so much of my attention for the past four years. Paula's psychic seeing of my four women, and her spiritual nature gave her the depth of perception to paint a cover, that might just sell the book. And this is only one of the talents of this multifaceted woman.

The natural language of black Americans is both rich and powerful. Many of the characters in this book would not have existed if they could not have spoken in their own natural way. I want to thank the many black Americans who inadvertently taught me their language, and I especially want to thank Andrew Thomas and Pat Sexton for carefully scrutinizing my accuracy, and Andrew for serving as the model for Amon, Tacuma, Aaron and especially Joshua.

This book would not have been published if it had not been for my readers; readers who gave me their excitement as well as both positive and negative feedback at its various stages. The prize goes to Chris Ohler, who read it in one sixteen-hour sitting. Second prize goes to Marika Blades, first, for listening to me tell the story as she was captive in my car on a long trip, and then for her excitement after reading it. I also thank Lee Verner, Nancy Jones, Joan Morris, Denise Herron, Sherri Southard, Pavla Miles, Stephanie Kendall, Pat Kemcrer, Julie Joy, Gay Reese, Judy Guernsey, Judy Pollack, Sherelyle Geen, MiltonWhaley and Nancy Fritz for their perceptive critiques. Milton and Nancy were espcially important during the early writing; during my first lonely year.

One last person needs to be thanked, and his contribution was without equal. This person helped me untangle the confused mess of trying to operate this computer. He very patiently explained what to do, how to do it, and then wrote it all down in **language I could understand**. God bless him. My son-in-law, Michael Bowman. And I need to thank his wife, my daughter, Terri Bowman, for her patience while our two heads bent over this machine, or a book that explained this machine, for hour after hour after hour. We were not much fun to talk to.

And many thanks to a higher intelligence that kept me hanging in there in spite of all the setbacks.

The

Fourth

Woman

Audrey Savage

"There is a destiny to fulfill"
Duanna p.19

CHAPTER 1

It was the dreams. Night after night, it was the dreams. For weeks, her demons had prowled through her nights. Her demons in female form. There were three of them. They named themselves. "Amanda," said one. "Duanna," said another. "Sabia," said a third.

They came and they went. They revealed themselves; they hid themselves. They darted at her from all sides. They stood solemnly in front of her. They talked voluminous words. They were silent.

She heard sounds: the groaning of slaves on a ship; the cacophony of the jungle; the screaming of a woman in pain; the moaning of lovers; the melody of a guitar playing the blues; the pounding of drums; the pounding in her ear; her scream in the night.

She saw the scenes: a burning cross on the lawn; white-sheeted men-like ghosts in the night; a man hanging - from a tree; a baby - dead and buried; a sword - coming at her; a fire burning - waiting for her; her scream in the night.

She knew them, one from another. Then she knew them not. Duanna with the olive skin and the natural beauty. Duanna, who skipped and played, with her long black hair flowing in the wind, and then died. Sabia, the magical, whose coal black skin shone as she wept for her enslaved lover. Amanda, soft and sensuous, buffeted about by the torments of circumstances she could not control.

All alive. So alive. All dead!

And earrings that swung from every ear. The same, yet different. Long. Shiny. Like tears, they hung from the ear. Symbols of love, never to be disconnected. Predictive of death to come.

And there were men. "Amon," he told her, as he stood tall in princely robes. "Tacuma," he said, wearing nothing. "Aaron," he whispered. Shy. Gentle. In love. Dead! The echo behind them all of "Joshua", "Joshua", "Joshua", "Joshua". They held out their arms. She floated into them. They disappeared. "Whyyyyyyyyyyyy?" she screamed into the night.

Then it was the one with the olive skin, standing by the sea. "Hear me," she said, "hear my words. Come to me before it's too late."

"I don't know where to come."

"Hear my words."

It was the quiet one, singing in the night. "Life is more than you know," she said. "Find it before it's too late."

"I don't know where to look," she said.

"Look to me."

It was the black one, of the ebony skin. "Find the magic," she said.

"Where is the magic?"

"In your spirit. In your spirit."

"Stop haunting me," she screamed in the night.

"We'll send you another," they said.

"One to give you magic," said the ebony skinned one..

"One to bring you to me," said the one of olive.

"One to help you live," said the one who sang in the night.

"Who is the other?" she said.

"We'll send her to you," they said in chorus.

And she was there - the other one

A mouth that moved, but spoke not.

And eyes! Eyes that pierced the very soul.

In a face as black as the one of ebony. And hair as white as the Chicago snow. Teeth that flashed in the wrinkled face. Old. As old as the wisest sage. And big! Bigger than the biggest of the men.

"Who are you?" she asked.

The wind howled. A clock ticked. There was a tap, tap, tapping on the floor.

"Who are you?" she asked again.

And then this other one went away into the darkness.

They were back . . . with the ebony skin, the songs in the night, and the earrings shining from their ears.

"Who is she?" she implored.

"Leeeeeeeeena," they said, as if on the wind. "Leeeeena. Find Leeeeeeeeeeeeena."

The wind howled.

Snow beat against the window.

She was up. Sitting at her desk. Crying. Pounding her fists on the hard wood. Afraid. "What do you want of me?" she yelled. "What do you want? You are driving me crazy!"

"Crazy. Crazy. Crazy," echoed through the room, bouncing from wall to wall.

"You're trying to send me back to the mental ward, aren't you?"

"Aren't you? Aren't you? Aren't you?" echoed through the room, bouncing from wall to wall.

She didn't know how long she sat there. She didn't know. Hours, perhaps. It was light before she got up from her chair. It was time to go to work. Snow was piling up on the Chicago streets; and the wind was sending its cold, cold message.

CHAPTER 2

Two days later, on December 15th in the year 1969, when the world was falling down around America's ears, Kate Andrews, consummate newspaper reporter, writer of books, and speaker in great demand, was standing in front of a house on South Damen in Chicago, Illinois . . . a house that contained the woman, Lena.

She stood there, with the wind - that famous Chicago wind - chilling her to the bone. She found herself in the midst of a sea of black faces, faces that stared suspiciously at her white skin; faces suspicious about what she was doing in their neighborhood.

She saw them without really seeing them. Her mind was on the woman inside that house: the woman, Lena. She was remembering how she had come to be here.

It was the morning after she had first seen Lena in her dreams . . . the morning after her three women had been so furious with her.

She'd come to work late, very late. Snow was clogging the Chicago streets and the bus had been interminably slow. Not only did she have those dreams to worry about but now she had to worry about being late.

She rushed into her cubicle, one arm out of her coat, kicking snow off her feet and trying to keep her damp hair out of her eyes.

"Late, huh?" said Leslie, her tall, lanky, cubicle mate, who'd shared that office space with her for seven years.

"Yes, and Ed will have my head. I was due to meet with him at nine."

"He's not here."

"He's what?"

"He's not here."

"Not here? Not here! He's not missed a day of work since the paper was founded in eighteen-ought-two, I'm sure. And he's never late."

"Well, he's not here."

"Will wonders never cease," said Kate, slumping down in her chair and pushing a lock of her damp hair out of her eyes. In her mind, Kate formed a quick picture of Ed: their short, squat, impossible editor, who never talked below a bellow, and was never without his foul cigar.

"It's a good thing you didn't manage to meet with 'his holiness' this morning. You look terrible."

"Thanks a lot, Leslie. I needed that."

"I'm serious. You haven't been looking yourself for almost a month now and I'm worried about you."

Kate sighed. Leslie wasn't telling her anything she didn't already know. Every time she looked into a mirror, she knew. She knew that the dreams, the sleepless nights and the worry about it all were taking their toll. She could see that her usually bouncy light brown hair was beginning to look bedraggled. The blue eyes that looked back at her from the mirror looked distinctly tired and the black circles underneath her eyes were deepening every day. ***And*** it was seriously affecting her good humor.

She slumped even further into her chair. "I know, Leslie. I know."

"You want to talk about it? . . . or not?"

Kate knew it was impossible to slide away from Leslie's intensity. Instead of trying she put her head in her hands and tried to fight back the tears. "I don't know. I. . . Leslie, sometimes. . . sometimes I think I'm going crazy again. I can't sleep; I haven't been eating; I've lost ten pounds I couldn't afford to lose; and I can't get them to leave me alone."

Leslie was trying to be calm after a statement designed to incur panic. Her imagination began working overtime. She had visions of some political hack Kate had written a story about dogging her footsteps night and day, calling her house at all hours, or generally making her life miserable. "Can't get ***who*** to leave you alone?" she said, much more calmly than she felt.

"The dreams. Three women, and another one. They won't leave me alone."

"Oh, I see," said Leslie, who didn't see anything at all. "Let's see if I've got it right. You're dreaming about three women and another one who won't leave you alone?"

"Yes. And they all want something from me and I don't know what it is," Kate wailed. "It's all so vague and distorted."

"As dreams usually are," said Leslie, trying to be practical, but pretty sure that Kate was not ready for her practicality.

"You see, they're all dead," said Kate... not only missing Leslie's practicality, but confusing the issue even more.

"The women?"

"Yes, the women." said Kate, as though Leslie would naturally know exactly what women she was talking about.

"Would you mind telling me what women?"

"The women in my dreams."

"Oh, of course." said Leslie. "Now I understand."

Kate took her head out of her hands and looked up when Leslie's sarcastic tone finally penetrated her foggy brain. "I'm sorry, Les. I guess you don't know what women I'm talking about."

"I certainly don't. You haven't been confiding in me for quite a while now

Kate dropped her head back in her hands. "No, I guess I haven't. It's been so awful and I've been so scared that I just couldn't talk about it."

"Of course . . . that's the best time not to talk about something. When you're scared and feeling awful."

Kate looked up again. "Stop teasing me Les. It really has been awful . . . and I just don't know what to do."

"Well, you can start by telling me about the women."

"Yes, I guess I can. You see, there are three of them. They've been . . . You won't think I'm crazy, will you Les?"

"I make no guarantees, Kate. All I can promise is to listen and you sure need someone to listen."

"Yeah, you're right about that."

"Now, just tell me about these women. You've got me hanging on the edge."

Kate laughed . . . for what seemed like the first time in months. "Well, see, they've been showing up in my dreams."

"Three of them."

"Yes, three of them. They are young and they are beautiful and they all want something from me . . . and I don't know what they want," said Kate, again losing her composure, looking at Leslie as if to say . . . 'Do something about these women.'

Leslie reached out and put her hand on Kate's arm. "Tell me what these women look like."

"Well one of them has long black hair and these big eyes and she always wears one of those . . . what do you call them . . . shifts, I think. Another one doesn't wear anything much. I think she wears a loin cloth some of the time. The other one has this long braid and she's black. She's the worst. She just gets really insistent."

Leslie wasn't sure she was understanding much more than she had before, but Kate was beginning to calm down. "And they all want something from you, is that right?"

"Yes, and I don't know what it is." said Kate, getting agitated again. I don't know what it is, and I know they are going to keep giving me nightmares until I understand. And I can't stand much more of this. I'm getting sick, Leslie. I'm getting sick. At first I was able to keep up with my work, but now I'm so tired and so distracted that I can't work."

Leslie tightened her grip on her friend's arm as if her grip would help Kate get the grip on herself she needed.

"Leslie, what can I do?"

"Haven't they given you any clues as to what they want of you?" said Leslie, deciding that she might as well join the craziness, realizing that she wouldn't get anywhere unless she went along with it.

"Well, last night they did, Yes. They were all so mad at me last night that they brought in this other women. They said they wanted me to see her. They said her name was Lena. She's old - maybe ninety - and she's huge: probably about three hundred pounds. She's very black, and I guess she's some kind of a psychic or something. They want me to find her; and I don't have a clue as to where to start."

"I might," said Leslie, in an incredulous whisper.

"I can't just look in the phone book under Lena, you know; that would lead me to zero . . . and . . . Leslie? What did you say?"

"I said I might."

"That's what I thought you said. Are you serious? Because if you are, you might just save my life."

"That bad, huh?"

"That bad. I think if I don't find this woman, my nightmares will send me back to the mental ward."

They laughed - both knowing it wasn't funny.

"Tell me, Leslie. Tell me," said Kate.

"Well, a couple of years ago, I tried to interview a woman named Lena, who looked just like the one you're describing. Good old Ed had heard about this incredible psychic, named Lena, who lived on the south side. He sent me out to do an interview. I went to her house and I saw her. But that's all I did - see her. She threw me right out of the house, pad and pencil in hand. As soon as I started through the door, her voice boomed out at me: 'You gits yourself out of this house right now! I ain talkin to no newspaper ladies. Git! Now!'"

"And Kate, I **got**. She is imposing, she is impossible: but I'm sure she's the one you're looking for."

"Oh, God, Leslie. That's all I need now: an impossible woman. She probably won't even see me."

"Hard to tell, but . . ." Leslie started rummaging through her desk. "I think I still have her phone number and address here. Yes, here it is." Leslie handed Kate a rumpled piece of paper containing an address on South Damen and a phone number.

"Just in time, Leslie. Here comes the cigar puffing down the hallway now."

The words were just out of her mouth when a head popped inside the cubicle. "I'll see you in my office . . . now!" said the head.

"I'll be right in, Ed," said Kate.

"Let me know how it all comes out," said Leslie.

"If I live, Leslie. If I live."

Leslie laughed, not at all sure but what Kate's fears might not be well-founded.

Leslie's forbodings had so intimidated her, that Kate's fingers shook as she dialed the number Leslie had given her, the number that felt so important that it would determine whether she lived or not. It was just after she had spent a grueling hour going over her inadequacies with Ed and she didn't need the trouble she was sure she was walking into. But the woman surprised her. "Where you been?" she demanded. "I's been richere by this phone two days now. You comes here Thursday roun 2 o'clock an I sees you." The phone went dead.

Now, on this Thursday, December 15th 1969, she was standing in front of a house - just a greying, white frame house with falling-apart steps. Nothing special. Just a house. And she was standing here because her feet had taken over her mind. They had decidedly frozen themselves to the ground. So she stood there, her feet unwilling to move, shivering under her heaviest coat. "Go in," she told herself. "Either go in or go home."

"I can't go in."

"Why not?"

"Becaues she'll unmask me. She knows who I am. She knows I'm not the superwoman I pretend to be. She knows how scared I am. She knows how much I hurt. She knows I used to be crazy. She'll unmask me for a fraud."

"Yes, she probably will."

"Then I can't go in."

"Then go home."

"I can't do that either."

"Then stand out here and freeze, dummy."

Kate walked to the door and rang the bell.

A small boy, around five, answered the bell. "You lookin for my Nana," he said. "She right in there." He pointed to an open door to the right side of the foyer.

Before she was even out of her coat, she heard the voice. The voice just boomed out at her from the indicated room. "You comes in here! Comes in here right now!"

Kate dropped her coat and ran.

It was Lena all right. It was Lena - the Lena of her dreams. Big. Imposing. Commanding even. And magnetic. Sitting in the same high-backed chair, holding the same walking stick . . . just like in her dream.

"Where you gits them earrings?" the woman demanded. "I sees em. I sees em hangin from your ears, fore you even comes in here. Where you gits em?"

Kate touched the earrings, a precious symbol of her love for a man now gone.

"Take em off and let me sees em," demanded Lena.

"I. . . I never take them off," Kate stammered.

"Then you comes over here so's I can be lookin at em," said Lena, pounding the floor with her walking stick. "Carry yourself over here."

Kate complied. Kate hurried.

The gnarled fingers of the old woman examined the earrings as if she knew them, nodding as she discovered their Egyptian writing at their widest part. But it was the blood-red rivulets, the long, red, blood-like rivulets that caused her breath to labor. "Where you gits them earrings?" she demanded again.

"A man named Joshua gave them to me."

"An he gots em from a woman with the name a Delia, who live in Miz'sippi, ain I right?"

"Yes, that's right!"

"You loves this Joshua man?"

"Yes. Very much."

"I knows them earrings."

"You know my earrings, Lena?"

"I been knowin them earrings mos a my life. An you needin to know em, too. I tends to see that you does."

Kate took her first full breath since walking into the room. "I thought I was in some kind of trouble for having the earrings."

"They's trouble all right but it ain the kin a trouble you's talkin bout. Now sits yourself down and we talks." Lena pointed to a chair a little to the right and in front of her.

Kate sat.

It was the eyes. It was those black eyes. They rendered her powerless. They looked at her and didn't see her. Yet they saw everything about her. Then they changed. They saw someone else who wasn't sitting in that chair. Someone far more important.

"How old is you?" Lena said after she had finished her perusal.

"Thirty-nine."

"When you born xactly?"

"October 15th, 1931."

"You been married but you ain married no more," Lena stated. "You gots youself two boys, but they lives with they daddy."

"Yes, that's right."

"You ain pretty," Lena said, finally seeing the serious blue eyes, the shoulder-length brown hair that always fell into her eyes, the overly-long Romanesque nose, the glowing white skin, and the soft, sensuous lips, once tight and drawn, but now softened by love. "But you got smarts. You ain puttin on no airs, paintin your face an sashayin roun like no fancy lady. I likes you. Yes, I does. I likes you."

Kate smiled for the first time since coming into the house. "Thank you," she said.

"You works for one a them newspapers?"

"Yes."

"You ain gonna write nothin bout me in your newspaper," Lena said with finality. "I don wan all kin a folks runnin roun here meddlin in my business. I gots nuff troubles as is. I don need no more. Hear?"

Kate laughed. "I promise not to write anything about you in my newspaper."

Lena's black face turned blacker. "Ain nothin to be laughin bout. I's ole an I's bout to go to the Lord, an I don need no more troubles than I's already got. I don need no folks snoopin roun here tryin to fin out bout me. No need to laugh bout that."

"Don need no meddlin newspaper," Lena muttered, this time more to herself than to Kate. "But one thing I knows for sure, chile, I ain goin to the Lord till you knows all your story. I's sure bout that. If'n he comma callin I got ta tell him, 'wait!' I's still takin' care a business. So don you be scairt, chile. I ain goin fore you knows all bout yourself."

A wicked thought crossed Kate's mind. "This woman's too cranky to die."

"An I ain cranky, neither," said Lena, banging her walking stick on the floor. "I's jus ole an when you's as ole as me, you don be wantin folks meddlin neither."

Kate's trust was complete. Her fear at least equaled her trust. Even her thoughts weren't her own with this woman.

Lena was talking again. "You's anguishin inside, chile. You's got a big hurt over this man, Joshua. You don need to worry none. He be back. He be different, but he be back. You worries youself sick cause you thinkin he done forgit you. He don forgit. He just actin the fool. When he done actin the fool, he be back."

"You's workin too hard cause a this hurtin over this man, Joshua. You thinkin if'n you works hard nuff, you forgits. You ain gonna forgit, an you be makin yourself sick if'n you don stop."

Lena paused for a moment, her eyes staring... staring into Kate, into the ghost of her past.

Kate was trying to forget what Lena had just said: that Joshua would be back. The pain burning in her belly hurt too much. The possibility of his return was more than she could bear. "You's been sick. You's been powerful sick. It were your daddy be makin you sick. He makin you sick cause he don love you. He cruel to you. You well rid a him. Now you ain needin to be sick no more. Lotsa folks lovin you now, cause you done good for em."

Kate's head wouldn't stop nodding. "Yes, Lena, that's right. All of that. It's right."

"I knows I's right. You ain needin to tell me."

"Lena, can you tell me about my dreams? I've been having these awful dreams."

"I knows you been havin dreams, chile, I knows. You's been dreamin bout folks dyin. Folks you don know, but knows you does know. Is I right?"

"Yes, that's right!" said Kate, amazed.

"We talks bout them dreams, chile, but firs we's gonna talk bout them earrings."

Kate touched the earrings, somehow so important to this Lena.

"Your man, Joshua, he done tole you he gits them earrings in Miz'sippi from an ole woman with the name a Delia. She be black, but she mos white. Din he tell you that?"

"Yes. Yes, he did."

"Well, chile, he did git them earrings from a lady with the name a Delia for to carry to you. But you had them earrings long afore that. You gots them earrings mor'n four hundred and fifty years ago from a man with the name of Amon."

Kate stared at Lena. "What do you mean?" Kate gasped.

"Jus like I says. A man with the name of Amon done give you them earrings mor'n four hundred and fifty years ago. You'n him live in Egypt then. But sump'n happen an you never gits to finish your love. You'n Joshua finishin it now."

The room resounded in silence. A minute, maybe more. Kate's voice, when she found it, was hoarse. She had to stop and clear her throat.

"Are you saying that I lived before and Joshua lived before and he gave me these very same earrings at a different time?"

"Tha's right, chile. You has them earrings when you was livin in Egypt an you has em in two more lives afor you gits em this time."

"Two more lives? That can't be. People don't live again, and then again, Lena. People only live once. Then they die. I don't believe this is my fourth life. I just don't believe it."

"It don matter what you believes, chile. You c'n believe whatever you wants. But tha's where them dreams a comin from. You dreamin bout them other lives. You sees a woman die when her chilin be killed. She die afor she be killed; is I right?"

"Yes."

"You sees a woman die with a spear in her heart, din you?"

"Yes, but. . .. "

"Ain no buts. Them women from your other lives."

Goosebumps. There were goosebumps all over her body. She saw them again. The other women. She saw them: she saw them walking; she saw them running. She saw them. . . . . dying! She covered her eyes not to see. "No, Lena! That's too much to believe."

"You don gots to believe if'n you don wan, but you gots to hear me. You be workin yourself into ***your*** death if'n you don hear me. You be workin an workin an writin an writin cause a them other lives. Cause a what happen to them other women what you been. You writing an writing cause they dead. They dead cause they women. They die cause they fights them folks what got the power. They die cause they women who be strong in they ownselves an folks don let em be strong. Kills em instead. This be what you mad bout, ain it? This be what you writing bout, ain it? When folks be vig'rous an other folks bigger'n them makes em weak an feeble?"

"Yes, but. . . . .."

"Then you gots to know bout them other women what you been. You gots to know bout em, so you knows who you is."

There was no sound in the room beyond the ticking of the clock.

Kate's throat felt raw. She tried to clear it.

Lena's raspy breathing filled the empty spaces.

"You gonna hear me now?" said Lena.

"I guess I'm going to hear you."

"Is you or ain you?"

"Yes. Yes, I'm going to hear you!" Kate was shouting.

"Well. . . I's glad you's come to your senses."

"What have I done?" Kate thought. "What have I agreed to?"

Lena knew what she had done - and was satisfied.

"Lemme tell you what we's gonna do. I's gonna take you back to them times you be livin afore. You gonna live them lives again. Don take you so long this time."

"Yes," said Kate, willing to agree to anything - all arguments drained away.

"Firs you gonna be Duanna an you gonna be living in Alexandria, Egypt. You starts livin there in 1503."

"Yes," said Kate.

"You bes be goin now. You comes back here Saturday, 2 o'clock, an we begins." Lena closed her eyes and spoke no more.

Kate stood up reeling from Lena's words about her past. Also feeling a terror about her possible future.

The next thing she knew she was walking down the front steps of the house. Then she turned around and went back inside. She had forgotten her coat.

CHAPTER 3

The argument was fierce. It was the same one, over and over again. Lena's words careened through her mind over and over again. Over and over, she made the decision not to go back on Saturday. Over and over, she changed her mind.

Now here she was - on her way, the bus bouncing and jostling her addled brain. It started again - the argument. The incessant argument with herself.

"This is insanity, that's what it is. Get off this bus now. Go home and read a good book."

"You're just scared."

"You're damned right I'm scared. I have a right to be scared. I feel like I'm on my way back to the mental ward. This is crazy!"

"What's crazy about it?"

"What's crazy is that I've agreed to see a woman who tells me I've got past lives. That's what's crazy."

"What's crazy about that?"

"Simple. I don't believe in past lives."

"What you believe has nothing to do with what's true."

"I don't want to hear that."

"You're getting hysterical."

"I'm not either hysterical."

"What then?"

"Scared. You're right. I'm just plain scared."

"I don't blame you."

"Thank you."

"And mad, too."

"Yes."

"What, exactly, are you mad at?"

"I don't want to do this."

"And what, exactly, scares you?"

"I've been living my life just fine. I'm successful. I've got enough money. I'm pretty happy. I don't need to know about any old lives I used to be."

"That sounds mad to me. What about scared?"

"Scared. Yes. Mainly, I'm afraid of dying. And I'm afraid of living her life. Part of it was horrible."

"Yes."

"And I'm afraid of what will happen when I come back to being me."

"Ah!"

"Don't be such a know-it-all. I'm going, aren't I? I'm going."

Today she went immediately up the steps and rang the bell. "No more time for indecision," she told herself.

Lena's scowl greeted her at the door. "So you's decided to come, has you?"

"I . . . " Kate started.

"Ain needin none a your 'scuses. You wanna know bout yourself when you was Duanna, or you wanna carry yourself back on home?"

Kate hesitated. Just a moment too long, she hesitated. Lena turned her head and banged her walking stick on the floor.

"Yes! I want to know! I want to know!" Kate said hastily. "Don't turn away. I want to know. I'm just a little nervous, that's all."

She gave up. The fight was gone out of her. She was going to be Duanna.

"Then you sits yourself down and we begins."

Duanna's history was reeling out of Lena's mouth before Kate was even in her chair. "When you was Duanna, you be born in 1503. You be livin in Alexandria. That be in Egypt. You knows bout Egypt?"

Kate nodded. In her head she saw a huge Gamal Abdul Nassar standing over the river Nile, building his Aswan Dam and dictating to all the little Egyptian people.

Lena acknowledged the nod and went on. "You was born during the season they be callin Inundation - sump'n like July here. Your daddy, he be named Zamen El Rashid an he be one a them thinkin types. He be workin at a university what they be callin Mouseion an he be teachin folks high-minded stuff bout religion an philosophy an such. Your mama, she be named Naditu an she mos a died havin you. She wantin you to be a son cause Zamen he don have no sons. Zamen, he don care nothin bout sons. He likes you cause you a girl."

Kate was doing her best to take in what Lena was saying. "Father, Zamen. Mother, Naditu. Born in 1503. I wasn't a son."

"They be namin you Enheduanna El Rashid but mos folks, they calls you little Duanna cause you so tiny. You got a sister they be callin Saragon an she be livin seven years an you gots another sister be callin Tiy an she be livin three years."

"Saragon and Tiy," Kate recorded.

"Alexandria a good place to be born cause it portant, too, cause it got them big palaces an lotsa temples an that university what your daddy be workin at. The owner a that city, he be named Alexander. He be buildin two a the biggest streets you ever done seed. They mor'n a hundred feet wide an they got them things what they be callin colonnades all along they sides for to shade them folks from the sun. That sun be powerful hot in Alexandria. They also got lotsa big houses they be callin villas for them rich folks to live in. You lives in one a them villas right there on that Mediterranean, cause your daddy, he be rich."

Lena's colorful description had Kate's imagination working overtime. She could actually see Alexandria on the Mediterranean with its two harbors, its palaces and its temples. For a moment, she even thought she saw the city's owner, busy building colonnades. She tried not to laugh outright at Lena's description of Alexander.

Lena wasn't waiting for Kate's imagination. Her booming voice rolled on. "Sides all that, they's got powerful mens runnin roun that city stirrin up trouble. They's all over the city, heads together plottin. They be jus like some a them black mens richere in Chicago what be havin their heads together plottin bout dope an such. Alexandria be like that, too. Trouble!"

"Sailin ships be comin to Alexandria from everywhere lookin for some a that trouble. They comes sellin stuff an takin stuff with em to sell other places. They comes sellin gold, an necklaces, an couches, an dresses an such. An they comes to git the poor folks what all huddles together in one part a the city to be part a that trouble. They gits them poor folk to steal from they brothers an from the rich folks an then they pays em tiny bits a gold for the thievin. Folks don git in no trouble for thievin in Alexandria cause the soldiers an the Sultan, that be like the po -lice an the mayor here in Chicago, they don see what they don wanna see."

Kate was amused at the unusual picture Lena was painting of Alexandria. Not exactly as she had read in her history books.

"Them sailors comin to Alexandria, too, cause they's lotsa wine drinkin an lotsa pretty ladies a sellin they bodies. But when you was Duanna, you don know much bout all them goins on, cause Zamen, he mos time be spoilin you rotten an he ain lettin you grow up much, neither. You don know nothin bout what goes on where them poor folk lives."

Lena stopped her monologue and closed her eyes. "Is she through?" Kate wondered. Apparently she was. She snapped her eyes open and said, "Now we's gonna go fin Duanna."

Kate panicked. Her hands were suddenly sweaty. Her heart started to pound. "Lena, wait! I'm scared!"

"Whachu scared bout? Ain nothin to be scared bout."

"Lena! You act like, every day, people just go back four hundred and fifty years into another life. I'm scared to do it. I'm scared of what's going to happen to me in that other life. I saw her in my dreams. It was horrible."

"Ain so horrible."

"Ain't so horrible, you say. Ain't so horrible? It looked horrible."

"Better'n you thinks. Duanna a spoiled little rich girl. Ain nothin much better'n that."

"I'm still scared of it. And besides that, what's going to happen to me when I come back? What about that?"

"You be the same. You be different but you be the same."

"Lena, don't talk in riddles. I need to know. I can't do this if I don't know."

"Ain no way I c'n tell you. Ain no way. Duanna be in you. Tha's all. Duanna be in you. She be in you now but, when you done with her life, you know she be in you."

"Then I'll know she's in me," Kate repeated.

"Tha's it."

"That's it." Kate did not feel reassured.

"Is you ready?"

"I'm as ready as I'll ever be," Kate said, pushing her hair out of her face. She sighed. There were to be no more delays. The inevitable had arrived. She wanted to leap from her chair and race out the front door. She wanted to leave Lena and Duanna and everything about their lives. She was terrified.

"Good. You jus relaxes while I gits ready."

Relaxing was out of the question. Her body wouldn't stop shaking.

Lena produced a long kitchen match from inside her dress. She lit a small lamp that was sitting on a side table - a lamp that looked as if it had generated genies in the stories of the Arabian Nights. A sweet odor wafted through the room.

Kate relaxed. Her head emptied. Thoughts disappeared. She stopped being afraid. Everything was wonderful.

Lena was talking. Kate knew there were words but she didn't know and didn't care what the words were. They floated into her brain and disappeared. She was floating right along with the words. She was all lightness, floating about in the air. Clouds swirled in her head. White clouds, grey clouds, beautiful clouds.

Lena was still talking.

Kate couldn't hear her. Everything was so nice. She was glad she had come. She floated. Up. Up. Down . . . and up again. Fluffy white stuff was outside of her just for her to float on . . . and inside of her just to keep her floating. She didn't ever want to leave this delicious place. Not ever.

But she couldn't stay. The fluffy clouds were permeated by Lena's words. She had to hear now. "You is now in the city of Alexandria. You is looking at Duanna, the woman you once was. Tell me what you sees."

Kate opened her mouth. Nothing happened. No words came. Nothing was there. She began to struggle.

"Stop agitatin yourself. Words comes when they does."

Now a picture was beginning to form. Out of the clouds came a girl. A pretty girl with dark hair. It was the first one of her dreams. It was Duanna.

Words began to come. "There's a girl standing in a room."

"How ole she be?"

"She's maybe fourteen . . . fifteen, at most."

"What do she look like?"

"She's very pretty. Long hair, almost to her waist, and straight bangs. Her skin is, uh . . . kind of olive. She's tiny, smaller than the people around her. She's dressed all in white . . . uh . . . except for a purple sash around her waist. She's wearing a veil over her nose and I can't see all of her face. But her eyes are luminous. They're like . . . uh . . . they're like two candles glowing in the dark. Those eyes, they're . . . they're . . . compelling me. Oh, Lena, I'm scared!"

"Ain no time to be scared. Look at her some more."

Kate took a deep breath and looked again. She noticed the girl's jewelry, first the gold brocaded slippers. Then the gold necklace with the purple stone. When she looked at her face she was aghast. "Oh, my God!" she said.

"What you seein now?"

Kate covered her eyes and refused to answer.

"Whachu seein now?" insisted Lena.

"Her earrings."

"Look at them earrings. I says **look** at them earrings!" Lena said leaning forward in her chair.

"They're mine!" Kate shouted. "She's wearing my earrings. The same ones I'm wearing right now!" Tears welled up in her eyes.

"Then who she be?"

"She's me!" Kate yelled. "Just like you said. She's me. Are you satisfied? I know she's me." A sob pushed its way through her throat.

"Yes, I's satisfied now." Lena sat back in her chair and was silent.

Kate's tears were coming unrestrained now, coming from some unknown place out of the pain of some unknown life. Fifteen minutes. A half hour. Kate didn't know how long. Time was beyond her capacity to know. Lena left her alone.

After a piece of forever, Lena spoke again . . . her voice gentle now. "Bes you talks with her."

"Yes," said Kate, knowing now that she had no choice, knowing that soon she would be seeing through those luminous eyes, having been impelled inside that tragic life.

"Go now. Talk to her."

"Yes," said Kate, moving into the vision that was in her head.

The girl smiled at her. "Welcome," she said. "I've been expecting you."

"You knew I was coming? I'm surprised. I didn't even know I was coming."

"You had to come. You have my earrings. We have decided. You are the one."

"But why?"

"So you won't die the way I did."

"I don't understand."

"The woman who has the earrings commits herself."

"Yes. Yes, I made a commitment."

"The woman who has the earrings has to be a special woman, because there is a destiny to fulfill."

"A destiny?"

"Yes, a destiny that brought me death."

"And the others?" Kate asked.

"Death, also. We had no choice. It was the times. But you . . . you have a choice."

"I have a choice?"

"Yes. You can decide to live out the destiny we died for, or you can decide not to."

"What do you mean?"

"Are you strong enough to go against the world to complete the destiny?"

"And if I decide to?"

"Then you have to live all of our lives, so we can teach you."

"I'm afraid."

"Yes."

"I'm more than afraid. I'm terrified."

"Yes."

"When I have lived all of your lives, then what?"

"Then you will know."

"Know what?"

"Everything you need to know."

"I don't understand."

"You wont - until the times comes. I can not tell you any more. We have chosen you. But you don't need to agree. If you are willing, we will proceed. If you are not, you can go back."

"I don't want to go back. I feel . . . maybe . . . like I belong here. Yes, like I belong here."

"Then you are willing?"

"Yes. I have a choice but I really **don't** have a choice. I suppose I decided all those years ago when I accepted the earrings. I knew then that there was something I had to do. Some things I had to say. Some things I had to finish. I think I knew then. Yes, I will live your lives. I will learn what you have to teach me. Then I will decide about my destiny."

"That's good enough."

"What do I need to do?"

"Begin by looking around you."

Kate's eyes searched her surroundings. "Is this some kind of celebration?" she asked, seeing for the first time all of the people, the splendidly-dressed people, the tables of food, the entertainment in the center of the room, the numerous slaves carrying goblets of wine.

"Yes, it is," said the girl.

Kate's eyes lit on an obviously important man. He was sitting on an ornate throne in the front of the room being fanned by six boys, each with a palm fan.

"The Pasha of Turkey," said Duanna.

"An ugly man," replied Kate.

"Not as ugly as that man over there."

Kate looked in the direction Duanna was pointing. The man was not only ugly, he was an offense.

"Who is he?" Kate asked.

"He's my husband. We were just married."

THE FIRST WOMAN

DUANNA

(1503 - 1524)

"It was a male dream . . . It was a female prison." p.57

CHAPTER 4

"It is time to come into me, to live my life," said Duanna. "Are you ready?"

"I'm ready," said Kate, now knowing the rightness of her choice, now knowing the absence of the fear that had plagued her for all these many days.

Duanna held out her hand.

Kate moved toward it, taking its smallness into hers. She felt the weight of her hair change. She felt her hair grow long and heavy. She felt her body grow smaller. She felt the silk against her skin. No. It wasn't silk. It was a different cloth, linen perhaps. She felt a sea breeze on her face. She felt her hair blowing behind her and her dress whipping around her legs. She heard Lena's voice. "Now you is Duanna an so you shall remain until her death. So it be's."

She kicked the sand with her toe. She picked up a rock and set it sailing into the water. Gone was the celebration with its hordes of people. Gone was the smell of sweating bodies. Gone was the entertainment, the wine and the slaves running every which way. All of this was replaced by the silence of nobody, by the regularity of the sea crashing against the rocks, crawling up onto the sand in finger-like wetness, and by her fury. Her fury at her father, at Tiy, at everybody.

"Tiy, you are hateful," she shouted into the wind. "All you talk about is Ninus. Ninus this, and Ninus that. I don't ever want to hear the word Ninus again in my life. You are so busy remembering Ninus, you forgot my birthday. Only the most important day in the world."

"And, father, you've spoiled my birthday. I wanted to be the important one. I wanted to sit in the center of the great room and have you give me gifts and have you sing and dance, just for me. I wanted you to tell me how important I am to be fourteen, how important I am because I am now a woman. That's what you did for Tiy when she was fourteen. But now you've spoiled it. You've gone and invited those ugly Ethiopian sailors. Why did you do that? Why did you do that?" she said petulantly. She kicked her foot into the sand, throwing up its wetness onto her white dress.

She walked up and down the beach, fury in her heart. The fury remained all afternoon . . . so long that she noticed that the sun was beginning to set before she deigned to go back to the villa.

When she finally arrived back at home they were all there waiting for her. The first to greet her were Gena and Illana, the two women who had cared for her since her birth. They were standing in the door looking worried. "Hurry into the great room." Gena said. "Your father is beside himself. Where have you been? "

"Out. Just out," said Duanna, tossing her head.

"Well, hurry." said Illana.

She refused to hurry. She looked at everything on her trip from the entry way to the great room. She stopped to examine the flowers in their vases and her lute laying on the floor. Gena was frantic behind her, trying to make her move. When she finally arrived in the great room she saw her father pacing the floor, and her mother sitting on a stool, frowning. Tiy ran toward the door, catching Duanna by the hand. "Where have you been?" she said. "Where have you been? Father is very disturbed. Hurry," she said.

"I'll hurry if I please," said Duanna.

"We were so worried," said Naditu. "Have you forgotten it's your birthday? You need to be in the bath."

"I hadn't forgotten," Duanna said coldly.

Zamen said nothing. He simply looked at her with a large question in his eyes. What was causing his little girl to be like this on this of all days? He had thought she would be delighted with his plans. She obviously was not delighted. "Your bath is ready. You must get bathed for our guests." he said.

She dawdled in the bath, demanding that Illana bring her more bath salts, refusing the soap they gave her, wiggling as Illana tried to dry and oil her body - determined to make them as uncomfortable as possible.

Her every move was designed to delay the inevitable. Delay the inevitable that is . . . until she saw the dress lying on her divan. Her birthday dress. Soft white on top, with sleeves that billowed out at the shoulders, and a full purple skirt that would swing softly around her legs as she walked . . . or danced. Next to the dress was a bright red sash speckled with shiny gems and by the sash lay a collar with black onyx stones.

Fury forgotten, she picked up the dress and raced out of the room. She had to show her new dress to Tiy. Tiy would be so jealous. She hadn't gotten anything that pretty for her fourteenth birthday.

Before she was even out of her room, she was interrupted by Gena. "You are to get dressed, mistress."

"I can't do anything I want," she said stomping her foot. "Not anything." She walked back into her room pouting.

When she finally arrived in the great room she looked very much unlike the spoiled little girl she had been portraying all day but very much the lady in a woman's dress.

Zamen couldn't believe his eyes. When she ran up to thank him he had to hold her away from him in amazement. He most of all was surprised at the results of his purchases. "My," he said. "You are as pretty as any of the Sultan's wives."

"Prettier," she said, as she pirouetted in front of him, prancing like a young colt.

Zamen couldn't hide his feelings. Pride and sadness mixed together in his breast. "Duanna, you will capture the hearts of every one of our guests tonight."

"I'm not going to capture anybody's heart tonight," she said, her fury returning. "I don't like slimy old sailors. They can keep their hearts to themselves."

Zamen laughed, feasting his eyes on his most beautiful daughter, so like Naditu in her small delicateness. So different from Tiy - strong, robust Tiy with the freckles and the sandy hair who was so much like himself. Briefly he thought of Saragon, little mother to them both - now with children of her own.

Memories flooded over him. Memories of his love for Duanna, of the feeling of her little arms around his neck, of holding her on his lap, telling her stories, of comforting her in the bad times. He remembered how they had almost lost her, before she was born. Naditu's body had been so weak and her labor so hard that Duanna had almost not made it into this world. When she lived, beyond everyone's hope, Zamen remembered how grateful he had been. He had promised, on that night, to teach her everything he knew. He remembered the nights they had sat under the flaming wall lamps writing with a quill pen on the parchment he brought home from the university, or reading stories he wrote for her, and later reading the books from the library.

Now, he was almost overcome by her beauty and the bittersweet possibilities of his plan for the night. "No time to think about that," he thought. The night was upon him. He heard Gena announcing their guests.

First to stride through the door was a man whose every muscle announced his presence.

Duanna's eyes widened at his tall darkness, at the eyes that surveyed everything in the room before lighting on her, at his long wavy hair falling to his shoulders in the current style of youth. Duanna quickly saw him as he would be, standing on the deck of his ship, the wind whipping his loose-fitting shirt, blowing his hair into disarray. As quickly as her eyes had widened, they closed again in a veil of disinterest.

Four other men followed in rapid succession. The majestic one was introducing them to Zamen and Naditu in a deep-toned voice that somehow filled the room. "My officers," he said. "It is these men who run my ship and are the secret of my success."

Naditu curtsied while Zamen welcomed them, each.

"He is handsome, isn't he?" whispered Tiy through her fingers.

"Who?" asked Duanna.

"The prince, of course."

"Better looking than most sailors I've seen." Duanna said lifting, ever so slightly, her veil of disinterest.

"How old do you think he is?"

"Oh, he's old. At least twenty-five."

"That old, you think?"

"That old. And probably boring."

"He looks important, doesn't he?"

"He looks full of self-praise, if you ask me."

"Shhhhhhhh. Here he comes." Tiy lowered her eyes, looking at the floor, as she bent to curtsy.

"Trying to act the lady," Duanna thought. "Well, not me."

He bent over Tiy's hand, touching it with his lips. "You look lovely tonight," he said. "A daughter to make Zamen proud. He tells me you are very musical. I hope I shall be privileged to hear you."

"Yes, Your Excellency," Tiy said, keeping her eyes on the floor.

Then he was there, towering over her, smiling at her, holding out his hand. "Amon De Bolla of Ethiopia, my daughter, Duanna," said Zamen.

Duanna smiled back and curtsied. Just a little, she curtsied. She held out her hand. Bravado sallied forth. Confusion reigned within. "You don't impress me," she told herself. "You may have a ship, and be rich, and be handsome but I'm not impressed. You're too full of self-praise. I wonder why my legs feel funny."

And there she was, looking into a pair of twinkling black eyes. He was bending to kiss her hand. "Why is my hand burning?" she wondered.

He was speaking. "You are as beautiful as your father has told me. Thank you for sharing your birthday with me."

"I am glad you are here, Your Excellency," she said, not for one minute believing her lie. Well, maybe for a minute.

The prince let go of her hand. He let go of her eyes. He walked away, leaving a strange void where his presence had been. He took a seat on one of the cushions scattered about the room and turned his attention to the grapes Gena was offering him.

"I feel funny."

Zamen introduced her to the other four men, the officers of the Prince's ship. She couldn't remember any of their names.

To be truthful, it was hard for her to remember what happened the rest of the evening. She and Tiy played their lutes, singing softly, while Gena served wine and Illana washed the feet of each of the men with oil. Tiy played the flute in accompaniment to Naditu's dancing. Duanna joined her mother for a synchronized duet. Naditu danced away, leaving her to dance alone.

Every eye in the room was on her. Duanna's heart leaped into her throat, knowing the prince was behind two of those eyes. Her knees were trembling. She forgot everything she knew about dancing. Disgrace stared her in the face.

Then, from some unknown place, she found strength and a pirouette unfolded. The purple of her skirt billowed, showing her firm, shapely legs. The darkness of the prince's eyes deepened and his breath quickened. New sensations flooded her body and her legs became empowered with new boldness. She snapped her castanets and her eyes flashed as she bent and swirled, bending until her head swept the ground, again. and again, and again. Righting herself, she shimmered to the increasing tempo of the flute, hands flowing in intricate patterns, hair streaming behind her.

Her eyes met those of each of the men, captivating them one by one. Tension filled the room. Her body twisted and turned in the patterns of an undulating snake, sensuously, beginning at her feet and moving up . . . up . . . up her body and through her head in slow rhythmic waves. Over and over again, with the timing of Tiy's flute, the willowy waves rippled through her body until she was literally throbbing. She could bear no more. She paused. Then slowly, ever so slowly, she began to swirl - gently at first, crossing the room with her movement, then swirling in front of each man, catching his eye, seducing him with her movements, her heart beating wildly. She saw their admiration. Everything was wonderful. Even her body became fuller as their eyes admired her.

She felt it . . . her body. It was expanding into the night.

The prince's eyes never wavered.

'Little Duanna' was disappearing.

She finished her last swirl in the middle of the room. As she raised both arms to the ceiling, a sound of triumph burst through her throat. She sank into a deep curtsy.

The room was full of silence.

No one moved.

Naditu and Tiy were agape. "This could not be Duanna, their Duanna, who had had two left feet during all of their training."

Zamen wiped a tear from his eye. There, on the dance floor, was his greatest hope and his worst fear. "Duanna has become a woman," he said gently.

The silence was awesome. For Duanna, deep in her curtsy, it was alarming. Tears sprang into her eyes. "Nobody liked my dance."

The room began to stir. The men murmured words of appreciation. The prince jumped from his cushion to her side. He grasped her hand and pulled her to a standing position. "You are beautiful," he said. "Never in all my travels have I seen the like." She felt his hand on her face, wiping away the tears.

She couldn't look at him. Before, she had looked. Now there was no more strength to look. Now it was **her** eyes that studied the floor.

"Don't look away, Dancing Duanna," he said. "You looked at me before. I liked the frankness that I saw there. Look at me now."

For the first time in her life, shyness ruled her. She could not look at him. Her eyes were glued to the floor.

"I cannot," she said.

His hand was under her chin, lifting her face toward him. Her eyes met his. Something was there. In his eyes. In hers. She knew nothing of love. She didn't understand.

"Now, that's better," he said. "Come and have dinner with me. I would like to know you better."

Duanna's tongue refused to unglue. "Thank you, Your Excellency."

"Please don't call me 'Your Excellency'. I am Amon. I would like you to call me Amon."

"Amon," she said, tasting the word. "Did you know that one of our most famous gods was named Amon - Amon Ra?"

"Yes. I do know. I know Amon Ra better than I would like to. My mother named me Amon after him. She had a mother's presumptuousness to believe I would be god-like. I wasn't in this world long before she knew she'd made a mistake."

Duanna smiled. Amazing! He no longer seemed full of self-praise. He no longer seemed so old. And Tiy was right. He was handsome. Her shyness began to disappear. She almost relaxed.

Dinner was full of questions: "Where have you travelled?"

"You travelled to Greece? To Rome? To Persia? Oh, my!"

"What do you do all day on your ship?"

"Don't you get tired of water, water - nothing but water - all the time?"

"Do you see lots of pretty women when you travel?"

"Ethiopia . . . why did you not stay there? Why did you come here?"

Gena interrupted her, handing her a goblet.

"What's this?" she demanded.

"It is wine, my mistress. Your father says you may have some for your birthday."

She tasted it. Her face was priceless. All screwed up with her eyes shut tight.

Amon tried to stop his laughter.

"Don't laugh at me, Amon," she said. "I've never tasted this before and now I know why. Ughhhhh! It's awful! Why do people like it?"

Then her face changed. Her eyes widened. She put her hand on her stomach. "OOOOOOOOOOOOOHHHHH!" she said. "Everything looks so different."

Amon laughed harder.

"Stop that!" she said.

"I can't, Dancing Duanna. You're too delightful."

Duanna's cheeks were in flames. "Stop laughing at me. It's not fair."

"I'll try."

"Besides . . . you didn't answer my question."

"What question was that?" he said, his face working hard to remove the amusement.

"Why did you leave Ethiopia? Why do you travel on your ship?"

Now the amusement left his eyes. Now instead of the twinkle, there was sadness - infinite sadness. His body changed, becoming tense and cold. He measured his words. "Life was good for me in Ethiopia. My father was leader of all men in Massewa, where we lived and I was taught by all the learned men. I was destined to be the next leader. But I couldn't stay to take my father's position."

Duanna saw pain now on his face and in his eyes. She put her hand on his arm. He didn't take it away.

"I . . . I had a wife," he said slowly. "Her name was Dameli. She died in childbirth three years ago. Since then I have travelled the Mediterranean, trading my gold for goods and the goods back to gold. I have not wanted to take another wife."

He was gone from her. Suddenly he was gone from her. He moved his arm out from under hers. Now it was he who studied the floor.

He turned polite. Chillingly polite. "I would like to take a stroll in the garden," he said. "Would you like to go with me?"

"Yes, if my father will permit."

"I will ask him." Amon rose to his full height and approached Zamen.

Zamen eyes softened as he perceived the success of his plans.

Amon and Duanna walked without talking, each lost in their own thoughts. Duanna was at a loss to understand her body. Many men had come and gone in the house of Zamen but none had caused her legs to want to buckle under her, had caused her to feel so strange, had caused her heart to beat so, had caused the flame now radiating from her cheeks.

The garden was becoming like a prison for her, with its high wall and dense foliage. It was trying to contain her within its brooding presence. She needed to run - run like the greyhound across the rocks and sand, underneath the moon, away from this strangeness of her body. Away from Amon's current chill.

"Let's go walk by the water," she said.

"Do I have to ask your father about that, too?" he said, only half in jest.

"No, not that."

Run was all her body could think to do with this strangeness. She gave in to her body's demands. She took off, the wind streaking through her hair, her dress flying behind her. "Catch me if you can," she said.

Not in the mood for childish games, he stood for a moment watching the sight of her, her black hair streaked with moonlight, her lithe body quickly outdistancing him. He was in the mood for childish games.

She raced through the sand and clamored over the rocks with the ease of an antelope. His larger body pounded the sand behind her. A mile, two miles . . . a long ways. Finally her movements slowed enough to enable him to catch her. With one burst of speed he caught her by one of her arms.

He caught her hand and held it. Now she didn't need to run away any more. He was back. The chill was gone. He was with her once more.

He curled her arm under his. "Now we will walk," he said. "Now I don't need to run," she said.

So they walked. Up and down the beach, they walked. He showed her his ship. "The Lioness," he told her.

"That's because it's got a lion on its bow," she said.

She stumbled over a rock.

He held her up.

A bird flew out of the darkness and startled them.

He showed her the North Star. "So we know where we're going in the night," he explained.

"Do you ever get lost?" she asked.

"Sometimes," he said.

"What's it like on a ship?" she asked.

"It makes a man forget," he said.

"Are you rich?" she asked.

"Yes," he said.

"Are you cold?" he asked.

"Yes," she said.

He slowed his walk. He stopped. His brow furrowed. She became afraid. Afraid he would go away again. And he did go away again. For a long time he seemed lost in thought. After what seemed like forever his brow unfurrowed and he spoke. "I will be in Alexandria for the next seven days before I must sail again. I would like to have the right to call upon you some of those days, if you would like and your father would permit it. Perhaps tomorrow?"

It was better than she thought. "Yes. Yes!" she said. "Let's go and ask father now." In a hurry, she started off down the beach.

"Don't run again," he said, grabbing a hold of one of her arms. "Let's go to ask Zamen slowly. My feet are too tired for running."

She curbed her excitement, suddenly realizing that she was acting the child. Now, she didn't want to act the child with this wonderful man.

Zamen graciously gave his permission.

Amon and his officers left the house of Zamen shortly thereafter.

The door was barely closed before Duanna raced to her father and threw herself into his arms. "It's wonderful to be fourteen," she said. "It's wonderful to be a woman. You gave me a perfect birthday surprise. Thank you, thank you, thank you!" She kissed him on the cheek and raced away, to bed, maybe to sleep, for sure to dream of Amon.

CHAPTER 5

Amon paced the floor of his cabin. Masts creaked above him and water slapped against the sides of the ship. Another man sat on a bench, turning his head from side to side, as Amon traced and retraced his steps. "She is good for you," said the man on the bench.

"I may have misled her," said Amon.

"She will make you forget," said the other.

"She is not like the other women. She is too fragile to hurt," said Amon.

"Seven days cannot hurt," said the bench man.

"Perhaps."

Duanna turned in her sleep. The dream did not penetrate. Another one followed.

She was playing extraordinary games. She was walking. She was running. She was skipping through white fluffy clouds. She was pulling off pieces of their fluffy vapor, packing them into balls and tossing them at imaginary playmates. She bounced on the cloud-made mattresses. She jumped into frothy mounds. She wrapped herself into diaphanous swirls.

She was not alone. There was a playmate, a boy, dark and handsome, with hair to his shoulders. He was playing her extraordinary games. He was catching her fluffy balls, joining her as she bounced and jumped, dancing with her, leading her through the vaporous masses to pirouettes and plie's, wrapping her in one of the diaphanous swirls, twirling her around and around and around. She danced out of the swirl, unwrapping and unwrapping and when she was free, he was gone.

She awoke to the sun - hot in her room. She languished, for a time, in her dream. Then she remembered reality. "Amon!" She jumped off the divan.

She spent the day bothering Tiy at her practice, Naditu as she pruned the garden and Gena and Illana at their work. The whole house breathed a sigh of relief when Amon strode through the garden gate in mid-afternoon.

Their first days together were even more than she had imagined.

They walked together - on the beach, where sea spray dampened her hair, to the market where he bought her trinkets and candy, on the streets where horses clattered and donkey carts creaked and swayed. They entertained each other, she blending her voice with the harp, he with his stories of his exploits at sea. They played together, she in wide-eyed wonder, he with fatherly gentleness. They even argued together. They touched, they laughed, they talked - nonsensically sometimes - seriously at others. He was amazed at her knowledge of the things she could know nothing about. She was amazed at his knowledge of the things he knew everything about. She wanted to be with him forever. He was not so sure.

She dreamed she was sailing away with him on his ship.

He dreamed of sailing away, watching her tiny body get smaller and smaller as his sails took to the wind.

She dreamed of touching him, talking to him, playing with him, day after day.

He dreamed of a woman-child . . . of playing with the child and watching the woman unfold. Nothing more.

Then one day, they went to the market.

It was a sea of chaos. The weather was hot and the people irritable. These people, they were everywhere - shouting, arguing about prices, pushing, shoving, stepping on squawking chickens, yelling at stubborn goats. Dogs ran loose. They barked at other dogs tied to the shops they guarded. Birds, red ones, red and green ones, yellow ones, multi-colored ones all chirped, twittered, or squawked from their hanging cages. Donkeys brayed as they struggled through narrow passageways, pulling carts that knocked over whole shops. Merchants stood in the middle of their rubble, shouting obscenities at the retreating carts.

Smells were overwhelming. There were the beautiful smells of the multiple flowers and the sweetness of incense floating through the air. These were mixed with the smell of the dung from the various animals and the sweat of the closely packed people.

It was in this sea of smells, sights, and sounds, that much of the intrigue of the city took place. Theft! Murder! Rape! Abduction! All took place daily. It was here that the seedy could find the well-to-do and make their transactions. It was here that slavers abducted their prey, imprisoning them in a pool of pleasure until they had no will left with which to escape. Even so, it was here that the legitimate came to bargain for their goods.

It was the very badness of the market that intrigued the good. Amon knew it well. Duanna was intrigued. They wandered the narrow passages, looking at the wares, talking to the birds, petting the animals and trying not to get knocked and pummeled by the masses of humanity. Women openly stared at Amon, and sailors, lounging about, winked at Duanna.

"Amon, old friend," they heard from somewhere in the crowd.

"Ah, Alonzo," Amon called back excitedly. "I have been looking for you," he said, moving in the man's direction. Then he turned to Duanna. "He is a man I must talk to, Duanna. Do you mind? Come."

Minutes later, Amon and Alonzo were engrossed in a business conversation. It wasn't long before Duanna was bored. She stood on one foot. Then on the other. She watched the people. She carried on an imaginary conversation with a parrot in one of the cages. Still the men talked, on and on as if they would never stop. She saw a woman in red dancing in one of the rare open spaces surrounded by an ever-increasing crowd of sailors and onlookers. She looked at Amon, engrossed as he was in his conversation. She wandered off to watch the lady in red.

Duanna's eyes opened wider and wider watching the woman, her red dress whirling about her thighs, her breasts clearly seen as she bent to pick up the coins the men were throwing, her eyes flashing seductively into the crowd, her castanets clacking to the swinging of her body.

Duanna didn't understand the experience she saw on the woman's face. She didn't understand the excitement of the men as they pushed and shoved and shouldered their way to get a better look. She didn't understand why the woman stopped dancing when a man held up a coin larger than the rest, nor did she understand the grinding of the woman's bottom as she moved toward the coin, laughing at the envy of the rest of the men as the two went off together.

Disappointed, she checked on Amon. He was still deep in conversation with his friend, Alonzo. Both men were talking more with their hands than with their mouths, she thought. She wandered on.

Amidst the colorful clothes, the mounds of figs, dates and apples, and the shining jewelry, Duanna noticed a strange group in the back of one of the shops. A toothless old crone was holding court over two muscular young men and a vacant-eyed girl about Duanna's age.

Duanna stopped and stared. The old woman was holding a crooked walking stick. She was using it as a weapon, Duanna thought. She was pounding it, pointing with it, and brandishing it about, striking one or another of the three at will.

Her face was ugly. Ancient and lined, toothless and evil, beady-eyed and beak-nosed. A dirty scarf covered her head and an even dirtier shawl, her body.

Her mouth never stopped moving; and her eyes never stopped darting around from boy to girl to members of the crowd. To Duanna! They stopped darting when they reached Duanna.

A tremor shook Duanna's body as those eyes settled on her, piercing through her smallness, making plans. The crone became even more agitated, stomping and pointing with her stick in Duanna's direction. A gnarled hand gripped the arm of one of the young men. The mouth moved faster.

The smell of danger made Duanna's legs move fast. "Amon," she called.

But she was only a few steps away when she found herself pinned against the chest of one of the muscular young men. He had his arm across her shoulders - stopping her progress. She smelled the ugliness of his sweat. She opened her mouth to scream. She felt the roughness of his hand as it clapped itself over her mouth. "Not so fast," breathed like a stench into her ear.

Duanna shouted through his hand and wrenched herself this way and that. He held fast. She could see Amon, still deep in conversation with his friend. "Amon!" she called. The sound of muffled silence followed.

Her eyes pleaded with the passersby. "Help me!" they said. Nobody helped.

Now he was whispering in her ear. "Just come with me quietly, beautiful lady. I'm going to give you something that will feel real good. You like to feel good, don't you? I bet you do. Just come with me and we'll see to it that you feel good all the time. Then you'll wonder why you didn't come peaceable."

She kicked him in the shins.

He yelled. He increased his pressure on her chest, pulling her backwards, her legs dragging on the ground. He was pulling her back . . . back . . . back . . . away from Amon, away from the people, toward the poison of the old crone. His words were coming like venom in her ears. "If you keep fighting, I'll have to take care of you right here. You won't like that as well. Just come easy-like."

Her struggling increased. She pulled and yanked, wrenching herself this way and that. Now the evil in his tone was sending chills through her body. "When we get back, I'm going to take care of you right away. You'll like it. They all do. And I'm going to like it, too. You're one beautiful lady. If I'm the one that takes you, I'm the one that gets you."

Duanna despaired.

Then she heard it. The voice she'd been waiting for. "Let that woman go!"

"Amon!"

"Let that woman go, you bastard, or I'll kill you!"

The man loosened his grip. Then he grabbed on, tighter than before. "What's it to you? This is my woman. She's runnin' off on me again. I'm teaching her a lesson."

"Son of a bitch! Let her go, I say or you **won't** live to regret it!" He advanced on the boy, his face contorting in anger. "Let her go!"

The pain across her chest released and the hand left her mouth. She raced toward Amon.

"We didn't mean no harm, sir. We were just going to talk to her. We don't want no trouble." Duanna guessed he was in plenty of trouble back with the old crone. She **hoped** he was.

She ran into Amon's arms. He scooped her up and held her like a child, while her body trembled, and her chest heaved with sobs. He collapsed onto a stool, rocking her, soothing her, taming her fears. By the time her crying had been reduced to a trickle, his shirt was plastered to his body, wet from her tears.

Now passersby paid attention. Now they clucked with disapproval at such a public display.

That night she dreamed of crones and sticks and dancing girls in red.

While he dreamed he was in love with a woman-child of long flowing hair.

CHAPTER 6

Each day was filled with adventures that were Amon. Every day was a day of unfolding mystery. Every look, every gesture, every smile touched her in some new place that was called woman. Stories of his life opened her eyes to a world she had never known. She fell more and more in love with the rogue in him, while stories from her learned imaginings opened his eyes to the woman she was. He fell more and more in love with a beauty inside of her that she didn't even know she had. Each day became more important than the last.

But each night was filled with torment. Dreams of a shadowy figure came to torture her. It walked between them. It caused him to furrow his brow, and his ship to sail away without her. Then she had to die. There was no more life without him. She simply had to die.

The name of the figure was Dameli.

But, on this night, her dreams were different. She dreamed she was his slave, shackled and in chains. She was his possession. He came and unlocked the shackles, setting her free. She dreamed he was the Sultan, with all the wives he wanted - all imprisoned in his harem. She was only one - and unimportant. He came and sent them all away, except for her.

She dreamed he was standing over her with a whip. He was telling her she was to have many sons. Only sons were important. Daughters were worthless and to be dispensed with. She bore him daughters. He loved his little girls more than sons.

She dreamed about a man who was writing rules on the wall. "Follow these or die," said the man.

It is your job to take care of me and make me feel important.

I have bigger things to do than worry about you. I have wars to fight and fields to plant and the Sultan to obey.
Sex is mine when I say so.

"I can't follow these rules," she said.

"I love you," he said. Then he tore down the rules.

She woke, wondering what that had been all about.She asked Zamen.

"The dreams seem to be saying something about what men usually expect from a woman, Duanna, but that Amon is not like that."

"He'd better not be," she said. "I'll never be a slave for any man." Her belief was so strong that she could never imagine anything but her total freedom . . . she could never imagine that someday she would be exactly that . . . a slave.

Amon's arrival put an end to all thoughts of dreams and meanings thereof. Her thoughts had turned to the two days left of their precious seven.

That day they had a picnic on the beach, then decided to again brave the market. More carefully this time.

The day passed while they aimlessly wandered the market.

"Look, Amon, aren't they pretty?" she said. A pair of silver earrings were swinging in her hand.

The look on his face horrified her. His eyes darkened and his brow furrowed. His face looked like angry thunderclouds. He stared at the earrings, but didn't see.

"Amon?" she said.

He heard nothing.

"Amon?"

His voice sounded strange. "Put the earrings back, Duanna. I'll buy you a pair of earrings, but not this pair." The thunderclouds lifted and he grabbed her hand. He half walked, half ran, as if crazed. He was pushing his way through the crowds, grumbling at anybody who got in his way.

Duanna was almost out of breath, when he suddenly stopped in front of one of the shops. He shouted at the bewildered man behind the counter, "Where's the man who was here before? The man with the jewelry?"

"I beg your pardon, sir?"

"I said, where is the man whose shop was here before? The man with the long beard? He sold jewelry. Where is he?" Amon was shouting louder now.

"Oh, yes. He's moved to the other side of the market. Over that way."

Duanna was running again, behind a more and more frantic Amon. He was racing up and down the narrow passageways, pushing people aside, muttering under his breath.

Smash! She ran into his back. He had stopped.

Now he was yelling at this shopkeeper. "Why didn't you leave your shop where it was?"

"Sire, it's been here for a week now. Where would you want it to be?"

"Back where it was, so I could find you."

"For you, sire, I will move it back."

Amon was staring at the man out of dark eyes. "I need to see some earrings. They are the ones I sold you a few weeks ago. I want to buy them back."

Duanna could almost see the wheels whirling in the little man's head.

"Ah, yes. I remember now. You did sell me some earrings. That was some time ago, isn't that right? I may not have those earrings any more. I believe I sold those to the Englishman with the dog. Yes, I may not have those earrings any more."

"Well, look, man, look!"

Slowly, very slowly, the man turned to some boxes he had in the back of his shop. One by one, he picked them up, pushing their contents around with a dirty finger. After each box, he shook his head, then discarded the box.

Amon became more and more crazed. He was pacing back and forth, back and forth in front of the shop, keeping his eye - like a hawk - on the man.

"Ah," said the man. "I believe these are the ones you're looking for. I was mistaken. It must have been the ruby ones the Englishman bought. Are these the ones?"

"Yes, yes," said Amon. "Quick, man, let me look at them. Yes, these are the ones." The demon had disappeared. He held them up for Duanna to see.

"Ohhhhhhhhhhhh," she said. There, dangling in front of her eyes, were pure enchantment. Gold, sparkling in the sun, looking all different colors at once: yellow, red, even purple. Gold hammered into the shape of a teardrop, probably two inches long and an inch wide at their widest. At the top, nearest the ear, were tiny rivulets of red, no more than an eighth of an inch in length. Lower on the earrings was the name **Amon** written in Egyptian letters.

"Ohhhhhhh," she said again.

"I will take them," Amon said.

"They are not for sale," said the shopkeeper.

"What?" said Amon, taking the man by the shirt front and literally lifting him off his feet.

"I . . . I mean, they are not for sale at the same price. I will need twice the price I paid you."

"That will do," said Amon, counting the coins from his pouch, dropping the earrings inside. He closed the drawstring and returned the pouch to his waist.

"Wait," said the man, believing he could get more money. "I made a mistake."

Amon was shouting again. "You have made one too many mistakes, including what I paid for these earrings. You are a greedy man. You'll take what I paid you or you'll have the earrings through your nose."

Duanna was racing again, as Amon stormed out of the market.

The merchant stood in the middle of the passageway with an upraised fist and a mouthful of obscenities.

Duanna was full of questions that she had sense enough not to ask:

"Why did you buy the earrings?"

"Why didn't you give them to me, like you have everything else you bought for me?"

"Why did you get so excited about this pair of earrings? There are other beautiful earrings."

"Why won't you tell me what's wrong with you?"

"You are going away in two days. Will you take me with you? What will happen to me when you go?"

"Duanna, do you love me?" he said, interrupting her head-full of questions.

"I . . . I don't know. I don't know about love. What I know is that when you're around, I feel funny. My legs get wobbly and they don't want to walk. My stomach wants to eat a lot and then it doesn't want to eat anything. And I make up stories about how we'll be together forever and ever. Is that love, Amon?"

He grinned. "I think so."

"Then I don't know if I like love. I don't want to go around with wobbly legs all the time. I'm afraid I'll fall down."

Amon laughed outright.

"Don't laugh at me, Amon."

"I can't help it. You're funny. But's that what I love about you. Sometimes you are so much a grown-up woman, talking about everything in the world, and sometimes you are such an innocent child."

"I'm not a child anymore. When I was fourteen, I stopped being a child."

"No, you're not a child. I couldn't love a child the way I love you, but sometimes you're still a child."

"You love me, Amon? You did say that, didn't you? You love me?

"Yes, I said that."

"Do your legs get all wobbly, too? Does your stomach feel funny?"

"No, little one. I love you a little differently than that."

He said no more. But Duanna didn't care. She wouldn't have heard him anyway. She was flying somewhere in the clouds.

After dinner, the Mediterranean again drew them to her. They walked hand in hand tonight in inky darkness. All the stars were lost under a cloud.

"There's a log over there, little one. Let's go sit on it," he said.

Now she was ready to hear. Now she had questions. "Amon, if your legs don't get wobbly, and your stomach doesn't feel funny, how do you know you love me?"

I know that I love you, because I want you near me. I want to touch you, to hold you close, to protect you from harm, to see you happy, to hear you laugh, to enjoy what you say to me, to have children with you. That's how I know I love you."

"Ohhhhhhhhhhh," she said.

"I didn't want to love you. I tried not to love you. I tried to enjoy you and have fun with you and not love you. I have known many women since Dameli died and I have loved none of them. I didn't think I would love you either . . . until these slavers tried to abduct you. Then I knew I loved you. I knew I could have killed them for trying to harm you, Duanna. And I have learned to love you more and more each day since then."

"Amon, what is it for a man to love?"

He took both her hands in his and looked deep into her eyes. "Love is being together in ways I'm not with anyone else. Love is finding my ultimate pleasure with you and you finding it with me. It means finding it more together than anywhere else, even though there is pleasure in other places. When I have love, you, see, I have everything else."

"Does that mean you want to possess me? Does it mean I have to follow your rules? Does it mean I have to give you sons?"

"Where did you get those ideas, little one?"

"I had some dreams."

"Ah, I see."

"Well, is it?"

"Well, for some men, all of that is so. Many of the men in my country and in other countries where I've travelled insist that that is what love is. Having a woman who will follow his rules, have sex with him whenever he wants, and give him sons so that he can feel important."

"To be like a slave?"

"Yes, to be like a slave."

"But what happens if she gives him daughters, or decides not to follow his rules? What if she doesn't want to make him feel important?"

"Then he just takes another wife who will follow his rules and give him sons."

She pulled her hand away from him and turned her head. "But that's not fair. Men are free. Why can't I be free, too?"

"You can be, little one. You are free now. When I saw you dance, I knew you were free. I want you to be free. I want both of us to be free. I don't ever want to possess you."

"Or make me follow your rules?"

"No. We make our own rules."

"Or want only sons?"

"I want daughters that will look exactly like you."

"And I want sons who will look exactly like you, Amon."

"Then we will have both, Duanna." His arms were around her. He pulled them both to a standing position. He bent and kissed her on the mouth. His lips were soft against hers and gently called her body to him. Something deep inside began to stir. It was like a birth. Something she had never known before, but now would know forever. It was commitment.

"Now I know about love," she said. "I love you."

"And will you marry me, your father willing?"

It was the woman in her that said, "I will, Amon. I will."

She rested her head against his shoulder and he stroked her long hair. They turned toward the harbor, the harbor that had just witnessed their words of union. Even the moon came out from behind a cloud, to celebrate.

"There is more I need to tell you," he said.

Duanna stirred in his arms. "Yes, tell me."

"I will be leaving Alexandria day after tomorrow to take care of my business - some things I have to do. I will be gone four or five months."

For the first time, Duanna knew the feeling of the stone in her stomach. While he was there, even holding her in his arms, she knew the stone.

"When I come back, we'll be married. I'll leave my home in Massewa and come and live in Alexandria with you. From then on, if I have to leave, I'll take you with me. I don't want to go now, little Duanna - now that I've found you. The last thing I want to do is leave but I have no choice."

In that moment, Duanna knew both sadness and joy. But she was too happy for sadness. She had tomorrow; and then in four or five months, she had everything. "Let's go talk to father now," she said, the child in her wanting to run, the grownup woman demanding she be demure.

Amon held her tightly until they absolutely had to leave to ask the permission they both knew would be theirs. 'One more day' stared at them from the waters of the Mediterranean.

CHAPTER 7

It was the best day of her life. It was the worst day of her life. They had a day. He would be gone. The woman-child in her was trying to decide. The frisky, willful, spoiled child of Zamen and Naditu was being pushed out by the newness of her womanhood. It was coming to her in the looks in his eyes, and in the sureness of his love for her. She felt it in her woman soul, the soul that was now making itself known to her, just as she was giving it away. Giving it away with full knowledge that this was the only way she could find it.

The day was quiet and contemplative. He finished his last-minute business in the city. They made plans for their wedding with Naditu and Zamen.

Zamen almost burst at their dinner celebration, in pride for his expanded family. Ninus joined Tiy, and Saragon came with her husband and little boy.

After dinner, it was automatic. They returned to the beach. To the log... their log.

Just an old log that had been washed up on the beach but now it was special because it was their log. They didn't talk. They were lost in thoughts, bittersweet as they were.

Amon broke the mood. He pulled the earrings out of his pouch and held them, enclosed, in the palm of his hand.

"Duanna, tonight I want to give you these earrings. I was such a fool to sell them to that man. I was despondent then and I didn't think I would ever want them again. They had cast a spell on me and all I wanted was for them to be gone."

"You see, they were Dameli's. After she died, I was so sure I would never find another woman to love that I got rid of them just to get them away from me. And I almost lost them."

He opened his palm and held the earrings up to the light of the moon. "There's something special about these earrings, Duanna. They can belong only to a woman who has been designated by the gods to wear them and they can be given to her only by the man who loves her. Once a woman wears them, it means her soul and the soul of her lover will be together forever, even through eternity. And once she wears them, she must never take them off, until her death. When it is time, she will know and she must find somebody to be keeper of the earrings after she dies - until the next designated woman is made manifest. Whoever is the keeper of the earrings will know who the next woman is when the time comes."

"Amon, am I the woman?" said Duanna, her eyes widening at his story.

"You are the woman."

"How do you know that?"

"Because I love you and you love me in a way few people know how to love."

"Yes," she said. Even in her innocence, she knew the truth of what he had just said.

"But, before I give you the earrings, I want to tell you everything, I want you to know their story. Then you can decide whether you want your soul to live throughout eternity with me."

"Amon, I want......."

"Shhhhhhh, hear my story first. Then tell me."

As Amon talked, Duanna was transported away from the waters of the Mediterranean, away from Alexandria, away from the Mediterranean... to Ethiopia. She was there. She saw it all.

It was dark. There was a fire. Two people sat in front of the fire. An old man with very grey hair, broad-shouldered and regal, wearing robes. And Amon, young Amon, without the lines of worry or the weather-beaten cxperiences of the sea. The old man was holding the earrings and he was talking.

"Son, you are to wed Dameli within the week."

"Yes, sir."

"I have seen the love between you; I approve. Your mother would have approved if she were among the living. And the spirits have spoken to me. They have given you to each other, to love forever, they said. They have told me I am to give you the greatest gift a man can give to a woman." He held up the earrings.

"Mother's earrings?"

"Yes. The gods have told me you must give them to Dameli to seal your love for each other."

The two men were gone. Duanna saw a woman - small, with lively eyes. She was running. She was happy. She was wearing the earrings. Amon was holding her. They were loving, at night, in a hut.

Days and nights pass; there is no child in her belly. The woman stops running. The happiness is gone from her eyes. She looks weak and frail. She goes from woman to woman in the village to find out what to do.

Amon holds her just as before. He loves her just as before. "I don't need a child, Dameli. I only need you. A child is not important."

Dameli does not hear.

Duanna saw the woman travelling deep into the forest, away from her home, away from Amon. She searches until she finds an old man, hidden away in a cave. They are talking together. He is nodding.

"You are not strong enough to bear a child and live," he is saying.

"Then I will not live," she said. "I must have a child for his love."

Now she was sitting in front of a fire, a putrid-smelling fire. The man is feeding the fire with herbs, bark and dead animals. Days and days she sits there.

The old man and the cave are gone.

Duanna sees the woman, running again into Amon's arms. She is happy again. Now she is big with child. But she looks even more frail, even weaker. Amon holds her even more gently now and loves her with more and more of himself.

Duanna sees frantic activity around a hut. The child is to be birthed. Amon is pacing, crazily, outside the hut. Screams of pain are coming from inside, as the child fights its way to life.

Duanna sees another man who paces, step for step, with Amon. His pacing is not crazy.

There is a cry, the cry of a newborn child.

Amon stops pacing and smiles.

"Wait," says the second man, the medicine man. "I will see them first. I will pass the spirits over them. Then you can go in."

Amon sits quietly on a stump, waiting.

A baby's scream of pain comes from the hut.

Then there is silence, deathly silence.

Amon does not move.

The medicine man comes out of the hut; blood is on his hands.

"Your son was born deformed. I killed him, as you know I must. You will have other children. Healthy children. You may go in now."

She heard screams of a new kind of pain, a pain from deep in Amon's belly. They ravaged the air. Screams to the gods. Screams of hate for killing his child. The screams came again, and again, and again.

Duanna saw Amon holding his wife in his arms, rocking her with his body. She is burning with fever.

Her eyes are opening. "Amon?"

"Yes, Dameli."

"Did we have a son?"

His eyes clouded over as he lied. "Yes, we have a beautiful and healthy son."

Then she was quiet.

"Amon, I must tell you the truth."

"What truth, Dameli?"

"I cannot live through the night. I saw a witch doctor many moons ago to help me have a child in my belly. He told me. But now that you have a son to love, I will die happy. Our love has given you a child; the child is more important to me than life. Be happy with our son, Amon." The effort has cost all her strength; now she cannot hear.

Tears are rolling down his cheeks. His body is shaking. He is calling out to the gods to take him, too.

Dameli is talking again. She is touching the earrings in her ears. "Take the earrings, my love. Find another woman to love and give them to her. Let her be the mother to our son. Let her love you as I have loved you; love her as you have loved me. Then my spirit will live in her as it will in our son."

Amon is taking the earrings out of her ears. He holds them up for her to see. He puts them in the pouch around his waist. "I promise," he said.

Dameli's breathing is harder and harder. Amon holds her and rocks her. Toward morning, her breathing stops. The fever turns to cold in his arms. Now it is sobs that come from deep in his belly.

Duanna sees his rage. She sees him destroying everything in sight. With his bare hands, he is destroying every possession he owns. He screams to the gods not to live. He is a crazed, mad man.

Frightened, children are running away from him.

Birds are leaving their nests.

Dogs are running in circles, afraid of the noise.

Men are trying to calm him.

Drums are awakening the village with the news of Dameli's death and the death of their newborn son.

Amon is staggering to his ship and flinging himself on his sleeping mat in his cabin.

"What are your orders, sir?" asks his captain.

"Sail! And never plan to come back here again," he says.

The captain sets the sails and the ship moves away from Massewa toward Amon's destiny; toward a life of no life.

Duanna sees a hollow-eyed and thin Amon being dragged from his cabin by the captain and three other men - forcing him into the sea air. He is gagging from the water they are forcing down his throat.

"It will do her no good if you die, too," said the captain. "Eat!" Then all the men were gone.

"I ate, Duanna. I don't know why. All I wanted to do was die. But I ate. They let me have the blackness of my despair for seven days; then they saved me from myself."

"Since then I have travelled the Mediterranean from Rome to Carthage, to Persia, to Constantinople and back again. I have bought and sold my goods in every city and country ringing this sea. I have traded with every thief I knew and with men I knew to be killers. I wanted nothing more than that they kill me, too. . . to send me to death with my beloved Dameli. I have involved myself over and over again in meaningless affairs with women. I have punished each of them by taking them to bed and then leaving them. And each woman has only increased my despair by reminding me of the promise I made to Dameli. For me, it was an empty promise. I had no son to love. I had no wife to love and I could not love another woman. I knew the earrings would never belong to another woman as long as I lived."

"Then the earrings became the focus of my despair. I could not stand to have them near me. Every minute that they lay in my drawer in my cabin, they reminded me of my love for her. I wanted to fling them overboard. I was afraid of my punishment in hell for destroyed their magic, so I sold them. I just sold them to the first man who would have them - the merchant you saw in the market."

"I didn't intend to love you when I came to your birthday celebration. I didn't ever intend to love you. I just thought you were interesting enough to lull away some of my time while I did business in Alexandria. First, it was your dancing that attracted me, then it was your wit and your learning. I think selling the earrings freed me from their hold on me, and allowed me to have fun with you. You helped me to forget Dameli, if even for a few hours."

"But when you were almost abducted by those slavers, I knew I cared for you more than I thought. Since then, I have been falling in love with you, more and more, every moment we have had together."

"Now I know how much I love you. I love you enough to give you these precious earrings. You have filled Dameli's place in my heart. You have her spirit. And now you have mine as well."

The story left him spent. Tears were rolling unchecked down his cheeks. He trembled.

The story had left her with a pain deep in her belly. She had no words to tell him what she felt. She took him in her arms and held his head to her chest. She touched his hair, letting him feel gentled with her touch. She wiped his tears with her dress. She rocked him until he stopped trembling, comforting him with her softness.

There they stayed in each other's arms, while the moon rose above the horizon, until it topped the masts of the ships rocking in the harbor.

"Duanna."

"Yes?"

"I want you to know one more thing. I will always carry Dameli in my heart and in my memory."

"Yes. As you should."

"But now my love for you is as strong as it once was for her. I will love you always. . . as long as you will have me."

"You will have me always, Amon."

"Will you wear the earrings, now that you know their story?"

"I will wear the earrings and never take them off. I will walk through this life and every other life with you. I will be with you through eternity."

"Then let me put the earrings into your ears."

Duanna reached up and removed the simple jade earrings given to her by Zamen. Amon pushed the wire of the first earring through her right ear. He said, "As I give you this earring, my spirit enters into you now and forever."

Something happened inside her. It was in her belly. It was strong. And heavy . . . and right. She took him in, his spirit; it was in her. She knew.

He pushed the second earring into her other ear. He said, "As I give you this earring, your spirit enters into me for now and forever."

Then it was as if lightning flashed around them - lightning . . . coming out of the clouds. There was a pain in her heart. A pain as though her spirit was leaving her. . . going to him. As quietly as it had come, it was gone. He had her spirit. She knew.

Duanna was too full of love now to be the child she once was. It was the woman who stood up from the log, moving toward Amon.

He pulled her to him with kisses on her nose, her cheeks, her forehead, her mouth, her neck. She loved it. She loved him.

He stood back, looking at her, the earrings swinging in the moonlight. "Yes," he said. "The poison in my soul is gone. I am free. And I love."

And the waves lapped against the rocks and the sand. Ships bobbed and weaved against the water. "Amon," she said. "I want our bodies to be as complete as our souls."

"I don't know that we can do that, little one. There is nothing I would rather take away with me tomorrow than the closeness of our bodies but you are a virgin. I can not violate your virginity now. We have to wait until our wedding."

"Isn't there a way, Amon?"

"Hmmmmmmmm. Maybe there is." He untied the belt from his tunic and dropped it to the sand. "Take off your dress and come to me."

Duanna slipped the linen of her dress over her head and dropped it on the log. Naked, she walked toward him.

He scooped her up in his arms and held her to him. He lowered his head to hers and kissed her gently on the mouth.

Duanna's body stirred.

He kissed her with more passion.

It was like a flame burning through her.

His tongue found hers.

The fire danced.

He was carrying her, away from their log, to a warm place in the sand. He nestled her among the grains, her tiny body enfolded within its warmth. He slipped off his tunic and dropped it, out of the way. He lay on his stomach next to her and began to touch her lovingly on the face, caressing her cheeks, moving her hair, strand by strand. He was touching her body where she had never been touched before. He was looking into her, into her eyes, eyes that trusted him in this moment.

She arched toward him. Her body rolled into his. She heard little sounds coming out of her throat, sounds she had never heard before. His hands were moving all over her body, sending sensation after sensation through her. She closed her eyes, to feel it all.

He knelt over her, closing out the sky, closing out the moon, closing out everything but himself. His face, so close to hers, moving. . . in rhythm. . . against her.

She felt it. A pleasure in her loins she had never known before. "Stay," she said. "Please don't go away."

Something was hard on him; and it was moving. . . gently. . . and with rhythm. It didn't go away. She strained against him. She wanted more. . . More. . . MORE. . . ..!

She was losing herself. Into her pleasure.

Lightning was going off all over her body. She pushed against him. Her body was out of control. He moved faster against her. There was something warm on her belly. Sounds came from their throats and blended with the wind and the waves and the crashing against the rocks.

Amon rolled away, pulling her body close to his. Sweat glistened in the moonlight as they were washed with the warm Mediterranean air and cradled in the soft sand.

"Our bodies are one now, Duanna."

"Our bodies and our souls," she said. "I love you forever, Amon." And the earrings twinkled, seconding her promise.

"For now and for eternity," he said.

They walked, arm in arm, back to the house of Zamen, silently saying goodbye.

Zamen saw them coming. Somehow he knew. He was proud.

The next day Duanna went to the dock with Amon and watched him board his ship. She stood, the wind whipping her dress and her hair, as he raised sail and began his voyage - away from her. He stood on the deck, his arm upraised in a silent salute, as the Lioness left its anchor. The earrings shone in the sun. Neither of them knew it would be years before they saw each other again.

CHAPTER 8

The events that tore them apart started within two weeks. For Duanna, this day was no different from the rest. Like a woman possessed, she wandered back to the beach . . . .back to the log. There to sit, staring into the horizon, into the water, out at the ships at anchor, indulging herself in her loneliness for Amon.

Her attention was so self-centered, she almost missed it. A ship had to pass almost under her nose before she looked up. Then she saw that ship after ship was entering the harbor, all at full speed. And there were masts as far as the eye could see. All were flying the same foreign flag.

Ships were passing directly in front of her, some dangerously close. She found herself looking down the barrel of huge guns. Men stood behind the guns training them on her.

They were shouting at her, calling to their fellows to come look, all in a language she didn't understand. They were laughing and slapping each other on the back, pointing at her.

Flames jumped onto her cheeks.

Ka Whom! It was from the guns of one of the ships near the palace.

Ka Whom! Ka Whom! A ship resting in the harbor was on fire.

Gone was her reverie. She ran, stumbling over the rocks, falling down, getting up again, this time with a torn dress and scratched hands and knees.

Ka Whom! went the guns.

She looked out at the ships, many with their guns trained on her.

She ran faster.

Halfway home, she saw Tiy running toward her. "Tiy, what is it?"

"You've got to hurry. Father is at home; and he wants to see us all right away. Hurry, Duanna!"

"Father? Home?" She looked out at the menacing ships.

Ka Whom! There was more fire near the palace.

They raced into the great room, out of breath. Zamen was pacing the floor. Duanna had never seen her mother look so worried.

Duanna flew into Zamen's arms. She felt a desperateness in his hug. "What's happening, Father? I saw the ships and heard the guns."

"The Pasha of Turkey is invading Alexandria. He wants to make Egypt part of the Ottoman Empire; and he's going to try to take Alexandria first, before he sails the Nile down to Cairo. The Sultan wants every able-bodied man to meet in the market in an hour, to fight off this enemy. All the women and children are to meet at the West Gate, where you will be taken to a camp in the desert. There you will be safe until we have fought off these barbarians. I want you to start packing immediately."

"I want to stay here with you, Zamen," said Naditu.

"I don't want to go either," said Duanna.

"If Ninus is going to fight, I need to stay and be near him," said Tiy.

"None of you are going to stay. The Turks are barbarians and noted for what they do to women. I would have no peace of mind knowing that any of you were here where one of these men could get their hands on you. I want you to go now. I want you to pack to leave. Gena, you will help. Illana, you will stay here with me."

Ka Whom! Ka Whom! sounded from the harbor.

"Hurry."

Naditu started to cry.

Zamen crossed the room to take her in his arms, to hold her, to kiss away her fears. Never in their twenty-seven years had they spent a night apart. The wrenching was deep for both of them. He smoothed her hair back from her face. "We'll be all right, Naditu. We'll have those Turks out of our city in three days."

But three days turned into a week . . . two weeks . . . three weeks . . . more.

The heat burned down on the women and children in the camp.

The wind brought dust and more dust getting into their eyes, their hair, their clothes. Cleanliness was impossible.

Water ran low; dirt caked their bodies.

Food was rationed, and many were hungry.

Nightly, women screamed and cried as news of the dead and wounded was carried into the camp by soldiers.

Children cried in loneliness and confusion.

The men quickly formed a rag-tag army, poorly equipped and devoid of training, but high in spirit and determination.

Professional soldiers fought off the early attacks and were successful.

In the night, Egyptian men boarded the ships at harbor and attacked the Turks at daybreak. Surprise caused the sinking of almost a third of the Turkish craft.

Later, more Turks poured out of the other ships and were sent retreating by the fire from the Egyptian guns.

Turks, who got close enough, were killed in hand-to-hand fighting.

But victory for the Alexandrian army was eluded by an endless stream of Turks emerging from the very bowels of these ships. Even though thousands of them floated face-down on the water, more and more kept coming, yelling at the top of their lungs as they advanced.

The Egyptians were becoming tired. Their ranks of soldiers thinned. The Turks were gaining ground.

The Egyptians were losing.

The Egyptians surrendered.

It took seven weeks.

An Egyptian soldier carried the news to the women in the camp. "Our men fought hard. Many of them died or were wounded to save our city. But now it is over. We are under the rule of the Pasha of Turkey. You will be glad to know that you will go home tomorrow and that most of your homes are unharmed. Turkish officers will be here to guide you. In the meantime, there are some new rules you should know about. The Pasha of Turkey has decreed:

"That our Coptic church will be outlawed. All citizens will be required to convert to the church of Islam and the worship of Allah."

There was a murmur of protest from the crowd.

"The position of women under our new rulers will be altered. Whereas before you have had the right to an education and the right to own property, this will be changed. The Pasha has ordered that all further education of women will be stopped; and all education of men will now take place in the Turkish language. Property belonging to women and their husbands or to women alone will now belong to their husbands alone; or if the husband is dead, to her son. If there are no sons, it will become the property of the government."

The murmurs grew louder.

"Finally, all women will now be required to wear veils whenever they are away from their homes or in the presence of men."

The murmurs were now angry shouts.

"I will post the list of wounded and dead."

Veils forgotten, the women with living husbands, fathers, brothers, and sons, rushed to the post.

Duanna and Tiy stood at the edge of the circle while Naditu made her way to the piece of parchment.

They watched her slump to the ground.

Duanna pushed her way through the crowd and flung herself over her mother's body, while Tiy read from the parchment. "Zamen El Rashid, killed in the battle of Alexandria on its last day, 1517."

Grief filled their tent that night. And stayed the next night, and the next, and the next, as they tried to live without the center of their family, the love of their lives.

By morning, Naditu was feverish and weak.

The Turkish soldiers were outside rounding up the women for the walk back to the city.

Rape was on their minds.

Soldiers raced through the camp on their horses, picking up young girls as they rode by, carrying them kicking and yelling, to the places of their intent.

Mothers tried to save their daughters and were struck down for the trying.

Girls cried out for pity.

Screams were everywhere as virgins were torn and bruised.

They emerged from tents, pulling their tattered dresses around them.

While soldiers stood in line, passing out the veils of chastity.

Duanna hated them, every one.

They half pushed, half carried the feverish Naditu as the caffel of women struggled its way back to Alexandria. Soldiers on horseback patrolled the parade, prodding with sticks those who slowed the procession. Girls cowered against their mothers, slim protection, as the soldiers made advances.

Naditu stumbled and fell. Duanna and Tiy were struggling against time to right her again, before they felt the force of a soldier's prod.

Suddenly there was a bellow from above. "Hurry it up there."

Looking down at them from atop a majestic white horse was one of the ugliest men Duanna had ever seen. He was bleary-eyed and bloated, with a dark complexion made darker by heavy black eyebrows and beard. His nose was large and reddened from the sun; and his lips were flaccid and almost colorless. His belly protruded from under his shirt; and jowls jiggled beneath the beard. He smelled of Turkish sweat and putrid alcohol.

Duanna's stomach turned. "My mother is ill; and it is hard for her to walk."

"I will see that you are relieved of your burden, if you will ride up here with me," he said, winking at her.

"No, thank you, sir. She's better now. We'll make it."

"I would like it if you rode up here with me," he said, his tone now insistent.

Duanna chose not to answer.

"What is your name?"

"Enheduanna El Rashid, sir," she said as quietly as possible, hoping he wouldn't hear.

But he heard. "Where do you live, Enheduanna El Rashid?"

"In the house of Zamen El Rashid, now dead," she said.

"If you will not ride with me, then we must meet again at another time," he said, spurring his horse until she reared, then galloping off in a cloud of dust.

"You made him angry," said Tiy.

"I don't care. He stinks. He would have made me vomit if I had been on the back of his horse."

"He would have helped us with mother."

"I'd rather carry her myself, Tiy. You ride with him if you want his help."

"He didn't ask me."

Later, Tiy was full of information. "I found out who he is, Duanna."

"I don't care who he is."

"Well, you will when I tell you. He's the Shamash, chief aide to the Pasha. He's going to be the most important man in Alexandria when the Pasha leaves to fight in Cairo. You should have been nice to him."

"Just leave me alone, will you? You could be a little more help with mother, instead of snooping around about that ugly old man."

"He said he'd see you again."

"Tiy!"

"All right! All right!"

Naditu did not heal. They kept a vigil over her around the clock, wiping the sweat from her body, reassuring her after her nightmares. Night after night, she woke up calling to Zamen, dreaming about his death, dreaming about his life, raging at the war, raging at the Turkish government.

Which was not through yet with the family of Zamen El Rashid.

It was a week after the miserable march home through the desert when Duanna saw a man on horseback, obviously a government man, tying his horse just outside the garden.

He was pounding on the door. "Open up for a message from the Pasha. Open up inside."

Gena raced in from the cooking room. "Shall I open the door, Ma'am?" she said to Naditu, who was reclining on the divan.

"Yes. No! Wait! Find the veils. Where are the veils?"

Tiy and Duanna went in immediate search for the hated veils. The pounding was getting louder. "Open the door in there!"

"Here they are," said Tiy.

"Now you may open the door, Gena," said Naditu.

A tall, gangly, dark-complexioned Turk pushed Gena aside as he entered. He didn't wait for politeness. "I have a message for Enheduanna El Rashid. Which of you is Enheduanna?"

"I am, sir," said Duanna.

He whipped out the roll of parchment he had under his arm, unrolled it, and began to read.

> **"The Pasha of Turkey decrees that on the morrow Enheduanna El Rashid shall marry the Shamash, chief aide to the Turkish governor. She shall leave the house of Zamen El Rashid in an hour to be brought to the palace for preparations. If this decree is not complied with in said time, the family of El Rashid will proceed to the prison and remain until said wedding takes place or until death."**

They were too stunned for anything but silence. It resounded off the walls and into their bellies.

Naditu finally found her tongue. "But she is already betrothed."

"It has been decreed," said the man, as if Naditu had never spoken. "She will marry the Shamash tomorrow. I will be back within the hour." He turned abruptly and walked out the door.

Duanna's screams filled the room. "No! No! No! No! I can't marry the Shamash. I can't marry that ugly man. I'm going to marry Amon." In her anguish, she fell to the floor, hands on her belly, and curled into a little ball. Wham! Wham! went her fists against the floor.

"No! No! No! Noooooo! I am to marry Amon."

Now the tears started. Great gushing sobs. "Amon. Amon. Amon. Please don't let them do this to me. Amon. Mother. Tiy. Please!"

This time it was Naditu who comforted . . . who took her in her arms, and rocked her. "You don't need to marry the Shamash, my baby. You don't need to marry that ugly old man. You don't need to." Duanna trembled in her arms.

"What are you saying?" Tiy whispered through clenched teeth.

"Shhhhhhhhhh," said Naditu.

Duanna heard. Even now, she knew what it would mean to her family for her to refuse. Tiy . . . Saragon . . . the baby . . . her mother . . . all in those dungeons they called prison. All sleeping on nothing but bug-infested dirt floors. All eating the gruel that they called food. All at the mercy of the guards . . . who raped at will. All starving. All dying. Time stopped for her in her trap. She knew there was no way out. There was no solution, but to walk into it.

She lay in her mother's arms, her sobs becoming whispers . . . her pain lying like a knife in her stomach.

In time, she sat up and wiped her eyes with the veil she still held in her hand. "I will marry the Shamash," she said. "I can't let you go to prison for me. You would not live in that rat-infested place they call the prison, my mother and Tiy; you shouldn't be punished for my sake. I will marry the Shamash. Tiy, will you gather my things?"

Naditu struggled her way back to the divan. She wasn't going to prison. But her relief was bittersweet. True, there would be no prison with bars and chains; but now she was in a prison of her loss, first of her husband and now of her youngest daughter. Both lost to the greediness of men.

Before the hour was up, a waif-like Duanna returned to the great room, carrying the few belongings she would take with her. "Mother, I have a message for Amon. He'll be back for me in two or three months. Tell him I love him; and that my spirit will always be with him, no matter what I'm forced to do. Tell him I will wear his earrings until death. Nobody can take that away from me. Will you tell him?"

"I will tell him."

CHAPTER 9

It was dark and it was gloomy, even with its light-colored marble walls and its attached oil lamps trying to make light what would not be light. Statues of the great and near-great ringed the central pool where children splashed and a girl bathed. Carved columns held up the ceilings; and women abounded in various stages of apathy.

Their dress designated their status: from wife to concubine, to attendant; from elegant to outlandish to plain. The activities varied from passive to dull to boring. Most lay around on divans, in stages of sleep. A few were playing with the art materials littered about. Some were painting their faces. Some were undoing the paint on their faces.

The harem of the Shamash.

It was designed with one purpose in mind. To serve its male master, its creator. To give him a bevy of women, whose only thoughts in their otherwise empty heads were to please him, to be beautiful for him, to vie for his favors against the other women, and to give him his sexual pleasures. He had designed it. He had created it; and he maintained it as an emblem of his self-aggrandizement.

It was the male dream. It was the female prison. It was a prison complete with its walls, its bars on the windows, and its prison guards - the eunuchs. Even the guards, those eunuchs, had been modified to serve the male dream. Each had been divested of his sexuality in order to provide the most and the least. They provided the most strength to keep any woman imprisoned who resisted imprisonment. They provided the least competition of intent that would violate the ownership of the master.

Duanna had learned these things at her father's knee. Now she was to live them. Now she was to be privileged to live the male dream. And her nightmare.

She was escorted by the deputy of the Shamash to the door of the harem, given entrance by the eunuch, and met by one of the plain women in blue. The woman curtsied and said, "My name is Iris, madam, and I will be your attendant." Then began her long trip through the collection of women, who stridently became alive at the entrance of their new rival. They converged, in pairs, in trios, or quartets, to eye and discuss her in every detail. They were not discreet in their whisperings. She heard every word.

"That's the one. That's his new wife."

"Too little to be much good - if you ask me."

"Needs more meat on her bones."

"Pretty little thing, though."

"She won't be so pretty when he gets through with her."

"Here she'll grow up fast."

"Why is he making her his wife?"

"He wants an Egyptian wife to show off to the Turks."

"He wants to be sure she doesn't get away."

"Egyptian women have a reputation for being independent. They teach them to read, you know."

"He'll get the independence out of her."

It was true. Duanna was home . . . in her prison.

Iris took her immediately to her apartment. It was just like the rest of those that circled the great room. Here, at least, was a window to the world. Here, at least, she could see out to the courtyard. Beyond that, it was a drab pair of rooms: long and narrow, with doors made of strips of colored beads to prevent isolation. In one room was a sleeping divan and in the other, some cushions and a make-up table.

She moved, as if dead, allowing Iris to do what she would. She didn't care. What was there to care about anymore? Life had been stolen from her. They had taken everything. They had taken, even, her dignity, for immediately Iris undressed her, leaving her naked. She washed and oiled Duanna. Then, with two other attendants, she began to fit her for the clothes she would wear on the morrow. They did whatever they wanted with her, putting on and taking off outfits, trying on shoes for size, holding necklaces and bracelets against her olive skin - to see which were the most attractive.

It wasn't until they came toward her with a new pair of earrings that she came alive. "No!" she said, grabbing at her ears and backing away. "Please let me wear these earrings."

Strategy seemed to be a dire necessity. She began to lie. "The last thing I want to do is defy the Shamash," she said, "but these earrings were a gift from my father, who died in the war. He would be so proud of me today if he were here, knowing I was marrying the Shamash. He would want me most of all to wear his earrings."

The three attendants put their heads together.

"We can't let her keep those earrings."

"We'll be in trouble with the Shamash."

"Maybe he won't notice."

"But what if he does?"

"He's usually too drunk to notice much of anything."

"But if he does notice, he'll beat us raw."

"The veil will cover them."

"Yes."

"Let her wear them, if it's that important."

Duanna was not going to lose her precious earrings; and the knot in her stomach unknotted . . . slightly.

She was given a silk gown to wear for sleep. "We will wake you in the morning for your happy day," said Iris, as she left for the night.

Duanna threw herself on the divan and cried until sleep rescued her from her hate and despair.

In the morning, Iris arrived with a tray. Duanna gagged at the very smell. She moaned and turned away.

"You must eat this, my mistress," said Iris. "It will make you fertile."

"Have the gods forsaken me? Isis? Isis, I need you now. Please don't forsake me. Fertile!"

She threw it out the window as soon as Iris walked out.

But it wasn't long before they were back, busying themselves with her toilet. They washed her hair and brushed it until it sparkled. They dressed her in her wedding outfit of white silk. White silk pantaloons and a white silk flowing blouse, with a purple sash and gold brocaded slippers. Then they proudly placed the veil over her face and led her to the great room of the palace, where she was met at the door by a triumphant Shamash.

"Ah, my Enheduanna. It is just as I said. We meet again."

She gritted her teeth. She refused to curtsy. "Yes, we meet again," she thought. "You win at your evil game. You now own my body. But you will never own my spirit. That is beyond your reach."

He propelled her through the hordes of ill-smelling, extravagantly-dressed guests to the front of the room where they were married by the Pasha. When it was all over, the hordes cheered for her fertility and wished the Shamash . . . .sons.

He left her at the side of the room in the care of a eunuch, while he and his guests ate great quantities from a table loaded with roasted goat, chicken and beef, oxen stew, steaming plates of barley cooked in olive oil, and desserts of figs, dates, and apples, as well as Turkish cakes baked especially for the Pasha. No wine glass remained empty, as slave girls raced about filling and refilling the goblets.

Entertainment went on through the day. The guests shouted obscenities at the dancing girls dressed in very little. They cheered for and against wrestlers, who grunted and groaned before falling on the floor. They shouted approval or disapproval of the acrobats, whose limber bodies were all over the arena.

As the wine flowed freely, some of the guests decided they were Sampson with long, flowing hair. They took on the wrestlers, shouting and snorting to their own defeat. Some decided they were Don Juan, and took on the dancing girls, raping them on the spot, to the cheers and jeers of the onlookers. Most decided they had wooden legs and fell drunkenly to the floor as the day went on.

Duanna, already sick, felt sicker.

Then he came to get her, to take her to his bedroom, to complete the marriage, to ravage her virgin body, to make her hate.

His room was large and full, mostly with a bed. Black. Canopied. And fearsome. The rest of the room was filled with cushions and a crock of wine surrounded by goblets.

As if he hadn't had enough, he poured another goblet of wine and ordered Iris: "Undress her and then leave." He settled his bulk onto one of the cushions to watch . . . to render her naked through the light silk.

Iris began with the veil, revealing a face, once trusting and naive, now frightened and bitter.

Then came the jewelry, piece by piece. The Shamash scrutinized each item as Iris laid it on the table. "Would Iris try to take the earrings? There would be a scene."

She didn't try.

Instead she pulled the blouse over Duanna's head, revealing satiny olive skin and small breasts.

The Shamash's eyes narrowed and pierced.

She tossed her long hair, trying to cover herself, but to no avail.

Iris finished by removing the pantaloons and slippers. Now she stood in front of him, naked, to be ravaged by his cruel intent.

She felt shame and humiliation at the bestiality she saw in his eyes.

Iris prolonged her agony by producing a hairbrush and pulling it repeatedly through her long hair . . . until he'd had enough.

"Leave now," he bellowed at Iris.

The brush clattered to the floor, as she ran out ahead of another bellow. "I told you to leave!"

He got up from his cushion, waving his goblet of wine, his ugliness getting closer and closer.

She wasn't sure her legs would hold her up.

"And now, my pretty, we will have pleasure like you have never known before; isn't that right?"

"Yes, my Shamash."

"Very good. You have been brought up well."

"Yes, my Shamash."

"Lay down on the bed."

From there, she saw his ugliness unveiled as he took off his robe and dropped it on the floor. With his eyes never leaving her face, he lifted his goblet to his mouth and drained it dry. Then he threw the goblet against the wall.

"To celebrate the joyous occasion of our marriage," he said.

He stood naked over her. She could see his organ in full erection pointing at her from under his bloated belly. She had all she could do to keep herself from turning away, from hiding at the sight of his ugliness.

Finally, the relish of his torture was replaced by his own greed. He crashed his heavy bulk down beside her. She rolled into him, as the bed sagged under his weight. He pulled her body against him, pushing himself between her legs. Now he was breathing his stench into her face. He was talking. "You had better prove to me, my pretty Enheduanna, that you have been with no other man or your life won't be worth the knife it will take to pierce your whoring heart."

Could he know about Amon? Would he know what they had done on the beach? Isis, please help me! she thought.

"Now open your legs, my Egyptian beauty. I will show you the wonder of Turkish manhood. Open your legs."

He was kneeling over her, his organ pointed and ready.

She saw it. She stared at it in all its horror.

He saw. "You like it, my pretty? Next time I'll teach you to play with it. But tonight . . . tonight I'm going to find out if there has been another man before me."

Before she could feel any more fear there was a tearing pain between her legs that refused to stop at her legs. She screamed. Over and over again she screamed. "Take it out! Take it out!"

The Shamash began to laugh. Then the pain was even more intense. "Take it out, my pretty? Take it out? Of course not. I'm not going to take it out. There is pleasure in there for me. Don't you like it?" he breathed into her face. "Don't you like it? You are my wife and you will like it. Lucky for you, there hasn't been another man. You're mine, all right, my pretty."

He plunged and shoved with all his cruelty, grunting and groaning on top of her. As she screamed in pain, he shoved harder - tearing and ripping until blood was seeping onto her legs.

Again and again she screamed.

Harder and harder he pushed, heaving over her for a small piece of forever. Finally he convulsed into satisfaction, and gave way to his drunken stupor, passing out on top of her. His total weight tried to suffocate her. He snored.

Duanna couldn't breathe. Pain was everywhere. Blood gushed from her insides. She clawed at him and pushed and kicked until he rolled off of her, snoring, onto his back.

She lost consciousness.

Later in the night, she tried to move and her pain woke her. Her bottom felt mushy; dried blood was on her belly and legs; and she felt as though she had been turned on a rack. Again the world disappeared.

The next time she knew anything, he was standing over her, bellowing for Iris. Iris raced through the door, tying on her apron as she ran.

"Take her away. Take this woman out of my sight. She's covered with blood. Take her away and clean her up. I don't want to see her again until she's healed."

Iris raced away looking for help, while the Shamash crashed down on one of his cushions. He took a long drink from his inevitable goblet of wine.

As she was carried through the great room, the gossipers were busy.

"Just as I suspected. Too tiny."

"Serves her right. These Egyptians are so sassy."

"She doesn't know yet what she needs to do to please his excellency. I don't think I'll tell her, either."

"And she thought she was so refined."

"He'll take the snob out of her."

"I heard she was betrothed to some Ethiopian prince before she came here."

"If she wasn't so high and mighty, he'd be easier on her."

"He'll do it again next time."

"Serves her right. Egyptian snob."

Iris was working feverishly over Duanna's semi-conscious body.

"Let me help," offered a plump, motherly-looking woman. Iris looked up to see Skhmet, the first wife of the Shamash, who remembered him before the harem, before the wine, before the requirements of being so grand. A woman who remembered a more gentle man, a man who had married her out of love . . . who had relished in his children . . . and who had been quite happy until the power of government had captured him in its entrails. She remembered this man before . . ..

"I'll get a tea of herbs to help the healing," she said.

Duanna tried hard not to - but they forced her to drink the tea. She sputtered and coughed as the liquid made its way down her throat.

When she was clean, and her wounds were anointed with salve, she lost consciousness into blissful sleep.

"I'll sit with her," said Skhmet. "She may need something."

"Yes, Madam," said Iris.

Skhmet watched her dream; watched her toss and turn and call out for Amon; watched her repeatedly put her hands to her ears and scream, "No! No!"

Amon was coming to her again and again to tell her she was no longer worthy of the earrings. She hadn't kept her promise. He was coming to take the earrings away. He could love her no more, because she was dirty and debased.

When he was not refusing her, she was refusing him. She had to tell him over and over again that now she couldn't marry him. Another man had taken her, torn her, left her dishonored and shamed.

The dreams went on and on. Over and over, she called out for Amon. Over and over, she tore at her ears. It was two days before she recognized where she was, who she was with, and that there was a new face standing next to Iris.

She groaned and turned her back on both of them. She refused to eat. She wouldn't drink the tea for her healing. She refused their conversation, their ministrations, their offers of love. She had decided to die.

She had decided to die - except that Skhmet was wiser than she. Skhmet had children of her own. She knew about love. "Who is Amon?" she asked.

Duanna's eyes widened. "How do you know about Amon?" she asked.

"You called out to him in your sleep. He is your love, isn't he?"

Duanna started to cry.

Skhmet knew how to help. She took her into her arms and let her cry out her pain, cry out her shame, cry out the fear that she had lost him. "He can never love me now," Duanna blubbered. "I have broken my promise to him. I don't want to live if he can't love me."

"How can he not love you? You haven't changed."

"Yes, I have. I have violated my promise to belong only to him. He'll never believe me now. He'll never want me now. He'll love somebody else."

"I would love you if I were him."

"You would?"

"You didn't do anything by your own choice. You didn't choose to marry another man. You didn't choose to have him violate you."

"No."

"I couldn't stop loving you for something you didn't choose to do."

"Oh," said Duanna, allowing these new thoughts to enter her addled brain. "I didn't choose, did I?"

"Of course not," said Skhmet.

"Then maybe . . . " she started, her tears drying a little. But no, she was not to be fooled. This woman was here to fool her. **She** knew the rightness of her dreams. "No," she said with even greater determination. "Even if I didn't choose, it's still the same. He can't love me now."

She dissolved into a new paroxysm of tears.

But Skhmet knew she had found an opening. She continued to poke and prod into that opening. "You know, Duanna, you are a lovely woman; much too beautiful and talented for Amon to stop loving you. When he comes back, he will know that you did what you did to save your family, not because you wanted to leave him. He **will** still love you."

Skhmet's words were beginning to penetrate. "Do you think so?" she sniffed.

"Of course," said Skhmet.

"Maybe when he comes back, he'll find a way to rescue me."

"Of course he will, but not if you die from not eating."

"Not if I die from not eating," Duanna repeated. "I have to live to see his ship come back or he won't be able to rescue me," Duanna said, talking more to herself than to Skhmet. "But I won't know when his ship comes back," she wailed. "I can't see the harbor from here."

"You can see the harbor from my room. You can watch from there anytime."

The wheels turning in Duanna's head were almost visible. The tears stopped streaming down her face. She looked up at Skhmet with a brand new face. This time it was with a new determination. "Then I shall not die. I will eat instead."

As soon as Iris could get it to her she was wolfing down a bowl of chicken stew and a hunk of bread. When the last crumb was inside her stomach she got up and walked to Skhmet's apartment to begin her vigil . . . her vigil of watching for Amon.

CHAPTER 10

The harem stifled her natural spontaneity. She lived in fear of the Turkish darts that came her way whenever she did anything. There was a constant buzzing of women, as they tried to eliminate this Egyptian presence from their midst. They segregated her for being Egyptian, for being pretty, for being young, for being a wife instead of a concubine, for being anything they didn't like. They congregated against her in their nastiness, leaving her bewildered, afraid and alone.

As if her wrenching separation from everything she loved wasn't enough, as though the brutality of the Shamash wasn't enough, now she had to put up with the isolation from women who should have been her friends. Her spirit, already broken, continucd to bc poisoned by her day-by-day exile.

Not only did they destroy her spirit but also they poisoned her body, with tasteless Turkish food, with the overwhelming odor of the eunuchs who passed in and out of the room, with the heavy Turkish incense constantly emitted from lamps that burned day and night, and with the strong-smelling perfumes worn by the women.

She spent her days in Skhmet's apartment watching the window to the harbor for a glimpse of the Lioness, her early evenings spent in abject fear of being recalled to the Shamash's apartment, and her nights in conflicting dreams. In some, Amon came to hold her in her terror, to soothe her, to make the lightning flash again. In others, he came to reclaim the earrings for her transgressions.

One day, out of her loneliness, came an Egyptian savior by the name of Alysha. The first time Duanna saw her, she thought she was looking into a mirror. She was looking at her own small, lithe body, her own long hair and wide eyes, and her own olive skin. But there the resemblance ended. Alysha was as street-wise as Duanna was naive. Physically, her sense of survival kept her strong, while Duanna's emotions tore her to pieces. While Duanna's thinking ran to abstractions and fantasies, Alysha's never went beyond the practical and concrete. It was if they were a study in contrasts in the same body. They were destined to be friends.

"Hi," said the mirror.

"Hi."

"Am I glad you're here. I haven't had anyone to talk to since I came and it's been awful. They don't like Egyptians much."

"I've noticed."

"I'd have been here sooner but the Shamash has had me in his apartment ever since the night of your wedding. How did you get here?"

"The Shamash saw me when we were all coming back from the desert. He sent a soldier to my father's house with a decree. And you?"

"Well," said Alysha, tossing her head. "You know how the Shamash is. Always eyeing the women with those piercing looks of his. One day just after the Turkish army got into Alexandria, he saw me in the market. I was dancing and giving those old Turks a look at a real woman, I was. And there he was on his horse, eyes piercing right through me. Scared me, he did. Scared all the men, too; because pretty soon they just drifted away. Then I got mad; because we'd been having a good time before he showed up."

"So then he just nuzzles his horse right up to me and asks my name and where I live. I told him my name was Alysha but I was scared to tell him where I lived. Then he sprung one on me I sure didn't expect. He asked me if I wanted to come and live in the palace with him. I didn't even have to think about it, I said 'sure'. Serving one man was going to be a lot easier than taking care of all those others."

Duanna's eyes widened at her suspicious thoughts. "What do you mean, take care of all those others?"

"Just what I said, take care of them. With sex. **You** know.

"You mean you were a prostitute?"

"Sure," Alysha said, tossing her head and throwing her hair behind her. "And I was a good one. I could make those men moan. First they'd moan and then they'd ask for more. The Turks were my best customers. The Turks with all their notions about veils and the sanctity of women. Bah. They lined up for me."

"But . . . but . . . didn't your family object to your selling your body?"

"Duanna, don't be naive. My family taught me. My mother has had men - as long as I can remember. Anu and me - that's my brother - were always being put out on the streets while mother took care of them. And if she didn't have any men around, we didn't have anything to eat except for what me and Anu could steal or earn by running opium for traders."

Duanna couldn't believe what she was hearing.

"I was only eleven when Mama's men wanted to have me instead of her. So then she started teaching me. She used to hide me in the corner of our hut so I could watch. That's the way I learned. That's the way I got all the tricks. And once I knew the tricks she put me to work."

"When the Turks came, and all you women left, Mama and me, we made lots of money. Mama and I kept them coming in and out of our hut like ants and when they were all gone, Anu would bring us some more."

This was beyond Duanna's imagination - to have men crawling all over her day after day - men like the Shamash.

"But, by the time the Shamash showed up, I was getting damned tired. When he said come live in the palace, I jumped. I was ready for plenty of food to eat, all the pretty dresses I wanted, and a soft bed every night. And the best part was there would be only one man."

For a moment, Alysha's eyes glazed over. "I sure do miss my Mama and Anu and all that fun we used to have. I'd go back to work in a minute if I were out of here."

Duanna's education was just beginning.

On another day, Alysha said, "Duanna, the trouble with you is that you think sex is sacred."

"Well, isn't it?"

"No. For me, it's just a business. I give them what they want and they give me what I want. Money. Simple as that."

"Oh, no, Alysha. It's not simple like that. Sex is for love. It makes two people feel like one. Like they belong together."

"Bah! There's only one reason for sex. For pleasure. And men are always wanting their little bit of pleasure. That's what they want us for. Since that's all we mean to them we might as well get what we need for doing it."

On a morning when Alysha came back from the Shamash's apartment, looking bedraggled and tired, Duanna was full of questions. "How do you stand the Shamash all over you every night?"

"That's easy. See, I don't care how ugly he is, how much he stinks, or what he does to me. All I want is for him to give me what I want. All I have to do is please him and he gives me what I want. All you need is a little practice and you can please him, too."

"No! No! No! I don't want to please him. I hate him! I hate him!"

"You'd better get over that, my naive Duanna. All you'll get for that is trouble. He thinks he's real important, like right up there next to God and if you don't pretend that you think so, too, you're in for a pack of trouble. He'll just keep on torturing you."

"But he's not important," insisted Duanna.

"Oh, yes he is. He's in a high place in government, right up there next to the Pasha."

"Well, all right. He's in a high place but that doesn't make him important. Only full of pomposity. Men who are really important don't have to act like that."

"True, yes, true, Duanna. But if you don't play into his over-inflated God-like belief in himself, he'll just keep on making you miserable . . . because he **does** have the power to do that."

"You mean I have to suffer because he thinks he's Allah or something?"

"Yes. And the sooner you learn that, the better it will be for you."

"So what I'm supposed to do is pretend that I believe he actually is right up there next to that god of theirs and satisfy his every need and whim in bed and then he'll be easy on me."

"Now you have it," said Alysha.

"Now I have it," said Duanna, sounding like she had just lost her last friend. "Alysha, I can't do all that. He's so repulsive."

"He is, isn't he?" Alysha laughed. Suddenly she jumped up from her cushion, spread her legs and stuck out her belly. "I'm the Shamash and this is the way I walk," she said, lowering her voice to a growl.

Duanna started to laugh. "And then he looks at you out of those bleary eyes and he lowers his brows like this."

"And then his jowls shake like this," said Alysha.

Then Duanna leaped off her cushion and started walking, belly protruding, feet apart, face in that characteristic frown with lowered brows and jowls shaking. "Here comes the Shamash. Big and important. Now everybody, love me," she said.

The sound that came out of Duanna's apartment was the first real laughter that had been heard in the harem in months, maybe years.

But she didn't laugh when the Shamash ended his reprieve, and called her again to his bed.

She found him slumped into one of his cushions, drinking yet from his inevitable goblet of wine. She was trying to remember everything Alysha had taught her to do. She remembered she was supposed to bow to him. "Good evening, my Shamash. I hope you are doing well this evening."

He ignored her attempts at politeness and leered at her. "Well, my Enheduanna, I haven't seen you for some time now, have I? I hope you're feeling better."

"Oh, yes, my Shamash. I am feeling much better."

His leer was turning into thunder. "I understand that after the night of our wedding, you tried to kill yourself by not eating; is that not so?"

"It is true that I did not eat for several days, my Shamash."

"And you are eating now and feeling better?"

"Yes, my Shamash."

"And you are ready to take your place in my bed?"

She lifted her chin and said, "Yes, my Shamash."

"Good," he said triumphantly. "Because, in order to see that you don't try that scheme again, I am going to see that you become with child. And in order to assure a child in your belly, I am going to have you in my bed for the next thirty nights. Won't that be wondrous?"

"Wondrous, my Shamash." Duanna wondered if her legs would hold her up one more minute.

From that moment on, Duanna's nights became a terror of suffering and brutality, followed by days of tears and despair. He took his pleasure with her with no thought for her whatsoever. Her pain, her injuries were of no concern to him. To Duanna, it seemed like he wanted to hurt her, wanted to see her face in agony, wanted to hear her cries of pain.

Some nights he would enter her with no preliminaries, and pump in and out . . . in and out . . . until he squirted his seed into her. This would immediately be followed by sleep and snoring. Shortly he would be awake and he would do it again and then again, until she was sore and bleeding. Some nights, he would order her onto her knees. Then he would come at her from behind, growling and slobbering like a dog. Some nights, he would stick his organ into her face and require that she suck it, pushing and thrusting until she gagged. He would lean back and laugh at her discomfort, then be right back for more. He would not stop until he was ready to jam himself into her bottom, to shoot his seed, to assure the child in her belly.

With each new atrocity, he would say," You like, my Enheduanna, don't you?"

She would clench her teeth and her fists and say, "Oh, yes, my Shamash."

But she had accidents. One night, she vomited in his bed, sending him bellowing for Iris. One night she bit him. He shrieked in pain. One night she passed out, leaving him heaving over an inert body.

After each incident, his torture increased.

Each morning, in the sanctuary of the harem, she released her torment in Skhmet's arms or to Alysha's less than understanding ear.

"All men misuse women, Duanna," Alysha said impatiently. "You might as well get used to it. Because that's what they think we're for. They think we're their playthings. First they buy us; then they think they own us."

"They buy me with money and they buy you with villas and palaces and servants. But it's the same thing. Once they pay their money, they believe they can do what they want. Whether it's for a prostitute like me or a lady like you. It's the same."

"No, Alysha, no! My father wasn't like that and neither is Amon. He doesn't think he owns me. He said so."

"Who's Amon?"

"He's the man I was going to marry, before I had to come here. He gave me these earrings. He said that as long as I wear these earrings, our spirits would be one."

"Spirits! Bah!" said Alysha, tossing her head.

"Wait, Alysha," and before she could think about it, she was telling the story of Amon and the earrings.

Alysha listened with skepticism. Occasionally, the story reached into an innocence hidden beyond her tough stance but then she would come to her senses. She was beyond innocence and glad of it.

Alysha would only accede to Duanna's notions with a shrug of her shoulders. "Well, maybe your Amon is different but I never knew a man like that. Spirits. Together for eternity. Never!"

Somehow, Duanna knew that Alysha understood.

But even Duanna's faith was being tested. She watched the harbor every day through Skhmet's window but there had been so sign of Amon's ship. Had he come back, and she'd missed him? Had he come back and gone away again? Maybe he hadn't come back at all. Maybe he was in prison somewhere. Maybe he was dead. Where was he?

Even with all her worry, her worst of times was over. After thirty days, the Shamash released her from her nightly torture. His virility, he was sure, had left her with child. Now his control was complete.

He was right. It wasn't long before her body began to expand to make room for the growing child. He preferred not to sully his growing sons with further seed; so he left her alone. For the first time, she realized what her baby would mean. It would mean a child to fill her loneliness, to love, and to teach. The Shamash had finally done something right.

Labor started early in the morning. It had already started when she woke up. It was all she could do not to scream out her pain. She curled herself into a ball and fisted her hands, trying to stop the sounds.

Iris took her immediately to the birthing room in another part of the palace. There she lay on a mat, sweat pouring from her body, writhing in agony with each contraction.

As the day went on, Duanna looked more and more to Iris to do something about her suffering. Iris was doing everything she knew to do. She wiped away the sweat with cool water. She brought in another attendant to fan her. She softened Duanna's worries by telling her she knew exactly how to bring a baby into the world. She'd done it many times.

Inside, she didn't feel as sure. "Something isn't right here. That baby is not moving down the birth canal. I wonder if my mistress is too small to birth this child. If she is, she'll surely die. And the baby, too."

Duanna's suffering went on into the night. Now she moaned and convulsed without letup.

Iris brought in two other attendants to help. They huddled together in a corner and spoke in whispered tones.

"How long has she been like this?"

"Since mid-afternoon."

"She looks weakened."

"She is getting weaker and weaker."

"Have you given her the herbs?"

"Yes, several hours ago."

"Nothing?"

"Nothing."

"I'm afraid she'll die if she doesn't birth the child soon."

"Yes. And such a young one, too."

In spite of their whispering, Duanna heard. "Conceived in violence, both mother and child dead upon arrival," she thought. "What justice!"

It was hard for her to breathe. "Iris," she said.

"Yes, my mistress."

"If I die, tell Alysha to take the earrings."

"The earrings, mistress?"

"She'll understand. Just tell her."

The words were barely out of her mouth when another pain convulsed her body. But this one was different. She felt less of it. She was beginning to float. She almost felt peaceful.

Then, from somewhere inside of her, came the words: "Push, Duanna, push. Don't give up. You can birth this child. Push out your little girl. She will make you happy. She will fulfill your life. Push, Duanna, push!" It was the voice of Naditu.

Iris suddenly came into action. Water broke all over the birthing mat.

"Help me," said Duanna in a weak voice. "The baby is coming."

"Yes, it is, mistress," said Iris. "Push a couple more times and you will have your child."

A tearing scream filled the room.

Duanna pushed, one more time.

The baby was born.

Duanna lost consciousness. The agony was over.

By the time Duanna again opened her eyes, Iris was standing over her, holding a squalling bundle.

"You have a beautiful daughter, mistress," said Iris.

Duanna's smile was weak but happy. "I will name her Amona," she said. But she couldn't hold her eyes open long enough, even, to look at her newborn.

The next thing she knew, it was the Shamash who was standing over her. He was smiling his sadistic smile. "I am displeased with you, Enheduanna. You have produced a girl child. I expected a son. Next time you will have a son." He turned abruptly and left.

She had never hated anyone more in her life.

In spite of her hate and her despair, the days went on, unchanging. The harem stayed the same. The women got older. Those who overindulged got heavier and more bloated. Those who did not just got more apathetic. Some had become her friends. Some still kept her at a distance.

She never left the stifling room except for festival occasions and occasional state visits, when she went all the way to the great room. She never saw Alexandria, or the market, or the harbor. She never heard the music, the sound of the Mediterranean, or the birds singing. She never heard from Naditu or Tiy and there was no news about them. Amon was lost forever. His ship had never come back to the harbor and she'd stopped watching.

One thing had changed. The Shamash. He called less and less for his women. His excess in food and drink were telling on him. He was fatter and it was harder for him to breathe. He was, if possible, even more slovenly. Sometimes, when she was summoned to his room, he would already be passed out on the bed. All she had to do then was wait until morning and leave. Other nights, he was too drunk to perform. Secretly, she gloated. Some nights, he would demand she play with his organ but before long he was snoring. That much she had learned to tolerate. Occasionally, however, none of these things were true and on one of those nights, her son was conceived. This birth was not difficult. She named her son Zamen, out of love for her father. The Shamash bothered her very little after that.

Amona was her bright light. Grown-up beyond her years, she learned very much like a younger Duanna. Duanna, very carefully, violated all the rules against education of females, by hiding art materials in her apartment, constructing Egyptian letters and making them into words for Amona to read. Teaching Amona gave her a reason to live.

With Skhmet to mother her, Alysha as her friend, and Amona to teach and to love, the days went on and on for Duanna.

CHAPTER 11

She was twenty-one today. She remembered, not long ago, when her birthday was a special day and celebrated. She thought back to her last celebration, her fourteenth. She winced.

But today was different than most days in the harem. There was all kinds of activity. Attendants were bringing new dresses in from somewhere. All the women were parading around in new finery.

Rumor had it that all of this hustle and bustle was in honor of some African chieftains who were looking for a military alliance with the Turkish government, and were bringing great quantities of gold to seal the pact.

Duanna was uninterested in the reason. She hated these drunken state affairs and would have stayed in her apartment if allowed. But, of course she was not allowed. So reluctantly she dressed and veiled herself and preceded to the great room with the rest, lining up according to rank, with Alysha on her left.

The potentates began to arrive, splendid in colorful African robes. They came through the door to musical fanfare, first one and then another. As the fifth man passed through the door, Duanna had all she could do to contain herself. It was Amon!

"Alysha, look!"

"Look at what?"

"Look at that man, Alysha. It's Amon."

"Are you sure?"

"Absolutely. It's Amon!"

She spent years of agony during the half hour or so it took the Africans to go through the curtsying and bowing and social amenities with the government officials and their wives. "Does he know I'm here? If he doesn't know, will he recognize me? Will he recognize the earrings? Will he see who I am under this veil? Does he want to see me? Does he still love me? Has he forgotten me? Has he taken another wife? If he doesn't recognize me, what will I do?"

He was there; he was standing in front of her. He had her hand. He was looking into her eyes. He was smiling. He knew she was there.

"Duanna, my love," he said.

"Amon," she said in a quiet little voice that wanted to shout from the top of the palace. She tried to know with her eyes if he still loved her. "Amon," she repeated.

He bent to kiss her hand.

And put a note into it.

As soon as it was safe, as soon as the men were settled on their cushions and supplied with wine, as soon as she couldn't wait one more minute, she opened the note.

> **"My little Duanna,**
>
> **I will be in the garden near the statue of Justine tonight when the moon shines its light on the masts of the ships at harbor. Please come. If you cannot find your way there tonight, I will be there every night at the same time; until you can be with me. My spirit has been with you these seven years.**
>
> **Amon"**

"Alysha, look," she said, handing her the note.

Alysha read it with mounting excitement. "What are you going to do?"

"I've got to find a way to get out. Help me, Alysha. I've got to get out."

"You know how dangerous that is," Alysha said, a frown appearing above her eyes.

"I don't care, Alysha. It's Amon. You must understand. He's found me. If they catch me, I don't care. Please help me."

"You know they'll kill you if they catch you."

"I know, Alysha. I know. I don't care. Just help me," said Duanna dancing up and down in her excitement.

Alysha understood about love, even though she didn't understand about love. "What do you want me to do, Duanna?"

"How can I get out?"

"You can't climb out the window. It's too high. If there were a tree there, you could go down the tree but there's no tree."

"The eunuch is always guarding the door. He would stop me if I tried to go out. "If the eunuch were asleep, you could go out the door."

"Yes, but I don't think that eunuch ever sleeps. Every time I see him he's prowling around our great room, sniffing out something. That won't work."

"Wait! You could pretend to be one of the attendants and get out the door that way. That eunuch is so dumb, he probably wouldn't notice."

"Yes! That's the way. I can change places with Iris. I'll wear her clothes."

"You can stay in the slave quarters until everyone is asleep. Then you can slip out to the garden."

"That'll work, Alysha. That'll work. Tonight I'll be with Amon!" She whirled around and around in her excitement.

"Be careful, Duanna. Be careful. Don't let the Shamash see you."

"Ohhhhh," said Duanna. "No. I wouldn't want him to know I was happy. I wouldn't want him to know that."

The festivities were agonizingly long and Duanna couldn't keep her eyes off Amon. When they were over and he was walking out, he caught her eye. She nodded.

Her plan worked exactly as expected. Iris was reluctant but after a fierce argument and the recognition that Duanna was not to be dissuaded, she agreed. Surprise of all surprises, the eunuch **was** asleep when she walked out the door. But, once outside, she began to feel panic. Her knees tried to buckle as she walked down the corridor. She realized she had no idea where the slave quarters were. How was she going to find them? It was dumb of her to have forgotten to find out from Iris. And what if she did find her way? What would she do if one of the other attendants decided to talk to her. What if they discovered who she was? What would she do then? Worst of all, what would she do once she got to the slave quarters? Where was Iris's bed? She couldn't exactly ask another attendant where her own bed was supposed to be. Then, if all of that turned out all right, what if she couldn't get back out again? What if they locked the doors or something? And if she did get out, what if she couldn't find the garden? What if? What if? What if?

Just as she was about to give up in despair, she saw one of the other attendants come out of the harem. Ah. She could follow her. One problem was solved. She just had to stay far enough behind that that other one wouldn't try to talk to her. Now, how to solve the problem of which bed? Cross that bridge when she came to it. Maybe if she stayed long enough in the toilet room everybody would be asleep, and she could just slip out. It would work. It would work. It just had to.

It worked. The moon was just rising enough to reach the masts of the ships in the harbor when she burst through the door into the garden and, almost without consciousness, was running through the garden, tearing off her turban and veil, toward the statue of Justine. Toward Amon. Toward her destiny.

He was standing next to the statue just as he said he would be. She ran into his arms. She wanted to cry. She wanted to shout. She wanted to jump up and down. She wanted to dance. She wanted him only to hold her. "Amon, Amon, Amon," she said, letting the tears run unchecked down her cheeks.

"Duanna. Duanna. My little Duanna," he said as his arms enfolded her against his chest. "I have missed you so these many years."

"I, too, Amon. I, too."

His lips were on her forehead, kissing away the salt of her tears, then wonderfully, ever so wonderfully, on her lips. He held her away, eating her up with his eyes. "I want to look at you. I want my eyes to feast on you. I want to satisfy the hunger for you I've had these past seven years."

"And my hunger for you. For seven years in this evil place, my eyes and my body have hungered for you. Night after night, my dreams kept me warm. Keep me warm now."

Amon pulled her to him. He kissed her mouth. He touched her body. Their passions mounted. He said, "I want to love you tonight as we couldn't when I was last with you in Alexandria. I want our bodies to be filled with each other."

Now Duanna started to cry in ernest. "I want that more than life itself, Amon. But you may not want me now."

"What do you mean, not want you? I can want nothing else."

"You see, Amon, I have been seven years the wife of the Shamash and he has violated me and brutalized me. He has torn up my insides. He has forced me to do things that made me vomit. He has left me bloody and dirty and no longer worthy of your love." She looked up at him, her eyes pleading for understanding, knowing he would not.

First she felt him tense beside her. Now she knew she had been right. Now she knew he did not want to be with her. She had been right. Her dreams had told her right. Despair took her over.

When he moved, he moved with such a ferocity that it frightened her. He hit the statue, he hit Justine with his fist. He hit it again and again. It was as though he was crazed. "I could kill him. I could kill him," he shouted. "I will, if I ever get my hands on him. I'll kill him. You shouldn't have had to suffer this man. I should have found a way. I shouldn't have let it happen."

"Amon," she said, laying her hand on his arm.

Her touch stopped his frenzy. He quieted, still breathing hard. When he was able to speak he said, "I love you, little one. What he did has nothing to do with that. I want you tonight, like I wanted you seven years ago - if you still want me."

"I do, Amon, but I was so sure . . . ."

It was his kiss that stopped her protestations, his kiss full on the mouth; his kiss that allowed their passions to take command of their bodies. They dropped onto the sand around the Justine. And Justine smiled at them in their happiness.

Amon touched her under her simple dress. He touched her and healed her in all the wounded places the Shamash had violated.

Duanna pulled at the sash that opened his robe, to touch him on the chest, to feel him once again in more than her dreams. He pulled her dress over her head. He dropped his robe on the sand.

He kissed her again, as the sand welcomed their bodies. He kneeled over her as she waited. He entered her body slowly, ever so slowly. She felt each sensation, one at a time, coursing through her everywhere.

When their coming together was complete, their spirits were rejoining, finding each other, quietly, delicately, with persistent power.

He closed his eyes, knowing his love for her, stronger even than for Dameli, stronger because of their years of waiting.

Duanna's insides began to demand. Her passions flared. She started to strain toward him.

He held still, letting her take him, letting her passions mount at her own rate, letting her come to him no faster than she wanted.

Then it was **his** flame that began to burn.

Electrical currents were surging through them both. "Amon," she said, as she strained against him, as she moved with more and more passion into their infinity.

Finally it was the lightning, jumping through her body, leaving her in flames, leaving her burning, leaving her with words spoken so softly she almost didn't hear. "Duanna and Amon for eternity."

And Amon planted his own seed inside her waiting body, giving her one of his greatest gifts. His full pleasure.

Now Justine seemed to bend and enfold the lovers in her shadow, while the sand around her body warmed and enshrouded them. The moon even winked, as it hid its light behind a uree, to protect their nakedness.

There they stayed, fulfilling the longing of seven years of separation and desire.

CHAPTER 12

Now they were ready for words. Ready to know the why of their separation. Amon held her against him as he sat leaning against the statue. "I want to tell you why I didn't come for you these seven years," he said.

"It doesn't matter," she said. "You're here now and that's all that matters."

"I need to tell you."

"Then I'll listen," she said, snuggling against his shoulder.

"I was about a week at sea," he began.

As he talked, it was easy to see pictures of his story.

She saw him on a ship commanding his men, manning the wheel, looking across the horizon through his spyglass, then seeing masses of other ships heading his way.

"Captain, come here and look," she heard him saying.

"Turkish warships, Your Excellency."

"On the name of the gods, could they be heading for Alexandria?" said Amon.

"I believe there was a rumor of war with Egypt when we were there last," said the Captain.

"Then turn the ship around. Duanna might be in danger. We need to get back to Alexandria. Turn the ship now."

"But . . . .your cargo, sir."

"Blast the cargo. We'll see to it when we find out what the Turks are up to. Turn us around."

"Yes, sir."

"Duanna, I made the biggest mistake of my life then. I mistakenly thought the Lioness could outrun the fastest of those Turkish ships, loaded as they were with cannons and munitions. But I was wrong. We had barely come about when I saw one of their ships bearing down on us."

Duanna's picture returned. The Lioness and a very large Turkish ship were battling at sea. The Turkish ship was much the stronger, sending shot after shot into the Lioness, setting it afire. Sailors were jumping into the sea. Amon, watching his ship burning and listing badly, waved the flag of surrender. Turks boarded the Lioness and rampaged through its decks, confiscating the cargo, then taking Amon captive along with what was left of his crew, and hauling them away in chains.

"We were kept in the hold of the Turkish ship, while it sailed back here. During the whole battle of Alexandria, while you were out in the desert, I was right here in the harbor, imprisoned in that same ship."

Somehow she felt comforted by that realization. He had been closer to her, during her ordeal in the desert than she had known. "If only . . . ." But there were no if only's. No. It had been as it had been. There were no if only's.

She went back to his story. Her next pictures were very dark. She had to let her eyes become accustomed to it before she could see his form, pacing back and forth, back and forth, in the hold of the ship. He was looking at some coins he had in his pocket. He was talking to one of the Turkish sailors, giving him the money.

Now she saw him climbing through an unlocked hatch and standing on deck. He was edging his way toward the side of the boat, keeping out of sight of a guard about thirty yards away. He had a rope and was tying it to the railing of the ship. He was about to let himself over the side.

Suddenly there was a bellow. "Where do you think you're going?" It was the Turkish captain.

Next she saw Amon's back bloody, as he was beaten with a cat-o-nine-tails. She winced as if those same cat-o-nine-tails were beating her.

Then she saw him chained to a post in the hold, where he stayed for days and days.

"When the battle was over, they took me back to Constantinople and threw me in prison."

She saw a dark, dank cave of a room with dirt floors and walls and only one open window, too high for him to see out, and just right to let in all the weather, especially the rain and the cold.

Again she saw him pacing the room. He was given some awful-looking gruel to eat. Gruel and nothing else. He refused to eat it. Later, she saw a much thinner Amon, and now he was eating it.

"I stayed in that dungeon for almost five years, Duanna. It was the most terrible experience of my life . . . worse even than losing Dameli. Then during the fourth year, I got sick."

Now she saw him lying on his mat on the floor, eyes hollow, body covered with sweat, rolling from side to side in his agony. She saw doctors coming in to treat him, but unable to make him well. She saw his legs buckle under him when he tried to walk.

Her next picture was of his captain carrying him out of the dungeon and onto another ship. He was rolling on a mat inside the cabin. He was almost dead. She heard him call her name.

"He took me to Massewa, Duanna, where he had me carried by standard bearers into the interior. He knew of a very learned medicine man, who might be able to cure me."

Duanna saw him now, lying in a hut, still weak and hollow-eyed, drinking cup after cup of a hot substance. A strange-looking man, old and with a long white beard was bending over him, shaking his head.

Months later, she saw him walking, in halting steps, between the old man and his Captain.

Later still, he was walking alone.

"Go to Alexandria," he was telling the Captain, "and find out what has happened to Duanna."

She watched the captain scouring the city of Alexandria. She saw him walk to the door of her villa and knock. The woman who answered was not Gena or Illana. To his question, the woman said, "I don't know anything about the girl, Sir.Since there were no sons in the family, this is now a government house. The mother died from shock, I understand. Her husband was killed in the war. You might try her sisters. There are two, I believe. They live in Alexandria, someplace."

"Naditu? Dead?" Tears welled into Duanna's eyes and then ran freely down her cheeks. She was no longer hearing what Amon was saying. Naditu . . . her beloved mother . . . dead. It was almost more than she could bear. And dying from shock? From the shock of losing her husband, and then her daughter, Duanna supposed. Suddenly Duanna didn't know where she was. The night was gone. Amon was gone. There was no statue of Justine nor the sand upon which she had just been loved. She lost herself in her grief. Tears, which had started as a trickle, suddenly became immense sobs.

Amon, who had been so emersed in his story, had failed to realize how his words had impacted Duanna. He stopped in mid- sentence when he felt the uncontrollable shaking of her body. He pulled her closer to him while she sobbed.

"Mama," she said.

"I'm so sorry," he said.

"I didn't know," she said through her sobs. "I haven't known anything. They have kept me from everyone. Naditu. Tiy. Everyone. I didn't know she was dead."

"I thought you knew. I wouldn't have told you in that inconsiderate way if I had thought you didn't know. I'm so sorry."

"I know Amon. Just hold me tight. For the first time since I came to this horrible place, everything is all right. Even Naditu, dead, is all right. Just hold me tight for a little bit more, and I'll be all right."

And there was silence under the statue of Justine while the moon continued its travels above. Until Duanna finally stirred in his arms. "I'm ready now," she said. "I want to know the rest of the story. I'm ready now."

"Are you sure?"

"Yes, I'm sure."

Her pictures reappeared as Amon resumed talking. Again she saw the Captain as he stood talking to another woman. Tall, with sandy hair. Was it Tiy? She looked so different. So old.

"Duanna was taken to the palace right after the end of the war," she heard Tiy saying. "She is in the harem of the Shamash, chief aide to the Pasha."

Now the Captain was talking to a palace guard, and giving him money. She saw the guard disappearing inside the palace. When he returned, he nodded.

"After several months of searching, my Captain returned and told me where you were. Then I was more enraged at the Turks than ever, but grateful that you were alive. I wanted to send you word but my Captain advised against it. He said it would put you in great danger; I devised another plan."

She saw Amon mining for gold, placing large chunks in a box, then setting sail with the box and many other African chieftains.

"Duanna, time after time, I despaired of ever seeing you again. When I found out you were alive, I knew I had to come here. I capitalized on Turkish greed. I offered them gold so I could get inside the palace. I knew that once inside, I'd find a way to see you again." Amon paused. "I may have put you in great danger."

"I don't care, Amon. It doesn't matter what they do. They can do what they will to me now; I don't care. I have wished every day for the past seven years to have you with me again. Now that I have, they can do what they will with me. It will have been worth it."

"We have to find a way for you to escape, Duanna. I don't want you to spend even one more night with that man. Come with me now. We can escape down the stairs to the water and capture a small boat out to my ship. We'll be out of the harbor before they even know we're gone."

"Wait, Amon. I have children - two of them. I must take them with us. The Shamash would kill them if I left without them."

"You have children?" he said.

"A girl named Amona. She is six. And a boy named Zamen. He is five."

"A girl named Amona," he said grinning. "No, we can't leave a child with a name like that. Is she wonderful?"

"As wonderful as her name sake."

"Then we'll wait until tomorrow. Can you get out again tomorrow?"

"I think so. Yes. I will. I know how to do it now."

"Good. I will be here again tomorrow night. Bring the children, and I will take you all out of this evil place."

The first rays of sunlight were beginning to peek over the horizon.

He held her once more. "Until tomorrow."

"Until tomorrow."

Duanna dropped her attendant's gown over her head, rewrapped the turban and replaced the veil over her nose, as she made her way back through the garden into the slave quarters. In the morning she slipped back into the harem to resume, for one more day, her life as the wife of the Shamash.

Iris was more than a little relieved at her return.

CHAPTER 13

Duanna was putting into effect her plans for escape. She had stolen an attendant's gown and turban from the slave quarters before leaving there that morning. All day, she had gone over her moves, detail by detail. Just before the children were taken for the night, she called to Amona.

"Amona, come here. I need to tell you something."

"Yes, Mama?"

Duanna settled the little girl into her lap. "Be quiet, very quiet. Don't talk. Just listen to what I tell you."

"I won't talk, Mama."

"Tonight we are going away from her, far, far away from here on a great ship. We will be leaving in the middle of the night with a man named Amon. He is the man you are named for. I will be coming to get you after you are asleep. You must tell no one; or we will be in great danger. Don't even tell your brother until we are ready to go. Do you understand?"

"Yes, Mama, I understand. We are to go away tonight. You will come to get us and I am to tell no one."

"And you must make no noise."

"I must make no noise."

For a long time after the children left, Duanna sat in the great room, saying goodbye. As much as she hated it, she still needed to say goodbye to the women who had shared her years of terror. "Goodbye, Skhmet," she said to herself. "You have been more than a friend. Without you, I might have died from not eating. Thank you for helping me live. Now I have Amon and I have the rest of my life in freedom. Thank you." She looked across the room at the motherly woman who had meant so much to her. Her gaze lingered there in appreciation until she felt the image of the older woman merge with her own. "I will have you in my heart, always," she promised.

Then her thoughts turned to Alysha. "Alysha, I wish I could say goodbye to you in person. I wish I could tell you the truth. I wish I could hold you and talk with you and laugh with you one more time. But if I do, I might endanger you, too. Please believe me: I will miss you. I wish you well, always."

When the attendants left, she left behind them. Nobody noticed. "Isis is with me," she said, taking her first deep breath of the day.

Once in the slave quarters she hid in a closet, an empty closet she had discovered the night before . . . and waited. She listened to the chatter as the attendants got ready for bed. She was amused at their gossip and their opinions of their charges. It seemed like forever before they were all asleep.

When everything was quiet, she moved her cramped body out of the closet and made her way out of the room. She crept down the hall to the children's quarters. She peeked inside the door. There, inside the door, was something she had forgotten. The night attendant. Her heart jumped up into her throat. She stood, as if frozen, with a door just slightly ajar. She was afraid to move and afraid not to move. When her heart quieted enough so she could hear, a familiar sound came to her ears. Snoring. It was snoring. "The gods are with me," she thought. "She's asleep and snoring loud enough to wake the dead." She opened the door the rest of the way and tiptoed inside.

This time, knowing exactly where to look, she found Amona lying on one of the small divans. She shook her lightly and woke her. "Go get your brother," she whispered. "And tell him to be very quiet."

"Yes, Mama," Amona said sleepily.

She didn't take one breath, she was sure, until Amona was back with Zamen in hand. The woman at the door continued snoring in rhythm.

"Be very quiet, my little Zamen," she said, " and come with mother. We are going to the garden, just the three of us, and then for a trip."

"To the garden," he said.

"Shhhh, yes. Take my hand."

The snoring stopped. Duanna froze - a child on each side.

It resumed again.

They tiptoed past the woman and out the door. Now there was only the maze of hallways to be travelled. Duanna breathed a little easier.

They padded their way through the halls - the same trip Duanna had taken the night before. Last night she had had smooth sailing. Tonight was not as easy. Tonight there was a guard. She saw him just as they were about to round a corner.

"Amona, Zamen, quick! Behind the statue!"

The guard marched down the hall, looking neither to the right or to the left. Duanna was sure he could hear her beating heart. Even worse would be a sound from the children. Nobody moved.

He safely rounded the corner at the other end of the hall. They proceeded.

Then she was free. They were through the garden door. Run . . . was what her legs wanted to do. Run . . . to the statue of Justine. Run . . . to Amon.

But she kept her legs under her, walking quietly, threading their way through the palm trees, through the patches of flowers, through the bushes, until she saw it. The statue. And there he was. Amon!

Her legs refused to be contained one more minute. "Hurry," she said, tugging at Amona's hand. Zamen stumbled.

Just as she righted him a shadow moved from behind the bushes. It blocked her way.

"Isis . . . why have you left me?"

It was the Shamash!

Duanna's stomach turned to stone.

From behind other bushes and trees came enough of the palace guard to fight the Egyptian army. "Take her and the brats to my quarters," the shadow ordered.

Brutal hands were all over her body. She kicked and screamed and wrenched herself from one side to the other.

One of them hit her in the stomach while another twisted her arms behind her. She doubled over and sank to her knees.

Four of them picked her up and carried her, spread-eagle, back to the palace. The others picked up the terrified children.

She tried to call out. She couldn't.

"Hold her right there," said the Shamash, once back in his apartment. "Stand her up. Don't let her fall."

The Shamash came up to her, until he was almost on top of her, his face black with anger, and his drunken eyes red with rage. He breathed his fetid breath into her face. He hit her across the mouth. Blood spurted onto her chin.

Her head spun from the blow.

"You thought you saw your prince in the garden just now, didn't you? You thought you were going to run away with him, didn't you? Well, my Enheduanna, the man you saw in the garden tonight was not your prince. He was **not** in the garden, tonight, because he is dead.".

"Dead . . . dead . . . dead . . . Your prince was **not** in the garden tonight, because he is dead." The words reverberated through her brain and sank into her very center.

The Shamash leered at her, his face even darker than before. "Yes, dead. Dead for his deceit and duplicity. His head cut off at the neck. You want to see his remains, my Enheduanna?"

Duanna turned her head. Turned her head away from the stink of this man. Away from his words. Away from the truth. Away from life itself.

He backed away. Now he was yelling at the soldiers. "Lay her there, on the table. Hold her arms apart and her legs open. You there, hold those children. They need to see just who their mother is. A whore! A whore! A deceiving whore!"

They threw her ruthlessly on the table, four of them holding her. Her legs felt like they were being yanked out of their sockets. He stood between her legs and ripped at her dress, until it was above her waist. He dropped his pantaloons, revealing his ugly organ, in full, angry erection.

"You look frightened, my pretty. Are you frightened? You wouldn't be so frightened if this belonged to the African prince, now would you? But it doesn't, my Enheduanna, because he is dead. Beheaded. For adultery."

He jammed his organ into Duanna's insides.

She screamed.

"Scream, my Enheduanna," he yelled. "Let the world know what a disobedient whore you are."

He jammed himself into her again and again and again.

She wrenched herself from side to side.

The soldiers held.

The children sobbed. Amona wrenched herself free and ran halfway across the room before the guards grabbed her.

The Shamash rammed himself into her again and again, until he finally shot his seed, his face contorting into evil ugliness.

"You will not whore on me again," he said, ripping her dress the rest of the way, beating her with his hands, enraged beyond rationality.

Until she fainted.

"Now take them. Take them all to the kitchen. At sunrise, they die."

He reached for his ever-present goblet of wine, tipped it back, and emptied it.

When she woke, the pain was worse than after her wedding. Blood was everywhere, dried on cuts and scratches, all over her body, and still oozing from her loins. She was black and blue. She was shivering from the cold, lying on the kitchen floor, still naked. She moved slightly and groaned. She sat up. It was just beginning to be light.

Amona wriggled past the guards that were everywhere and threw her arms around Duanna's neck. "I love you, Mommy. Why are these men hurting you?"

Duanna had no answer. "I love you, too, Amona. Be brave, my baby!"

It wasn't long before the Shamash reappeared, his clothes rumpled, his hair hanging in his face, black eyes threatening, and still reeking of wine. "Take her to the garden," he ordered. "Take them all."

Rough hands again half carried, half dragged her back to the garden. The sun was just coming over the horizon. It had been just 24 hours since the scene of her joy.

"Stand her up against the wall," the Shamash shouted.

"I am ready to die. I cannot live this way anymore. Not this way. Not even for the children. I hope they will be well taken care of but I am ready. Do what you will," she thought.

"Now stand the children next to her."

"Not the children," she screamed. "They are innocent."

"But you are not," he howled, his face again contorting into ugliness. "You will watch them die, whore. You will watch them die! Even your son . . . you will watch die. Even your son."

"The girl first," he ordered the soldiers.

Duanna collapsed.

"Stand her up," he ordered. "You are going to watch. You are going to be punished for your adultery."

One of the soldiers ran at Amona with his sword. He ripped her through the genitals and belly. She crumpled to the ground.

Duanna's screams filled the air until every tree, every statue, every flower, every bird and every piece of sand reverberated with the sound.

"Now the boy," commanded the Shamash.

But Duanna didn't know. She was dead. Dead. Dead of a broken heart and the brutality of men. It mattered not, that the sword went through her after it killed little Zamen; for she was already gone. Pain could reach her no more!

CHAPTER 14

Duanna's body was taken immediately to the catacombs to be mummified. The news of her death flew through the harem like wildfire. Alysha begged the eunuch to take her for one last look at her friend.Standing over the body, Alysha couldn't stop her tears. They streamed unchecked down her face. They even made her angry. Maybe she wasn't as tough as she pretended.

"I wish you well in death, little Duanna. I wish you the happiness that you've missed in these past seven years. I hope Amon is with you in the spirit world."

She leaned over and kissed Duanna on the forehead, quickly taking the earrings out of her ears. "I know you would want me to do this, Duanna. I know they must be given to some other person, who loves as you did. I will see that they get to the right person. This much I can do for you, my friend."

Back in the harem, Alysha held the earrings up to the light. The longer she looked at them the more she was sure. "Something isn't right," she said. "Something has happened to these earrings. That's ridiculous, Alysha. Put these earrings away. Earrings don't change. Just put them away and forget them."

She headed resolutely for her apartment. Half way there she stopped again. Again she held the earrings up to thc light. "There is something different. Now I know what it is. It's the red rivulets. They're longer than they were. And I don't remember these rivulets ending in red pools. These pools look like tiny droplets of blood. . . . Can't be." she said. "Must be my imagination."

"But maybe not," she said to herself later, as she again held the earrings up to the light. "She always said they were magic earrings."

CHAPTER 15

Kate lay on a mattress, curled into a little ball. Tears streamed down her face. Lena sat beside her holding her walking stick. A space heater glowed, and candles flickered in the darkness. Through the window, street lights were shining.

A clock was ticking on the wall.

It was Sunday.

"Is time to come awake now, chile. Ain no need to be stayin in Duanna's body no more, cause she done gone to the Lord. You bes be back in Chicago now. We's got some doin to do fore you goes home an bes we be's at it."

Kate slowly opened her eyes. She stared into the darkness. Turning to Lena she silently pleaded with her to return Duanna's life. Lena's unbending gaze told her that she could not.

Now the tears turned to sobs. She turned her back on Lena and buried her head in the mattress, sobs wrenching their way through her whole body.

Lena was silent.

When the sobs seemed never-ending, Lena leaned over to pick her up, like she would a frightened child. "Come here, chile. Let me take care a your miseries. I's an expert at takin care a the miseries for folks. I been doin it long as I remembers."

Kate twisted away from Lena's grasp. "Don't need to be taken care of. I can take care of myself."

"I sees."

Kate was immediately sorry. She turned over and crawled into Lena's arms.

Lena cradled and rocked and began to sing an old plantation lullaby in a cracking voice.

Kate stopped fighting and gave in to Lena's protection. She began to feel soothed. Her sobs waned to a trickle, leaving damp spots on Lena's cotton dress.

"Why did she have to die, Lena? Why did she have to die? Why was the Shamash so cruel?"

"He don know no better," said Lena. "Mens gots rights in them times to kill who they pleases. If they wife don please em, they kills em. Easy as that."

"Easy as that," Kate repeated. "First he forces her to marry him; he makes her life miserable for seven years and then, when she has a chance to be happy, he kills her."

"Tha's right. Tha's the way it be's in them days."

Lena went back to rocking and humming, and Kate to grieving for the loss of her first life.

Finally Kate stirred. "What time is it?"

"Bout six o'clock."

"Only six! It seemed like I was asleep longer than four hours."

"You was. It be six o'clock Sunday."

"Sunday?"

"Umhmmmmmmmmm. You was sashayin roun Egypt for mor'n twenty-four hours."

"Oh, Lena, I've got to get home."

"I knows. Jus you sits here a bit longer till you's ready. Then you goes home."

Kate knew there was no use arguing with Lena so she settled in, letting her pain and grief ebb into the woman's arms.

It was eight o'clock before Kate got home. She went immediately to bed, to sleep a dreamless sleep. It would be mid-January before she made another visit to the house on South Damen. All Lena would tell her was her next life was an African woman named Sabia. "This must be the one with the ebony skin," she thought.

CHAPTER 16

For the first few days after Kate's life as Duanna, she didn't have time to think about it. Ed, her over-stuffed, over ego-inflated, hard-headed editor, had taken this particular time to give her extra assignments. She had worked every night until midnight all week.

Thoughts of Duanna had popped into her head off and on - but there was never time to really think about it.

Finally Saturday rolled around and she could be alone with her thoughts. Over her morning coffee, she finally allowed scenes of Duanna's life to parade through her mind. Duanna's happy family, her protected upper-class life, her classical education, her life by the sea, Amon, becoming a woman in his arms, the death of her father, the harem with all that meant, her death.

Nothing made any sense. Kate couldn't see the key to any of it for her own life. For hours, she ruminated. Scenes of Duanna's life swirled in her head. Amon . . . the Shamash . . . the market . . . the old crone . . . the harem . . . the Lioness . . . Naditu . . . her log . . . their log . . . the harem again. What was it all about? Nothing made any sense.

She put her fists to her eyes to keep them from burning. She wanted to pour water over her head to stop the spinning.

What to do? What to do?

A thought flashed through her mind. "Call Lena. Lena will know!"

"Oh, my God," she thought. "I can't do that."

"Why not?" asked her other self.

"I'm afraid!" she said.

"Afraid? A big girl like you? Afraid?"

"Yes I am. She's so . . . so . . . "

"Powerful?"

"Yes, powerful. She knows everything and she won't help me with anything."

"She helps you. You just don't like the way she helps you."

"Oh, I hate you. You're always so right."

"I am, aren't I?"

"Shut up. I'll call her. I'll call her."

She picked up the phone and with shaking fingers she dialed.

"Whachu want?" was the sound she heard over the wires. Hardly reassuring.

"Lena . . . this is Kate."

"I knows who you is. Whachu want?"

"Lena . . . I've been trying and trying to figure out what this has been all about . . . Duanna's life, I mean. What has it been all about for me? She's just not like me. She was young . . . and rich . . . and naive. She was a spoiled little rich girl. I was never any of those things. I never even knew what it was to be young. What am I supposed to understand?"

"An whachu want from me bout that? I was thinkin you was smart. Smart nuf to be figurin out bout Duanna's life."

"But, Lena, I've tried . . . and I can't."

"You cain't?"

"No."

Silence. There was a deadly silence on the phone. Kate even suspected that Lena might have hung up, except that she had heard no click.

She finally ventured a thought: "Well, there was the harem."

"What bout the harem?" came Lena's rasping voice.

"It was a prison. It was like . . . it was like my house when I was little."

"An the Shamash?"

"Well, he - he was like my father. Brutal . . . mean . . . making everybody miserable."

"An now you knows," said Lena. "You ain needin to bother me no more."

Kate knew the conversation was over. "Wait. Lena," she said. "Don't hang up."

But, too late. This time she heard the click, and then the incessant monotony of the dial tone.

Kate reluctantly hung up the phone. She put her head in her hands. "Lena scares me even more than my father," she thought ruefully. "Well, maybe not quite as much as my father."

But the hard part was over. She had made the call. Now all that was left was to make sense out of what Lena had said. Thoughts of her young life started to run through her mind, countered with thoughts of the harem.

She saw the prison of the harem . . . the bareness of the rooms, the bars on the windows, the eunuchs guarding the doors, the loss of all that life meant except the life lived inside the bars. And all of it ruled over by the whims and cruelty of the Shamash. Then she saw her father. Full of whims and cruelty. She saw her house . . . a prison. Yes, a prison. A prison of the soul. She saw her mother no less a prisoner.

She saw the harem again, with all of its barrenness, ruled by the ugly hand of the Shamash.

She saw her miserable life in her house, ruled by the ugly hand of her father.

The light was dawning. "I think I see it. I think I know. Lena, I think I know. Duanna was supposed to teach me about prison. The prison of my life. The prison my father made of my life."

And there was Lena's face again, scowling at her. "An you thinks you is out a that prison?"

"Yes. Since college. Since Jenny, I . . . ."

"You's thinkin you's free."

"Yes, I . . . ."

"Harumph."

"I'm not free?"

"Well, is you?"

Now Kate had to think hard. What was freedom? The right to do what she wanted without restriction, as long as she accepted the responsibility of the freedom. If she accepted that responsibility then she had freedom. At least that was what she had been telling her audiences all these years.

Now she started to think about responsibilities. "I've certainly been responsible," she thought. "Responsible to that damn newspaper and to my writing. But not to much else. I've certainly not been having any fun. I've not been taking care of myself very well. Too much coffee, too many quick meals on the run. Not enough sleep. Work, work, work? Responsible, all right. Responsible to my work. But free?

"I guess not. Joshua made me free. Now that he's gone, I guess I've put myself back in prison. Only this time, it's the prison of my work instead of the prison of my father's making."

She could almost see Lena's face. "Now you's gettin mos as smart as I's thinkin you was."

"Damn, Lena," she said elatedly to the imaginary face she was now seeing in her head. "Damn. Duanna is trying to make me see that I'm still in a prison of my own making and that I've got to get out."

"Now you's smart."

"And, by God, I'll do it. As soon as I catch up on all my work at the paper. Then I'll do it."

Now she could see Lena's face laughing at her. "When you gonna do it?" the face was saying.

"Like I said, Lena, as soon as I get all my work caught up at the office."

"When you gits all that work done you be doin at that office."

"Yes, that's right."

"An you thinks you's gonna do it if'n you waits that long?"

Now it was Kate's turn to grin. Lena was right . . . as usual.

CHAPTER 17

Christmas had come and gone, the New Year was celebrated, and Chicago was suffering from a week of below-zero weather as Kate again climbed the crumbling steps to the house on South Damen. Again she was suffering from her struggle with skepticism. It had plagued her for almost a week now. Duanna's life had faded, as she went back to the reality of what was going on in the nation in this first part of 1970, back to her typewriter at the Daily News, back to fighting with Ed; her woman-baiting editor who was forever on the other side of every important issue. As the nation seemed more and more out of control, he delighted in making his staff suffer from tighter and tighter restrictions. How could she think about other lives when everyday life was so chaotic?

She rang the bell.

Lena was ready; she must have been ready for some time. She was impatiently tapping her walking stick on the floor when Kate walked in. Lena didn't even give her time to sit down. "Is you ready for Sabia (Suh-bye-ah)?" she said, leaning forward in her chair.

"I think . . . I think I'm ready for Sabia."

"Well, is you or ain you?"

"Yes, I'm ready for Sabia," laughed Kate uneasily.

"I's glad to hear that. I's thinkin you's doubtin again."

"Aren't I allowed to doubt, Lena?"

"You c'n doubt all you wants, but them womens ain gonna leave you any peace till you knows who they is."

"So I'd better hop to and forget everything I've been taught to believe all my life, is that right?"

"You c'n forgit or you c'n member . . . ain gonna make them no min."

"Sometimes I wish it was someone else they'd decided to haunt. Not me. Sometimes I wish I could go back to my peaceful life and forget about Duanna and forget about Sabia, or anything else about lives other than the one I'm living right now. Sometimes I think I've got all I can do to take care of what I'm about right here."

"You wanna know bout when you was Sabia, or you wanna keep fussin bout it?"

"Yes, I want to know when I was Sabia." Kate was shouting now. "I want to know."

"Then when you's through hollerin at me, we begins."

Kate was chagrined. "I'm through."

"You's sure?"

"I'm sure."

"Good; then I's gonna tell you somethin bout yourself when you was Sabia afore we goes back to Africa an be's Sabia again." Lena settled back in her chair.

"When you was Sabia, you be African an that be different from when you was Duanna an you livin in Egypt. What mos important when you was African was survivin. Survivin in a worl what don care bout whether you survives or you don. You don spend your time readin an writin an ponderin stuff like Duanna do. You spend your time wonderin when the nex hard time's gonna come an if'n you be roun when them hard times be over. What be portant to you ain who buildin them palaces an who wearin them pretty dresses. What be portant to you be when the nex rain gonna come to water them crops so's y'all c'n eat, an is them diseases an plagues gonna take all them babies from you in death. Eatin an livin be portant. It ain thinkin an figurin. When you African, you ain the thinkin kin'. You be the livin kin'."

Kate had no trouble bringing back a mental picture of Duanna in the huge palace of Cleopatra but the simplicity that Lena was describing as Africa was harder.

"In Africa, it be the gods an the spirits what be decidin bout how your life gonna be. If'n you pleases them gods an them spirits, then life be's good. If'n you don please em, life ain so good."

"Where you lives in Africa, they be one big father god what rule the worl an he be named Nyambe (Nigh-am-be) an they be a mother god, an she be named Ala (Ah-lah). She in charge a the earth. Then they be the gods a rain, sun, moon, birth, death, harvest, an such. All them gods - they work with them two big gods."

Kate's imagination was working overtime. She saw a family of errant little gods and goddesses running around in loin cloths, with father Nyambe and mother Ala trying to keep order.

"Then they be the spirits of all them ancestors what don be back in a new chile's body yet. They be floatin roun. Sides them spirits of trees an animals an rivers an such. They all gotta be pleased so life be's good. So all them African folk gotta follow lotsa rules an show respec for all them spirits cause them spirits - they be all over."

Now Kate was adding spirits of ancestors and trees and such to her family of gods and goddesses. If she thought it was confusing before, now it was worse. And they all had to be pleased or those poor earthlings were in trouble.

"African folk, they be different from them white folk. White folk, they ain a feelin folk. They a figurin folk. They all time figurin stuff out in they heads. African folk, they feels it with they insides. When you was Sabia, you feels the insides of everything: yourself, your peoples, them trees, them monkeys, the river, the fire, everything! Them white folks, they don know nothin bout that. They don know nothin bout them spirits an how to respec em."

"All this be portant when you be Sabia, cause you born a special chile. You grows up magic, you does. You gits messages direct from them gods, an them spirits for to give to them other folks. You so portant when you was Sabia, you more portant even than the witch doctor."

"If I'm important as all that, I think I might like being Sabia," she thought.

"When you was African, you lives in a village they be callin Nahut (Nah-hut). Tha's in them eastern parts a Nigeria. You's livin by a river they be callin the Benue (Ben-you). An that meet up with the river Niger (Nigh-jer) an that river done go all the way to the ocean."

"Them French an them Portuguese an them English white folks, they be tradin there for a long time. They's tradin for ivory an gold an stuff, but mos they tradin be done for slaves. They gits African folks to prey on they brothers an they sisters, an then they sells em for slaves. In Nahut, you don know nothin bout that; cause them white folks, they don travel that far."

Kate was glad she wasn't going to have to know about slaves. "This life has been in turmoil enough since the civil rights movement started," she thought. "Maybe my life as Sabia will be more peaceful."

"You be born in 1762 an you be from the tribe of Ibo (ee-bow). They's a peaceable tribe. Your mama, she be called Najuma (Nah-jew-mah) Olu (Oh-lou) an your papa, he be called Diallobe (Die-a-low-be) Olu. You lives in one a them huts they be makin from the mud a the Benue an toppin with them grass an them reeds they be callin thatch. This here thatch be protectin you from the sun what be terrible hot an the rain what come down terrible hard."

"Your mamma an your papa, they be mos proud to have you cause your mama, she don have no chile for mos a year after she be with your papa. When Najuma don have no chile, your papa mos have to take another wife, it bein the custom in them days. They mos proud to have you, too, cause you a magic chile. You know stuff you don know. When you be Sabia, you be like me in that way. Them gods an them spirits, they favors you."

Suddenly Kate saw herself as another Lena. It scared her some. To be truthful, it scared her a lot.

Lena stopped talking. The silence in the room was broken only by the tick-tick of the clock.

Kate was reveling in the notion of being magic. Of being as powerful as Lena. Then a new picture crept insidiously into her mind. Cannibals and pygmies and wild animals all eating each other up. She remembered her children's story *Little Black Sambo.*

"Lena, I'm not sure I want to be African way back in the 1700's. From what I know, Africa isn't very civilized now and it must have been nothing but savages then."

"Life be more civilized than you thinks. Folks lives together in harmony mos the time. They hunts, fishes, harvests, cooks, eats, loves, celebrates an grieves jus like mos folks. Then they prays an they sacrifices so's what come natural don get em."

"But what about sex? Aren't they promiscuous?"

"Ain promiscuous. Sex come natural to em an they celebrates it. Ain taboo like here but they ain promiscuous, neither."

"Ummmmmmmm. Well, what about sacrifices? Do they sacrifice human beings to appease the gods and spirits?"

"Onliest time folks be sacrificed be when they bein punished. An they needs be mos bad fore that gonna happen."

"Who decides about the punishment?"

"Mos time it be the Council of Elders; sometimes it be the witch doctor. He s'pose to know mor'n the res."

Kate was surprised. "Council of Elders?"

Lena was through explaining. "Ain gonna be no more talkin. Gonna have visions now." She pointed to the mattress in the corner of the room, the same one that had held Kate when she was Duanna. "You lays yourself down over there, now. Saves havin to carry you later."

As Kate lay down, Lena lit the sweet-smelling lamp and began to chant:

"Ka kung, Sala, Faranga
KaKanga, Ranga, Baluaranga
Ala, fitu, Sala, Sala, Sala
Kate Ka Kung Aranga. Ka Kung Aranga
Ka Kung Aranga, Sala Famungaranga
Sabia."

And on and on and on.

Kate's thoughts of Africa disappeared. Pygmies disappeared. Grandiose thoughts of being like Lena disappeared. She was back in the clouds, that were floating around and above. Try as she might, she could not keep them out of her head. The white stuff seeped through her brain until she was all white - furling and unfurling in front of her eyes.

Sounds penetrated the clouds. Sounds flowed over her, calling her to come. The sounds of a river rushing downstream, crashing over rocks; the incessant sounds of the forest population, monkeys chattering, wild hogs crashing through the underbrush, birds squawking. The sound of drums - drums pulsing, throbbing, reaching deep into her belly. All calling her to come.

She could see them. The men behind the drums - working, sweating, enjoying.

She saw huts . . . about fifty of them . . . some large, some small. She saw people in various shades of black, dressed only in loin cloths, walking about. Some were carrying loads on their heads, some carrying children on their backs. She saw the river. She saw the dark jungle where monkeys chattered. She saw fields of brown grass and small cleared areas of healthy crops. She heard the buzz of conversations.

Then she saw a man, a man different than the rest: grey-haired and robed with an air of prominence. He appeared out of the forest and was hurrying toward the largest hut.

The drum beat changed, apparently announcing his presence. A second man burst out of the big hut, also robed, but with a face decorated in scars and red paint. His surprise was obvious, his welcome warm.

Lena's words interrupted Kate's fascination. "That man with the paint - he be Asina (Ah-see-nah), the chief of Nahut. He a good and fair man. The other one he be Yusufu (You-su-fu). He a medicine man and conjurer of spirits. He from the village of Balewa (Bale-ee-wah), bout one day journey from here. Listen. They's talkin bout you."

First she heard Yusufu's educated and deep tones. "Asina, I've come with news. The gods sent me a message. Your village will be blessed with a child, a child who will grow to be more powerful even than myself. It is to be a girl child to be named Sabia. It is to be born of Najuma and Diallobe Olu. She is to be conceived in three moons, during the feast of Ala."

"That is good news. Najuma has started no child in her belly since she has married Diallobe, for more than one rain now. There has been pressure for Diallobe to take another wife. Our village spitfire, Nekayia (Neck-aye-ah), has her eyes on him and is determined to have him. She will, too, unless Najuma becomes with child."

"That would have been a terrible mistake. He will have his hands full with one wife and this child. Asina, the gods have sent me with instructions. Would you call Diallobe and Najuma here?"

Asina called to a young boy passing by. "Get Najuma and Diallobe immediately," he said. The boy disappeared and almost immediately reappeared with two people - two people who obviously belonged together. Their proud steps told the world how healthy they were, how strong they were, and how much they loved each other.

The man was tall and strong, ebony black, and wearing only a loin cloth. His muscles rippled with power and coordination. The woman was his slightly smaller identical reflection. Each had soft lips, broad noses, watchful eyes, and close-cropped wooly hair. Struck by their physical power and internal beauty, Kate's breath quickened. There was grim determination on the face of the man, while a frown creased the woman's forehead.

"Tha's your mama an papa comin now," said Lena into her ear. "They's thinkin they in trouble bout no chile in her belly. They's thinkin Diallobe's gonna have to marry up with Nekayia. They's ready for a fuss."

The pair disappeared into the hut and all was quiet.

But not for long. Kate could hardly miss the commotion from the other side of the compound. It started with a fearsome sound, part moan, part wail, part scream. It was coming out of a body all painted in grey and white stripes, so thin his ribs were showing. His hair was long, tufted by leather thongs, and standing straight out from his head. He gyrated and jerked in a frenzied dance before a fire. Fire lights and shadows danced off the paint on his body.

Lena was informing again. "That be Cacanja (Cah-can-jah). He powerful mad cause them folks in Asina's hut makin plans without him. He jealous and mad. He don like Yusufu much nohow an now he special mad causa this message he bringin. He don wan no magic chile in his village. He evil to the core, this Cacanja. He gonna be trouble. Trouble!"

Kate felt the trouble. The man was fearsome and looked vindictive. "I'm in trouble before I'm even conceived," she thought.

A young boy came running up to the fearsome man. He was trying to get his attention. He stood in front of him and called his name. When there was no answer he waved his arms. Then he raised his voice and shouted. He did everything but stand on his head to get the man's attention. Nothing worked. Cacanja had decided to be difficult. He was acting the part of the reluctant lover. Finally the boy took a stone and threw it at him. Cacanja came out of his gyrations in a rage. But come out of his gyrations, he did. He went immediately to Asina's hut.

Once Cacanja was inside the hut, Kate heard a combination of low tones and strange sounds. She had a vision of the battle taking place. When it was all over and they walked out, four people smiled and one looked dour indeed.

Asina signalled the drummers. They immediately picked up the pace, to tell the villagers that the time had come to meet in the compound. Villagers poured out of huts, came in from the fields, left the well, and hurried to the compound.

Together, Asina and Yusufu made the announcement while Cacanja glowered.

The drums quickened their tempo.

The villagers celebrated with a night of dancing and palm wine.

Except for two.

Cacanja - who danced his own dance, his dance of anger and retaliation in front of his own hut, in front of his own fire, and in front of his own evil charm.

And Nekayia - the most sought-after woman. Who wanted only Diallobe and who was willing to cast her witch's spell to get him.

Nightly, she had been sitting over her Najuma form, working her mojo of no child in the belly. And daily, she flirted with Diallobe in the compound, openly seductive.

Now there was to be a child. She hated the child. Now and forever! The child interfered with her plans. And she was not a woman to have her plans interfered with!

THE SECOND WOMAN

SABIA

(1762 - 1783)

"When you African, you ain the thinkin kin' You be the livin kin'." Lena, p97

CHAPTER 18

"It be time for you to live Sabia's life now, chile. Is you ready?"

"I'm ready."

"You's gonna find her underneath the big baobab tree jus outside the village. Go now."

Kate saw her, a naked child of about five. She was a replica of Najuma and Diallobe in a young body. She had the same health, the same strength, and the same sense of internal beauty. She was sitting with her eyes closed and her back against the tree.

"You sees her?" questioned Lena.

"Yes."

"Who she be?"

"She's Sabia."

"An who else she be?"

Kate sighed deeply, as her reality again slipped away from her. "She's me."

"You sits by her."

Kate found herself sitting quietly beside the child.

Without opening her eyes, Sabia spoke. "You have come to me from the gods to enter into me and to live my life with me. Come into me now. I am speaking with the gods. Their message is strong."

Kate immediately had the sensation of shedding clothes, becoming smaller, and knowing her hair and face had changed. The strength of Sabia Olu's body became hers. She was no longer Kate Andrews; she was Sabia now - until death.

Kate Andrews had become a forgotten memory, to be replaced by a howling in her head and a vision of trees bending, swaying, cracking at the base, falling about. A vision of roiling river water; huts crashing into bits of rubble. A vision of screaming people torn off their feet and bashed into trees or thrown into the river unable to swim. A vision, grotesquely silent, but for a strange warning: "The wind. The wind. Beware of the wind as the sun sets this day."

"The cave. The cave. Go to the cave and take your possessions with you. Go to the cave."

"Tell the villagers go to the cave. Many will not listen. **They will die.** The wind will come as the sun sets this day."

Sabia blinked open her eyes and shook the vision from her head. She scrambled up from beside the tree. She had to tell Najuma. The late afternoon sun fanned her panic. There was no time to be lost. Her little legs carried her swiftly through the trees and huts. She found her mother pounding grain outside the Olu hut.

"Mama," she cried. "We are all going to die."

CHAPTER 19

Cacanja's jealousy exploded. "What?" he screeched. "What? A big wind? Sabia told you there will be a big wind? On this day, before the sun goes behind the earth, there will be a big wind? And the people are to go to the cave?"

"I have heard nothing of a big wind. The gods have not told **me.** Bring her here. Bring her to me! Bring that wretched child to me!"

Najuma couldn't move. Cacanja had petrified her to her spot.

"Go!" he yelled into her face.

Startled into mobility, Najuma fled.

Cacanja didn't wait. He called for the drummers. "Call the villagers," he demanded.

As the drums began their message, he raced into his hut. He stopped his frantic movement only long enough to smear his body with red paint, letting it drip about his face in a frightening array of splotches.

The unusual call of the drums brought the villagers hurrying. They ran from their work posts to the compound, fearful of what was next.

They found Cacanja, deep in a grotesque dance. He leapt and whirled. "Ah eeee. Ah eeeeeee!" he screeched, pummeling the earth with his fists. He called to the gods, naming them each.

Swirling and bending, leaping to the heavens, he called "Nyambe! Ah eeee! Nyambe. Nyambe. Ah eeeee!"

Landing with a thud, prostrating himself in the dust, he called "Ala! Ah eeeeeeee! Ah eeeeeeee! Ala! Ala! Ah eeeeee!"

Leaping to his feet, whirling, swirling the dust around him, he called, "Damballah (Dumb-bah-lah)! Ah eeeeee! Damballah, Damballah! Ah eeeeeeeeeeeee!"

The villagers stared in terror. This was his dance of punishment. Someone was to be penalized. Who was it? It could be anyone. Cacanja never needed a reason. They looked around at each other. Who had committed the crime? Who had aroused Cacanja's anger?

In the middle of a whirl, Cacanja descended to a halt, pointing his finger, his stillness like a statue. The villagers held their breaths. All heads followed his pointing finger.

Sabia sat between Diallobe and Najuma, looking back at the pointing finger. She was confused. What was all this fuss about?

"Haaaaaaaaaaaah," the villagers drew their breath as one.

"This child," Cacanja screeched. "This child claims to have had words with the gods, claims that there is to be a big wind. Big enough to blow down our huts and smash our canoes. This child claims that the wind will come this day as the sun goes behind the earth. She claims that we are to act like terrified antelopes and go to the big cave, carrying all that we own. This child claims to have words from the gods that I do not." By now it was more than his finger that was shaking at a confused Sabia. It was his whole body. But he had succeeded. The villagers were distraught. They were torn and divided. They debated among themselves.

"I remember the wind from twenty rains ago."

"Aunt Yerba died in that one."

"It took two rains before all the canoes were rebuilt."

"I'm afraid."

"Cacanja didn't get this word from the gods about the wind."

"It was prophesied that Sabia would be more powerful than Cacanja."

"She's only a child."

"I'll do what Sabia says."

"I'll not be terrorized by a child."

Asina heard it all. He stood up.

Everyone quieted.

Asina needed to be careful not to make the situation worse. He had opposed Cacanja before, with disastrous results. Yet, right now, he feared for the safety of the village.

"Perhaps," he said in his resonant, well-modulated voice, so much the opposite of Cacanja's screech. "Perhaps the gods have chosen two messengers for our village. Cacanja is one and Sabia is another. It could be they have chosen this message to pass through Sabia as her first test, a test of her ability to be of service."

Antagonized, Cacanja began chanting.

Asina simply talked louder. "I'm going to the cave under the hill as the sun ends its journey through the sky. If no wind comes, nothing is lost. If Sabia's message from the gods turns out to be the truth, we'll all be safe. I invite you to gather your possessions, tie down your canoes and join me in the cave."

He left no more room for discussion. He walked majestically out of the compound.

The villagers were stunned. Many didn't know what to do: to stay with Cacanja and risk the wind, or to go with Asina and risk Cacanja.

Cacanja whirled and howled in his dance of sacrifice.

When the time came, Asina led little more than half of the villagers to the cave. Cacanja was still gyrating in the compound, dancing his dance to ward off evil weather.

There was no sign of a storm in the sky.

Even those who trudged toward the cave wondered at the wisdom of their decision. They looked many times at the clear sky and saw no sign of a storm. They looked back at the angry, gyrating Cacanja and remembered how many times he had later taken revenge Then they looked at the determined back of Asina and tried to trust in his wisdom. Sabia, skipping along with the group, was smelling the flowers, picking up and throwing stones and playing with her ever-present friend, Tacuma (Tah-ku-mah). Watching her childish behavior, many wondered if they weren't being foolish. More than one thought seriously of turning back.

In spite of their reservations, they all settled themselves in the cave to wait, their questions silently turning through their minds. Which of their leaders would emerge triumphant? Would their homes be destroyed? Would their loved ones and friends who chose to stay behind die?

Sabia was totally unconcerned with the fuss she had created. She scuffled and tumbled on the cave floor with the seven-year-old Tacuma, the tall lanky son of Bayo (Bay-you) and Jawarah (Jah-war-ah), who lived in the hut next to hers. They had been together constantly since Sabia had been tiny. Seeing them together was often a village entertainment: watching them explore their world, Sabia hardly able to walk, toddling along, trying to keep up with Tacuma's more experienced step, their first clumsy attempts to climb the sentry outposts, seeing them covered with mud from the banks of the Benue, Sabia's babyish attempts to cure the wounded animals they brought back from their explorations in the forest, or Tacuma's attempts to teach the wide-eyed Sabia how to master the spearing of fish. Right now they could have done without Sabia's prediction that had delivered them into their doubts.

Asina was watching the weather and letting the villagers know the state of the sky. His first reports were of nothing eventful. "The gods are blessing us," he said. "There is no sign of a wind." Those who had loved ones still in the compound were relieved.

Then his face changed. He was frowning. "The sky is darkening," he said. The villagers stiffened.

Without warning, it began. First it was a howl, like the howl of the fiercest trapped animals. Nobody moved. Then, for a moment, everything was in chaos. Frightened mothers gathered equally-frightened children to their bodies.

Then came more sounds - trees crashing to the ground, objects whose momentum sent them banging into anything in their path. Babies cried, frightened by the noise. The sounds seemed never-ending. Crashing! Falling! Crashing!

Sabia clung to Tacuma, their playfulness ended.

The deafening blasts of the wind reached into Sabia's soul to terrorize her. Tacuma's arms offered protection. Something was happening to her. Something new. A bond. There was a bond now, linking them together. It was like a chain, connecting their two bodies. It was safe.

Then, over the roar of the wind, she heard words. "Tacuma will be your mate. Cherish him mightily."

While those in the cave huddled together, frightened, but safe, the villagers below were dying. No place was safe. Huts shattered around them. Trees toppled in their path. Canoes flew through the air, striking them, felling them on the spot. The wind shoved them from place to place. Some rolled into the Benue and were smashed against rocks and drowned. Some were crushed by falling objects. Some were rendered unconscious by careening missiles. Everything moved. Nothing was stationary.

What followed was even more frightening.

Silence.

Not a bird twittered. Not an animal moved. Not a tree rustled.

The inside of the cave was equally as silent. It was as if they had all stopped breathing. No one moved.

Asina was the first. He picked his way gingerly to the mouth of the cave. He looked out. Destruction was everywhere. When he came back, his face told the tale. They knew what he didn't say. What he did say was, "I believe the gods are through with their destruction and it is safe for us to return to the village."

Now they worried. What would they find out there now? Then they saw it: the devastation. It was difficult to pick their way through the debris to get back to the village.

What greeted them was more terrible than their worst imaginings. Many of their huts lay in shambles. Those that were left standing had no roof. Ruined canoes were scattered all over the compound. Debris was everywhere.

Mangled bodies lay about. Some were dead. Some moaned in deep pain. A few villagers were still standing. They took halting steps, hanging their heads in shame at their stupidity.

Cacanja was nowhere to be seen.

The villagers stared in numb silence at the annihilation of everything.

Asina was taking note of what was left standing and what was destroyed. Then he took charge. "Bring the wounded to my hut as quickly as possible. Wrap those who are dead and take them to the burying ground. Kasimu, get your spear and protect our dead from the animals. We will bury them tomorrow. Tonight we have to take care of those whose spirits are still with us. Move quickly now."

In their despair, they began to move. They moved through the village, listening for the moans of those lying wounded, searching through the rubble for those dead. They found a man lying under a fallen tree, chest crushed. He screamed as six men lifted the tree and pulled him out. A woman was found unconscious, half in and half out of the water, a baby lying face down beside her. A child, skull crushed, and dying, was cradled in the arms of an old grandmother. There were repeated wailings as loved ones were found dead, intermixed with cries of joy for those found unharmed.

Then Cacanja emerged from the forest. He strutted through the devastation, apparently without shame or humiliation.

Asina was bent inspecting one of the dead when he saw him. He lost his usual composure. He shouted. "I should send you to the crocodiles, you . . . you . . .. It was your jealousy and your antagonism that caused all of this. You should join the dead."

Now Cacanja lost his strut. It wasn't Asina's threat that frightened him. It was loss of power. The child, Sabia, had trespassed. She had trespassed into what was rightfully his, into the unknown. And she had been right. Now he had lost face. And she was to blame.

He glowered at Asina. "It was the gods that sent the wind . . . to punish us. They told me. They sent me a message. They told me they sent the wind to punish us for our sins. They are angered. We didn't send them enough sacrifices. They sent the god of the wind to force our sacrifice."

"Don't tell me about sacrifices," Asina roared. "You caused this death. Not the gods. You and your jealousy caused it. Look around. Look around and see what you did." Asina was so angry he was shaking.

"The gods demanded this sacrifice," Cacanja yelled back. "I couldn't have stopped it."

Asina wanted to tear the man limb from limb. Instead, through clenched teeth, he pronounced his punishment. "From this day forth, you shall become teacher to Sabia," he hissed. "You will teach her all you know."

Cacanja stared at Asina, his mouth open. "I'd rather go to the crocodiles," he growled.

"And you will, if you defy my order. You will teach her everything! Furthermore, from now on, all predictions and pronouncements, you will make together."

Cacanja glared.

"And if you decide to be uncooperative in any way, I will see to it that you are crocodile meat. I have spoken. Now take this man to my hut and treat his wounds."

Villagers who had witnessed the scene silently cheered.

Cacanja seethed. Before, he had been jealous and felt a grudging rivalry. Now he was possessed. He wanted her dead. "Asina, for now you win," he muttered under his breath. "But only for now. You are getting older. One day. One day I will have my chance. Sabia will be punished. My time will come. So be it!"

CHAPTER 20

Sabia became the learner. Cacanja and Yusufu, the teachers.

On this day, sweat beaded on her forehead and spun from her naked body, as she swirled and gyrated to Cacanja's driving force.

"Dance, Sabia, dance. Dance until you see them," he screeched.

"Call them to you. Call the gods to you."

"Call Ala!"

"Call Nyambe!"

"Call Damballah!"

"Call them, Sabia!"

"Dance until they come to you."

"Faster!"

"Harder, Sabia."

"Dance, Sabia."

Until she dropped, exhausted, to the dust.

"Sit quietly and let the gods come to you, Sabia," said Yusufu. "Close your eyes. Breathe in the smoke from the fire. The gods will come to you. They will tell you what you need to know. Listen to them. Breathe deep, Sabia. Sit quietly."

Until the vision in her head was clear and a god spoke.

The first one spoke, "One of the panthers is crazed. He is a danger to your village. He will prowl tonight in search of food. Tell the men to post extra sentries. Without extra sentries, the panther will kill one of your babies."

And so it was. As the panther leapt from his tree that night, he was killed by one of the spearmen.

Another god said, "Tell the men to fish around the second bend of the river near the old stump. There they will catch enough fish for three days."

And so it was and everybody ate fish for three days.

"Dance!" yelled Cacanja. "Dance the dance of birth. It is Aole's time."

And she danced . . . until she saw it.

She saw Aole squatting over a pile of clean rags, her belly huge with child . . . heaving as she moans and grunts . . . until she expels the child from her insides.

She hears the scream as the baby's head emerges from Aole's body, followed by the rest . . . dropping, bloody and squirming, into the pit of clean cloth, while Aole collapses onto her mat.

She hears the cry, as the birthing woman whacks its tiny behind and lays it, gasping and hungry, on Aole's stomach.

She feels the peace, as Aole suckles the child until, soon, both are asleep.

She emerges from the birthing hut just as the drums are announcing this new arrival and the villagers begin to converge to dance the celebration.

Sabia thought of a child of her own.

Yusufu was teaching her to use her body to heal. He showed her how. He had to. A woman came screaming into his hut as they sat. "My son! My son. He was mauled by a cat. He is dying. Save him, Yusufu. Save him."

They ran to the place where the boy lay . . . in agony . . . blood gushing from his leg and from a gash across his chest.

Yusufu took charge. "Sabia, get water. Woman, shut up that noise." He tore a piece of his robe and tied it around the leg to stop the bleeding.

Water was brought and Yusufu washed the wounds. Wounds clean, he sat cross-legged, eyes closed, with his hands over the jagged openings on the boy's skin. The child was green and ashy. He breathed as though near death.

The woman howled and struggled in Sabia's grasp.

Yusufu sat, his body quivering.

Sabia could almost see it! The electricity coming from his hands, the healing heat of those hands.

Sabia contained the woman as she kept up the noise. "Help him, Yusufu. Help him. Don't let him die. My only son. Don't let him die."

The boy's eyes fluttered open.

The ashy color was gone.

He smiled.

Yusufu dropped to the ground, exhausted.

"What happened?" said Sabia later, as they sat by the fire.

"I generated heat in my belly and sent it out through my hands to heal. You can do it too, Sabia, but do it only if the situation is most grave because it takes everything away from you. All your strength. Use herbs and poultices for your healing unless the situation is most grave."

"You are a most learned man, Yusufu. Thank you for teaching me."

The drums announced a death, the slow mournful rhythm of death.

"It is time to dance for Grandma Zola," said Cacanja. "She has gone to the spirit world."

Sabia danced.

Later Sabia looked at her, lying alone in her hut, eyes closed, body cold . . . her usually busy mouth finally closed.

The children she had loved gathered around with tears for no more stories, for no more scoldings, for no more bits of sweet food passed surreptitiously into their hands when the other elders weren't looking.

Sabia danced the dance of death, until she knew death. Until she saw Grandma Zola leave her body and go into the world of spirits, where she would wait until it was time. Where she would dictate to the living world from her lofty spot. Where she would wait until it was time for her to live again. Sabia danced the dance of death.

"Call to Damballah," said Yusufu. "He is the most powerful of all the gods. Stronger even than Ala. He is the god of death and the god of life, not to be angered. He can be angered, sometimes to the point of death when the natural earth is violated. He is the god of the serpent. Call to him, Sabia."

She sat in front of the fire, seeing the flames leap and die, and leap again. She called his name. "Damballah, my friend. Come to me. Damballah of the coiled body. Damballah, who holds the world together with those coils, coiled time after time, around the earth. Damballah, you who can destroy. Damballah, you who can protect. Damballah, come to me."

And there he was, hissing and coiling in the fire. He was talking. "You are learning well, Sabia. I am pleased with you, my child. Soon you will no longer be one who learns but the one who teaches."

Yusufu nodded.

Sabia grinned.

And with Tacuma, she was everywhere. Day after day, they spent in the rain forest, in the river, swimming or fishing, in the canoes paddling up and down, laughing, teasing, playing, touching . . . being children together. Being like their elders together. Knowing the time would come when they could mate. Unknowing of what to do with their growing bodies until then.

"I have a sling for you," he said one day as they walked in the rain forest. "I will teach you to hunt. All you do is put a stone in the middle of the sling, like this. Then twist the sling with your wrist, like this. At just the right moment, let the stone go and try to hit the center of the tree." His stone, of course, struck the center of the tree.

"I can do that," she said, grabbing the sling. She placed the stone, as instructed. She turned it around and around, letting go just at the right time so it would hit the center of the tree, just like Tacuma. It didn't hit the center of the tree. It didn't even hit the tree.

"Here, let me show you again," said Tacuma, trying to take the sling.

"No, I can do it myself," she said.

It was many suns before she hit the tree.

It was almost a moon before she struck the center.

Tacuma was patient.

Sabia was determined.

On the day she brought home her first kill, Diallobe was not pleased. "Girls do not hunt," he told her. "That is men's work."

"I must do all work," she told him. "I must know men's work and women's work as well."

"I could forbid you to hunt," he said.

"I would hunt anyway."

"Then you would be guilty of disobedience."

"Yes, my father. I would be guilty of disobedience, as well as of hunting."

They stood almost eye to eye. Sabia was tall for her ten rains.

Diallobe was silent, knowing he could not win. "You may hunt," he said.

"Thank you, father."

All of which produced a quantity of small birds, wild turkeys, and later, when her aim was without deviation, a wild pig or two for the family.

Sabia dreamed: a woman with skin the color of the antelope and hair as black as hers, but longer than the tail of the cow. This woman came to her in her dreams. She made her hair swish as she talked. Golden earrings glittered from her ears.

"Sabia," she said. And it echoed through her night. "Sabia. Sabia. Sabia," said the echo.

"I know you," said the woman.

"I know you," said the echo.

"We are one," said the woman.

"One. One. One," said the echo.

Then she disappeared.

Sabia knew her . . . and she knew her not.

"Come back," she said. "Come back. Come back. Come back," echoed through her dreams.

But not until later did she come back.

Sabia told her dream to Tacuma.

Tacuma knew about the earrings.

Even though his dream had been different, he knew about the earrings. The man in his dream was strong of build and powerful of voice. He spoke to Tacuma from his ship with the wind in the sails. He said, "Get them from Giaka. He has them. Get them from Giaka and give them to Sabia."

"Get what?"

"The earrings, of course."

"Of course. The earrings."

Tacuma didn't understand the dream, but he knew he had to be prepared to buy a pair of earrings from the trader on his next trip. He knew it was important.

The next day when Sabia found him, he was making his drum, hollowing it out from a large log, covering it with the hide of a goat. The drum sound was deep and low.

"Why are you making a drum?" she said.

"To trade with Giaka."

"For what?" her ever curious self wanted to know.

Tacuma knew he was in trouble now. "I can't tell you," he said.

She pouted, she cajoled, she threatened, she insisted, but none of her maneuverings would extract the reason from Tacuma's sealed lips.

Giaka came every year just after harvest to trade his trinkets and cookware for food and gold. He came from Morocco, a white man, a dark white man, with long softly-curling hair and a mustache, wearing robes and no shoes. He was the only white man to brave the mosquito-infested river, to bring the villagers what they needed.

He had the earrings.

The transaction was easy. Somehow Giaka knew the earrings were for Tacuma and Tacuma knew he must have them. "I have been making a drum for you . . . to trade for the earrings," Tacuma said . . . hoping his drum would be enough. "Sabia will wear them."

Giaka looked carefully at the drum. He turned it this way and that. He thumped it again and again. He held it to his ear as he thumped it. He shook it, checking for loose pieces of wood inside the hollow that would affect the sound. He was a shrewd man, this Giaka. He knew he must sell the earrings to Tacuma. He knew he would have the earrings forever if he did not make this transaction, but he was determined to get as much for them as the market would bear. "Is this all you have?" he finally asked, his dark face looking disapprovingly at the drum.

Tacuma's face fell. He wasn't going to get the earrings. "Yes," he said. "That's all I have."

"Then I can't sell you the earrings." Giaka started to walk away.

"Wait!" said Tacuma, frantically searching his mind for something else he could trade. "Wait. I have a carved stick."

"Can't say as I need a stick, but let me see it anyway."

Tacuma ran frantically to his hut to retrieve the stick. Retrieved, he looked at it with despair. He knew Giaka. Giaka would never accept this lowly stick for such a precious trinket as the earrings. But it was all he had.

But Giaka did accept the stick. He knew his market. He knew he was lucky to get the drum. It was a good drum. One of the best he had seen. The stick he could throw away later. It was his pride that had to be assuaged. The stick assuaged his pride.

Now Giaka had to explain. "These earrings are magic," he said. "The magic of trouble to those who are not supposed to wear them and the magic of life to those who are."

"What do you mean, Giaka?"

"Many women have tried to wear these earrings since the Egyptian beauty and her lover vowed their eternity together with these earrings as the symbol. None have succeeded. Each woman who has put them to her ears has torn at herself, because she was burning like fire. Now no trader wants to carry them, because they are no sooner sold to a woman than they are re-sold back to the trader. All the traders know their curse. But Sabia's ears will not burn."

"Sabia is the right woman?"

"Yes, Sabia is the right woman."

Giaka went away with Tacuma's drum, and his stick. And Tacuma buried the earrings where they would be safe . . . until he took his mate . . . not knowing that that would be much sooner than he expected. Much sooner than was allowed.

Now, late into the night, when Sabia was asleep, he could be seen whittling and carving.

One day he presented her with a bow and arrow.

"Oooooooh," she squealed.

Now the days were interchangeable between the sling and the bow.

He taught her to shoot. "Just place the arrow in the bow, like this, aim, and pull back," he said. "Then let go. Like this." He demonstrated. His aim was perfect. He hit the tree dead center.

"I can do that," she said. "Let me try."

A family of chattering monkeys kibitzed from the tree as she fitted the arrow into the string, aimed at the same center, pulled back and let go. Just as she let go, her arm jerked crazily and the arrow shot straight up into the air, into the midst of the chattering monkeys, scattering them in all directions.

Tacuma started to laugh. "Ha, ha, ha, hee, hee, hee." He doubled over.

"Stop laughing at me, Tacuma. Stop it."

"Ha, ha, hee, hee, hee." He was holding his stomach.

"Stop it," she said, throwing herself into him, sending him to the ground. There they became a mass of arms and legs, rolling and tumbling over the ferns and the moss, banging into trees. Laughing. Pummelling. Happy.

He finally pinned her shoulders to the ground, imprisoning her with his knees. She gave in to his imprisonment. She became motionless. He was triumphant above her.

She was absolutely still, looking at him.

He was absolutely still, looking at her.

Slowly he dropped his face, and touched his lips to hers.

She closed her eyes.

All was quiet, except for the monkeys looking on.

Then he jumped away from her, as though burned by fire.

"Where are you going?" she said, confused. "Come back here! I liked it."

"I liked it, too, but I can't come back."

"Why not?"

"Because I feel funny."

"I feel funny, too," she said. "I like feeling funny. Come back and do it again."

"I can't."

"Why not?"

"Because I feel funny in my member," he said. "My father, Jarawah, told me not to allow my member into you until after the mating dance. He was very firm about that."

"Come back anyway. Jarawah won't know."

"No, I can't. We must not. We have to wait until it is time."

Sabia jumped up from her forest bed and started for home, bow and arrows in hand. "Well, I don't want to wait. I liked it. If you don't want to do it again, I'll go find Kandia. He'll do it."

"Wait, Sabia. Wait! I'll do it again, but just once more. Then we'll wait for the mating dance."

Sabia stopped her head-long dash and waited.

Tacuma placed one more soft kiss on her mouth, while she struggled to hold him to her. He stayed as long as he dared. Then he unhooked himself from her embrace and moved away from her. "No more until we are mates, Sabia. No more," he said with all the resolution he could muster. He refused to look at her disappointed face. He was going to refuse any more arguments. "I bet I can beat you home," he said, knowing the challenge would distract her from her determination.

"Bet you can't."

They ran, through trees, over logs, and ferns, splashing through puddles, to the edge of the rain forest. When they emerged, hand in hand, Sabia was beaming. She was going to ask the gods. They would tell her how to change Tacuma's mind.

CHAPTER 21

Their relationship was a problem. It defied the customs of the village - girls stay with girls, boys with boys, until the dance of mating. Until the time when life-long partners are chosen. Tacuma and Sabia would not follow the custom.

The women, who gathered around the well every day, gossiped.

"She is becoming a woman."

"They are walking on unsafe ground being together like that."

"The gods will punish them with child if they are not careful."

"He is teaching her to hunt, did you know?"

"To hunt? Diallobe should stop her."

"She will not be stopped. She says she must know about hunting."

"It is not for women to hunt."

"She says she must."

"She is trouble."

Tacuma was taunted unmercifully by the other boys. They mocked him at every turn and challenged his manhood when they could. They were unmerciful in their insults. Most of the time, Tacuma was oblivious to their jibs, until one day when he was incited by Konata, the largest and most aggressive of all the boys.

On this day, Tacuma was walking across the compound when, without warning, Konata loomed in front of him. Several of the other boys hovered in the background.

"So, where's your little playmate?" sneered Konata.

Tacuma ignored him and continued walking.

"I'm talking to you, coward," Konata said, blocking his way.

Tacuma was forced to halt. "I heard you," he said.

"Then don't be rude!" Konata said, into his face. "Answer me!"

Tacuma knew the challenge was to fight. He didn't want to fight.

Konata made not fighting impossible. He spat in Tacuma's face. "I said, where's your playmate?"

Now Tacuma knew he was to be shamed in front of all the other boys. Now he knew why they were there. They were waiting to cheer the larger Konata on to victory. They were waiting for him to show his weakness, to further deprecate his relationship with Sabia.

He decided.

Up came his knee into Konata's groin, with a simultaneous fist to the nose.

Konata yelled in pain and doubled over, holding his private parts. He fell to the ground, gasping for breath. Blood was streaming from his nose.

Tacuma calmly stepped over him and walked home.

Later, he was brought before the Council of Elders for fighting and severely reprimanded; still the taunting gang of boys had a new respect for him and spoke to him with admiration. Eventually, even Konata showed him a grudging respect.

Najuma, especially, worried about how Sabia and Tacuma violated tradition. She worried that they might violate the most sacred tradition of the Ibo. The time was coming when she needed to talk with Sabia about Tacuma.

It happened when Sabia was just over thirteen rains. It happened on the day she ran into the hut waving a bloody cloth. "Mama, look. I'm a woman now. Look."

Najuma beamed. "Yes, you are. You are a woman now. And I'm proud of you. You are a woman, just as Yusufu predicted. Just as the gods told us. Now there are things you need to know."

"About what, Mama? What is it I don't already know?"

"You need to know about Tacuma."

"About Tacuma, Mama?"

""Yes. Diallobe and I have watched you since you were a baby, playing with him, learning from him, loving him. We know he is to be your mate."

"Yes, Mama, he is."

"Does he excite your body?"

Sabia turned away from the question. She knew that now it would be Najuma who would warn her. "I feel strange sometimes, when he is with me," she said, still not wanting to talk about it.

"You know you need to wait to satisfy your body until you are united by Asina. You need to wait until you choose each other at the mating dance. You cannot let his member enter you until then. You must not become with child until after you dance the mating dance. Custom is very strict about this. Nothing else will be tolerated."

"I know, Mama."

But everything conspired to make her break her promise.

The sounds of Diallobe and Najuma loving in the night. The sounds that penetrated her sleep, causing her to have passionate dreams of Tacuma.

The sight of other lovers. Kasimu (Cas-ee-moo) and Toulupe (Tah-lou-pay) entwined together in the bush, Kasimu covering Toulupe's body with his own, as they squirmed and writhed together.

The drum music at festival dances that pulsed and throbbed through her, joined her body to their rhythms, and created a passion she could only express in the dance. What was worse was watching couples aroused, disappear into the bushes.

All of this caused a burning at her center for Tacuma.

Sabia knew she could not hold back her passions much longer.

It was shortly after she had passed her fourteenth rain when the gods spoke. She was sitting in her favorite spot, at the foot of the baobab tree.

"Go to Tacuma. Your time is now."

Sabia's eyes flew open in surprise. They were telling her what she wanted to hear. Was she hearing right?

"Go to Tacuma. You must mate with Tacuma soon."

This was what she had been waiting for. But this was too good to be true. She waited. She was sure there would be a different message. None came.

She tentatively asked the gods the question she only wanted to be answered in the positive. "Am I to be with Tacuma before the mating dance?"

"We have spoken," they said in unison.

She jumped up and ran toward the compound, searching for Tacuma. She found him by the river, patching his canoe.

"Tacuma," she said, out of breath. "The gods have given me a message."

"Yes?" he said, smiling at her happy face.

"They have told me . . . " she had to stop. She was panting.

"Wait. Catch your breath," he said. "I'll still be here."

Laughing at her own urgency, she slowed her breathing and tried again. "They have told me that we are to be united now. We don't have to wait any longer."

Tacuma stared at her, his mouth open. His mind was racing with conflict. There was tradition. He had to wait. There was desire. Do it soon. There were his father's warnings. Keep your member from her. There was her teasing seductiveness. She was so beautiful and seductive standing there. After all, was she not the message from the gods, standing before him in a woman's body?

"Do the gods promise to keep us safe?" he asked.

"Oh, yes. They have promised," she said, telling him only half a truth. He had been so stubborn.

Tacuma relented. He desired her too much to be cautious. Taking her hands, he looked deeply into her. "The night of the feast of Ala?" he asked.

The feast of Ala could not come too soon.

It was the drum that announced the beginning of the feast, the feast that gave thanks for all that belonged to the earth, and celebrated the passions of the people. Sweat glistened on the bodies of the drummers as they worked in the hot sun. They chanted as they worked:

> ***"Oh na ma za zi zim***
> ***Oh dee jaa . . . . . . .de jaaaa.***
> ***Ma no ho bah di zulu zim***
> ***Oh dee jaa . . . . de jaaaa."***

The rhythm was easy. Later, as the sun traversed the sky into the dark night, the tempo would quicken, compelling the people to know their earthy substance.

Today Sabia didn't need the sound of the drums. It was her day. She was ready.

Diallobe waited for her outside the hut. When he saw her, this grown woman, so tall, so muscular like Najuma, so vibrant and intense, with breasts that swayed as she walked, it was hard to remember that it had been just fifteen rains since she had been conceived. He remembered the sweetness of the night. He remembered the prophesy they had been fulfilling. He remembered the promise of the child . . . this child . . . this grown child he was now so proud of.

He held out his hand; they walked together to join the others, already milling around inside the compound, tasting the delicacies prepared for the feast and sipping the palm wine that hung in a leopard skin from a tree.

Diallobe stopped at the leopard skin, filling his gourd. He handed it to her. She tasted for the first time, the palm wine that was tradition at all celebrations. A warmth began at the pit of her stomach and crept stealthily into the rest of her body. "I like it," she declared, taking another sip.

"Be careful of how much of this you drink," he said. "It will change your feelings. Some is nice but a lot will make you sick and crazy."

"I'll be careful, father," she promised. But the promise disappeared as she was captured by the rhythm of the drums. The pulsations demanded of her . . . required of her . . . the movement of her body. She couldn't stop herself. Her strong legs carried her to the center of the circle of unmarried girls, where she danced, her legs weaving a graceful sinuous pattern in the dust.

Later, as the tempo of the drums quickened, so also did the force and vigorousness of her dancing. Sweat beaded on her glossy body as she swirled and strutted to honor the earth. To honor Tacuma. To honor herself.

Dusk fell. Lighted torches cast alternate shadows and light on the dancers. Passions and desires were rising. Sounds came out of their throats, rising above the beat of the drums. Still Sabia danced.

Then she felt him, standing by the side of the dancers. He was waiting for her - tall and straight and beckoning.

She swirled out of the circle of young girls. He grasped her hand and they ran, stumbling, through the brush and into the mouth of the cave, the very cave where she had first known of their bonding . . . of their eventual mating. They dropped, panting, onto the soft sand, knowing now their destiny. Tacuma reached behind him and lit a small torch.

Sabia rested her head against his shoulder, her body shivering from the cool dampness of the cave and the heat of her passion-filled body. The drums throbbed in the background, caressing her mind, giving more urgency to her need for Tacuma's body, demanding that they begin.

Wordlessly, they both rose, each throwing off their belts, allowing the drumbeat to dictate their movements. They undulated toward each other. Together . . . then apart . . . touching . . . not touching . . . knowing . . . not knowing.

Only the throb of the drums entered their consciousness as his member touched her again and again . . . only to move away. Returning . . . moving away . . . returning . . . in rhythm to the pulsating tempo behind them.

Sabia arched her back, thrusting her hips forward to meet him. She circled her hips around his member . . . catching it . . . to touch . . . to pleasure. She was quivering . . . shaking . . . waiting.

They dropped onto the sand.

He rolled over her, on his knees.

She parted her legs. "Enter me," she said. "Enter me now."

"Yes," he said, as his member began its slow journey to the bottomless pit of her desire, pausing at her maidenhead.

"It will hurt," he said.

Her cry of pain was followed by a gasp of pleasure as he filled her completely with his body. With his soul.

She thrashed wildly. She couldn't get enough of him. She grasped his body with her arms, hungrily searching for his lips.

His kiss, so deep, so passionate, brought both to their moment.

The drums beat to the surging of their bodies.

With one enormous thrust, her desire was met. Her body became his in one pulsating moment.

Tacuma planted his seed inside her.

Their hearts beat to the rhythm of the drums as they lay in the soft sand, bodies spent, hearts content. The torch flickered over their naked bodies.

The drums continued to throb.

Sabia nuzzled her head into Tacuma's shoulders, knowing, now, her contentment and wishing for forever.

But Tacuma was becoming restless. Forever was too long for him. There was a surprise hidden in the sand and he was ready for her to have it.

He squeezed her shoulder and rolled away. "I have something hidden here," he said. "A gift for you." He dug briefly in the sand, then holding up his find so it glowed in the light of the torch.

Sabia's eyes and mouth widened at what she saw. "It's the earrings. Those are the earrings."

"What?"

"Those are the earrings. They belonged to the woman in my dream. Remember, Tacuma. The woman with the antelope skin. She was wearing those very same earrings. What are you doing with them?"

"I got them from Giaka, the trader. I traded my drum for them. He told me they were magic and that you were the only woman who could wear them."

"I don't understand, Tacuma. Why me?"

"Because the magic of the earrings is the magic of love. It is our love that makes the earrings right for you. I had a dream, a dream about a man on a ship. He told me the earrings belonged to you."

Sabia was quiet. Her mind was full of pictures. The woman from her dreams appeared. She was talking about love. She faded away. Then there was a man standing on a ship. He was holding the earrings in his hand. He disappeared. Then she saw woman after woman with the earrings in their ears. She heard them scream in pain as they tore them off. As the screaming women disappeared, the woman of her dreams returned. "We are the same," she said. "The earrings are yours." She saw Tacuma holding the earrings.

Now she understood. The earrings had been hers before. Tacuma had been hers before. Their love had been the same before. It was the love between them that made the earrings hers now. As long as the earrings belonged to her every other woman who put them on . . . who lacked the same kind of love that belonged to her and to Tacuma . . . would tear at their ears in eternal damnation if they tried to wear them. Now she understood.

"These earrings . . . they unite us for eternity, Tacuma," she said. "Our spirits, when they leave our bodies, will wait to enter life again until we can enter together."

"Eternity is what I want with you," he said. "I am not afraid of eternity, are you?"

"Not as long as you are with me," she said.

"You know that once I put them in your ears, you cannot take them off for the rest of our lives together."

"I know," she said quietly. "I know, and I am ready."

Tacuma held them up for her to see one more time, for she would not see them again, once they were in her ears. "Ohhh," she said, somewhat dazzled by their beauty in the torchlight. She reached for them and held them between the palms of her hands. She ran her fingers along the edges and over the red lines. Suddenly she felt her hands hot, a burning hot. She didn't need the goddess to tell her. She knew it was the power of the earrings and of their story that was etching its way into her hands . . . her healing hands. She knew, at that moment, that these earrings were indeed hers. There was no question. They belonged to her and to her destiny.

She removed the ivory from her own ears.

Tacuma pushed the wire of the first earring through her right ear. He said, "As I give you this earring, my spirit enters into you now and forever."

Strangely, she felt heat in her belly - no pain, just heat. She was excited. "I felt it, Tacuma. I felt it."

"I, too," he said.

Then Tacuma pushed the second earring into her left ear, saying, "As I give you this earring, your spirit enters into me now and forever."

Sabia felt a sharp pain in her heart. Tacuma started and put his hand to his chest.

They knew. The flame had passed from heart to heart.

"We are now as one," proclaimed Sabia.

"Bodies and souls as one," said Tacuma.

They faced each other in the torchlight, hands touching. Sabia could feel the weight of the earrings swinging in time with her movements. They were full of satisfaction.

As the drumming ceased for the night, Sabia and Tacuma emerged from the cave, hand in hand, not the same as when they entered.

Najuma saw . . . and worried.

CHAPTER 22

Dreams. Sabia was having dreams. Fearful dreams, sent from the gods, that left her weak and afraid. What they were telling her, she did not know.

The first dream came to her four nights after the feast of Ala. So thoroughly did it frighten her that she told no one. Not even Tacuma.

They all began the same way, with a howling in her head. That in itself was frightening. Once the howling began, she would be lifted from her pallet and carried away, to be deposited in some strange place.

On the first night, the gods sent her on a long journey to another land. There, she found none of the brooding masses of trees, none of the sounds of the animals that forever made up the noises of her life, no expanses of tall grass filled with antelope, hyenas, and flocks of birds. There she found fields and fields full of bushes of cotton and a some buildings interspersed among the fields. There she saw her black people bending over those plants, filling and dragging large bags of the fluffy stuff.

Everything was confusing. These were her people but nothing was right. First, the covering on their bodies was alien. The women wore long white dresses smudged with dirt, that were tattered and torn and the men wore dirty pants and shirts. Second, they spoke in a strange tongue and yet when they sang, they sang the familiar songs of Africa. There was great sadness when they sang. It broke her heart to listen. Then she noticed that their eyes stayed downcast while they worked and their movement was oppressed. They were lifeless and without freedom.

Suddenly her attention was drawn to a young man toppling over in the dirt. He was holding his stomach and retching. He lay on the ground, moaning and writhing. She didn't understand. No one came to help. The pickers noticed, but did not move.

Farther downfield, a strange-looking man riding a large animal raced to investigate. Sabia was amused and somewhat repulsed by his pale skin and round body. His skin was the color of the albino and the hair sprouting from his face and head was a preposterous straw color. Dismounting, he swiftly approached the sick man.

He carried a whip and was angry.

His victim, terrified by the sight of him, begged for mercy. Sabia was ashamed. "African men do not beg nor ask for pity. They are too proud. What manner of African is this?"

Tragically, this lost African had sold his pride too cheaply and was paid with the kiss of the whip. The ugly one struck him again and again. His body jerked under each cutting lash. He was beaten until he was a bloody, broken wound gasping for breath and his screams were reduced to pleading whimpers. After a very long time, even the whimpers ceased and what was once a man lay near death.

After one last vicious kick, the overseer mounted his animal and rode away. The other black people dared not help what remained of the man. They kept on picking. Suffocating fear hung in the air.

The singing stopped.

Sabia woke, sweating and afraid.

All day the dream haunted her. When she went to sleep that night, she hoped the gods were finished with her - so sufficiently frightened had she been from the night before. But they were not through with her. The howling came again. Again she was lifted from her pallet and flown somewhere into the night - into the land of the strange people.

Tonight, she saw many buildings, buildings that dwarfed the huts in her village. Some were so big that all of the huts of Nahut could be piled inside. She saw many of the pale-looking men walking around among the buildings. Some were riding the big animals. She shook her head to clear her vision. Was it her imagination? Was it real? She kept seeing whips in their hands. But there were no whips. Her imagination.

She did see pale-looking women, wearing lots of clothes. Why wear all those clothes when it was so hot? And why were they so stiff when they moved.

She looked at the buildings. There were so many. Building after building after building. Where the buildings stopped, she saw water. The big water! And there sitting on the water was one of the big canoes. 'Ships', Yusufu called them. When she looked again at the ship, she gasped. It was full of her own people, her own black people. They were all in chains. They were coming out of the mouth of the ship, hobbling. The pale men were whipping them, wanting them to move faster.

A terrible odor assailed her nostrils, the smell of disease. These ebony men and women were sick.

The pale men whipped and bellowed until all of the black people were herded into one of their buildings. A small shiny stick was turned in the door. The black men and women were inside the buildings and could not get out. She heard their fearful cries of pain.

She felt their cries, deep in her belly.

Later, there was a commotion. People were gathering, jostling, laughing, shouting hello's. A pale man was talking from a platform. "Traders must be in town," she thought. She moved closer to see his trinkets. Out of the corner of her eye, she saw a black man being dragged from the building. Then she knew. She knew what was for sale.

They were selling her people!

The horror of it hit her stomach like a stone.

Each black man made naked was poked and prodded and shamed before the crowd. Then sums of money were counted into a bucket and the man was dragged away. When the black man didn't want to go, the pale one hit him.

The horror was worse with the women and children.

Sabia woke sweating and afraid.

Sabia knew the gods were not through. She knew this torment was going to keep on until their message was clear. By the third night, she didn't want to sleep. Scenes from the other dreams wouldn't leave her mind. Exhaustion finally claimed her and she slept.

Again there was the howling. Again the currents carried her away but this time, she was still in her own land. The forest, the sounds of animals, the grasslands, the big water, they all belonged in her own land. But there was something new. It was made of stone and it sat on the edge of the big water. Black men and women were inside. They were waiting. Waiting for what?

Then she saw it. The same pale-looking men with whips. They were whipping the black men and women onto a ship.

Was she seeing right? It couldn't be. But it was. Black men with whips! Herding! Chaining! Whipping! She screamed in anguish. Not her own people! Black men betraying their own? It was true - black men betraying their own!

Without warning, she was in the blackness of the big canoe. She was underneath the tramping of feet and scraping of chains. The stench was overwhelming. Her eyes couldn't see until the gloom lifted. Then she saw them. She saw them chained together, one after the other, back to front, back to front, back to front.

They were bleeding from the whips and defecating on themselves. The pale-looking men were bringing them putrid water, and food unfit for a rat.

She woke, sweating and afraid.

All the next day, Sabia begged the gods: "I've had enough," she cried. "Don't send me any more." But she knew they would.

This night, when the howling came, she found herself in her own rain forest. For the moment, it was almost natural. The monkeys were chattering. The baboons were showing off. The birds were squawking and screeching and the bush fowl were scurrying here and there. It seemed the horror might be over.

But no! There they were. Four men, three of them her own black men. There was only one pale man. What did they have in their hands? Not whips this time. Sticks! Wicked-looking sticks. 'Guns', Yusufu had called them.

They seemed to be tracking something. How stealthily they moved! Not a twig broke under their feet. Not a sound came from their lips. "That animal is as good as dead," she thought.

Then she saw the prey. Horror filled her body. It was not an animal. It was four black hunters. Two were young, like herself, and two older. They were setting their traps, unaware.

The hunters had become the hunted.

Four men, three black and one pale, were now the hunters.

How quickly the hunted were surrounded - each with a gun in his face.

The hunted stared, uncomprehending, at the big sticks.

One started to run.

There was a terrible noise; fire spewed out. The runner stumbled, poised for a moment in mid-air, then crashed to the ground. Two of the others started toward him. They stopped, as the fire sticks came closer. Movement ceased.

The pale man angrily strode toward the fallen boy, turned him over with his boot, then kicked him in the head. The boy was dead. He was to be left there - booty for animals. Those alive were bound together with a thong, neck to neck. They were marched toward the river. There they were thrown into the bottom of a canoe.

Sabia came closer to see the faces.

Her scream pierced the night.

In the bottom of the canoe were Diallobe, Jarawah and Tacuma. The dead boy was Ato, Tacuma's brother.

CHAPTER 23

Her scream pierced everything. Najuma was awake. Diallobe was awake. She was up and pacing furiously from one side of the hut to the next.

"What does it mean? What does it mean? What do my dreams mean?"

She paced.

She paced some more.

She entreated the gods.

"Answer me," she yelled. "Tell me what it is you want me to know."

She sank back on her pallet, her head in her hands. "Why don't you tell me?"

Diallobe saw that there was no danger. He went back to sleep.

Najuma squatted at her daughter's level and waited.

Sabia said nothing.

Then the answer came. "Go to Yusufu."

"Of course," she said, jumping up. "Mama, I've just had a message from the gods; I don't know what it means. I need to go to Balewa to see Yusufu. He will tell me."

"How long will you be gone?"

"I'll be back in three days."

"When will you leave?"

"At sunup. I'll get my things ready now."

"It is the time of the wild boar. Be careful!"

"I will, Mama."

Najuma turned away, returning to her pallet.

"Mama?"

"Yes?"

"Tell father not to go hunting while I'm gone. There may be danger if he hunts. Will you tell him?"

"I'll tell him," said Najuma, her eyes heavy with sleep.

Sabia gathered her things: her sling for small game, her bow and arrow in case of danger. She put food into her goat-skin bag and left the hut. She squatted near the door, waiting for the first rays of the sun.

She looked lovingly at the hut of Tacuma next door. "I wish you were going with me, my love. I will miss you these three days. Please don't go hunting until I get back."

She was sure that her warning to Najuma was enough.

Her trip to Balewa was without event. Just as the sun was going down, she arrived at Yusufu's tent. He was squatting outside with several men of the village smoking his pipe. He rose and threw his arms around her. "My child, my child. What is it that furrows your forehead and brings you to me this day?"

"Yusufu, something terrible is going to happen. The gods have told me in my dreams. It may be that Diallobe and Tacuma are in mortal danger."

Yusufu nodded, puffing on his pipe.

"The gods are telling me that all our people are in danger. Pale-looking men are here in our land to steal them away to another land and our own black men are helping them."

As Sabia sketched in the full details of her dreams, Yusufu's frown deepened.

"I'm glad you came to me, my child," he said in his learned way. "This is a grave situation - grave indeed. Slave traders have never before trespassed this far into the interior."

Sabia was shocked. "You mean pale men have stolen our people before?"

"For a very long time, Sabia. But, always before, they confined their treachery closer to the great Niger. Up until now they have never been able to navigate the Benue and our black men were not interested enough in their gold to help them. Something terrible must have changed all that. Your dreams must be a warning from the gods that our people are in great danger."

"You can explain my dreams then?" she asked.

"What you saw in your dreams, my child, was slavery."

"Slavery? I don't understand."

"What you saw was the white man owning all of those black men and forcing them to his will."

"But what gives the white man the right to own us?"

"His guns, those wicked sticks that you saw," explained Yusufu. "You see, he is very willing to be cruel and to frighten our people into submission. But even more important, he believes he has the right to do it."

"But, Yusufu, why would anyone think that stealing people from their homes and loved ones and then beating them bloody is right?"

"I'm afraid the white man does. His soul is weak, my child. He does not see things as we do. He cares not for the life of everything and everyone as we do. He cares about his accumulations. Whatever furthers his accumulations, he believes is right."

"But what has that got to do with his soul, Yusufu?"

"If his soul were stronger, Sabia, it would tell him that stealing other people was wrong, not right, as he believes. Then he would care about our people and not hurt them."

"Can we do anything about his soul, Yusufu?"

"No."

"Then what can we do?"

Yusufu was spent. "That is for the gods to answer, my child. Now we must sleep."

Sabia was tired. Yusufu was right. Tomorrow was soon enough.

Yusufu brought out a mat for her. Immediately she went to sleep. There were no dreams. There was no horror. Just peaceful, dreamless sleep.

In the morning, when she awoke, Yusufu was building the fire. Just as they were about to sit Yusufu poured into the fire two drops of his powerful liquid. Flames immediately leapt and danced in an array of colors. Sabia and Yusufu closed their eyes and became as in a trance.

Images began to march through Sabia's head. They had the same nightmarish quality as her dreams. Cruel men, one after another, each with a whip, paraded across her eyes. Each was breaking his whip over the back of a black man or woman. As this parade disappeared another vision took its place. She saw a circle of pale men, each holding one of their dangerous sticks, surrounding one frightened black man. Another vision: the big canoe sailed across her eyes. She could hear the moans and cries of her people imprisoned inside. She saw them angry and hating, pulling against their chains. They were hungry and thirsty. They were dying of starvation. Bodies were being thrown overboard and eaten by the big fish.

Black women were being forced to submit to the pale men. They cried out in pain at their brutality. There were virgins in terror, their bodies invaded and torn, without the healing passions of love. The self-centered maliciousness of the men terrorized even the older, more experienced women.

Black women began bearing children, not of their own kind. There were children with no father to claim them or teach them the ways of the men in this world. There were children with strange-colored bodies and hair - not belonging anywhere. Black men were seduced by the pale women, then thrown into burning oil for their crime. The sexual brutalization of the black women continued.

There were hundreds of big canoes, all carrying her black people into slavery. Thousands of her people marched out of those canoes in chains.

There were black men tied to ropes and swinging in the air. White men beat them to unconsciousness with whips. She saw them running from their tormentors. Dogs attacked and dragged them back to more humiliation and torture.

Her people were crying, screaming, hungry, dying, while the pale men watched and didn't care. She saw:

The whips.

The guns.

The whips.

The guns.

The whips.

The guns.

She was going mad; her mind exploding with images that threatened to consume her. She could not watch anymore. Her eyes flew open.

Dizziness assaulted her as the light of the day and the scenes of the compound hit her. She got up, stumbling and lurching, until she made her way to the edge of the village. There she wretched up everything that was in her. It was green and vile and smelled of sickness. She collapsed in the shade of a tree to regain her strength.

The sun was at its midpoint before she was able to return to the fire. She was just sitting back down when Yusufu opened his eyes.

"I'm afraid I didn't have the stomach for what I saw, Yusufu," she said. "I just expelled everything that was inside of me."

"I'm not surprised, my child. What the gods have told me is very hard to stomach. Let's thank them for their wisdom and go inside where it is cooler."

He sounded so without spirit, as though he did not have the answers either. He sounded so gloomy.

Sabia waited. The sun had moved some distance before he spoke.

"The gods have shown me what you already know, Sabia, and what I hoped I would not see. They have shown me that the white man is a devil; that he does not care whom he betrays and that he is interested only in plundering our Iboland with his whips and his guns. He has even put a curse on our own black men with the promise of gold. Now we have to be ever wary of our own; because he is helping the white man to snare whole villages into slavery."

"The gods tell me that our black traitors will be punished in their own time, when they have worn out their usefulness. The white devil will betray them and they, too, will be cargo on a slave ship. Until then we can not stop them."

Sabia felt awful. "Is there no hope?"

"Only a little. We can not stop the white devil. But we can slow him down. We can give him a hard time."

Sabia felt a little hope. "How?" she said.

"We will use the drums to warn all of the villages to be careful of strangers, black or white. We will tell them to be ready, to post more sentries, and to prepare for surprise attack. We will tell them not to go outside their villages alone, but to travel in large groups and always to be prepared for attack."

"So what we have to tell them is that they have no freedom to move about in their own land?" said Sabia, angry now.

"I'm afraid so."

Sabia exploded. "He has no right! He has no right! The white devil has no right!"

To a surprised Yusufu, she leaped up, ran out of the hut and into the compound. She screamed to the heavens. "He has no right! Nyambe! He has no right. Bring on the wind and destroy the canoes. Damballah, move the earth and destroy the villages and fields. Ala! Make him suffer. Take his children, his possessions, his loved ones. Keep this plunderer from our land!"

She started to whirl and gyrate as if she were Cacanja, swirling up the dust in the compound, shouting to the gods.

Yusufu watched her pain, wishing he could do more.

With one last leap, she crashed to the ground, bending her body to the earth in silence. Her anger was spent.

Dirty tears streaked the face that looked up at Yusufu.

He helped her up and together they walked back into the hut. There they sat in communal bitterness toward this plague against which they had so little power.

Yusufu lit his pipe. Puffs of smoke circled the hut. He was restless. He broke the silence. "I need to talk to you about something else when you're ready."

The explosion was over. Her insides were quieting. "I'm ready," she said.

"Sabia, I've been watching you grow since you were a baby. I've been your teacher. You have been an amazing pupil. Now I see you on the eve of your womanhood and I know you are ready for the fullness that you are. You are ready to be all you have learned, in service to the people."

"Thank you," she said shyly.

"I have heard from the gods that I will join the spirit world soon. It is important that you be ready."

Sabia thought that all of her emotions had been used up but now there was more. There was a wrenching in her heart. She reached for his gnarled hand.

Yusufu choked. It was hard for him to go on. "It's important that you go on with my work."

Sabia was so touched and so saddened that she had to force her words. "What do you want me to do?"

"I want you to make yourself available to the men and women of our villages. I want them to know they can come to you in time of need. I want you to take care of their sicknesses of mind and body. Will you do this, my child?"

"I am honored, Yusufu, but I am not worthy."

"That is wrong. You have been worthy for a long time now. And the older you get, the more power you will have - until some day you will surpass even mine."

Sabia doubted his words.

Yusufu went on. "I want to help you all I can. I'll give you the recipes for my potions. One that will heal the mind. Another we threw on the fire this morning. When you use it the gods will be provoked and they will give you the answers."

Yusufu touched a charm he always wore around his neck. "And I want you to have this. When I go to the spirit world, I will have a messenger bring it to you. You'll walk the rest of your life with my spirit."

Sabia couldn't stop the tears of gratitude. Her hand tightened on Yusufu's.

They sat, with no more words, this young girl with her youthful vitality and this old man with his experience and wisdom.

They sat silently while the sun traversed the open sky. It was Yusufu who broke the silence. "Sabia, there is one more thing you need to know."

"What is that?"

"You need to watch out for your enemies."

"Enemies?"

"Yes. Cacanja. You know he is your enemy."

"Yes. I know about him. Even while he teaches me, he hates me."

"Good. I'm glad you know. But be vigilant, my child. He is very cunning. He could take you by surprise. I know he will not dare do anything while I'm alive but when I pass on . . . talk to Asina. Make him your protector. Cacanja will respect Asina."

"I promise to talk to Asina."

"But you have another enemy you may not know about."

"Another one?"

"Yes. It is the woman, Nekayia. You need to be even more careful of her."

"Nekayia?"

"Nekayia. She may be even more dangerous than Cacanja, because she does not speak or show her hatred."

"I've wondered about her, Yusufu. I've felt her hatred but I've never understood it. Why does she hate me?"

"Her hatred is very strange and very deep. It goes back to before you were born. It seems that she wanted to become your father's second wife. She thought he would take her because Najuma had not conceived. When we predicted your birth, Diallobe had no further use for her. She has since harbored hatred for you."

"That explains it. I've wondered and wondered about her. I'll be careful of her, too, Yusufu."

"Good. My mind is relieved. If you're careful of those two people, you will live a long and happy life and be of great service to many."

Tears were again misting her eyes. "You have been my teacher," she said.

Then two pairs of eyes were wet with tears.

When Sabia left Balewa the next morning, the drums were beating out the message of the work of the white devil. Now along with her sling and bow and arrow, she carried a gourd containing Yusufu's potion for invoking the gods, recipes for other potions, and the sadness of knowing she would never again see Yusufu alive in this world.

She half ran, half walked on her trip back to Nahut. All she could think about was Tacuma. There was so much she wanted to tell him. Once home, she did not see anything in the village but his hut. Blindly, she ran to it.

Najuma and Bayo, Tacuma's mother, were gossiping. They saw her coming. Sabia hardly stopped long enough for Najuma's hug.

"Where is Tacuma?" she asked urgently.

"He has gone hunting with his father, Ato, and Diallobe."

Sabia slumped to the ground, unconscious.

CHAPTER 24

Sabia stopped living that day. Gone was her sunny disposition, her friendliness the villagers had come to expect, her zest for everything around her. Her mind was lost in darkness, a darkness that came and went, then came again, not to go away.

It happened, as in her dreams. Diallobe and Tacuma, Jarawah, and Ato never came back to Nahut after their hunting trip. Ato's body was found two suns later, with a hole ripped in his chest. There were many signs that her dreams had been fulfilled. Hunting equipment was scattered about. A piece of chain was left lying on the ground. The bank of the river showed where a canoe had been beached.

The search party brought Ato's body back to Nahut. It was only then that everyone believed and knew their grief. Darkness descended over the villagers' minds. For Sabia, the darkness came much sooner. For her, the outcome had never been in question.

In her darkness, she saw only one face . . . Tacuma's. His memory overpowered her mind with total relentlessness. Over and over again the night in the cave played through her head. The delicious feelings of her body, his touch, her desire, the thrill of their culmination, the earrings, their pledge of eternal love.

Each time the scene marched through her head, it was followed by the emptiness, the open wound of loss. It tormented her from all sides and would not leave her alone. The darkness!

Sabia's stillness in the hut stayed for almost a moon. Now Najuma was grieving two losses. Sabia was letting herself die by starvation. She was thin and hollow-eyed and listless.

On this day, Sabia sat, as usual, with hunger crawling at her stomach, her mind a total blank. Then, just as if the gods were trying to reach her, a thought crossed her mind. "I haven't started to bleed."

She noticed the thought and went back to darkness.

Suddenly brightness engulfed her mind. Her eyes popped open. "I haven't started to bleed!" she repeated. "I should have, suns ago. Mama told me that not bleeding means only one thing. That I am with child. Could it be? Could I be with child? Tacuma's child?"

Life surged back into her body. She got up, stumbling, and ran toward the door. She squinted into the sun, almost blinded. She forced her weak body to the foot of her old baobab tree. She dropped to the ground, ready to ask the gods.

Najuma watched it all, astonished.

Sabia wasted no time. "Tell me," she asked of any spirit who would hear her. "Tell me. Am I with child? Am I with child?"

None spoke.

She waited.

Silence.

Then there were words. "Tacuma's child is in your body. Tacuma is gone from you but you will have his child to love."

Sabia jumped up, forgetting how weak she was. She twirled around and around in her excitement. "I am going to eat. I am going to live. I am going to have Tacuma's child."

She found Najuma pounding grain in front of the hut, tears running down her face. "Mama," she said, coming up behind her. She put her arms around Najuma and held her against her own skin. "I have been selfish," she said. "I have been so lost in my own grief, I have forgotten yours. I am sorry."

Najuma patted her hand. In that moment she couldn't talk. Feelings welled up in her. Perhaps life was not over after all. Perhaps . . . ?

In that moment, life resumed for both of them.

Sabia surprised even Najuma. She was more than her old self. She was full of life. She had a new vitality. She had a happy glow.

Najuma mistakenly decided she had forgotten Tacuma.

One day Najuma brought it up. "Sabia," she said.

"Yes, Mama."

"We need to talk about your future. Now that Diallobe and Tacuma are gone, we need to decide."

"Yes, Mama." Sabia clearly didn't want this conversation. She knew what was coming.

Najuma began carefully. "You know you will be fifteen rains soon."

"Yes, I know."

"That means it is time for you to take on a woman's responsibilities: a hut of your own, a husband, children."

"Mama, I . . . "

"I know you still grieve for Tacuma and I know it is soon but the mating dance is coming up in a few moons and you will be expected to dance in it."

"But, I . . . "

Najuma was determined. "Kandia seems interested in you. You could get to know him better."

"Mama, I'm not going to choose a mate."

"You're not?"

"No, Mama."

"But you must. It is the custom. You are fifteen rains and all women choose a mate at fifteen."

"I am not going to, Mama. I am not going to choose a mate, now or ever, now that I can not have Tacuma as my mate."

"But Tacuma is gone and as good as dead," Najuma said, forgetting Sabia's grief in her own determination.

Sabia winced at her mother's words, and a tear formed in her eye, but she talked on. "Yes, Tacuma is gone and that is why I will not choose another mate. You see, Mama, whether he is here or not, I am still mated to Tacuma."

"What do you mean?"

Sabia put her hands to her earrings. "Do you see these, Mama?"

"Yes."

"Tacuma gave them to me on the night of the feast of Ala. They have a history. Only couples who are willing to unite for eternity can have them. I made that pledge. I made that pledge to unite with Tacuma for eternity. For eternity, Mama! And that is why I can not choose another mate."

Najuma wasn't giving up. "But you do not have to keep that pledge now. A pledge given to a boy who is gone does not mean anything."

Sabia was exasperated. "Mama, there is another reason, an even more important reason. I can not choose a mate, because I am with child. Tacuma's child."

Now it was Najuma's eyes that stared in horror. "You are what?"

"I am carrying Tacuma's child."

"May the gods save us."

"So you see, Mama, I can not dance to choose a mate. I already have one. It is Tacuma. And he is for eternity."

Silence.

"Then . . . then . . .," Najuma started, gathering her courage. "Then . . . you will just have to get rid of the child."

"Mama, that is madness. I am not going to get rid of Tacuma's child."

"If you have this child, you know the whole village will exclude us. They will exclude Bayo, too."

"I know, Mama but I want this child. I love this child. It is Tacuma, and it is me."

Najuma started to cry. "I can not stand to be excluded now. Not now. Not after I just lost Diallobe."

"I know that, Mama. I understand. But please understand me." Sabia touched Najuma on the shoulder. "I know it will not be easy but I have no choice. I love Tacuma. I almost lost my mind when I found him gone. Now I am happy again. Now I am happy because I am going to have his baby. Don't you see? Now I will have his child. He will be with me. Please try to understand, Mama."

Najuma did not understand. All she knew was that the villagers would exclude her if Sabia had a child before she had been properly mated. All Najuma knew was that she could not tolerate exclusion now that Diallobe was gone. Exclusion would mean more loneliness than she could stand. Exclusion, now that she no longer had Diallobe, would mean that she would, indeed, go mad. She must have the other women to talk to . . . to be with her in her grief.

But she said nothing. She knew now that argument was hopeless. To avoid it, she nodded.

And she knew the child must not be born.

Najuma waited. She waited until Sabia was asleep. Then she slipped out of the hut, making her way across the compound. She knew where to get help.

From Cacanja!

Someone else was interested in her movements across the compound that night. Unknown to Najuma, a stealthy figure moved through the compound behind her, a figure whose eyes and ears had not missed her argument with Sabia or her late-night movements. As Najuma reached her destination, the figure slipped behind a tree - to listen and to watch.

Cacanja was sitting cross-legged in front of his fire, its flames throwing demonic shadows on his body. He greeted her with a scowl.

Tonight she wasn't intimidated. "Cacanja, I need your help."

"What do you want?" he said, annoyed at the interruption.

"Sabia is with child. Tacuma's child."

The scowl left his face. Now he was interested. "Go on," he said.

"She insists on having it. I have told her the consequences, but she insists. She insists she will have it anyway. I don't want exclusion - for her sake."

"What do you want from me?" growled Cacanja.

"I want you to help me eliminate this child from her belly. I want to make her realize that Tacuma is gone and that she must choose another mate."

Inside, Cacanja gloated. This was exactly the turn of events he needed. He almost rubbed his hands together in anticipation.

Instead, he grumbled, as though overworked by her request. "You expect me to help you eliminate the child from her belly? You expect me to help you?"

"I will pay whatever you require."

"What you have may not be enough for services such as this."

Najuma was not to be dissuaded. This was too important to let Cacanja's pettiness interfere. "I will give you anything," she said.

" My requirements are high."

"I will pay them."

"I require the remains of the expelled child."

"You shall have them."

"I require your absolute silence."

"I will be absolutely silent."

"I require your she-goat."

Najuma gulped. Giving up the she-goat meant deprivation for the family until one of the ewes became old enough to replace it. She hesitated . . . but only for a moment.

"You shall have the she-goat," she said. The deprivation of food was nothing to her in comparison to the deprivation she would feel if the villagers carried through their exclusion of her.

Still Cacanja hesitated. How else could he toy with this desperate woman. "This is no small job you are asking me to do," he said. "This will take my most powerful potion, and many suns of prayer to the gods. This is difficult work. I am not sure I want to do this for you."

"Oh, please Cacanja. I will give you anything else you wish. I must not be excluded. I must not."

Cacanja pretended he was beginning to feel compassion for the woman's position. "You understand that this is not something I would do for just anyone . . . but since you are the wife of Diallobe, now dead . . . . . . "

"Yes, yes. I understand. Please help me."

"Well, perhaps I can help you," he said, still acting reluctant. He slowly got up from his position in front of the fire and disappeared into his hut. After a long period of time he returned holding a small gourd filled with liquid.

"This potion, along with my advocacy to the gods, will cause Sabia to expel the child in one moon. Give her two drops at each meal. No more. No less. Exactly two drops. It will poison the child and kill it. It will make Sabia sick, too, but not sick enough to die. She will recover as soon as the child is expelled. She will think her sickness is from the first days of carrying the child. You will help her think that. Do you understand?"

"Yes, I understand," said Najuma. "Two drops at each meal . . . no more, no less."

"And I shall have my price?"

"I will see to it, Cacanja."

Najuma slipped away as she had come, now carrying her salvation; not knowing the destruction she would wreak with her brand of salvation. As she left, the shadowy figure moved from behind the tree, having heard everything. The figure joined Cacanja at the fire. There they talked in low tones until the moon disappeared behind the Benue.

It was Nekayia.

Najuma returned to the hut, hid her precious gourd, and slept peacefully until morning. The dread of exclusion was no more.

The next day she began to poison Sabia's food.

Within a week, the poison was working. Sabia's eyes were bleary and her face was drawn and ashy. She said, "Mama, I think I had better stay in the hut today. I am not feeling well."

"It sounds like that child in your belly is doing exactly what it is supposed to do. In the beginning, they are likely to make you sick. Rest. You will feel better later on."

But Sabia didn't feel better later on. She felt worse. She didn't get up that day or the next, or the next. Within seven suns, she was shivering from fever, sweat pouring from her body. Her sickness went on and on.

Najuma kept her covered, gave her lots of water to drink, and put two drops of poison into every meal.

It had been almost a moon since the poisoning began when Sabia thought she saw an apparition. It stood in the doorway in the form of a man. It was surrounded by light.

"Who are you?" she said, blinking into the sun.

"It is Lumumba. I have come with a message from Yusufu," said the apparition.

Sick as she was, she was able to smile. "How is he?"

"He is dying and he has sent you this."

She reached for what she saw dangling in front of her eyes . . . Yusufu's charm She struggled upright to grasp it from Lumumba's hand and hang it around her neck. Immediately, as the charm touched her bare skin, she felt it. She felt the surge in her insides, a surge of new power. It began in her belly and moved out to her fingers until her fingers felt as though they were on fire. Her legs started to quiver as though she could almost get up from her pallet and walk. She knew what was happening and it filled her with both sadness and pride; sadness because she knew the great man was dying, and pride because she now had Yusufu's spirit to give her new strength.

"Thank you, Lumumba," she said through parched lips. "I shall wear it always in tribute to his spirit. I shall wear it always in appreciation for his great learning and power. I shall wear it always in the hope that I can be half the 'man' he was."

Lumumba was aghast at what he saw before him. It had only been two moons since he had seen Sabia happy and healthy, visiting his own village of Balewa. Now it was difficult for him to speak to the skeleton he saw lying on this pallet. Now he understood Yusufu's other message. He went on speaking. "Yusufu says, also, to tell you not to eat any more of Najuma's food; for it is poisoning the child in your belly."

Could she be hallucinating? Najuma? Poisoning her child? She put her hand to her neck to feel the charm, to test the hallucination. The charm was there. She was not hallucinating. Najuma was poisoning her child.

"Yusufu says to tell you that she got the poison from Cacanja."

Sabia fell back on her pallet. "Cacanja. Of course. Cacanja."

"He wants you to know he learned of it too late to save the child. It is already dead. You will expel it in two suns."

Sabia turned away. Sobs wrenched themselves out of her. Through her fever, she saw the faces of those she had loved. Diallobe, Tacuma, Yusufu, Najuma, her child. They came. They faded. They came again. They all faded away. "Don't leave me!" she yelled at the retreating faces.

The messenger looked perplexed. "But I have to get back to Balewa before the sun sets. I must leave now."

But Sabia didn't hear.

She was sobbing. A word echoed through her feverish brain. "Alone . . . Alone . . . Alone . . . !"

"Yusufu wishes you strength to carry on your work," the messenger said, as he backed toward the door.

"My work . . . my work . . . my work . . .."

In two suns, as predicted, she expelled the child. Dead!

Cacanja was there, to take the remains.

Luck was with him. He now had the information and the means to Sabia's end. It was here, in this leopard skin. He went home to prepare her future. He poured the remains into a clay bottle, setting it very carefully in the center of the hut. The leopard skin, he buried underneath his pit of fire. There they would be, to work their evil, to further his plan to eliminate her from his life when the time came. To forever remind him of his hatred and jealousy.

That night, he was in full head-dress and body paint, whirling like the wind, in front of his fire, calling on the gods to do his command.

As Sabia slept and Cacanja danced, Yusufu died. The full strength of Yusufu came into her, just when she needed it most.

The sun was already at midpoint when Sabia woke the next day.

She shed tears for her child.

And a few more for the complicity of Najuma.

Then she got up, to sit in the sun - stronger than she would have believed.

She refused Najuma's offer of a healing potion.

Within seven suns, she was up to doing what she needed to do.

CHAPTER 25

It was on a day that Najuma was washing clothes. She was busy pounding the wet cloth against a rock.

After seven suns, Sabia knew she was strong enough. She went to her mother.

"Mama, I know that you and Cacanja killed my child."

Najuma stopped in mid-movement. She stood like a statue.

"Did you think you could poison me, kill the seed that was growing in me, and almost kill me without my knowing it?"

"I . . .." Najuma turned her head away. Away from the truth.

"Look at me, Mama. Look at what you accomplished. My father and my lover are both gone, even though I told you to stop them from hunting. My baby, who gave me back my life, has been poisoned. And then I learn my own mother has collaborated with my worst enemy."

Najuma looked at the ground. To look at Sabia was impossible.

"Oh, I understand why you did it. You were afraid. The opinions of the villagers were more important to you than my happiness. And now, not only is my child dead, but Cacanja has all the information he needs to do his will against me whenever he is ready."

Najuma felt wretched. "I did not think about all that."

"No, you did not, did you? Only about your position in this village. And tradition. You wanted me to mate with a man I do not love so I could follow tradition. Cacanja wants me to mate as well. He thinks I will lose some of my power in the tradition of wife and mother. Then he can regain some of his."

"Well, I want you to know and I want Cacanja to know that I am not going to follow tradition. Again, I tell you that I am not going to mate, now or ever. Tacuma is gone, but my soul belongs to him. And that is the way it is."

Now, for the first time, Najuma recognized the enormity of what she had done and what could not be undone. Tears filled her eyes. Shame filled her heart. "Sabia, I am sorry. I see now that I was wrong."

"Yes, you were wrong, my mother. And I am the one to pay for your mistakes."

"I am so sorry. I wish I could take it back. I wish that more than ever. But I can not. Could you find it in your heart to forgive me?"

"Some day I may. But not now. I understand the fear that caused you to do it. I wish you had understood my love."

Then Najuma knew. For the first time, she knew how profound was the love between Sabia and Tacuma. Now, she remembered her own love for Diallobe. She remembered her joy when Sabia was conceived. She remembered her happiness in her growing daughter. At that moment she knew hopelessness. Her eyes pleaded.

Sabia saw the look and softened a little. Not to forgive. Just to soften. "I will be leaving tomorrow to move into my own hut, Mama. Yusufu has charged me to go on with his work and I can not do it where I have been betrayed. I will ask the gods to bring me forgiveness and perhaps they will. Until then, I will work alone."

Najuma wept and Sabia hurt, but . . .

Their bond was broken.

Sabia left her mother as she had found her, at the river washing clothes. She had more work to do. She went to find Asina. He was there, in front of his hut, as if waiting for her.

His smile wrinkled the scars and paint on his face. "How are you, my child? It is good to see you over your sickness."

Sabia came right to the point. "It is my sickness that has brought me to you."

"Yes, my child?"

"Cacanja and Najuma have been poisoning me."

"Cacanja and Najuma?"

"Yes, Cacanja and Najuma. You see, I was carrying Tacuma's child in my belly when he went away. When Mama found out, she conspired with Cacanja to rid me of the child so she could save face and prevent exclusion. He gave her poison to kill my child in exchange for my baby's remains. Now Cacanja has the power to murder me."

Asina's frown deepened as she talked, his mind concentrating on her sin; not on her dilemma. "You were carrying Tacuma's child before the mating dance?" he said severely.

Sabia was ready for him. "I was and I'm proud of it. Don't tell me I did wrong because I was not wrong. But if you want to condemn me and have me excluded, I want to know now, before I start my work here in Nahut. If you condemn me, I will take my work to another village."

"You went against tradition and that is wrong."

Fire danced before Sabia's eyes at his intransigence. "It is not wrong. If I had not defied tradition, I would not have known Tacuma, ever. I would not have known, even for a short time, his child in my belly."

"I see," said Asina. "You do not believe that your defiance of tradition was wrong."

"No, I did no wrong."

Asina was torn. She had defied tradition and she deserved to be punished for it . . . but he knew she had already been punished. Tacuma . . . dead. Her child . . . dead. He decided to forgo punishment in this case. "I believe I understand," he said.

"Then, do you condemn me?"

"No. You've already been through enough. You do not need to have me condemn you."

"Then I will work in Nahut."

"I am glad, my child. I am glad."

"But to do it, I need your help. I will need your protection from Cacanja's cunning."

"Yes, I see that you do. He has already put you in danger once. I do not want you endangered again. I will talk to him right now." He stopped a boy passing by. "Bring Cacanja to me as quickly as you can."

The boy hurried away.

"Thank you, Asina. I will leave now, before Cacanja gets here."

The two enemies crossed paths as Sabia left and Cacanja came. His eyes burned, as if to scorch her with the fire of his hatred. She looked back out of her knowledge.

She knew Asina would protect her as much as his power allowed, but she also knew she was not completely out of danger.

Later, she saw a frenzied Cacanja, in front of his fire, dancing around a clay pot.

At the same time, she moved her few possessions into her new hut, the hut of Grandma Zola - which was still filled with all of that grandmotherly warm spirit.

The next day, she wasted no time in getting to work. The activities of the white devils were still eating at her insides. In spite of Yusufu's gloom, there must be a way. Now she thought she knew what it was.

She started by building a fire. She waited until the flames licked at the wood and there were embers glowing underneath. Then she used Yusufu's potion. He had told her the gods would give her the answer. Now she knew the question.

The flames leapt high and the color was splendid. Sabia settled in. She asked her very important question. "Show me where the white devil is working. Let me know where the white devil is now." She closed her eyes to wait.

Then she waited. For a long time she waited. She waited long enough to be discouraged. She became afraid. The gods weren't going to tell her.

Then she saw them! Twelve of them. Nine were black, and three were white. How furtively they walked. How strategically they dispersed themselves around the village. How careful they were that no villager could escape. How quietly they talked in a language she didn't understand. "Bantu (Ban-too)," she thought.

Watching, her dark thoughts almost overwhelmed her. "Oh, how I hate you, you black men! You are worse, even, than the white devil. At least, the white devil has the excuse of stupidity. You have nothing but your greed."

So strong was it, that her anger almost interfered with her purpose., She had to forcefully calm herself in order to do what she had set out to do. Once calmer, she could see what the gods were showing her. She peered at the surroundings. "What village is this? It is small. Smaller than Nahut, and away from the river. It is near a lot of rock and there are only a few trees. Where is it? What is its name?"

Villages passed through her mind that had that kind of terrain. "There's Chepkempoi, Koumba, Bada. Is it Oding . . . that's it! Oding!"

She jumped up. She went immediately to the drummers. "Quick," she said. "Send a message to the village of Oding. Tell them there are twelve slavers outside their village. They will probably raid it tonight. Tell them that nine of the men are black and three are white. They are spaced inconsistently around the village. Suggest that they send their best spear hunters out to find their locations, and surprise them from behind. Say Sabia of Nahut sends this message. Send signals that speakers of Bantu will not understand."

The next morning before she was awake, there came a return message. "Sabia of Nahut," it said. "The people of Oding salute you. Five of the devils were taken with a spear. The rest ran off in disorder. Our village is spared. The gods be praised."

Sabia glowed, while . . .

Cacanja simmered . . . and

Nekayia sulked.

From then on, Sabia asked the gods daily for the location of the white devils' work. Regularly she found them poised to seize more unsuspecting villagers. Nahut's drums were busy forewarning. To individuals, groups, hunters, farmers, and whole villages, the air was filled with Sabia's messages. The white men didn't understand what was happening. They were killed in ambush. They were caught and imprisoned. They were constantly surprised by educated counter-attacks. So successful was she that, within three rains, slaving among Ibo villages had almost stopped.

Her name, constantly drummed through Iboland, brought her a success of another kind. People came from villages far and wide for her healing services. Daily they poured into Nahut.

Women brought their children with open sores, runny eyes and noses, distended stomachs, embedded thistles, convulsions, rashes, fevers, and multiple bruises.

Men came with long, jagged gashes from hunting accidents, muscles cramped from waiting in abnormal positions, bellies hurting from too much celebrating, pain in their members, broken bones, vomiting.

Women came with burns from their cooking fires, pains in their sex, complaints while with child, questions of how to prevent more children, questions of how to have more children, and the never-ending question: "Why am I so tired?"

They came with unsolvable problems:

"Sabia, my child won't eat."

"Sabia, my wife complains all the time."

"Sabia, my husband has stopped hunting and working in the field."

"Sabia, the beautiful Folami (Foe-lahm-ee) is trying to seduce away my Moriba (More-ee-bah)."

"Sabia, my mother won't leave me alone even though I'm married and have three children."

For the sick, it was a salve for this one, an herb for another, while a third was wrapped in a cloth dipped in a poultice. To the next, she gave advice. Often she advised a different diet, vegetables to supplement their usual grain and meat.

For the unsolvable problems, she advised, cajoled, questioned, and modeled new solutions.

Sometimes, she used her hands to heal, generating the heat and health from her own body as Yusufu had taught her. She did this only when the disease was extreme because it exhausted her. When she didn't know what to do, she asked the gods. Yusufu's potion was her last resort.

Sometimes she was tired. Then she clasped Yusufu's charm in her hand and asked the great man for strength. Often, in the night, she saw his grey head and heard his kindly learned voice. He always renewed her strength.

And so it went for Sabia for the next seven rains.

Toward the end of her sixth rain since leaving Najuma, she had a surprise visitor. Nekayia darkened her door.Nekayia, the seductress, who had tried to win Diallobe and failed. Nekayia, the most sought-after woman in the village during her youth. Nekayia, who had finally settled for Muwato (Moo-wah-too), the handsome and accomplished grandson of Asina, two years her junior and for whom she had borne five children.

Muwato had been destined to be chief of Nahut one day. He was to have married the daughter of the chief of Sanga. He had given all that up to marry Nekayia. Now it was widely known that he was unhappy with Nekayia and was seeking a second wife. He would have had one except for Nekayia's viciousness. Their stormy marriage was common village gossip.

Sabia was immediately suspicious. Yusufu's words came back to her. "She may be more dangerous than Cacanja because she neither speaks nor shows her hatred."

True to form, Nekayia was all smiles and duplicity today. She began to pout. "I want you to see Muwato," she said. "His lovemaking is a disappointment to me. Most of the time he can't even get his member to rise. I think something is wrong with him and he needs to talk with you about it."

Sabia felt distrust in every pore. "Talk with me about it?"

"Yes, I think something is bothering him and he needs to talk about it with someone."

Sabia decided to come to the point. "Nekayia, you surprise me."

"Oh? Why?"

"Because if it's Muwato who has the problem, why didn't he come? And then I wonder why you ask a person you hate to help with such a delicate situation?"

Nekayia, for a moment, lost her composure. "I. . .I. . used to hate you, yes, but I do not hate you any more. That has been over for many rains," she said coquettishly. "I hated you because your birth stopped my marriage to Diallobe but now I am happy with Muwato, and I have not thought about hating you for a long time."

"Hmmmmmmm," said Sabia. "Lies," she thought. "But I think I will just play along and see what is going to happen."

"Tell Muwato to come and see me whenever he will."

"Thank you, Sabia. I know you can help him. He has lots of problems."

"And you are most of them," Sabia muttered under her breath as Nekayia left. Sabia was too suspicious to let it go at that. She walked quickly to the door and watched Nekayia walk hurriedly to Cacanja's hut, where she went in without invitation. Hushed tones emerged. It was midday before Nekayia left. "Ah ha," said Sabia. "Cacanja has an ally in his wish to send me to the spirit world."

"Trouble is brewing!"

CHAPTER 26

It happened quite by accident. It was on a day, a quiet day, when she had no burning questions for the gods. It happened not long after she moved into her own hut.

She found a way to be with Tacuma.

On this day she wanted to experiment with Yusufu's potion - to know more about its workings. She built a fire, waited for the embers to be hot, then threw on two drops of liquid. The flames leapt and danced as expected. The colors were ever-changing, as expected. But there was no message.

She sat . . . and she waited . . . but there was no message. Nothing! There was only emptiness in her head.

She closed her eyes to take away weariness, for she was very weary. When she opened them she could not believe her eyes. There was a form emerging. It was a familiar form . . . a head . . . only a head. This was no god that she knew. They were playing tricks on her. They must be. Because . . .

It was . . . it was . . . Tacuma.

He looked haggard and sick, but he was smiling. "I did not get a chance to say goodbye," he said wryly.

"Tacuma!" She jumped up, ready to run to him. She stopped herself just before she headed into the fire. "He's real only in my vision. He's not real to hold, to touch, to love. He's real only at the mercy of the gods." She stopped herself before she singed her legs.

Then she took a look at him and saw his haggard face. "Tacuma? What have they done to you?"

"No worse than they have done to all of us, Sabia," he said. He began to tell her his story . . . his horror story.

As he talked she began to see the scenes he described inside the fire . . . around his head. She saw him tied, neck to neck, with a thong, to other men and marched through the jungle. She saw his feet, bloody from the marching. She saw him piled into a canoe, with other men piled around and on top, until he could hardly breathe. She saw him whipped until his back was nothing but open wounds. She saw him dragged in front of white men, and poked and prodded in his private parts. Stinking food was fed to him. He was lying in his own defecation. He was chained to a board next to a man, who was next to another man, who was next to another man, like fish in a net. They were on board one of the big canoes, going over the big water. The canoe was pitching and rocking and the men were expelling everything from their insides.

He was still talking. "I may not live, Sabia. Many of the men who started with me are already dead, including Jarawah."

"Tacuma!" she screamed. "You can not die."

"Sabia, I may not have a choice. My body can not live with the torture of the white man much longer."

"But, Tacuma . . . "

"I've come to say goodbye and to free you from your promise. The promise of our souls living together for eternity."

Sabia could feel her heart breaking. "Tacuma, I do not want freedom. Knowing that our souls are travelling together has been what has saved me since you have been gone. For a time, I didn't want to live either. I knew a time of blackness that almost killed me. I wouldn't have wanted to live at all without feeling your spirit with mine, as mine is with you. Do you feel my spirit, Tacuma?"

"I feel it. I know that it has been your spirit that has kept me alive until now."

"Then let it keep you going a little longer. You are not through with life. I lived. So can you."

"You do not want freedom from your promise?"

"No. I want to keep our promise until I die. Then I want to keep our promise as we are together in eternity. I do not care what happens to our bodies."

"Then I'll do all I can to live."

Sabia was satisfied..

His face began to fade from her eyes, to be replaced by the emptiness in her soul. The part of her that had died when he was taken had revived for a time - too short a time. Now it had died again.

But a new thought was forming. "The gods let me see him once. Why not again?"

She ran for more wood for the fire.

She built it up, until it was again roaring. Then she threw on more liquid. Now she worked with intention.

"Damballah! Damballah Oueddo. Come. I need you, Damballah," she intoned. "Come to me. I need you now."

The flames flickered, then danced higher. A shadow began to form in the center of the fire. Smoke billowed upwards, then cleared. She heard the hissing of the serpent. Then she saw him coil and oscillate within the fire, flames dancing about his head.

"Damballah, thank you for coming. I need you now."

"You have done my work well, my child. You have interfered with the intentions of the white devil, who is unfairly plundering your people. My help is yours."

"Thank you, Damballah. I need help with Tacuma. He is being destroyed by the white devil. He thinks he is dying. I want to find a way to help him heal. Will you help me?"

The serpent coiled and recoiled. Flames shot out of his mouth, his eyes glinting in anger. His hissing words spit forth: "The white devil will pay for his treachery. I will see to it."

"But will you help me?" pleaded Sabia.

"Yes. I'll help you," he hissed. "Wait one more moon; then sit as you are in front of this fire. Call forth Tacuma on the big canoe; then send your body to him. You will find him in great pain and almost without will. Heal him then and he will live. Heal, also, Diallobe, for he, too, suffers greatly."

"Thank you, Damballah. Thank you."

The serpent hissed forth more words. "You can be with Tacuma in this way whenever you want - with only one restriction."

"I can be with Tacuma whenever I want?"

"When you want - with one restriction."

"What is that, Damballah?"

"The restriction is your own health. When you cross the miles out of your body to be with Tacuma, it will take from your strength. Do not let your strength suffer, or you will not be able to do your work..to fulfill your destiny."

"I know, Damballah. I won't default on my destiny."

"So, space your time with Tacuma so that you will have your health. Do not let your time with him drain away your strength. Give yourself time between trips to come back to health."

"I can follow that restriction, Damballah. To be with him at all is more than I expected."

"I wish you well, my daughter."

Sabia reverently bent to touch her forehead to the ground. When she straightened, Damballah was gone.

In exactly one moon, Sabia was ready. She lit the fire, threw on two drops of the potion, and sat. Into her vision came the big canoe. "Send me to Tacuma," she said over and over again. "Send me to Tacuma."

Then she felt it. Her body lifted from its place and flew. Her body sat in front of the fire. But it lifted from its place and flew.

She landed in darkness. A stink struck her nostrils: a stink made up of vomit, unclean bodies, and human feces. It was so overpowering it made her wretch. Sounds consumed her. The sounds of men: screaming, sobbing, asking for mercy, gurgling in death. The suffering sounds of the men reached into what was now the leadened pit of her stomach. As her eyes became accustomed to the dark, she saw them. Man after man chained together, lying on boards, bodies covered with welts, pleading eyes looking out of hollow sockets, faces haggard and sapped of strength.

Her eyes searched for Tacuma. In this sea of human deprivation, she searched for Tacuma. She called his name. She saw a man weakly raise his head.

"Sabia, is that you?" His voice was hoarse and hardly recognizable.

"Tacuma." Again she had the unrelenting wish to run to him, to touch him, to hold him in her arms. But she resisted. Instead she said, "I have come to help you live."

"Live? Live in this hell-hole. Look around you, Sabia. Would you want to live? The only air we have to breathe is this foul stink. The only movement we are allowed is the few times they choose to let us up those stairs to the deck. The only food we are given is unfit for any man. The only drink is the foulest of water. They whip us unmercifully. My body is full of festering sores. I don't know anything but pain. If I live, it will be to suffer more injustices at the hands of those white men. Why?"

She did look around. Tacuma was right. What was there to live for? But she knew he must. Somehow she had to give him the will. She had to give him the strength.

"Tacuma, hold out a little longer. Don't give in to the will of these white devils. Live! Not for them, but for you. For us. So our spirits can be together. You are near your destination. Then you will have fresh air and food. You can make it. Live!"

"I can make it," he said weakly.

"I came to heal your wounds and relieve your pain. Live for our spirits, Tacuma. Live!"

But Tacuma didn't hear. He had lost consciousness.

Sabia started to work, as Yusufu had taught her. She generated heat in her belly, convulsing until it reached her hands. She worked rapidly over his body, touching all the festering places, clearing away all of the running pus. Her last charge was into his belly where starvation threatened. She sent it - the heat - from her body to his, to give him what food had not.

She left without knowing whether the healing had worked.

She went to find Diallobe. She found him unconscious in another area of the canoe. She worked quickly over him, using her last bit of energy, to eradicate the worms she saw invading his intestines.

She returned home, exhausted, as Damballah had warned her. It took seven suns before she was able to work. It was more than the loss of her physical strength that got in the way of her recovery. She was also brooding. Brooding about the appalling sights and smells of the men on the big canoe. Her spirit was full of hatred for the white man who mindlessly perpetrated his atrocities.

It was many moons before Sabia tried again to be with her love. She had thought about him constantly, but much of the time afraid. She wanted nothing more than to be with him, but he had been so despondent . . . as though he didn't want to see her. This time would he try to turn her away? Would his despondency turn into rejection of her? Was he, perhaps, angry at her for saving his life? Would he know she was there, or was his illness so severe that he would not recognize her? How was he? What was his state of mind? Did he still love her? These questions had haunted her every day and made her afraid. But finally she could wait no more.

This time she found him in a tiny building, lying on some straw on the floor. It was so like her dreams. Lots of little buildings, lots of fields of cotton, tobacco, and corn, and one huge building held up by two huge columns in the front. She saw him asleep in the tiny building. She gently called his name.

Panic. It was panic she saw. His eyes flew open. His body cowered, as if expecting to be hit. Then he saw her. "Sabia," he said. He covered his face and looked away from her. "You should have let me die on the ship," he said. "You should have let me die. What is living for, Sabia? What is living for? For this? This is no better than the ship. Here the only life is to work from the time I wake in the morning, until I crawl into this straw, exhausted, at night. I'm either working or sleeping or being beaten by the white devil that owns me. He rides around all day on his horse, whip ready for anybody who doesn't satisfy his slightest whim. He treats me as if I wasn't there, as if I had no mind and no feelings. Why didn't you let me die?"

Sabia decided to ignore his rantings. Instead of talking she crawled into the straw beside him and nestled him against her, as he had so often nestled her in their happy days. He rested his head against her shoulder. She began to rock, gently lulling his body into quiescence. Tears trickled onto Sabia's breasts. It was his tears that showed her the enormity of his despair. In Nahut no disaster was big enough to make a man cry . . . yet he cried.

She held him and rocked him, soothing his body, healing his new wounds, loving his spirit. When he fell back into a deep and restful sleep, she kissed him on the forehead and returned to her body in Nahut.

Again she knew the exhaustion, the despondency, the horror of what she had seen.

The crops that had been seedlings had grown to tall perfection, and been harvested before she went again to find her love. Arriving in the strange land, she looked for him in the same little building where she found him before. But he wasn't there. She searched everywhere. Panic was overtaking her before she found him in a tiny room inside the big house, the one with the columns holding it up. He was asleep on a strange-looking object that was raised off the ground by four posts and squeaked when he moved.

She watched him as he slept. She saw no wounds on his body, and his face looked peaceful. "Things are better," she thought. "Yes, things are better."

"Tacuma," she said. "Tacuma, it is Sabia."

His eyes fluttered open. "Sabia!" He jumped out of the contraption. He gathered her into his arms and held her. "I know I am dreaming but I do not care. If I am dreaming, I do not care. Sabia. Sabia. Sabia."

He held her away from him, letting his eyes feast on her. The earrings shone in the moon's rays. He touched them. He let his hand run gently over her face. He softly touched her lips. He bent to kiss her.

His member rose to touch her, filling her body with passions she had not known since the night in the cave. Her lips filled with heat and she pulled him closer. He kissed her, hard on the mouth, while lowering her body to the softness where he slept. Their hunger for each other was so great that there was no waiting. Quickly, he slipped inside of her. Their bodies writhed and thrashed while the bed squeaked underneath them. In their joy she was transported into blissful rapture. Too quickly the convulsions took them over, erasing the pain of the horror between them. They collapsed in a heap, feeling the satisfaction denied them for so long. They lay contented in each other's arms.

It was Tacuma who broke their blissful silence. "You forced me to live, Sabia and I am glad."

"So am I," she said, knowing nothing in the moment but contentment.

Tacuma squeezed her shoulders and smiled. "Life is not good, yet, for me but it is much better. The lady of the house took a liking to me one day and brought me into the big house to work. The work is easier and now I have no more beatings."

"Tacuma, I do not understand why the white man needs to beat you. What is in him that causes him to be so cruel?"

"Remember the panther who was so crazed that she was threatening our village and would have killed one of our babies if we had not sent a spear through his heart?"

"Yes."

"Well, I think the white man is like that. He is crazed inside and the only thing he knows to do with his crazed feelings is to strike out with them. Like the panther, he rages at whoever is around."

"But what makes him crazed, Tacuma?"

"I think he is lonely. He doesn't know how to be close . . . close to the earth, or the trees, or the animals. He doesn't even know how to be close to his wife and children."

"He is lonely and that makes him crazed? Is that it, Tacuma?"

"I think so. He is angry, because he is lonely. He can't take his anger out at the real reason he is lonely because that is himself. So he is angry at the easiest prey around, his Africans. Niggers, they call us here. He says his niggers are just like animals and beating is the only way to train an animal."

Tacuma stopped talking. "Someone's coming," he said.

"Tacuma, quick. Listen to me. Now that you are well, you can come to me. Come to me in Nahut."

"But how?"

"When you are ready to come, close your eyes and call to Damballah. Then wish yourself in Nahut. Say these words: 'Take me to Sabia in Nahut.' Then wait until the flying takes over. Come to me in six moons. I'll be waiting. I must go."

Just as Sabia disappeared, the door burst open and Tacuma's 'massa' stood in the door. "I heard you talkin an I heard the bed squeakin," he bellowed. "If'n I find one of my wenches in this room, I'll whelp your ass." He strode into the room. He overturned the tables and chairs and swept with his stick under the bed. He glared into the corners and under the pieces of furniture. When he didn't find anything, he was furious. His menacing body stood over the bed while he brandished his stick. "I don't know what ya did with er, but when I find who it was, you'll both get twenty lashes." He stormed out of the room, slamming the door behind him.

Tacuma started to laugh. "Ha ha ha hee hee heee." He couldn't stop. He risked the massa's re-entry and a beating with the stick for the crime of laughing. "Ha ha ha hee hee heee." Right now Tacuma felt the healing of the laughter. It had been a long time.

The men were in the fields planting before Sabia knew him again.

It was a night when the moon shown on the Benue. She was asleep on her pallet. Suddenly she knew he was there. She was ecstatic. He had learned to do it, to bring his body to her while yet staying at his place of enslavement.

She held him. They loved.

Her sounds were heard by the villagers passing by. They smiled and winked at each other, and wondered who the mystery man was. They were glad for her because she had had no man since Tacuma.

From then on, she returned no more to the place of his enslavement for he had found the way. Now she had the contentment of her work and the contentment of occasional visits from her 'mystery lover', as the villagers had come to call him. Nothing more was said about him. Sabia didn't say. The villagers didn't ask.

CHAPTER 27

Muwato was becoming a frequent visitor to Sabia's hut. His years with Nekayia had left him lonely. In Sabia's company he found solace . . . sometimes more than solace. Sometimes he felt sparks, even lightning flashes . . . feelings he never knew with Nekayia, his wife.

In spite of her knowledge of Nekayia's complicity with Cacanja . . . her sense of foreboding, Sabia liked having him visit. He was relief from the sickness she saw day in and day out. She liked talking to him. She looked forward to seeing his handsomeness darken her door.

She so enjoyed him, she simply forgot to be careful.

He came and he went. He talked and he was quiet. He raged and he was peaceful.

He said many things:

"I do not know why I am here."

"Sometimes I want to take my hands to her throat and shake her until she is dead."

"She is so cruel to the children and vicious and underhanded with me."

"Sometimes I go to the river - just to get away."

"She rages at me then throws pots and gourds and pestles."

"I should not have chosen her at the mating dance."

"She was more exciting than any of the other girls of the village."

"I was young and Sanga was too far away."

"I was not sure I was worthy to be groomed as the new chief."

"Sometimes I could take my hands to her throat and shake her until she is dead."

"My member will not rise, because I do not want to give her pleasure."

"I do not want pleasure from her."

"I would go away, except for the children."

"I fear what she would do to them if I left."

"Nekayia is jealous when I show any interest in the girls of the village."

"I am trapped. I can not stand to stay and I do not dare to leave."

It was of his bitterness he talked. Of his love, he said nothing. These thoughts he kept to himself.

"I would like to take you as my second wife, Sabia."

"I would not care how much Nekayia raged."

"I wish you did not wear those earrings."

"I wish Tacuma was not still in your mind."

"I think I love you, Sabia."

"For you my member rises."

Sabia told him, "Go to the forest and find a small tree that is dead. Tear it down, limb by limb, and break each limb against the trunk. Pretend the tree is Nekayia. Pretend that you have your hands around her throat. Tear at the tree until the rage is gone from you. Do not go home until you can go in peace. Do this every day that she provokes you to want to shake her until she is dead."

"I am to rage at the tree instead of Nekayia?"

"It is safer."

And with each visit two pair of eyes watched from the compound, carefully noting the time between his entrance and his leaving. With each visit this pair garnered more fuel for their diabolical scheme.

Sabia had lived twenty-one rains the morning she heard the mournful message. The drums were sending their announcement of death. They were calling the villagers to the compound. Sabia knew whose soul had gone to the spirit world. It was Asina. Her old friend, Asina. He had told her it would not be long. He was prepared, he said. But the tears streamed down her face at the sound. He had come to mean so much to her, for without Najuma he had become more than a friend. He had become her only family. Like a father he had been her confidant as well as her protector. She knew she would miss him mightily.

She joined the others in the compound.

It was Jomo, Asina's son, who made the announcement. "All work will stop," he said. "We will spend the day in respect for my father's soul, and in celebration of his ascent to the spirit world. We will sit in respect near my father's body until Cacanja dances the dance of death after the sun has gone past midday. Then we will carry my father to the burying ground, where he will lie next to my mother. When his body is safe from the animals, we will all celebrate his spirit with dancing and palm wine. Please begin your time of respect now."

Sabia wondered, "Who will be the next chief? His son, Jomo, or his grandson, Muwato? Muwato is certainly the more able," she thought. "Jomo has never taken much interest in village affairs. He has always been the wrestler and the hunter. He has never had enough serious thoughts in his head to take over as chief."

As planned, Cacanja danced his dance of death. Asina was then buried amid the wailing and lamentations of the women and the silent reverences of the men. The procession back to the compound was sad and mournful. Once back, the drums quickly changed their forlorn beat and shifted their tempo to that of celebration, the celebration of the beauty of the spirit that was Asina. Palm wine emerged from huts and flowed freely. The villagers were in high spirits.

Cacanja had more on his mind than the dance of death. More than the celebration of Asina's spirit. The time he had waited for, had planned for for so many years . . . this time was now.

Today he would carry out his plan to be rid of his hated rival. Today he would return to power. Today Sabia would be the second soul to go to the spirit world.

The villagers would collude with his plans.

He knew they would collude because they were full of palm wine and dancing.

As dusk approached, he signaled to Nekayia. "Begin," he told her.

Nekayia left the compound.

She returned, carrying a small gourd containing one of Cacanja's potions . . . not meant to kill . . . just to drug.

Surreptitiously she poured just a drop of the potion into the wine of two of the merrymakers . . . who never noticed. They continued to drink. She immediately reported to Cacanja.

The groundwork was completed. Now it was time for him to play out his part. His first move was to create a frenzy of activity outside the circle of celebrators. He began his calculated movements . . . movements that could not escape attention. Drummers paused. Dancers stopped in mid-step. All eyes turned toward the commotion.

What they saw was . . . Cacanja . . . covered with green and white paint, whirling as if he were the big wind, parting the crowd as he twirled. He whirled and gyrated until he was into the center of the compound, until he was spinning in front of the burning fire. There, he synchronized his motions to the rhythms of the flames, teasing the fire, inviting it to burn his body if it would.

Punishment! This was his dance of punishment. The villagers knew what that meant. Who is to be punished, they wondered? Am I the one? Are you the one? What have any of us done? What is Cacanja's reason? But then, Cacanja never needed much of a reason.

They watched, their feelings mixed with horror and wonder. He swirled around the fire once. Twice. Again. And then again. He dropped to the ground, sweating and panting. He planted himself there like a grasshopper, ready to leap. Then slowly . . . ever so slowly . . . he circled inside the crowd, glaring at each of the villagers as he passed.

Suddenly he screeched and pointed his painted finger.

"You!"

Everybody craned their necks. Who was it? Who was to be punished? Each Thanked the gods that they were not the one.

Then a surge of sound came from the crowd.

Nobody believed. It couldn't be true.

He was pointing at Sabia.

She stared back at his accusing finger.

"You!" he screamed again. "You are a witch. Yes, a witch. A witch who is seducing the men of this village away from their wives."

Sabia didn't understand. She was feeling strange. Her head was fuzzy. She couldn't think. She didn't comprehend.

Cacanja resumed his circling.

He stopped, this time in front of Adiaha, one of the women of the village. "You!" he screeched.

Adiaha trembled at his pointing finger.

"What sounds have come from Sabia's hut at night?"

"Sometimes she moans as with a man," gasped Adiaha.

Cacanja nodded. He continued to circle. He stopped in front of the boy Diaba. "You," he shouted, again pointing his painted finger. "What sounds have you heard?"

"I have heard the same thing. I have heard her moaning, as with a man."

Cacanja's screeching reached its highest pitch. He bent and charged toward Sabia. "These two have heard you. They have heard you in your hut, as if with a man. Could it be that others have heard it? Tell me, Sabia, have others heard it?"

"Who has heard it? Step forward."

The villagers murmured, as many of them moved toward the center of the compound.

"Do you deny what everybody has heard?" Cacanja screeched.

Sabia didn't answer. Something was wrong with her. Her head was whirling and she felt sick. She didn't understand.

Cacanja went back to circling. The villagers went back to anticipation. The anticipation was fulfilled for five young married men. "You, you, you, you, and you!" he screamed, pointing his finger at Nkosi, Taiwo, Seitu, Yero, and Erasto. He grabbed each by the scruff of the neck and pushed them toward the fire.

"You have been with her," he screeched at Nkosi.

Nkosi shook from the accusation. Cacanja's reputation for showing no mercy was well-known. "No!" he shouted. "I am not the one!"

"You have been with her," he screeched, as he turned to Taiwo.

"No! I've been only with Nalo." He pointed to his wife.

"You," he shouted at Seitu, then at Yero, then at Erasto in turn. "It was you."

"No!"

"No!"

"No!"

He surprised everybody. He believed. He left the five alone and went back to circling. How slowly he circled, looking into the eyes of each of the men. He paused in front of one after another.

With each pause, everybody held their breath.

It seemed as if forever that he accused each in turn.

Finally his movement stopped and he stood absolutely still.

The eyes of every villager stared at the one.

"You," he screeched. "You have been the one. You. The grandson of the great one who just died. You, who are being considered for chief. You, who already have a wife and five children. You have been the one."

It was Muwato!

Muwato blinked. Cacanja was there, a green and white Cacanja. But what did he want? Muwato's head wouldn't tell him. It was not acting right. He couldn't think. He didn't know what was going on.

"Do you deny it?"

Muwato blinked again but couldn't answer.

Mercifully, his tormentor disappeared. He was at the other side of the circle. He was pulling Sabia from the crowd. He was shoving her toward Muwato.

They stood, staring at each other, recognizing, but not recognizing. At Cacanja's signal, the drummers began a sensuous sound.

Trance-like, Sabia and Muwato moved closer to each other, as if lovers, as if they had no choice.

The villagers watched, also trance-like, unbelieving.

Then it happened and Cacanja saw. "Look," he screamed. "It rises to her." He was pointing his painted finger at Muwato's member.

They looked. As if through one pair of eyes . . . they looked. His member pointed. In shock, they murmured among themselves. Everybody knew the gossip. Everybody knew Muwato's member could not rise, even for Nekayia, his wife.

"Nekayia," Cacanja shouted. "Look!"

Nekayia stumbled through the crowd, weeping as though persecuted. "I see it," she wailed. "I am betrayed. Betrayed by she who claims that her spirit walks with Tacuma for eternity. Betrayed by she who has no children hungry and crying for their father. She who has no compassion for me who is hungry for my husband. Sabia is guilty."

The evidence was strong. The day was late. Cacanja's tirade and the day's celebration inflamed them.

But Sabia was a favorite. A witch? Doing evil? Hard to believe.

Cacanja had waited long enough. He accused. He turned first to Muwato. He bent into his face and leered at him. "You've allowed Sabia to seduce you, haven't you?" he yelled.

Muwato's head nodded, unknowing.

The villagers gasped.

Cacanja was satisfied.

Now he turned to Sabia. "Witch! Aren't you? You're a witch. Everybody's heard you. Now everybody's seen you. You're a witch who has seduced Muwato."

Sabia shook her head. Something was happening here. Cacanja's screaming was penetrating into her mind. Vaguely she saw the villagers staring at her. Vaguely she saw Muwato standing in front of her. Clearly, she heard Cacanja's accusation. She used all her strength to focus her mind, to clear the fog from her head, to pull herself out of her drugged state.

"NOOOOOOOOOOoooooo!" she screamed at Cacanja. "I've been with no man in this village."

"Ah haaaaaaa," Cacanja cooed. She had just said what he needed to hear. "Taiwo, bring me the grey pot from my hut."

Returning, Taiwo handed Cacanja a round grey ceramic pot with a lid.

"Ah eeeeeeeeeo. Aheeeeeeeeeo. Aheeeeeeeeeeo. Aheeeeeeeeeo," screamed Cacanja, the sound so piercing that it reached into the bellies of each and every villager. He raised the pot to the sky. "Aheeeeeeeeo. Aheeeeeeeeeeeo." Again he circled, leering into the crowd. He stopped in front of a frightened Najuma. "You know what is in this pot, don't you, Najuma?"

Najuma was shaking. Everybody saw it. She was shaking.

"This is the remains of Sabia's unborn child, is it not? Sabia's unborn child, killed by her own hands with poison. Is that not right, Najuma?"

Najuma was too frightened to deny Cacanja's half-truth. "Yes," she said, almost under her breath.

"What?" said Cacanja.

"Yes," said Najuma, louder this time.

"Let the villagers hear," shouted Cacanja.

"Yes!" Najuma almost screamed.

Accusing eyes turned on Sabia.

"Let us see if she has been with no man - as she claims," cackled Cacanja. "You there, throw her to the ground and spread her legs. Let us see if she has her maidenhead."

Men surged forward. Rough hands threw Sabia to the ground. Finger after finger went up her sex. Now there was no gentleness - inflamed as they were by Cacanja's accusations and the day's celebration. A chant arose from the men. "Throw her to the crocodiles. Throw her to the crocodiles."

"No. Not so," said those who believed her innocent. They took up another chant. "A trial by fire. A trial by fire. Prove her guilty or innocent. A trial by fire."

Cacanja, flush with success, was willing to win with a trial by fire, so sure was he. For now he had the villagers on his side. "Build up the fire," he ordered. "Bring her a robe. We will find out whether she's a witch or not."

The men threw more wood on the fire. Its flames leaped toward the sky while the coals underneath turned iron-poker hot. A woman brought her a robe. Gone was the effect of the drug. Now she saw everything. Now she saw what was on their faces. The villagers actually believed her guilty of seduction, even branding her a witch. Cacanja's evil was strong, surpassing everything she had done in the past seven rains. Their faces showed it. Anger. Confusion. A thirst for punishment. But, yet, for some, compassion and disbelief.

Many disappointed her.

Cacanja roughly pushed her toward the fire. "Walk," he said. "Prove your innocence."

"I'm not going to die, Cacanja," she said. "Your evil plot is going to fail."

"Not this time, Sabia. This time it is I who will win."

"And what will you win?" she said, facing Cacanja with all her power.

And the villagers heard.

Then she turned toward them and shared her prayer. "May the spirits of Yusufu and Asina walk with me in this moment. May Ala help me prove the truth. And when the truth is known, may Damballah see that the truly guilty are punished." She looked directly at Cacanja.

She put her hands on Yusufu's charm, the charm she always wore around her neck. She stood quietly in front of the flames, the flames that were now leaping toward the trees. She was breathing deeply. She dipped into herself to bring forth a wall of cold, which she formed around herself. Her body felt icy, her feet numb, and the robe clung to her body as if wet.

The villagers watched: some with the anger conjured by Cacanja, some with disbelief that this was really happening, and some with fear and a growing realization that they had been tricked.

She took her first step. When her foot touched the embers, the coals hissed, as if water had been poured on them.

The villagers were silent.

Her second step. The flames drew away from her, as if drawn by a magnet. She pulled the robe around her and glared at Cacanja.

The villagers turned, some also to glare.

Her third step. The flames which had been leaping high, died down, until they reached only her ankles.

The villagers collectively stopped breathing.

Her fourth step. A flame leaped like a giant finger at Cacanja, who missed being singed only by his agility.

Damballah had answered Sabia's prayer. The finger of guilt had clearly pointed and now the villagers recognized, as if one, who was guilty here.

Her fifth step. With this one she stepped out, unharmed, on the other side of the flames. She stood triumphant. There wasn't a sign of fire on her body, not a piece of soot darkened her robe, not a blister burned her foot, not a scorch could be seen anywhere.

A cheer rose up through tight throats. Relief was rampant. "Not guilty! Not guilty. Not guilty!" they chanted.

The drums began their sound of celebration.

The villagers, released from the drama, began to dance, glad that their favorite had been vindicated. Cacanja was sly, but Cacanja was not their friend. Their friend was safe . . . and even more important . . . they were released from their complicity.

But just as quickly as the movement had begun, it stopped.

There was a whirring sound in the air.

Sabia slumped to the ground.

For a moment there was absolute silence in the compound. Not a villager moved.

Then a form hurled itself through the crowd. It was screaming. It was Najuma.

Najuma hurled herself onto the prone body, shaking and pummeling; screaming out of control.

Other villagers surged forward, some to console the insanity that was Najuma, some to see to Sabia.

Two of the men turned Sabia's body upright. As the villagers looked on a gasp arose from their insides. Sabia was bleeding from the heart, where an arrow had pierced through.

Sabia was dead.

Nekayia stood behind a tree at the edge of the compound with a bow in her hand.

Chapter 28

The villagers didn't move. Horror rippled through the crowd. Sabia's fallen body stared at them from where, a few moments ago, a triumphant breathing woman had stood. Najuma threw herself over the body, sobbing hysterically.

The villagers were sobered now. The horror embellished itself in them as they thought about the Sabia they knew, the indomitable spirit, the gentle caring, the wit and the humor, the sicknesses she relieved, the understanding she offered, the advice she gave, the diet she improved. **And** her work with the white devil.

Shame filled the compound. The drums beat in turn with their shame.

Cacanja saw the change in mood. He made haste, slinking away to his hut.

Nekayia dropped her bow and slipped from tree to tree, going home . . . feigning sleep.

The villagers were waking to their truth. They started to do what they had to do. The women returned to their huts, coming back with oil and a clean cloth. They anointed Sabia's body. They wrapped her in clean cloth.

Muwato carried her to the burying ground, followed by the shamed villagers. Each took their seat to wait. To mourn. While Hyenas sounded off. While owls hooted. While crickets sang.

As the night wore on, the villagers could not stop the sleep that took them over. One by one they slipped away, to sleep. When dawn neared, it was only Muwato who kept the lonely vigil. Even his eyes closed, wanting sleep. He fought to stay awake.

His head began to bob forward. He jerked himself awake, knowing that there was movement in the rain forest . . . human movement. No. There was no movement. He shook his head, deciding he had been dreaming.

Wait! He had not been dreaming. There, standing over the body, was a shadowy figure that looked remarkably like Tacuma. The figure stood, looking down at the body. Then it bent and touched the dead face. Muwato saw love. He felt a tearing sadness.

The figure faded away.

Muwato got up and walked to the body.

He looked. He looked again.

It was true.

The earrings were gone.

He stood absolutely still, not seeing, not hearing. Then, how quickly he moved. He took the charm from around his neck, the charm he always wore. He placed it on Sabia's forehead. He backed away from her with reverence. He turned and ran to his own hut . . . there to retrieve his spear.

He crept to the hut of Cacanja, entered noiselessly, and drove the spear through the sleeping man's heart.

"Nekayia, you're next," he said.

'SABIA'

CHAPTER 29

Kate opened her eyes. She shook her head to relieve the groggy feeling. She sat up. Sitting on the edge of the mattress, she pulled her knees into herself and stared at the floor. She ran her fingers through her hair.

Lena watched, silently.

Kate got up and walked to the window and looked out, seeing but not seeing. The pane steamed up as her breath touched its coldness. Cars passed. A man walked by - old and bent.

Wham! Her fist hit the wall next to the window. Wham! Wham! Wham!

The pain in her clenched, bleeding fist was a welcome release from the deeper hurt inside. Leaning against the window, forehead pressed against the pane, she felt the cold glass against her skin.

"Goddamn her! She shouldn't have died, Lena. She shouldn't have died. She was smarter than that. She could have known what Cacanja and Nekayia were up to. She could have stopped it. She had the power to do that." Kate turned and walked to Lena, demanding an answer. "Why did she die? Why?"

"Maybe she s'pposed to die," Lena shrugged.

"Supposed to? Shit! And just who decided that? Cacanja and Nekayia? The gods? Who, for crying out loud?"

"Whenever you gits yourself through with this fit you's havin an sits yourself down, I tells you."

Ignoring her, Kate angrily began to pace. Back and forth. Back and forth. Each time she came to the window, Wham! Her fist hit the wall.

Kate glared at Lena, as though it were Lena's fault that Sabia died. As though it were Lena's fault that her baby had been poisoned. As though it were Lena's fault that slaves existed. Wham! went her fist.

Whirling away from the window, Kate looked ready to pounce on Lena . . . and then . . . almost in mid-step . . . she stopped. She stared at Lena as if seeing her for the first time, seeing the black face and the lines of life that were etched there. Seeing the woman who wouldn't be sitting in this chair in this room in the city of Chicago if it hadn't been for those very slavers who had poisoned Sabia's life. Shame swept through her.

Kate dropped into her chair and looked at the floor, apology in her every body line.

"You's done now?"

"I'm done now. I'm sorry."

"You wanna know bout Sabia dyin?"

Shame was instantly replaced with a crying need to understand, a crying need to have Lena explain. "Why did she let Cacanja and Nekayia kill her?" she asked. "She was so powerful she could have stopped it. Why did she choose to die?"

"It don be bes for Sabia to live no more. It bes for her spirit to go to another body."

Kate didn't like what she heard and the anger was loud in her voice. "Whose body could possibly have been more precious than her own?"

"Tacuma's chile."

"Tacuma's child?"

"Tha's right. Tacuma's chile."

"But . . . but . . . ." sputtered Kate.

"Tacuma's massa, he furious with him cause he don take no wife. One day he takes a gun to Tacuma's head; an he say 'If'n you don cover this wench right now I's gonna kill you.' Then the massa, he stan over Tacuma while he bed her, till a chile be on the way. Sabia knows bout Tacuma's chile. She don tend to die, but when she do, she carry her spirit richere into that chile's body."

"So she could be close to Tacuma?"

"Tha's right. She don need to work no more in Nahut. Her work be finished there. She done outwit them slavers. She done took care a her folk. She done showed em her spirit. She through with it an it be time she happy herself."

"Now I see. It was really time for Sabia to die."

"If'n you din be havin such a fit, you'd a seed it fore now."

Kate grinned sheepishly.

Lena went on. "Tacuma, he done have a girl chile, but the mama, she die when that chile be born. Tacuma, he done raise that chile mos by hisself. He know that spirit a that chile be from Sabia, so he namin her Fela (Fee-lah). Fela meanin 'Love be saved.' When Fela grow up, Tacuma gived her them earrings he got when Sabia die."

"My earrings?"

"Them earrings you gots in your ears right now."

"What happened to them after that?"

"Fela done pass em down to her chillen but ain nobody fit'n to wear em. Then you gits em when you was Amanda Rochelle Blake."

"When I was Amanda Rochelle Blake," Kate mused.

"I tells you bout when you was Amanda Rochelle nex time you comes. Now I's tired, girl. You bes go home cause I's goin to sleep richere in this chair if'n you don."

Kate smiled and got up. "You're wonderful, Lena." She leaned over and gave the woman a hug.

Lena huffed and drew herself up in the chair. "Ain no need for you to be huggin on me now. Git yourself on home."

Kate was sure the Lena was delighted. She laughed, knowing she was finally one up on the old woman.

"You gits on home now," Lena blustered.

Kate let herself out the front door, managing the steps into the street below. There she took a deep breath of cold air. Her body felt vital and strong. "Sabia, I'm glad I know you," she said, wiping the last traces of tears from her face. She started to run for the bus that was pulling up at the corner.

Chapter 30

Kate was angry. Lena's explanation for Sabia's death was fine; yes it was just fine. But Kate was still angry. To be truthful, she was mad, just fuming mad. As a matter of fact she was mad at everybody. She was going about ready to fight with everybody.

And she did. She argued with Ed - a not uncommon occurrence.

She argued with Bryan over some detail about the boys.

She even argued with Leslie and they had **never** argued in the seven years they had shared office space.

What was bothering her had nothing to do with Leslie, or with Bryan, or even with Ed. What was bothering her was Sabia. It was plain and simple. It was Sabia. Lena's explanation had not moderated her feelings one bit. Sabia should not have died that way. She was too smart . . . too strong . . . too magical . . . to have been victimized by that fool, Cacanja. "She had no business dying," fumed Kate. "She still had work to do. Her people still needed her. They needed her strength . . . her magic."

"And besides," she continued, "what does Sabia's life have to do with me? A magical medicine woman with enough strength for seven women, for god's sake. That's not me. Never has been and never will be. Absolutely not!"

"And no. I'm not going to call Lena about this one."

And, then, there she was . . . her other side . . . her other argumentative side. The side of herself she so hated because she was always right. There she was sitting in her brain ready for a fight. But this time Kate was ready. She was ready, even for her. She had been preparing all week.

"So what does strong and magical have to do with you?" she heard her other side say.

"Goddamn it. If you spoke like a southern black woman, I'd think you were Lena."

"Never mind the smart-ass remarks. Just answer the question."

"Nothing. Absolutely nothing. Being strong and magical has nothing to do with me. I've never been strong in my life."

"Now wait a minute. Did you hear what you said?"

"Of course, dummy. I said . . . I said . . . . Well, no. What did I say?"

"You said that you had never been strong in your life."

"That's right. I have never been strong. I am not a strong woman. On the contrary, I have run away from life like a scared rabbit."

"Oh, have you now?"

"Yes."

"What about Ed, have you run away from Ed?"

"Well, no."

"What about your work, have you run away from your work?"

"No . . . but . . . "

"What about your education, have you run away from that?"

"No, but none of that counts."

"Oh? None of that counts?"

"No. I've always run away from what counted."

"Like what?"

"Well, like my father for instance."

"And what would have happened if you had faced him?"

"I'd be dead right now, that's what."

"Well?"

"Well, what?"

"Just well, that's all. Just well."

"I'm not going to respond to that. Well what?"

"You're not listening to yourself again."

"I am, too. I said I'd be dead right now if I had faced my father."

"That's right. That's what you said."

Suddenly the argument stopped. Both voices became quiet. In the quietness she let herself realize that something important was going on here. What was it? What was her other side trying to tell her?

"Well?" Her other side could only be quiet for long.

"Are you trying to tell me that if I had been strong and confronted my father I would be dead by now?"

"I didn't say that, but somebody did."

"You're right. The one time I did confront him he almost killed me."

"So there you are."

"But all my life I've thought I was weak. I was quiet. I didn't have any friends. I couldn't socialize. I didn't have any boyfriends."

"Etcetera . . . etcetera . . . etcetera, right?"

"Yes. And Sabia was anything but weak."

"She was."

"She was not. When I was her I felt strong all the time."

"What about after Tacuma was stolen, and she lost her father? As I remember, Sabia lost it after that."

"Oh, yes. That."

"Yes, that."

"But she had a lot of provocation."

"And you didn't have provocation while you struggled with your father?"

"Yes, but it wasn't the same."

"Are you hearing yourself. It was the same. Think about it."

Kate thought about it. What was the same about it? It was true that after Tacuma was taken Sabia wasn't able to do anything. But then, there was really nothing she could do. Tacuma and Diallobe were already gone. And then, about her father, she couldn't do anything that either. If she had, he would have killed her. Yes he would have killed her. So, if she had fought with her father she wouldn't have survived to tell the tale, or to worry about Sabia or anyone else. Hmmmmmm. "Are you saying that sometimes it's strong to be weak?" she said to her other self.

"Exactly. That's exactly what I'm trying to get you to see. It would have been idiotic to have acted with strength . . . to have fought with your father. So you didn't. But as soon as you had the means you started to fight."

"Like with the Doctor?"

"Yes."

"And with Ed?"

"Him, too."

"And with Bryan?"

"Yes, with Bryan. And more important, you always fight for what you believe."

"Yes, I do that."

"And you do it in front of any audience you can muster. That takes courage."

"I . . . I . . . I guess it does."

"And magic, too."

"Oh, now wait a minute. Now you've gone too far. Sabia was magical. She was born magical and she used it all her life. But that's not a word that describes me."

"Oh?"

"Stop that. Strong. Courageous. Maybe. But magical. No. I'll never accept that."

"What about the magic you weave when you speak. All the unlikely people you've convinced with your words. That's magical."

"Yes, but . . . ."

"What about your books? Your columns? All the people who write to you and say 'right on. You've touched me in a place that counts.' What about that?"

"But that's not . . . "

"Well, what is it then?

"It's . . . it's . . . . Oh, I don't know."

"Almost nobody can do that."

"They could if they wanted to."

"But they don't want to. You do."

Kate had to reflect on that for a moment. Her other side was right. She did want to. She had been driven all her life to speak out about one thing or another. Even when she was young she was driven.

Her other side was leaving her no time for reflection. "Not only do you want to, but you succeed. You have the strength to speak out, and when you are speaking you weave a magic, just like Sabia wove a magic with what she did. The people you speak to need your magic, just like they needed Sabia's magic way back then."

"Oh. Well. When you put it that way."

"Whew. Finally. You can be so stubborn."

Kate was still being stubborn. "Wait a minute."

"Now what?"

"There's something wrong with this argument. Everything I've ever done has come from weakness. All this strength came about because I was scared. And that's pretty weak."

"So?"

"So? What do you mean, so?"

"Just what I said. So."

"So it doesn't matter where it came from, right?"

"Right."

"All that matters is that I'm strong now and that I produce something magical."

"Now you've got it."

"Now I've got it, you say. Now I've got it. Why is it that now that I have it I feel outsmarted somehow?"

"Because I just outsmarted you, that's why. You are strong and you are magical, but sometimes you're not too smart."

Kate laughed in spite of herself.

"And now you know it."

"And now I know it," Kate said, wondering if she really did know it.

"Now you know it . . . and remember what Lena said about all of this."

Kate didn't remember. "What did she say?"

"She said that the only thing that is important about all of this is that you come to **know** who you are."

"Yes, she did say that. She said I had to live all of these other lives so I will know who I am. Yes, she said that."

"So, now that you know it, I'll be right here to remind you - in case you forget."

"I bet you will. Yes, I bet you will. You'll probably be on me every minute to see that I don't forget."

"No, not every minute. That will give you a big head."

"Ohhhh, I hate you. Why don't you go away. I need to get some sleep."

"First, say 'I'm strong'."

"Okay. Okay. I'm strong."

"Now say 'I'm magic'."

"Now that's too much."

"Don't argue. Just say it."

"Damn it. All right. I'll say it. I'm magic. I'm magic. Now can I got to sleep?"

"Feels good to say it, doesn't it?"

"Yes. Yesyesyes. Now go away so I can get to sleep."

"All right. I'm going."

"Thank God. I thought you'd never leave."

"I'm leaving. I'm leaving."

"Good. Goodbye. . . . . "

"Kate?"

"Oh, God. What now?"

"Sweet dreams, Kate."

"Ooooooohhhhhhh. Go away. Just go away."

CHAPTER 31

Kate picked her way among the puddles of water spotting the sidewalk in front of the house on South Damen. "Damn puddles," she thought. "Now I'm going to be later than I thought. Lena will be furious. Not a good way to start my life as Amanda Rochelle."

Six weeks. It had been six weeks since her last visit to Lena. Spring was coming to Chicago, and with it a cold, drizzly rain and fog. The rain was settling in her hair and soaking through her jacket. To top it off, a young boy rode by on his bicycle bent on hitting every puddle. Mud splattered from his tires to her jeans. She jumped away, and immediately into another puddle. All she could do was stare at him, astonished.

So much had been happening in Chicago and in the nation in the last six weeks that work had kept her away. She'd been covering the now-famous trial of the Chicago Seven . . . and it had just ended. Nobody knew, any more, which side was right and which side was wrong. The defendants had acted deplorably and the judge had acted equally as deplorably. The trial had ended with indictments and jail sentences for five out of the seven defendants, and the lawyers as well. Bail was even denied for the defendants. Vice President Spiro Agnew, deplorable in his own right, had denounced defendants and lawyers alike as anarchists and misfits.

Kate had been especially interested in the fact that the Supreme Court had ordered immediate school desegregation in Mississippi. Ed had sent her down there to write human interest stories on the degree of tension and the hurriedly set up private schools.

Although she hadn't gone to the inquest, there was a furor over the death of Mary Jo Kopechne at Chappaquiddick Island and the possible guilt or innocence of Senator Ted Kennedy, brother of the late president.

And a brand new television program was making her late for the trial in the morning. It was called Sesame Street.

All in all, it had been a busy six weeks. Now events had settled enough for her to continue her journey through time. She rang the bell. Through the window she heard Lena's voice. "You gits yourself in here right now, fore I whips you with this stick. Din your mama teach you no manners bout keepin folks waitin?"

The door swung open. Kate hurried inside, dropping her wet jacket as she ran. She stood in front of a belligerent Lena.

"Where you been? I's been waitin an hour now."

Kate knew it hadn't been an hour. She knew it was no more than ten minutes.

Lena banged her stick on the floor. "Where you been?"

"Lena I . . . ," Kate began.

"Don be tryin no scuses. Sits yourself down now an we begins. An stop that drippin all over my floor."

"I think I need a towel to stop the dripping."

"Ain got no time to git no towel. Gittin a towel cause Manda to git away from us. You jus needs to be wet. An stop that drippin."

Kate stifled her laughter.

"You's ready for Amanda?" Lena asked without asking.

After being cold and wet and late, Kate wasn't sure she was ready for anything.

Lena abruptly closed her eyes. Kate used the time to take a tissue out of her purse and wipe the water from her face and hair. Surreptitiously, she removed her shoes and edged her wet feet toward the warmth of Lena's heater. Feeling a little more comfortable, she relaxed.

"When you was Manda Rochelle Blake, you was the bes woman ta sing the blues a that time. You comin afore the likes a Ma Rainey an Bessie Smith an Big Mama Thornton an such. You was singin your heart out afore Bessie Smith ever born. An you knows them blues. You knows em real good. Every black chile knows them blues but you gits em early, cause a what done happen to your mama afore you was born. An you gits em from Duanna an from Sabia, too."

"When you was Manda, you was born in 1883 in Natchez, Miz'sippi. Natchez ain like mos towns. It mos like two towns. Part a the town be on the bluff where all them rich white folks lives in them big houses with them servants and they Nanny's an such; an then they be the part they be callin 'down under'. Down under them bluffs be the flats by the Miz'sippi. Tha's where all them poor folks live in them ramshackle cabins. Up top be all rich an proper; an 'down under' be full a hell-raisers totin them guns an them knives. Streets 'down under' be filled up with them gamblin places and them ho houses. An they gots them honky tonks an them juke joints where folks be dancin an drinkin that gin an carryin on all night. You kin believe, in the mornin, one or two a them folk be dead. Tha's the way it be 'down under' in Natchez."

"Manda, she live down under, by the river, close to all them goin's on. Manda live in one a them fallin down shacks with three rooms an a porch up front. It got a kitchen up front, the livin' room in the middle an a sleepin room in the back, but folks sleeps in all them rooms. Your mama, she be named Clara Blake; an she jus a little thing, bout five foot three, an she ain none too strong. She bout twenty-six when you be born. Your papa, he be named Lewis Blake; an he plenty strong. He work on them boats what run up an down the Miz'sippi. He be loadin an unloadin. They callin him a roustabout. Tha's what he do. He rousts everthin about. You gots yourself two brothers an two sisters. One a them sisters be ten when you be born, an she like nother mama to you. She be called Earlie Mae. The other sister, she be only two, so you grows up with her. She be named Sarah. Jesse, he your oldest brother, an he be eight when you comin long. Your las brother, he be Curtis. He be six when you bein born. You closest to him cause you'n him play them blues together."

"Your life be full a what us black folks knows bes - them bad times. By the time you was born, that war be over an we be's free. But we ain for real free. We's still slaves to them white folks, jus tryin to make nuff money to live. An them white mens, they ain gonna part with much a that money to no colored folk. Payin us colored folk money for our labor jus ain his way."

"Equality ain his way, neither. That government be forcin em to do it after the war an it scares em. It scairt em so bad we ain been equal since. But us black folk got somethin ain no white folks got; an tha's lotsa love. You had lotsa love in that house with Clara an Lewis. So you din know too much bout them bad times . . . leastwise till your papa dies."

Lena stopped talking. Kate shifted in her chair trying to extricate herself from the clamminess of her clothes. The clock ticked. A minute. Two minutes. "Tha's all I gots to say," Lena announced. "Wha's you ponderin now?"

"Uh . . . I was thinking about the blues singers I've seen. They always seem so free, and like they're having so much fun."

"They does have fun. Us black folks gots to do something to get away from them hard times; so we makes up the blues an sings em like we enjoys em."

"It's a happy sound, Lena. Why do they call them the blues?"

"The blues ain happy. They full a lament, but we jus sings em happy. Ain no sense in us moanin an a groanin bout what we cain do nothin bout. So we jus states the fac's an has fun while we's doin it. Then we goes on our way. We feels better fer the doin it."

Kate laughed. "I sure hope Amanda teaches me one thing that I can bring back to this life. I hope she teaches me to sing. Right now I can't sing a note on key."

"Don know bout that but you sings em good when you's Amanda. You gots to hush up now while I gits myself ready." The room quieted. Lena closed her eyes. Minutes passed. Lena began to hum. Opening her eyes, she leaned over and lit her lamp. The pungent smell wafted into Kate's nostrils and she began to feel sleepy.

"Lay yourself down cross that bed now. We's gonna go to Natchez to see sump'n what happen to Clara afore you was born."

Kate slipped onto the mattress and immediately began to shiver.

"Wha chu shakin for? You ain scairt, is you?"

"No, Lena. Not this time; I'm not scared. But I am cold. Could I have a blanket?"

"Land sakes, you white folks is puny." She immediately pounded on the floor with her stick and yelled, "Abraham! You comes in here with a blanket right now."

Her great grandson scampered in carrying a colorful quilt.

"Throw this here quilt over the lady," directed Lena.

Now, warm and comfortable, Kate began to drift off to the sounds of Lena's chanting.

"Ka kung, sala, faranga.
Kakanga ranga baluaranga
Sala, fitu, sala, sala, sala,
Kakanga ranga baluaranga
Sala, fitu, sala, sala, sala
Kate, Ka hung aranga, ka hung aranga
Ka hung aranga, sala famungaranga . . .
Amanda."

Kate turned dreamily on her mat, her thoughts enveloped in fog. Without warning, words pounded into her ear - words that frightened her.

"Come 'ere, woman!"

"I said, come over here!"

Kate was in a strange place. It was night and there were no lights on the streets. Buildings were ramshackled, dark and foreboding. Most were store fronts and rooming houses, old and unpainted. Dark doorways were receptacles where a man could hide ... and wait ... for his prey. There were few people anywhere.

Then she saw him. Big. With powerful muscles. A face with steely blue eyes leering at someone, and a shock of dirty blond hair falling into those awful eyes. His clothes were smudged with dirt. He was leaning drunkenly against a door frame.

"You hear me, woman? I **said**, come 'ere."

Kate heard footsteps. The footsteps were moving rapidly. She could hear the click of heels on the boardwalk, a boardwalk raised by logs about two feet above the damp earth. Then she saw the owner of the footsteps, a short, slight, black woman, in a worn cotton dress, carrying a paper bag full of something. She was a pretty woman but now she looked tired . . . and frightened. She was walking past the man, trying not to run, although she must have wanted to run.

"Tha's Clara, your mama," came Lena's voice in her ear. "An that white man, he Big Eddie Brown. He work on them river boats. He ain up to no good."

The man moved with the agility of a much smaller person. How quickly he was behind the women, pinning her arms to her back. Her bag of food dropped to the ground, spilling its contents on the boards. His grip was cruel and she winced with pain. "You been sashayin by here every night a wigglin that ass a yours. Tonight your nigger ass is comin with me."

The woman screamed a blood curdling scream. A group of men standing on the corner looked, and did nothing. The man clamped a rough hand over her mouth. The sounds became muffled but did not stop. She wiggled and struggled, finally landing a solid kick on his shins.

"Ahhhhhhhhgg," he yelled, letting go of her arms. She grabbed the moment to escape. "Goddamn it, woman," he yelled. "No you don't. You ain't gettin away from me." With one lunge he had her again. This time he pushed her up against the wall, holding her by the front of her dress. He breathed into her face. "Don't you try to get away from Big Eddie. I'm havin your ass tonight, nigger. You ain't goin nowhere but with me, understand?"

Clara was too terrified to speak or move.

Satisfied, the man pushed her through one of the doorways and up a flight of stairs.

"Go with em," came Lena's voice.

Kate followed. They entered a dimly lit room, bare except for a rumpled bed and a chest pushed against the wall. Dirty curtains hung at an even dirtier window.

The man threw Clara onto the bed, then bent over her, pinning her arms to the mattress. Through clenched teeth he said, "Don't you move or I'll beat your nigger ass bloody." Standing, he reached up and ripped a curtain from the window and began to tear it into cords. The fear in Clara's eyes excited him all the more.

Clara moaned and turned away.

She felt the full force of his hand across her face. "I told you not to move."

Blood spurted from a cut across her cheek. Clara moaned again.

"Shut up your nigger mouth," he yelled, as he began ripping the dress from Clara's body.

Clara struggled and grabbed at her clothes.

The man punched her in the belly.

Clara lost her wind. There was no more struggle. As she gasped for breath, her eyes took on the look of a wild woman, caged and helpless.

"Now," he said, as he began to tie her arms to the bed posts. "Now we'll see what kind of a fine lady you are. Movin that ass of yours every night down from that hill. Sashayin down that street like you owned it. Now we'll see who owns that fine nigger ass." Finished with her arms, he tied her legs in like fashion. She was lying spread-eagle on the bed.

The man stood, and inspected his work. He inspected every part of her body. "Not bad for a nigger bitch," he said, as he removed his pants and shoes. His dirty shirt and socks remained.

Clara's eyes widened when she saw his organ, engorged and long, in full erection.

The man's laugh was demonic. "Yeah. Look at it. Big, ain't it? Bigger'n any nigger buck. An just waitin for its pleasure. Just waitin for you. Just waiting. Look at it!"

Clara stared. Horror crept through her small body.

"Do you like what you see, woman?" he yelled. "Do you?"

He raised his hand to strike. "I asked you, do you like what you see?"

"Please let me go," Clara pleaded.

Hand ready to strike, he yelled again. "It's better'n any a them nigger bucks you been fuckin; ain't it, woman?"

"Oh, God! Don do this," cried Clara in despair.

He crashed down onto the bed on top of her, straddling her body, brutally tearing into her with one movement.

Clara's screams were only muffled by his chest, as they bespoke her pain . . . while her blood spurted onto the bed.

Cruelly, he pushed himself deep inside her. "You like it?" he said, raising his face, breathing stale liquor into her nostrils.

Cringing away from his foul odor, Clara whimpered.

"You like it!" he said again, pushing his hugeness deeper into her.

Clara wished to die. Anything to escape this stinking, sweating horror.

"Tell me, Goddamn it. Tell me."

"Yeeeeeessssss!" she screamed.

He pushed and thrust, smashing his whole body on top of hers, his face contorting into a combination of rapacious intent to hurt and his own pleasure. He was breathing heavily. "Tell me you love it, whore!" he hissed through panting breaths. "Say, I love it."

Clara only groaned.

"Say I love it," he bellowed, thrusting deep.

Clara screamed in pain.

"Say I love it. Say it."

For Clara the nightmare was over, she had lost consciousness.

Seconds later, the man spurted his seed into her. He collapsed on top of her, panting. Then he rolled over, laying on her arm and leg. "And now your nigger ass knows one bigger'n them nigger bucks you been fuckin."

He lay, spent, his breathing coming back to normal. He took a last deep breath, and rolled over her, reaching for his bottle of whiskey on the chest. He took a long drink. Then for the first time he looked at Clara. Dried blood was on her face, and more was seeping from the gash on her cheek. A bruise, darker than her skin, had appeared on her belly. Blood was oozing between her legs. Eddie looked alarmed. "You ain't breathin," he said, as he rolled away from her. "Oh, shit! Goddamn cunt! I'm gettin out of here."

He got up, reeling drunkenly. He took a long swig from the bottle, set it down and pulled on his pants. The bed creaked as his bulk crashed down on it while he put on his shoes. Again he looked at Clara. "Well, Goddamn. You ain't dead. Just passed out." He got up and reeled toward the door. Then he turned back. "Shit. I'd better untie this nigger so she can go home. I don't want no trouble."

The moon was high overhead before Clara regained consciousness. She rolled over, not knowing where she was. The pain in her body reminded her. Moaning, she tried to sit up. Each time she tried, it was as if a hand pushed her back onto the bed. She felt panic. "I's got to git home. I's got to git to Lewis," she mumbled through swollen lips.

She rolled her body slowly toward the edge of the bed. Pulling herself up with the help of the chest of drawers, she inched into a sitting position. Her head reeled. She fell back onto the bed. She moaned again. She turned over on her stomach and crawled to the other side of the bed. On the floor she saw the remains of her clothes. She reached for their shreds, but couldn't quite get them. She pushed her body over the edge of the bed until she could just get a hold of her dress. Moaning as she moved, she sat up. She slipped what was left of her dress over her head. She discovered the long rip from top to bottom. Standing unsteadily she pulled the dress around her and stumbled toward the door. At the top of the stairs she clutched at the handrail. "Ain gonna make it down them stairs on my feets. I's gonna fall fore I's two steps down. What does I do? What does I do?" In desperation she sat down. Then she knew what to do. She eased herself down the stairs, a stair at a time, on her rump. Once on the street she held to the sides of the buildings to stay upright. She was propelled by only one thought. "I's got to git home. I's got to git home to Lewis."

Holding on to walls, street posts and fences, she half walked, half crawled her way the mile to her house. Almost home, she lost strength. Blood was still oozing from between her legs. She fell to the ground, now crawling over the stubbles of grass and stones, called out, "Lewis. Lewis!"

A tall, strapping, coffee colored man ran out of a house and toward the sound. Seeing him Clara gave up her struggle. She lay, spent, on the ground.

"Clara! Clara! I's so worried. Wha's happened to you, baby? Wha's happened?"

Clara gave in to her tears.

Lewis scooped her up in his powerful arms and carried her home. He saw her face, he saw her torn dress, he saw her bleeding from her most private parts. He knew.

He laid her carefully on the bed. "Lay still now," he said.

"I's goin for some water."

"Lewis?" she said, holding out her hand.

"I hears you, baby. I hears," he said, sitting back down on the edge of the bed.

"Hold me. I's so scared."

Lewis laid his strong body next to hers and held her, caressing her feverish forehead, pushing her hair from her face, touching her lovingly.

"Who done it, baby. I jus needs to know, who done it?"

"Man call hisself Big Eddie."

"White man?"

"Yes."

Rage filled his body.

Clara lost her pain in merciful sleep.

Lewis edged himself off the bed. He headed for the kitchen where he pumped some water, putting it on the stove to heat while silently his insides churned. Water warm, he returned to the bed. He washed the blood from her face and loins. He cleaned the dirt from her hands and knees. He lovingly touched the bruises, trying to heal them with his hands. At last he covered her with their quilt and kissed her on the forehead. He returned to the kitchen.

Once out of her presence he lost control. With tears streaming down his face, he howled in anguish. His fist came down on the table again, and again, and again. Dishes clattered as they were jarred from the table. Some crashed to the floor. Still the sound came . . . the howl . . . uncontrollably from his throat, and his fist beat the table.

"I swears," he said through gritted teeth. "I swears to you on this night, Big Eddie Brown. I swears to you on Clara's bruised body, that I's gonna kill you. I swears it, Eddie Brown. An when you's dead I hopes your soul rots in hell." The fist continued to beat.

Abruptly it stopped in mid-air. Four pairs of frightened eyes stared at him from the doorway. Lewis's angry face looked back at them. Earlie Mae held the baby. Jesse and Curtis stood one on each side of her. Curtis was the first to move. Running into his father's arms he said, "Sump'n comin' to git us. I hears it growlin."

Sarah started to cry.

Jesse and Earlie Mae crowded around. Jesse, ever the brave one, said, "Papa, le's git it. Gimme the knife an I c'n git it."

"Ain no need to git it," said Lewis. "Was me makin them noises."

"You?" they said in unison.

"Your mama, she hurt bad. I's feelin crazy. I's makin them noises."

"Mama?" they said, again in unison. Curtis headed toward the back room.

"Curtis! Don you be botherin your mama now, hear. She sleepin. She be all right, but she sleepin. Don you bother her."

Curtis stopped in his tracks. Reluctantly he returned.

"Now I's gonna tell you what you gots to do. I's goin to work in bout an hour. Earlie Mae, you gonna be in charge a Mama. Whatever she needin you gits it for her, hear? An don be lettin her outa the bed."

"I hears, Papa."

"Jesse, you run on up to the Jessups an you tells Mz. Jessup your mama been hurt an won be comin to work, maybe a week."

"An Curtis, you leaves your mama be. She needin her res. You leaves her be. Hear?"

"I wanna see Mama," he blubbered.

"You kin see her when I comes home. Till then you leaves her to Earlie Mae. Sides, you gots to ten to Sarah."

Curtis scowled and kicked one foot against the other. "But Papa . . .."

"Don' fuss with me!"

"Yes, Papa."

"An Earlie Mae, you watch over Sarah, too. Don let her bother Mama neither, hear?"

"Yes, Papa. Mama gonna be all right?"

"Don know for sure. She hurt pretty bad, but I reckon so. Now gits back to bed till mornin come. I's needin to ponder."

Four pairs of feet padded toward the center room.

Lewis leaned his head on his hands as his children trooped out of the kitchen. Shortly his head dropped onto the kitchen table, and he slept.

Nine months later Amanda Rochelle was born.

Kate retched on her mat.

Lena watched without passion.

THE THIRD WOMAN

AMANDA ROCHELLE

(1883 - 1912)

"Us black folks gots to do somethin to get away from them hard times so we makes up the blues an sings em like we enjoys em."
Lena p182.

CHAPTER 32

Kate was awake. The fog was gone. Her body was taut and poised for danger. Her stomach was full of rot, rot that was trying to erupt onto the mattress.

Lena was pounding the floor with her stick. When Abraham raced through the door, she said, "Git a kitchen pail for this lady. She pukin all over the floor."

Immediately the boy was back with a pail, holding it under Kate's mouth.

In one, long retching moment, the rot that had accumulated for every woman who had ever suffered the outrage of having her body invaded by the vermin of a man who thought he had the right . . . that rot was in the pail.

Kate was breathing hard. She wiped the sweat from her forehead.

She flopped back on the mattress, pulling the quilt over her. She was shivering.

"Oh, Lena," wailed Kate. "That was awful."

"I sees."

"That poor woman!"

"That was your mama."

"And that man, that Big Eddie, he was my father?"

"You comin from the seed a Big Eddie, but he ain your papa. Lewis be your papa. Ain no never min to Lewis whose seed you be comin from. He still your papa."

"But didn't he hate me, knowing I wasn't his?"

"He don think bout that. He only thinkin bout gettin back at that man, Big Eddie, for Clara. It be Clara what hates you. She sick all time she carryin you, an she scairt. She scairt your skin be white; an she even more scairt you be a boy chile an be like Big Eddie. But when you comes out a girl chile with dark skin an nappy hair, an you bein happy the way you was, she learn to love you. Maybe she even love you mor'n the res, she tryin to make it up to you an all. You an Clara real close. But you ain so close to Clara as you is to Lewis. You be the pride a Lewis, playin an singin the way you does."

"So everything was really all right."

"No! Nothin ain all right. Clara don never be the same again. She lose her spirit. An Lewis be broodin an puttin pennies and nickels away in a jar savin for that gun for to put an end to Big Eddie. Clara, she scairt Lewis gonna do it, an Lewis scairt he ain gonna git the chance. Big Eddie, he scarce roun Natchez for a long time."

"An Jesse take to fightin. He git hisself a knife an he throw it, an he throw it, an he throw it at this here hangin sandbag on the riverfront. He say he ain gonna let no white man come on him or on Clara no more. He git so good, he coulda sliced out that white man's heart with one throw. He kep that knife with him every day while he carryin Clara back and forth to the Jessups."

"But you'n Curtis, you don know nothin bout them goin's on; cause you'n him carin only bout playin that one-string an singin them blues."

"A one-string? What's a one-string?"

"Folks down in Miz'sippi, specially them folks what live in the Delta, they too poor to be havin them guitars. So they makes theyself a one-string. Is jus an ole board an a broom what be layin roun somewhere ain bein used. They takes that wire from roun the straw an tatches it to the board. Then they fines an ole bottle an runs it up an down under that string; an then they plucks away. They makes that one-string wail, they does. Curtis'n you plays every day on this one-string afore you gits a guitar. Tha's all you knows . . . playin an singin. You ain worryin none bout the woes a the family."

"But jus cause you don know bout them woes, don mean you don know bout them blues. They in you. They in your eyes what be sof an gentle like. They's full a the pain a all them colored folk. Them eyes knows. They knows bout folks all time keepin on tryin but cain't never win, an them feelin's a rage what come when folks never git no place for all their tryin. An them eyes knows bout bein used an abused, cause tha's where you comin from. So you sings what you knows; an you'n Curtis, you makes that one-string sing jus like yourself. Singin them blues, tha's what you does."

"I think I'm going to like being Amanda," said Kate.

"Times you will, an times you won. Don make no never min whether you likes bein her or not. You's her; an tha's that. An bes you be gittin to her afore she gits away."

"I'm ready."

"Jus close your eyes, an you sees her."

"I do. I see a strong-looking girl with tan skin and hair braided close to her head. She looks about seven or eight."

"She be eight."

"Ummm. She's got on a white dress. It looks like it's made out of sacking."

"Tha's what it be. Lewis gits that sackin from the boats."

"She's playing that instrument, that one-string. There's a boy with her, older than she is - about fourteen. He has one of those instruments, too."

"That be Curtis."

"She's singing. Her voice . . . it's . . . it's not like a child's voice. It's much too low and too throaty. She sounds older, maybe fifteen or sixteen."

"She gots an ole soul. Ain no time for her to be a chile."

"Oh, she just looked up. I can see her eyes now. They're so intense . . . like . . . like they know things. They're beckoning to me, Lena. I'm supposed to see out of those eyes."

"You go sits by her an you tells her you's here."

"Yes."

Amanda stopped singing. Without a word, she held out her hand. Kate took it.

Now she saw. She saw Clara kneading bread at the kitchen table; Lewis watching, drinking coffee from a steaming cup and asking: 'Where Earlie Mae at?'; Jesse, sitting on a stool near the kitchen door whittling on a piece of wood; Sarah chopping vegetables for the soup bubbling on the stove; Curtis and Amanda making music, making intricacies with their voices, combining . . . disconnecting, talking to each other with their one-string, laughing.

In the middle of their laughter there was a sound . . . the sound of footsteps on the porch.

A man, slightly bent, with salt and pepper-colored hair, stands grinning at them through the screen door. He is carrying a guitar.

"Smokey Joe!" Instruments abandoned, they both ran onto the porch.

Laughing, he picked up Amanda and hugged her to him. "Mandy, Mandy, Mandy, jus look at you. You's gettin to be mos as big as your mama. An that singin a your'n. I heard ya, I did, all the way down the street. Bes little singer in all Miz'sippi, I betcha."

"Oh, Smokey."

"An as pretty as a picture. Tomorrow I comes by with some paint an I paints ya on some paper, I does."

"An Curtis, how you be?" Setting Amanda down, he threw his arm around Curtis's shoulders.

"I be fine, Smokey."

"I brought ole Tessy fer ya to play," he said, patting the guitar.

"We plays it. We plays it," said Curtis excitedly." We make it sound better'n that one-string."

"I wants to hear you play it first," said Amanda.

"Shore will. We's all gonna play it."

"Smokey Joe!" said Clara, wiping her floury hands on her apron. "We ain seen you in an Eagle's piece. Come on in. Stay to eat?"

"Don min if I does," said Smokey, wrapping his arms around her, hugging her until she squealed. "My, my, my, my, but you's gettin better lookin every day."

"Hear what you's sayin," Clara said, pushing him away.

"Ain she gittin finer every day, now, Lewis?" he said, keeping her to him, holding her around the waist.

"Shore is," said Lewis, clapping Smokey on the back. "I's glad you's here. Wants to talk with ya shortly." He dropped his voice to a whisper. "Bout that guitar for Mandy an Curtis. I's got the money now."

"I takes care of it. I gitcha the bes one in town. Sarah, there. What chu doin workin so hard over that stove? Come here an give ole Smokey a hug. An Jesse, whachu makin, so busy over there in the corner. An where's that Earlie Mae . . . gittin to be such a fine lady these days?"

Clara scowled. "She foolin roun with them boys down the street. She don stay home no more. I's worried she be in trouble, she don quit doin that."

"Earlie Mae be eighteen now, ain she? She s'posed to be foolin roun with them boys. I members you was married when you was eighteen, ain that so now, Clara?"

"Sixteen," Clara said, looking shyly at Lewis.

"Sixteen, an you ain sorry one minute, is you?"

"No, I ain."

"Well, then, don be cuttin Earlie Mae out a what you got."

"I ain stoppin her from nothin, Smokey. I's jus worried. Sits yourself down now; an I brings you some coffee," said Clara, heading for the pot on the stove.

"Play us a song, Smokey," said Sarah, finishing with her chopping and joining the group.

"Yeah," said Amanda and Curtis in chorus.

"Play the one bout the gamblin man," said Curtis.

"Song bout the gamblin man," mused Smokey. "Don rightly know as how I members it."

"You members it, Smokey. "Member? 'I once knew a man named Lightnin John, an gamblin was his game.' Member?" encouraged Curtis.

"Members now." Smokey picked up the guitar and held it to his ear while he tuned it. "Ain hearin too good lately," he said. "Got ta git it right up here fore I knows them notes be right."

"Okay, now. Here I goes." He began to pick and strum. "Cain sing no more. Voice all crackly now. I's jus' gonna tell ya:

"I once knew a man named Lightnin John,
An gamblin was his game.
Always ridin them steamers,
Forever, the dreamer.
To challenge him, they came.

Yes, I once knew a man named Lightnin John,
Who played his game of chance.
Who bet his wad,
On the turn of a card,
And made the ladies dance.

Oh, yes, I knew him, this Lightnin John.
An a mighty bad man were he.
His wages to win,
Were the wages of sin,
Tha's the only way he knew to be.

Lightnin John were a very bad man.
He played them cards close to his heart.
He was drinkin bad gin,
With the cards marked to win,
He knew how to play them smart.

But Lightnin John were a very bad man,
With a weakness for a woman refined.
When he was able,
To win at the table,
It was always with her, he dined.

But bad for this man, was a fancy man, Dan.
Who owned the lady, refined.
With Dan, John got greedy,
Bet more than he needed,
And was caught in the game of the mind.

Dan was the smarter, suspectin the cheatin
Caught Lightnin in the lie.
He pulled out his gun,
Shot into the sun,
Left John on the floor to die.

The lady that caused it, the death of the gambler,
Shed a tear as her lover went down.
But the riverboat patrons,
Din agree with the matron,
Cheered Dan on for round after round.

Oh, yes, John was a gambler, ridin the steamers
Takin his life in his han.
And now there's no grievin,
They's rid of the theivin,
At the hands of the fancy man, Dan.

For John was a bad one, and no one would miss him.
Not one minute since he was gone.
Not for one minute,
Would anyone miss him,
Not big bad Lightnin John.

No, not big bad Lightnin John."

"Yeah. Yeah," cheered Curtis. "You members. Whachu sayin you don member?"

"Play some more. Play some more," called Sarah and Amanda clapping and stomping.

"Play some more? I comes to talk to your mama an your papa. I ain gonna bang on this here guitar all night. You plays it," he said, handing the guitar to Curtis. "Anyways, i's time to hear Mandy sing."

"I plays it," said Curtis, hardly able to sit still he was so excited. "I loves this here guitar, Smokey." He began to strum. Amanda hummed along.

"MMMMMMMMmmmmmmmmmmmmMMMMMMMMMMMmmmm"

"They calls him Big John, the gamblin man.
An they calls him Lightnin for short.
With cards up his sleeve, he won every man's roll
An every woman's heart.

MMMMMMMMMMMmmmmmmmmmmmmmm."

"Tha's good, Mandy," exclaimed Smokey Joe. "You keeps on singin like that; an you be playin in the bes jukes from Chicago to New Orleans."

Amanda beamed.

"Curtis, play it now."

Curtis slid his fingers up and down the strings until the guitar wailed. With Amanda scatting with him, he did not put the guitar down until Clara announced dinner, over an hour later.

Seven beaming, happy and contented faces sat about the table.

"I gots me some food, I gots me some music, an I gots me some friends," said Smokey, chucking Sarah under the chin. "Ain nothin more I be needin."

"Amen," said Lewis, ladling soup into everyone's bowl and tearing off chunks of Clara's home-baked bread.

CHAPTER 33

There he was, standing on the bow of the steamship Saint Louis as it limped into Natchez port. Big Eddie! Looking the mean man he was. The Saint Louis would be drydocked for three days. Repairs on its engines, so they said.

Hatred seared through Lewis's body, as if it had been yesterday that he'd seen Clara crawling home on her hands and knees, bloody and bruised. As if it had been yesterday that he had frightened his children with his despair. As if it had been yesterday when he had made his promise to avenge her destroyed body and soul. "Tomorrow you dies," Lewis snarled. "You dies for the hurt you give my Clara, an the res a my family, an to any other woman you ever done like you done my Clara. Tomorrow you takes your las breath. Now I's got a gun, thanks to you; an I knows how to use it. One shot an you dead. Sorry you won know what done kill you; sorry you won die slow an tortuous like what you done to my Clara, but fas gits you dead."

Lewis went home. He had things to do. He retrieved his gun from the drawer where it had been hidden for more than eight years. He searched through another drawer until he found his supply of bullets. He laid both gun and bullets out on the kitchen table. He checked and cleaned his gun; then he placed the bullets in the cartridge. He snapped the safety catch. Satisfied, he pocketed it, feeling its weight against his leg.

Next he searched for a place to hide it. "Cain let Clara know bout Big Eddie. Cain let her see this here gun. She say: 'don do it, Lewis.' She cry an carry on." Lewis searched the house for a place to hide the gun. "Gots to fin a place so's I can git to it easy in the mornin." He wandered all over the house but no place was quite right. Gun in hand he walked outside. "Under the porch," he thought. There he found exactly the right spot tucking the gun in a crevice under the front steps. "Nobody sees it here, an I grabs it firs thing in the mornin."

Lewis was preoccupied and untalkative that evening. To be truthful he was acting downright nervous. Immediately after supper, he went to the porch, checked to see if the gun was still in its place, then sat on the porch swing planning each of his moves. Dishes done, Clara came to join him. "You ain talkin to me tonight. Sump'n wrong?" she asked.

Lewis didn't answer.

"Lewis!" Clara raised her voice. "I's talkin to you."

"What you say, baby?"

"I say, sump'n wrong?"

"Nothin wrong. I's tired, tha's all. An two new boats comin in tomorrow gonna make me work late. Been thinkin bout all that work I gotta do. I's thinkin they's too much work an ain nuff pay. Smokey Joe'n me n some a the other coloreds talkin bout tryin to get more money."

Clara's eyes widened in alarm. "Whachu thinkin you gonna do?" she said.

"We's thinkin bout forcin em to give us more pay."

"Now how you think you's gonna do that?"

"We jus' don' work, tha's all."

"You do that, an they jus give them jobs to someone else."

"We ain gonna let em do that."

"Jus how you thinks you gonna stop em."

"We jus goes down to them boats with guns an don let no one else work."

Clara's fear was mounting with every statement. "You gits yourself killed if'n you does that. Things is good now. You's workin; I's workin. We's got a roof from the rain, an we's got food for the chillen's to eat. Don mess with it."

Lewis sighed. He had done what he set out to do. Diverted her mind from what was on his. "Don worry bout it none. We ain gonna do nothin yet. We's jus thinkin bout it." He squeezed Clara's thigh. She put her hand on top of his. They sat quietly, the porch swing squeaked with every slight movement.

Lewis started looking around with new eyes. He could see the children inside. He could see Curtis and Amanda alternately playing their new guitar. He could see Sarah sewing a patch on one of her dresses, listening. He looked at Jesse finishing the supper dishes, grumbling with each dish. He could even see Earlie Mae down the street talking to her beau. His heart swelled with pride." If all go okay, I be here tomorrow, an the nex night, an the nex, an the nex. If'n it don . . . Well then . . . " he thought.

"Le's go to bed," he said to Clara, putting his arm around her shoulder and squeezing her.

"Afore the chillens asleep?"

"Umhmmmmm. Right now," he said, dropping his hand beyond her shoulder, gently touching her breast.

Clara stood. "Whachu reckon them chillen gonna think?"

"What they allus thinks," he said, chuckling. He lifted her into his arms.

"Whachu doin this for?" she laughed.

"Cause I's lovin you," he said, as he lead her through the kitchen into the back room.

"Whachu doin?" Jesse asked.

"Jus lovin your mama, tha's all."

The four of them smiled knowingly. It wouldn't be long before the old bed in the back room would be creaking, and Mama would be moaning.

That night their love was full of tenderness and passion, Lewis knowing it might be their last time. But to him it didn't matter. What mattered right now was to avenge the crime against the person he loved the most.

Clara's sleep that night was unbroken, so satisfied was she deep in her soul.

Lewis spent the night pacing . . . planning. Lewis knew Big Eddie's habits. He knew where he would be. Kelly's Tonk. His white friend, Charlie, would help him, help him without knowing. Charlie would get Big Eddie out of the Tonk and Lewis would shoot him from across the street. Simple as that.

"Got to talk to Charlie, tell him I needs to talk to Big Eddie. Got to member my gun. Tha's all." The next day could not come too soon.

Work dragged. Lewis was in a fever, waiting. Charlie had agreed to help him without knowing what it was all about.

But Charlie worried about Lewis. "Big Eddie's trouble," he said. "You sure you know what you're doin?"

"I knows what I's doin. You jus git him out a the Tonk. I takes care of the res."

"You want I should wait around in case of trouble?"

"Naw, you jus go on home. Won be no trouble."

"Okay." But Charlie was not as sure as Lewis. He knew any black man trying to talk to a white man was trouble.

In the late afternoon, Lewis caught a glimpse of Big Eddie leaving the Saint Louis. He patted the bulge under his loose shirt, reassured that his gun was still in place. He began to worry. "Maybe Big Eddie ain goin to Kelly's Tonk. Maybe he don stay till I git there. Maybe he don come outside for Charlie." Minutes dragged. Lewis checked again to see if his gun was in place. He glanced up to see if Charlie was still working. He looked at the sun. How many times during the day did he repeat these movements. He had to be especially careful. He didn't want Charlie to know how important this meeting was to him. He didn't want Charlie to be suspicious.

Finally it was time. "Ready, Charlie?"

"Ready."

"Jus git Big Eddie out of the Tonk. Then you c'n go home."

"Gotcha. You sure you don't want me to stay?"

"Naw. I's gonna be fine."

Lewis's mind was cold. All day he had fueled his hatred for Big Eddie with thoughts, thoughts of Big Eddie thrusting himself into his Clara, Clara crawling home, blood oozing from her body, Clara crying when she learned the man's seed had given her a child, hating the man, hating the child, Big Eddie teaching her despair.

While Charlie did his work, Lewis placed himself across the street deep in the shadows. From his position he could see anybody standing in front of the Tonk with no difficulty. He didn't have long to wait. Charlie had moved rapidly. There he was, Big Eddie, standing on the sidewalk. Unfortunately there was a woman with him. They were laughing and hanging on each other. Lewis didn't like the woman being there but he wasn't about to change his plans. He watched coldly as Big Eddie looked up and down the street. Words boomed forth. "Where's the bastard wants words with Big Eddie? Where is he, Lottie? He won't show up if he knows what's good for him, hey, Lottie?" And they both laughed long and hard. "Wish he'd show his ass. I've got better things to do than stand out here." Eddie lurched forward, and ran his hands up the woman's dress.

"Eddie! Not here!" she squealed.

Righting himself, Eddie pulled a flask from his pocket and took a long swig. He handed it to the woman. Just as she tilted it to her mouth two shots rang out.

Eddie slumped to the ground, blood gushing from his head.

The woman screamed; then she, too, fell forward, the flask spilling its contents on the walkway.

People poured out of the Tonk. Up and down the streets windows flew open; heads popped out. A carriage stopped. Its occupants stared.

Lewis slipped between two buildings and headed for the river where he discarded his gun. Then he walked, trying to settle himself. His mind was racing. "Din mean no harm to the woman. Jus had to be sure. Coulda killed him with one. Second shot jus for sure. Got ta git home. Clara be frettin. But I cain go home till I's not so scairt. She know fer shore, then . . . But I better git home. I better git over this bein scairt."

He was about two hours later than usual.

"I's got supper waitin for you on the stove," Clara said, as he hugged her. She felt something different in his hug.

Desperation.

"Ain hungry, baby. Sweat took it all out a me today. I jus ain hungry. Le's go sit on the porch while I cools off."

And they sat, while he held Clara's hand . . . waiting for his destiny.

CHAPTER 34

Destiny was unfolding at Kelly's Tonk.

"Big Eddie is dead; the woman is still breathing."

"Git the doctor. Go git the doctor quick."

"Gimme your handkerchief. Lemme see if I can stop her bleedin. My best woman. Bleedin to death on this Goddamned sidewalk. Who did it? Anyone know who did it?

"Don't know. He got away. No one saw him."

"Git out of the way. Stand back. Can't you see these people need air. Stand back."

"Where's the Goddamned doctor?"

"Get back. Didn't you hear me?"

"Doctor's here. Let him through."

"The man's dead. The woman's got half a chance. Help me get her in the carriage. Take her to the hospital."

"Hold that cloth over the bleeding."

"Careful with her. Don't jerk her around."

"No need. She's dead."

"Who done it? Who the hell killed my best woman?"

"Don't know. No one saw him."

"He was talkin to a man name of Charlie Unger just before he came outside. I saw him."

"Well, go get this Charlie. Don't just stand here. Go get him."

"Everybody. Get back inside. Nothing more we can do here."

"Drinks are on the house."

"I'm Charlie. You wanted to see me?"

"Who the hell shot Big Eddie and my best woman?"

"Don't know about that."

"Don't tell me lies. You were the last one to talk to him. Who shot him?" Charlie found himself held up against the wall, lifted off the ground by his jacket.

"Lewis Blake. Lewis Blake told me to get Big Eddie outside. He wanted words with him. It was Lewis Blake."

"Who knows Lewis Blake?"

"I do. He works on the boats. Nigger."

"You know where he lives?"

"Sure do."

"Damn nigger killed my best woman. Any of you men ready to come with me and get that Lewis Blake?"

Chairs were knocked over as the men scrambled to get in line. For a chance to get a nigger who killed a white woman, they would all stand in line.

An hour later a bottle was hurled through the kitchen window as Lewis and Clara slept. "Lewis Blake, come out here now, or we'll burn this house down."

Lewis shot upright in bed. This was it. His worst fear had come to pass. There was no more waiting . . . no more wondering. He jumped into his pants and ran through the children's room into the kitchen. There they were. White hooded men with torches, riding back and forth in front of his house, horses neighing. Just as he got to the kitchen an explosion ripped into the porch. The men on horseback were shouting. "For killing a white woman, you die, Lewis Blake! Come out here now. The next bomb we throw won't be on the porch!"

In his years of planning, Lewis had known that this was a possibility . . . this horror of white-sheeted men menacing his house and his family. He had known. It was no secret that this was what happened to black men who offended. But before, he had not known the full terror . . . the full ugliness of it all. Now he knew. He stood in the kitchen, watching the spectacle outside . . . the horses trampling in the dust; whinnying and neighing, the flickering of the men's torches bouncing off his kitchen walls, the obscenities shouted into his home, the fear in his loins.

Suddenly Clara was behind him.

Then the children were up. Amanda was first, streaking to the kitchen window. Curtis and Jesse held back, avoiding the rocks that were hurtling into their room. Sarah clutched at Jesse.

The neighbors gathered on their porches.

Clara screamed. "Lewis, it ain true! You din kill no white women?"

"By mistake, Clara. I din mean to kill her. I meant to kill Big Eddie, an he daid. I done avenged you, an he daid. She jus standin nex to him, tha's all."

"Lewis Blake, three more minutes and we burn this house."

Clara was uncontrollable. She kept screaming. "Now you daid, too, Lewis Blake! Why'd you do it? Why? Why? After all this time?"

Lewis yelled to the man outside. "I's comin'. Wants to say goodbye to my family." His voice trailed off. Nobody outside cared.

A stone landed in the middle of the kitchen. "Two minutes, Blake."

Lewis pulled Clara to him and held her as the flames from the fire on the porch flickered on the kitchen walls. "I loves you, baby. You be all right now, hear? Do it for me, baby."

"Come here, Mandy, Sarah. Take care of Mama, hear? Jesse, Curtis, you the men in the family now. Jesse, see if you can git my job at the boats. They needin someone now."

"Earlie Mae ain here. Tell her I loves her."

Lewis walked through the door just as one of the men was lighting a bottle full of gasoline. He let the flame go out in his hand.

Eight guns pointed at him. Three men dismounted. Lewis was thrown to the ground, his arms and legs tied cruelly tight. He was thrown over the back of a horse. A man laced his arms and legs together. He tied a rope to both his arms and legs and secured it under the belly of the horse. "He ain't gonna fall off now."

Earlie Mae rushed up just as they started to lead her father away. "Papa! Papa!" she screamed.

"I loves you, baby. Don you shame your mama now, hear?"

A foot crashed into the girl's belly just as she tried to race toward her father. She fell to the ground. "Get out of here, bitch, before we take you, too."

One of the hooded horsemen began yelling at the families huddled on their front porches. "Don't you forget this; any of you who think you can quarrel with a white man! If you do, you'll be the next ones to be dead! Don't you forget it!"

They rode off, torches streaming behind them.

Clara slumped to the kitchen floor.

Earlie Mae bent over double as she made her way into the house.

Amanda stood at the window staring, not seeing . . . seeing everything.

Sarah came and put her arms around her.

The next day a search party of neighbors found the body of Lewis Blake hanging from an oak tree south of town.

Amanda was the first to see him.

CHAPTER 35

"**Papa's** ***gone now, Mama weeps and cries.***
Papa's gone now, Mama weeps and cries.
Found him on the hangin tree, where the
white man got him tied.

Committed a crime, so the white man said.
Committed a crime and now he's dead.
Tied up and dead on the hangin tree.
Tied up and dead on the hangin tree.
Dead! On the white man's hangin tree.

Loves our papa, so the children weeps and cries.
Loves our papa, so the children weeps and cries.
Nowhere to go now, we mights well lay down and die.
Committed a crime and now he's dead.
Tied up and dead on the hangin tree.
Dead! On the white man's hangin tree."

Amanda's song hung heavy over the kitchen. Gloom had descended on the house in the weeks since Lewis' hanging. Amanda spent her days staring out the kitchen window, seeing the holes made by the rocks, the shattered porch, and remembering the white-hooded men, the sounds of their terror, the torches burning, the brutality of the night . . . her father hanging from the tree. Her remembrances always ended with the picture of her father swinging from the hanging tree. Then they would start all over again . . . holes from rocks, shattered porch, torches . . . . All day she stared out the window, rarely moving, rarely talking. Some times she picked up her guitar and sang her father's song.

Clara had taken to her bed, refusing to eat. Nightmares besieged her. White-sheeted men chased her. Lewis hung from a burning cross. Her house was in flames; the children burned inside. The barrel of a gun was pointed in her face. Big Eddie was wrestling her to the ground, forcing her again, demanding the hated words from her: "Say 'I love it.' Say it!" Time after time she woke up screaming, always to see the worried faces of one or more of her children wiping the sweat from her body, replacing the covers, bringing her food, soothing her.

Jesse was trying to take on the mantle of manhood worn so easily by his father. Rejection assaulted him with every attempt. He had taken the message of Clara's illness to the Jessups. Misses Jessup herself had come to the back door. "Tell your mother there will be no need for her to return to work here. I don't want the wife of a murderer working for me," she said and slammed the door in his face.

He had gone from there to the loading dock to try to get his father's job. Jesse had no more than set foot in the work area when the supervisor appeared. "What do you want, boy?"

"I's thinkin I could get my father's job."

"No job for you here, boy. Throwin those knives the way you do, you're growing up to be a killer just like your father."

'A killer just like your father. A killer just like your father.' The words reverberated in Jesse's brain. His hand came up in a fist.

The man backed away. "Get out of here now, boy, before I call the guard."

Jesse left, rage overtaking him. His fist crashed into a pile of boxes sitting on the dock.

"Guard!"

Jesse ran.

Sarah had turned mean. For her, everything was Amanda's fault. She taunted Amanda unmercifully. "Is your fault papa die. He still alive if'n twern't for you." Amanda did not understand what Sarah was talking about. Her grief was too great to try.

Earlie Mae was throwing up in the sink.

"You's with chile, girl," Jesse accused. "Onliest time I be seein girls throwin up is when they's with chile."

"Hush your mouth. Don let Mama hear what you sayin. She bein sick an all. Sides, I's sick 'causa bein kicked in the stomach." "Yeah. Tell me bout it. From bein kicked in the stomach." Jesse teased.

Earlie Mae had no comeback. She was back at the sink throwing up.

Curtis gathered food where he could. "Jesse, quit your fightin with Earlie Mae, now, an git your pole. We's got to go fishin so's we c'n eat tonight."

But food became scarcer and scarcer, even with Jesse and Curtis hunting and fishing every day. Even with the neighbors helping out.

Curtis was in despair. He saw everybody getting thinner, black circles appearing under their eyes. One day he squared his shoulders and said, "I gits us some money. I sells this here guitar." He was almost out the door before he heard Amanda's cries.

"Noooo! Curtis. Wait. Wait! I's got a better idea. Le's take this here guitar down to the river, on the Esplanade. We c'n sit on the corner. You plays. I sings. We gits money in a cup like ole' blind Willie."

"We ain blind."

"No, but we's hungry. Le's try."

They came home with $1.37. They poured the pennies and nickels on the floor and counted them. For the first time since the night of horror, the children laughed.

The gloom began to lift.

Clara had a new dream. A figure all in white floated in her head. The figure held out her arms to Clara. She enfolded, cradled, rocked and crooned until Clara was easy. "Mama?" Clara asked.

"Yes, chile. Is me."

Clara struggled. "Mama, Lewis . . . ."

"I knows all bout Lewis, chile. I knows. Is all right."

Clara eased back.

"You gonna die, too, if'n you don eat."

"Wants to die, Mama. Don wanna live no more 'thout Lewis."

"Whachu sayin? The bestess reason to live is sittin right now in your kitchen, tryin they bes to ac like they's growed up. Five of em. Five of em needs you. Now they ain got no papa. Lawd have mercy on them chillens if'n you leaves em, too. Amanda needin you mos'. She nothin but a baby."

"Mama, if'n it don be for Mandy, Lewis still be alive."

"Don you talk like that. Manda don have nothin to do with Lewis dyin. You hears me, chile?"

"I's hearin you."

"Now you hears this. When you wakes up, you starts eatin. You eats that soup them chillens got for you. An you eats every day, till you gits yourself strong again. You hears?"

"I hears, Mama."

"You gonna do what I says."

"I do what you says, Mama. When I wakes up I eats till I gits to be strong again."

"Zactly! An no more a them dreams you been havin. You hears that, too?"

"I hears that too, Mama."

"Good. You res now while I rocks you. Sleep peaceful till you wakes up. Then you eats."

"Then I eats, Mama."

It was Sarah who sat with Clara that night, her most peaceful night since the gloom descended.

The next morning she allowed Earlie Mae to feed her some soup. It was a month to the day since Lewis had died.

In three months she was at the back door of the Jessups ready to go back to work. She knocked, timidly, worried about her reception.

Sadie Lee, the Jessup's cook, whose girth attested to her accomplishment of her craft, filled the doorway. Shock . . . and joy filled her face. "Clara!" she said, enveloping Clara into her own big body. "I thinkin I's never gonna see you no more. Come on in. Come on in. I's gonna call the Misses."

Clara watched Sadie Lee's big body navigate through the kitchen and into the sitting room. Shortly she was back, a scowl darkening her face. "The misses say no need for you to come back here to work. She say she don wan no wife a no murderer in her house." The stern look softened. She took Clara's hand. "I's scairt she a thinkin that way. I hear her talkin after the hangin. She say 'Serve that Lewis right. Any man go roun killin white folks don deserve nothin better'n hangin.' I hear her say so myself. An I hear her tellin Mr. Jesse, no need for you to come back here to work even when you was well. He musta forgit to tell you, you bein so sick an all. I's sorry I's the one to tell you, but the misses, she don listen to no arguments."

Clara collapsed at the kitchen table. She put her head in her hands. "Oh, Sadie Lee, I don be spectin this. Now what does I do? What does I do now, Sadie Lee? I cain keep spectin my chillens to bring in all the money. What does I do now?"

"I tells you," said Sadie Lee. "I hears tell they's a job at Truefel's couple days a week. Pay ain so good, but no need for Miz Truefel to know bout Lewis. At leas it be somethin."

"Thanks, Sadie Lee. I's goin right over."

The next day Clara went to work for the Truefel's. Three days a week at seventy-five cents a day. Jesse worked at odd jobs. Amanda and Curtis sang every night on the streets. The family was no longer hungry.

But the family was getting bigger. Earlie Mae made her announcement. "Mama, I's with chile."

Clara scowled.

"Justin'n me, we wants to get married. C'n he come live here with us? He work an he help us."

Clara's scowl lifted. "S'ppose it be okay. We needin another man roun here now Lewis gone."

"Thanks, Mama. I tells him."

So the family expanded by two. Justin and Earlie Mae's baby girl.

Amanda changed her vigil for her father from the kitchen stool to the hill, where she sat under his hanging tree. Every day she climbed the slope, guitar in hand, to guard his lonely spot.

CHAPTER 36

Amanda, at twelve, was a budding woman; tall for her age. Sleek. Her movements were as graceful as a panther's. Like the cat, there was a slowness about her, a deliberateness. Like the cat, she was always in possession of herself. She had a 'waiting' sense about her. And when something did happen, she would move quickly and with sureness. Her hair, long now, was in one braid down her back. Her face was gentle and animated with feelings. Yet her eyes looked inward to the location of her pain, the pain that forced her to look out again at the pain of others, to see it, to connect with it, and to sing about it.

Almost daily she climbed the hill on the north side of Natchez, to sit underneath her father's tree; to watch the Mississippi roll by; to find tranquility in the movements of the water; to see the boats; the tugs, the steamers, a few flatboats; to watch the fishermen on the shore; to pick at her guitar and sing the new songs . . . sometimes the old. To know this hill as her favorite place.

Nobody, not even Curtis, Curtis who was part of everything in her life, shared this hill with her. Curtis was part of their work in the streets, the new job two or three nights at Papa Jacks' Juke Joint and most of all, her music. Her music. There were no words to describe the sharing of her music with Curtis, the oneness they felt when they worked, the compliment they were to each other.

But the hill beneath her father's tree was hers and hers alone.

Mama knew about her trips to the hill. They had argued about it one day. Amanda remembered the conversation.

"Don know why you spends so much time on that hill where you fin' Lewis."

"Don know neither, Mama. Jus likes it there."

"Strange, you goin there so much."

"Ain strange. Is quiet, an I thinks bout things."

"Don know what you got to think bout so much."

Amanda was pleased. "Mama's fussin with me again," she thought. "I's glad. Means she mos herself now. Good thing, too. She so busy an all. Now she ain got time to think bout Lewis, what with workin at Truefel's every day an bein gramma to them four little ones. Them two a Earlie Mae's is scamps sure nuff. An Jesse's two, they Mama's hearts. Onliest thing she got to worry an fuss bout now is Sarah. Good thing cause she be needin sumpin to fuss bout. Justin workin every day down on the boats an Jesse livin out on Saint Catherine Street with Flory. Her min be eased, Jesse bein married up so good. Flory's papa ownin that store an all. But that Sarah, all time runnin roun all night, nobody knowin where she at, runnin her mouth like she do at me when she home, tha's a worry. Seems like I cain do nothin right for Sarah no more."

"Today ain no day to fuss bout Sarah," thought Amanda. "I wants to be sittin on my log, jus sittin an a strummin, an watchin them folks by the river."

"They's a log under a tree, down by the Mississippi
They's a log under a tree, yes, down by the Missippi
On that log, tha's where I wants to be.
Sittin an singin, tha's where I wants to be."

Amanda hummed as she walked. "A sittin an a singin, tha's where I wants to be."

Once on her hill, the world seemed just right today. The sun shone down, warming her body. The trees rustled their leaves while she sang. The blasts from the steamboats punctuated her lines.

"I's sittin on my log now, tha's where I wants to be.
I's sittin on my log now, tha's where I wants to be.
A sittin an a singin, where nobody cain hear me.
Jus' a sittin an a singin, where nobody cain hear me."

Amanda chuckled at herself. She upped the tempo of the guitar.

"Good mornin, blues. Blues, how do you do?
Good mornin, blues. Blues, how do you do?

You come an took my daddy, what more can a
poor woman do?
Yeah, what more can a poor woman do?"

Abruptly, she stopped playing. "I hears sumpin," she thought. "What do it be?" She sat very still, listening. She waited. Then she waited some more. "Ain nothin," she said to herself. She went back to strumming her guitar.

She stopped again. "Leaves fallin from this here tree," she said. "An I does hear a noise."

All of a sudden her heart started to beat, up tempo. It seemed as if a lump as big as a grapefruit had grown in her throat. Her legs started to shake. "Sumpin ain right. I's got ta git home."

She dropped her guitar and jumped away from the log. She started to run toward the edge of the bluff. Then, out of the corner of her eye, she saw the source of the sound. A white boy jumped from the tree and was chasing after her.

She tried to make her shaking legs move faster. "Mama, you's right. I ain gonna come here no more. I's sorry I been comin here. I din know no white boys be after me. I's sorry, Mama."

"Wait," the boy yelled. "I'm not going to hurt you. Please don't go away. You forgot your guitar."

"My guitar. I din member my guitar. Gots to git it. Cain run no more. Gots to git my guitar. Mama, help me."

Life itself wasn't as important as the guitar; although she wasn't sure she would have a life after that white boy got a hold of her. But she did stop running and turn back. She saw the boy coming toward her. She was trembling.

"Please don't run away," he said, as he came closer.

"I ain runnin. You's got my guitar."

"Oh, here," he said, handing it to her.

Amanda looked at him suspiciously. He looked about her age, maybe a little older. He was taller than she, with broad shoulders and a narrow waist and hips. There was a shock of blond hair that sat in an unruly tangle on top of his head. He had deep blue eyes.

"Whachu doin up in that tree?" Amanda demanded.

"Well." The boy cleared his throat. "I've been coming here for almost a month now," he said. "I've been hiding in those bushes over there and listening to you." He pointed to a clump of bushes about twenty feet from the tree. "Today." He cleared his throat again. "Today I decided to tell you how much I like listening to you."

Now that Amanda had her guitar she was again ready to run at the first sign of danger. "You been hearin me a month now, hidin in them bushes?"

The boy cleared his throat again. Then he began speaking in a low and melodious voice. Before he was through with the sentence his voice had turned high and squeaky. "I was afraid if you knew I was there, you wouldn't come back."

Amanda's laughter rang out. "You ain talkin right. Wha's the matter with you?"

The boy cleared his throat again. "I think . . . uh . . . " Again his voice cracked and went from low to high. Again he cleared his throat. "I think this voice is just as afraid to talk to you as I am," he said, looking defeated.

At that, Amanda started to laugh uproariously. She couldn't stop herself. The idea, the very idea, of this white boy being afraid to talk to her. She kept on laughing. The boy laughed, too, although somewhat self-consciously. After all that laughter the atmosphere cleared. Fear was replaced by an awkward silence. They stood facing each other, arms dangling, Amanda gripping her guitar as though it would protect her.

The boy broke the moment by stepping forward and holding out his hand. "My name's Aaron. Aaron Spellman. What's yours?"

Amanda looked at the hand. "Oh Lawdy, what does I do now?" she thought. "Is I supposed to touch it? I ain never touched no white folks afore. I wonder, do it feel slimy an cold?" She continued to stare at the hand. Then, in one quick movement, she reached out and touched it.

Startled, she jumped back, pulling her hand away. "Name's Amanda," she said. "I's got to be gettin home now."

"Will you come back again?" His voice was full of eagerness.

"I comes here mos days."

"Would it be okay if I came, too?"

"This hill don belong to no one. You c'n come to this hill same as I can."

"Will you be here tomorrow?"

"S'pose so."

"I'll come too and sit over in the bushes if you don't want me near you."

"S'pose you can come, too. An s'pose you can sit somewhere sides them bushes."

The boy's face broke into a smile. "Then I'll see you tomorrow."

"S'pose so."

But Amanda didn't return to the hill the next day. She didn't return for three days. Her thoughts were clear. "Ain no sense you sociatin with no white boy. You stays home, an maybe he goes away." But someplace deep inside, she knew that whenever she went back, he'd be there. Still she wanted to go back.

In three days, Amanda had to go. "Wants to be on my hill. Cain let no white boy keep me from it. Maybe he gone away now."

But there he was, sitting under her tree, chewing on a piece of grass. He didn't see her until she was almost upon him. Startled, he jumped up and looked directly into her eyes. "You're here," he said. "I was afraid you'd never come back."

Amanda began to study the ground. She didn't like the way he was looking at her; a funny, warm confusion surged through her as he looked directly into her eyes. "I's here, an I's gonna play this here guitar for a while. You c'n sit over there by the tree if'n you wants."

Amanda tuned the guitar. She strummed a few chords to check the tuning. Then she strummed rhythmically, sliding and bending her strings until the guitar began to sing. She hummed along.

> ***"I woke up with the blues this mornin,***
> ***Blues come on the train.***
> ***Yes, I woke up with the blues this mornin,***
> ***Blues come on the train.***
> ***Thought my baby'd come to get me,***
> ***But the train bring nothin but the pain.***
> ***OOOOOOOOOOooooooooooooooOOOOOOOOOOOOOoooooOOO.***
>
> ***I got the empty train blues.***
> ***Where did that man a mine go?***
> ***OOOOOOOOOOooooooooooooooOOOOOOOOOOOOOoooooOOO.***
> ***Yes, I got the empty train blues now.***
> ***Where did that man a mine go?"***

Amanda played non-stop for two hours. Fear was her motivation. She barely stopped between tunes. "Don got nothin to say to no white boy. Got to keep playin," she thought.

Aaron watched intently, listening to every word. Periodically he tried to say something, to tell her how much he liked listening to her, but she wouldn't stop long enough to hear him.

After two hours, her fingers burned and her hand ached. Her voice was beginning to crack. She jumped up from the log and said, "Gots to go home now."

"So soon?" he said, his face a picture of disappointment.

"Now," she said, packing her guitar in its case.

"Will you be back tomorrow?"

"Don know. Could be," she said, looking at him out of the corner of her eye.

"Okay if I come back?" he said.

"Don nobody own this hill."

"I'll see you tomorrow."

This time Amanda waited a week. "That boy, he be gone by now," she thought, as she trudged up the hill.

But he was there, sitting as if he had never moved, back against the tree, still chewing on his piece of grass. This time he heard her coming. His face lit up. He scrambled to his feet and came toward her. The closer he came, the more his face changed. He looked shy and unsure. "Can I help you carry your guitar?" he asked, reaching out for it.

"I's been carry'n this here guitar mos my life. I c'n carry it some more."

Immediately she was sorry. He looked so disappointed.

"I was afraid you weren't ever coming back," he said.

"I din know neither. I's scairt a you. You a white boy, an I don know what to do with no white folks."

Aaron's eyes flickered. He cleared his throat. He tried to talk and his voice screeched up high. He stopped. He cleared his throat again. He stopped trying. Finally, he croaked out, "I'm scared of you, too."

"Why you scairt a' me?"

"I don't know." He frowned while he pondered the question.

"Is it cause I's colored?"

"No," he said. "It's because you're special."

"Special? What you mean, special?"

"I mean I like you a lot and I'm afraid you won't like me."

"Why you likes me?"

"Because your special. That's all I know."

Amanda laughed. "I likes bein special," she said, resuming her walk toward the tree.

He fell in beside her. "Then can we be friends?" He sounded desperate again.

"S'pose we can."

Amanda went home that day feeling strange. She liked him. She did not like him. She was afraid of him. She was all right with him. She would never go to the hill again. She wanted to go back tomorrow.

"I's got a friend now, sits under this tree with me.
I's got a friend now, sits under this tree with me.
He's got the bluest eyes, anyone ever did see.
MMMMmmmmmmmmmmm OOOOOOOOOO EEEEEEeeeeeee."

Day followed day, week followed week. Every time Amanda went to the hill, she wondered if he would be there. He always was. She brought her guitar. She played for him. He brought books; he read to her.

"I c'n read," she said vehemently one day." I could read afore I was even four years old. I went to school with Sarah. I went all-time to school, afore my papa die when I was eight. I c'n read them books."

"Why don't you read to me for a while, then," he said.

"What this word say?" she asked, unfamiliar with the first word.

She read as she sang . . . with excitement and truth. She had a way of singing that spoke truth even when the words were untrue. From that day on, they read to each other. Amanda sometimes took his books home to read. She would sit on the porch swing, book and paper on her lap, reading page after page and writing down the words she did not understand.

Her world expanded beyond the confines of Natchez.

"My papa die on this tree," she told him one day about six months later.

"Your papa? On this tree?"

"He kill a man one night. Someone who hurt him long afore I was born. I don know what the man do, but he hurt my papa real bad. Papa, he don mess roun when he finally fin' the man. He kill him right off with a gun. An a woman, too, so they says. Mens in white hoods comes to our house that night an takes my papa away. They burns a cross in front a the house, an they throws stones an bottles inside the house. They ties up my papa an brings him here, an we fin's him hangin the nex day. I was firs to fin' him." As she talked tears started trickling down her cheeks.

Aaron took her hand in his. She cried harder. He put his arms around her and held her against his shoulder. She sobbed out her grief. She finally lay trembling in his arms, tears spent.

"Ain never talked bout that afore," she sniffed, when it was all over. Slowly she pulled away and sat up, facing him.

Aaron pulled a big white handkerchief out of his pocket and dabbed at her eyes.

"I's got to blow my nose, too," she said.

"Here, take the handkerchief."

She blew and blew and blew until the handkerchief was soaked. She stuffed it into her pocket. "Cause they's gonna be more blowin," she said.

There the handkerchief remained until Clara washed it a week later. The initials A.S. were clearly embroidered in the corner.

Clara was waiting when Amanda came home later that day, handkerchief in hand. "Where this comin from?" Clara demanded.

"Where what comin from?" Amanda said, thinking about something else.

"This here handkerchief."

"Oh! That be Aaron's handkerchief. I be blowin my nose with it."

"An jus who this Aaron be?"

"He a frien I meets up with on the hill. He a white boy."

Amanda was totally unprepared for Clara's outburst. Clara began to scream. "A white boy! Whachu doin with a white boy? You cain have no white boy for a frien."

Amanda stood absolutely still. She was stunned by the force of her mother's words.

"Din I bring you up right? Don you know bout white folks? Din I teach you right?"

"You teaches me, Mama, but this boy, he be different."

"Ain no white boy different. They all the same. Poison, tha's what they be."

"No, Mama. This one different. We been friends since spring come, an it be mos Christmas now. He ain hurt me yet."

"He don hurt you yet, Manda Rochelle, but you min me, he will. You truck with them white folks, an they will."

"No, Mama. He promise."

"Promise don mean nothin to no white boy."

"He different, Mama."

"He ain no different from the res. Wait an see. He ain no different."

The subject was closed.

Clara fretted and fussed every time Amanda came home from the hill, but Amanda never wavered. Her trips continued unbroken. She went on playing her blues for Aaron and he went on reading for her. They shared their secrets, played together, and grew closer every day.

And Amanda was becoming more and more a woman.

CHAPTER 37

Curtis was tuning up. Papa Jack's was smoke-filled and noisy. Sixteen now, Amanda was ready.

"You's gonna sing fer us tonight, Mandy?"

"Shore is, Jake. Jus waitin for Curtis here to be ready."

"Curtis, if'n she don be your sister, bet you be beddin with her. She mighty pretty."

"I's got myself a lady, Ansel. Finest lady you ever did see."

"Better fer beddin than Mandy."

"Don know bout that. Mandy ain for beddin."

"I'd bed her in a minute if'n she say she do it."

"Ain gonna let cha, Ansel. Maybelle'd have her rollin pin to me if'n you done that."

"Yeah, an a gun to my head."

"Bes you forgits the beddin."

"Bes I do. You shore is pretty, though."

"Buy ya a gin, Mandy, baby?"

"You knows I don drink none, Willy."

"Buys ya a pop, then, if'n you comes and sits with me when you finishes."

"I sees."

"Curtis, when you gonna be ready? We's waitin out here fer the music."

"Jus sits your fat ass down, Hambone. I's ready when I's ready."

"Well, we's ready now."

"Is you gonna sit down now or ain you?"
"I's sittin. I's sittin."
"I's ready, Mandy. Wha chu wanna do?" said Curtis.
"How bout 'The Blues Jus Done Come Down?"
"Here we goes, folks," Curtis announced.
"We's waitin."

"Hear me now; them blues jus done come down."

"We's hearin ya, baby."

"I say, won cha hear me now, them blues jus done come down."

"What brung them blues down on ya, Mandy?"

"My baby wen an lef me, an the blues jus move right in."

"That man mus a been crazy."

***"He lef me for Chicago. Gone on the river boat Queen.
He lef me for Chicago. He the bes man I ever seen."***

"Mus a been a no good man to a lef ya like that, Mandy."

"Yeah. I'd a never lef ya."

"Play it, Curtis," said Amanda.

"An the blues jus done come down now. Hittin me night an day."

"I's willin to take care a them nights fer ya, Mandy."

"An the blues jus come on down now. Ever since my baby wen away."

As her low throated sounds disappeared into the night the crowd was immediately on its feet stomping and whistling. "We'd go git that man fer ya, if'n it'd make ya happy."

Mandy beamed while the more stoic Curtis pretended to ignore the noise of the listeners by busily trying to tune his strings . . . that were already tuned to perfection.

"Curtis'n me, we gonna do a lowdown shuffle fer ya, now. Everybody up an dance."

"Moanin low, don cha hear that train whistle blow?
Moanin low, don cha hear that train whistle blow?
Nothin but that train, to bring my baby low."

"Yeah. Sing it, baby."

"Sing it, Mandy. We's moanin witcha."

"Wants to git some money, for to buy me a diamond ring.
Wants to go git some money, for to buy me a diamond ring.
Wants to git on that train, to see what Memphis can bring."

"How bout this here ring, Mandy? You c'n have this'n any day."

And so it went, hour after hour, night after night at Papa Jack's.

During their break, Amanda saw something that disturbed her. She whispered to Curtis. "Ain that Sarah over there with that man?"

"Shore is. An all dolled up, lookin like one a them street walkers."

"Stop it, Curtis. She your sister."

"She my sister all right, but she actin more like a lowdown whore lately."

"I's goin over an talk with her."

"Don git too close, she scratch your eyes out; the way you two's been actin lately - like two cats fightin over the same Tom."

"Curtis, cut it. Ain gonna listen to you talk like that."

Amanda headed for her sister's table. She stopped midway. "They's gone," she said. "Damn! How they git away so fas? Oh, there they is, goin out the door. Hey!" she called.

Sarah didn't hear . . . at least she didn't stop.

Amanda was immediately out the door after her. They hadn't had a chance to get very far ahead. As a matter of fact when she burst out of the door she saw them just across the street. "Hey!" she yelled again, starting after them. Then she saw. She halted in mid-step and her heart fell. Now she knew what was happening. The two of them were going in the door to the hotel, the hotel used by the street walkers. "Oh my God," she said, leaning against the wall of Papa Jack's, her mind racing. "Sarah? Sarah doin it for money? My sister Sarah? Damn! What's I gonna do? Sarah in trouble bad."

"Well, ain you the pretty one, standin out here by yourself. I's comin to keep you company, baby." The voice was coming from a man staggering toward her - his body in a crazy tilt, a bottle in his hand.

Amanda quickly slid along the wall, edging away from this man's craziness, until she was back inside. She was breathing hard; first from her knowledge about Sarah, and then from her close encounter with that man's drunkenness. Papa Jack met her as she came in the door. "Man over there wants to see ya. Curtis already talkin to him."

Amanda peered through the smoke to where Papa Jack was pointing. Right now, the last thing she wanted to do was to talk to any strange man. "That white man,"she said.

"That white man. Calls his self an agent. Name's Sam. Been comin in here fer bout a month now, listenin to you'n Curtis."

"What's an agent, Papa Jack?"

"Man what gits folks jobs, then charges em fer the gittin."

"S'pose he wantin to git Curtis'n me a job?"

"S'pose so. If'n that what he be wantin, don you be fergittin who give you your firs job now, hear?"

"I ain forgittin, Papa Jack."

Amanda approached the table. As she approached, the white man saw her coming and stood up to greet her.

"Mandy, this here be Sam Leapold. He say he be an agent, an he wantin us to play Saturday night on the riverboat 'Natchez'."

"How do you do, Mr. Leapold," Amanda said, eyeing his out-stretched hand with suspicion.

"Nice to meet you at last, Miss Amanda. I've been coming in here every chance I get to hear you two. You've got quite a talent."

"Thank you, sir."

"Here, take this chair. I'll sit over here. It's like your brother said. I can get you two a job, come Saturday night. The riverboat, 'Natchez', will be docking here and they need a couple of performers to fill in for two who are sick. Oh, here's my card."

Amanda glanced at the card. It was a white card with a black silhouette of a man blowing a trumpet. The name 'Sam Leapold, Agent' was printed under the silhouette.

"Ain they jus white folks on them riverboats?" she asked.

"Yes, the passengers are white. Of course, Natchez residents can come on just for the entertainment if they want to."

"But none a them residents is colored , is they?"

"Well, no."

"Curtis'n me, we plays for colored folks."

"Mr. Leapold here say he think them white folk might like our music if'n they ever git to hear it," said Curtis.

"Umhmm. That's what I've been telling Curtis. If you played for a white audience, it wouldn't be too long before they'd be clambering to hear you. Why, you could work on the riverboats whenever they tie up in Natchez."

"If'n we does it, whachu gonna pay us?"

"What about $15.00?"

"Fifteen dollars?" said Curtis and Amanda in unison. "We's only makin $2.00 and tips workin here," explained Curtis.

"How much a that does you take?" questioned Amanda, remembering Papa Jack's words.

"Well, right now I won't take anything," said Sam. "Let's just see how it works out. If you like it, I'll get you other jobs. Then I'll take ten percent of whatever you make."

"So if'n Curtis'n me works on the Natchez an we makes $15.00, you takes $1.50. Is that right?" said Amanda.

Sam's look of surprise didn't go unnoticed by Amanda. "I's good at figurin, Mr Sam," she said. "So don go tryin to cheat us."

"You wants to do it, Mandy?" said Curtis.

"We ain never played for no white folks," said Amanda.

"Yeah, but if'n we makes $15.00 every week plus what wc makes here at Papa Jack's, Mama could quite workin at the Truefels. She ain gittin long so good no more, an she tired an needin to quit workin."

"Tha's right. She do," Amanda said, contemplating. "If'n it mean Mama can quit workin at the Truefels then I say we does it."

"Okay, Mr. Leapold, we tries it," said Curtis.

"Shake on it," said Sam.

It was the next night that Amanda confronted Sarah. Sarah was finished dressing and about to go out the door when Amanda walked in. Amanda immediately told her what was on her mind. "Sarah, why you doin whachu doin?"

Sarah paused in mid-step, mock surprise on her face. "Whachu mean, lil sister, why I doin what I doin? Whachu thinkin I doin?"

"Don you play dumb with me, Sarah. I sees you dollin yourself up like a cheap hussy, goin off nights an not comin home. I sees you drinkin that gin like you don be gittin no more."

"So what if I do, little sister. Is me tha's doin it, ain you. An sides, what does you care?"

"I cares. I don like seein you shame yourself this a way."

"So ... when do it be that you start carin bout me, huh? You ain never carin nothin bout me."

"Whachu mean, I ain carin nothin bout you?"

"Jus what I be sayin. You ain never carin nothin bout me. All you carin bout be Curtis an that guitar an that music you makin. Ain nobody in this house carin nothin bout me. I ain nothin to nobody. But you, little sister, you bein their pride. They carin bout you the moment you been made. Mama with her mopin roun an worryin, an Papa savin up for that gun to git that man with. An time you born, they makin you so portant. They coos an they coos over you, an they plays with you. I gits none a that. An you an Mama so close. I sees how close you is to Mama."

Amanda backed up, eyes widening.

Sarah kept talking. "Nobody roun here treatin me portant like they doin you. But now I learns how to be portant. I plenty portant to them mens out there. They treats me kin an gentle. They gives me money and buys me pretty things. Ain one a them don treat me better'n any a you roun here."

"Sarah, I . . . ," Amanda began.

But Sarah wasn't hearing any more of what Amanda had to say. She was already on her way out the door. "Sides, you got no min talkin to me, all-time messin with that white boy." The screen door slammed behind her.

Amanda stared at the door. Sarah's words were whirling in her mind: 'I ain portant to any a you. All you carin bout is Curtis an that guitar . . . Mama's mopin an worryin. Papa savin for that gun. Now I learns to be portant.'

"What she mean: Mama worryin an mopin? What she mean: papa savin for a gun to get that man with? Don know what Sarah be talkin bout. I sees if'n I c'n fin' her gain on the streets tonight. Gots to fin' out."

But Amanda didn't see Sarah again for a week. By then, other things had taken her mind.

Saturday arrived and she and Curtis boarded the 'Natchez' with some difficulty.

The first thing that confronted them was a big burly white man guarding the entry to the ship. "No colored folks allowed here. You walk on down there. That's where the kitchen is."

No amount of explaining helped. Curtis and Amanda wended their way to the stage via the kitchen.

Sam was worriedly waiting for them. "I didn't think of that," he said when they explained why they were late.

A magician was already on stage playing to a sea of white faces. Half of the white faces, the women, were dressed in colorful finery with hats garnished by huge feathers that waved over their food as they concurrently ate and seemed to talk non-stop. The men were all in suits with shirts that had ruffled collars and cuffs. All these white faces were sitting around large tables covered with white cloths. Food was everywhere. Colored waiters were moving from place to place with bottles of wine, refilling glasses. Conversation was quiet and polite, but persistent. Nobody paid much attention to the hard-working magician. They clapped politely when he finished.

"Curtis, I's scared," said Amanda. "All them white folks. An look it. We's got to git up on that stage."

"Jus pretend you ain' up on no stage. Jus pretend you's at Papa Jack's an you's seein Hambone, an Ansel an Jake out there. Then you be all right."

"I tries. I pretends to be sittin in the corner at Papa Jack's. I pretends we ain on no stage. You scared, too?"

"I shore is."

"How bout I sings to you, stead a to them white folks."

"Be fine. Le's go."

Curtis quietly played the first tune alone while Amanda stood toward the back of the stage. When he finished there was only a smattering of applause.

Amanda's fears were heightened by their disinterest. It was all she could do to push herself forward on the stage . . . to join Curtis. When her mouth opened to sing she thought, surely, she would be greeted by silence. But come out it did.

> ***"Wonder how long, jus how long that train been gone.***
> ***Ouu, Ouu, Ouu, wonder how long, Oh jus how long that train been gone.***
> ***My daddy's gone away now, he been gone so long."***

Curtis's guitar started to wail. People were looking up from their meal, staring at them. Forks were quietly placed back on the table. Conversation quieted.

> ***"Daddy, Daddy, Daddy, why does you treat me so bad?***
> ***Daddy, Daddy, Daddy, Oh, why does you treat me so bad?***
> ***Yeah, Yeah, Yeah, you the bes man a poor girl ever had."***

"Do it again, Curtis; they seems to be likin it," Amanda said, surprise all over her face. Curtis's guitar sang out while Amanda moved back.

> ***"Oh, yes, now I wonders jus how long, jus how long that train been gone.***
> ***Ouu, Ouu, Ouu, Ouu, I wonders jus how long that train been gone."***

When they stopped and the guitar quieted, there was not one bit of conversation left in that room. Sam Leapold, standing in the back of the room, led the applause, applause which was long and loud.

Amanda sang for over an hour. Curtis's guitar had never been finer. Each time they tried to stop, the audience took up the chant. "More. More."

"Le's try one more, Curtis."

When at last they left the stage, the audience was on their feet, stamping and cheering. "Them white folks cheerin jus like they does at Papa Jack's," Amanda said, as Sam pushed them back on to the stage for bows.

"Wha's bows?" Amanda wanted to know.

"Just get out there and let them see you. Go!" said Sam, giving them a push back onto the stage.

Amanda became shy and awkward standing there while all the people cheered and whistled. Curtis was full of composure. He was bowing at the waist and smiling. "Thank you. Thank you. Come on girl, bow!" he whispered. Taking her hand, they both bowed. "Thank you," he said. He pulled her off the stage just before she started to cry.

Success began that night. Sam was going to get his ten percent.

CHAPTER 38

The afternoon was peaceful. They were lying in their usual poses, side by side, on their stomachs, staring at the river, lost in their own thoughts.

"Aaron, Sarah'n me been fightin."

"Mmmmmmmmmmmm?"

"I say, Sarah'n me, we been fightin. Is you hearin me?"

Aaron rolled onto his back to face her. "Yes, Mandy. I'm listening."

"You ain."

"I am now," he said, his grin impish.

Amanda traced the lines on his chest with a flower in her hand. She paused, taking in his body, well over six foot now. He was, as usual, without his shirt, the muscles of his broad shoulders and chest outlined against the grass. He was bronzed from the sun, tanned almost to the color of Amanda. His eyes twinkled mischievously, ready to play or be serious. His unruly blond hair fell into his eyes.

"What about Sarah?" he said.

"Sarah gittin into trouble. She pickin up mens down by the river. She lettin em take her anyway they wants. She doin it for money, Aaron. I's worried bout her."

"How old is Sarah, now?"

"Le's see. I's mos sixteen. She eighteen now."

"She's old enough to do it if she wants," said Aaron.

"Wha's bein eighteen got to do with it?"

Well, nothing, I guess. But you can't stop her once she's eighteen."

"Oh, I ain gonna stop her nohow, cause she be determined to do it, but she say her doin it be causa me."

"How so?"

"She say she ain portant in our house. She say I git all the tention cause I special somehow. Then she say I don care bout her. It ain true. I does care bout Sarah."

"Sarah is saying she doesn't get attention?"

"Yeah. Then she say I don care bout her."

"Could Sarah be lonely?"

"Lonely?"

"Umhmmmmm. It sounds like she doesn't feel part of the family."

"Wha chu mean?"

"Well, you say that she thinks she doesn't get any attention because you get it all. That's the way it is at my house. I don't get any attention, because my brother, Hal, gets it all. My father glories in Hal. 'He can fight like a man', my father says. 'My how that boy can hunt', my father says. 'He stalks that animal to its death', my father says. Now, Hal is learning my father's business. 'Going to be a big business man,' my father says. Then he sticks his fingers in his belt, puffs out his chest and leans back on his heels. He blows big clouds of smoke from that cigar he smokes and claps Hal on the back and winks and says 'Want to go with me Saturday night?' When Hal goes with him on Saturday night he always comes home half drunk with his clothes all rumpled and he smells like cheap perfume."

"I's glad you don wanna go with your father an come home smellin like that."

"I don't want to do any of it. I never could learn to fight. Too clumsy, I guess. And I hate hunting with them. I hate what they do to the poor animals; they're so cruel. And I don't want to be in my father's business. I hate his business. I hate the way he treats the people who work for him. The two of them are always doing things together . . . are always pushing me away. Most of the time I'm glad to stay away, because I don't want to be doing what they're doing. But then I'm lonely. When I'm not on this hill with you, I'm lonely."

"An maybe Sarah be lonely too."

"Umhmmmmm. Like she's outside of the family and everyone else is inside."

"So she do somethin bout it. She fin's mens what like her an makes her feel good. Then she don be lonely no more?"

"Sounds that way."

"MMMmmmmm," said Amanda, rolling over on her back, laying her head on Aaron's shoulder. He slid his arm around her. They lay still resting on the grass while the clouds traversed the sky above them.

"Sarah goes out and finds men so she won't be lonely any more," Aaron said, "like I found you, and now I'm not lonely any more."

"Ain the same thing. I ain sellin my body to you. We's jus friends."

'We's jus friends.' The words hung in the air like a cloud hanging overhead waiting to discharge its rain. 'We's jus friends.' An untruth . . . they both knew it.

"Aaron."

"Umhmmm."

"You know what I jus say?"

"Umhmmm."

"It ain true. Times I up here on this hill with you, my body git to goin crazy. An then I knows we needs to do somethin bout it."

The unspeakable had just been spoken.

"Aaron?"

"Yes, Mandy."

"Why ain you sayin somethin?"

"Because I don't know what to say."

"Say wha's in you."

Aaron sat up. He pulled a piece of grass from the ground and started to chew on it. Then he leaned back against the tree and pulled Amanda to him. He held her with her head against his shoulder. He spoke the words, the terrifying words they had both been avoiding, always settling for a friendship that was beyond friendship. "I love you, Mandy. I love you more than I know how to say. When we're not on this hill together, I think about you all the time;, how you look, how you smile, how you feel when I touch you. I think about how you are, how warm you are, how honest you are about everything, how much fun you are to be with, how deep you are when you think about things. Then I get scared. I feel so unworthy. I want you to love me so much that it hurts me inside. I can't explain it. It's like . . . . ..uh . . . it's like I hurt whenever I think about you because I want you so bad and I know I'm not supposed to have you. And I know that having you is so much more than I deserve. Then I'm afraid that tomorrow you'll be gone. Do you understand?"

"I understands that you love me."

"Do you also understand how much that scares me?"

"Causa what folks be sayin bout us?"

"No. Well, yes, that, too. People will make it awfully hard for us to love each other, but it's more than that . . . it's . . . "

"Why do it got to be all that mixed up?" Amanda interrupted. "I's happier here with you than any other time. I knows I loves you. Now you tells me you loves me. Sump'n goin on in your min that say lovin me ain okay?"

"Oh, no! Loving you is the best thing that ever happened to me. That's what I want you to understand. I don't care what people say or think."

"Then what does you care bout?"

Aaron hung his head. "I . . . Mandy, I . . . . Well, you're so special to me, I can't even find the words. See, what I feel . . . is . . . well, like I'm not good enough for you. That's what's bothering me. I just know that I'm not good enough for all that you are."

Amanda was silent. Her fingers drew figures on the grass. "You loves me then?"

"So very much. So very much that I'm petrified every time we're on this hill that you won't come back, or you won't like me any more, or you'll tell me you're getting married."

"I ain gonna do that! I ain gonna marry up with no one. I's comin to this hill long as I lives. If'n you comin, too, we be's together."

"I'm coming, too, so I guess we'll be together."

Amanda's body relaxed against his shoulder. She was grinning. "Then you's got to love me with your body, cause tha's what we does when we loves."

Aaron's body stiffened as if he'd been hit. He said nothing.

"Aaron. I say you's gotta love me with your body, cause tha's the way we does when we loves. Why don you say somethin?" "Mandy . . . I . . . I . . . I . . . " he stuttered.

"Aaron, what be the matter?"

"Oh, Mandy, I want to. I want to love you with my body. I want to feel your skin next to mine. I want to hold you so close we won't know which is you and which is me. I want to kiss you everywhere. I want to . . . but . . . "

"But what?"

Aaron was silent. His face contorted into a grimace. He began to tremble.

"Aaron?" She slipped out of his arm and turned to face him. "Aaron? What?"

"I don't want to hurt you the way my Daddy hurts colored women," he blurted. He put his head in his hands, his body still trembling.

"How he do that?"

"He has sex with them all the time, Mandy. A different colored woman all the time. Once when I was about eight, I ran into his room, and he was in bed with Mama's servant. And then later he bragged about it. Told me that was what every man did. Told me now I'd seen what a man does. Then I asked him about Mama. He slapped me on the back and said, 'White women are fragile, son. Better to take the colored wenches. They like it better and don't give you any trouble about it. 'Find a good one,' he said. 'Keep her for a while, give her a few coins and she's happy. If you have a child by her, just say it isn't yours, boy; just say it isn't yours.

Then he looked at me, proud like, and he said 'You're going to grow up just like me, son. Just like me.' And then he clapped me on the back again. Mandy, it made me sick. I went to the bathroom and vomited."

Amanda wiped away a tear forming in the corner of his eye.

"I knows tha's what the white mens does. I sees em huntin down by Papa Jack's. I sees them colored women goin with em, too. I sees em goin into that hotel. I knows what they does, but we's different."

"It isn't any different, Mandy."

"Yes it is. You ain your Daddy an I ain jus some ole colored wench."

Aaron was hearing but he wasn't hearing. He couldn't hear because his whole body was shaking. Violent spasms were contorting his body. Shame was filling him: the shame of his father and the other white men who had taken women like Amanda against their will, shame for the centuries of white men who had taken colored women, shame for himself for wanting Amanda's body.

Amanda watched his struggle. She felt his trembling and somehow knew his shame. She knew his shaking body was purging his soul of crimes he had never committed. Purging his soul of the rot, the rot that kept him from loving her clean . . . purging his soul of the rot so that he could let his love for her come to her . . . clean. Deep inside, she knew this. Her soul stirred as she watched his struggle.

Suddenly the struggle going on on the hill was not only his struggle. She was in the midst of another struggle. She found herself back in another time, another love. She found herself near an ocean that was sweeping the shore. She was seeing the moon over head. She found herself different. She was one of two people silhouetted against the light of that very moon. First she was saying hello to a very powerful black man, then she was saying a sad goodbye. In this other place and this other time she was loving this other man exactly as she now loved Aaron.

Words were forming in her head . . . a voice was telling her. "No force on earth is strong enough to keep you from him. No force." said the voice.

Now she was trembling. She had never heard words in her head before. These words were absolute. Absolutely insistent. She knew they were right.

His trembling was subsiding. He was slumping against her, weak now, but back in control. She held him, rocked him, caressed his face and hair. He dropped his head into her lap. She caressed his hair. She rubbed his back.

He shivered.

Amanda enclosed him with her arms, bent down and covered his bare back with her body. Her breasts pressed into his back through the thinness of her dress.

He sighed.

She nuzzled against his neck.

They were still for a long time.

Gently he rolled on his back. She was directly over him. He pulled her head to his and kissed her, tasting her full lips. "It's time, isn't it?" he said.

"Is time."

"I've never done this before. I don't know much about it."

"I knows bout it." she said. "I sees Mama an Lewis doin it. An I sees Earlie Mae an Justin. I even sees the girls'n boys behin the shed. I knows bout it."

She sat up, reached for the bottom of her dress and slipped it over her head.

Aaron's eyes widened as the beauty of her body was revealed to him . . . the wide shoulders, the full breasts, the blackness of her nipples, the darkness of the aureoles around them. Her chest was heaving and her soft belly invited him.

Slowly she leaned toward him, her arms on his shoulders, her body coming closer and closer until it was brushing against his.

He closed his eyes.

Amanda moved her legs over his body until they were touching, her softness to his hardness. She began to rock.

Aaron pulled her face down to his and kissed her, holding his lips to hers while she rocked against him. "Ohohohohohhhh," he moaned. "Oh, Mandy."

Her long braid brushed his face as she moved.

She sat up. From his position on the ground he could see the rocking beauty of her body silhouetted against the sun, he could see the shadows on her skin caused by the interference of the trees. He could see her eyes sparkling, her body moving in rhythm with his.

Amanda's eyes closed. Her face softened. Her lips parted. Her movements increased. Quickly she bent over him, grasping his shoulders, her lips struggling to find his. Her knees clasped the side of his body as she dug herself against him..

A surprised and delighted squeal escaped her throat.

"Something's happening," Aaron said, as he thrust himself off the ground as though he could join her softness with his hardness.

"Oh, God," he groaned, as his seed exploded against the cloth of his trousers. "Oh, God," he repeated. "Mandy, Mandy, Mandy. Oh, my Mandy." He held her to him as his body writhed against her.

Amanda dropped her body onto his, her heart trying to pound its way out of her chest.

Aaron's arms held her with firmness.

And there they stayed until their hearts ceased trying to leave their bodies.

Now Amanda was content. They had done what she knew they needed to do to cement their love.

She rolled over and settled herself into the crook of his shoulder while his arm pulled her closer. Their breathing quieted. The sun beat down through the trees throwing shadows on their bodies. Aaron closed his eyes.

Amanda amused herself by tracing the lines of his face with her fingers. His nose twitched. She giggled. He opened his eyes. He pulled her to him and kissed her deeply on the mouth.

"I love you so much, Mandy. I don't want anything to ever separate us, even for a week. Not even for a day."

"Ain gonna be no separatin. We's jus gonna git better'n better."

"Better'n better," he repeated. He kissed her on the nose.

She stirred. "Is bout time for me to go home, now," she said. "I's workin at Papa Jack's tonight."

"Sing one song for me tonight?"

"I sings this one for ya."

> ***"I's got a man now, with the blue, bluest, blue, blue eyes.***
> ***Oh, yeah, I's got a man now with the bluest of blue, blue eyes.***
> ***An the way he loves me, mos wanna make me cries."***

Slowly she got up and slipped her dress over her head. Aaron watched her before he, too, got up and retrieved his shirt hanging from the tree. Then a thought struck his mind. "Hey, isn't it almost your sixteenth birthday?" he asked.

"Shore is. Day after tomorrow."

"Will you be here?"

"I be here."

"Good. I've got a special birthday present for you."

"Whachu gonna give me? Tell me," Amanda teased.

"I won't tell you until your birthday."

"You tells me now," said Amanda, tickling him on his chest.

"I'm not going to tell you now. Quit that. Ha ha ha, hee."

"Ain gonna quit till you tells me."

"I'm not going to tell you now, but I'll give you something else right now."

"Whachu gonna give me right now?"

Aaron pulled her into him and kissed her, holding her body fully against his. When he released her, he ran toward the bluffs. "Can't tell you now. It's special for being sixteen."

Amanda waved and smiled. She turned and trudged toward the flats.

CHAPTER 39

Two days later, Amanda climbed the hill, slowed by the weight of her guitar. Run was what she wanted to do but as much as her body said 'run' her legs dragged like weighted pegs. "Whatsa matter with me?" she thought. "I feels funny. Ain no time to be feelin funny. Today I's sixteen." But her eyes held to the ground. They wouldn't look for Aaron.

He was already there, back against the tree, chewing on his inevitable blade of grass. He was watching . . . waiting for her head to come up over the side of the hill. When he saw her shadow, he jumped up from the tree, running. She barely had time to set her guitar on the grass before he scooped her into her arms and swung her around and around. "I love you, I love you, I love you," he said. "Now I can tell you how much."

Amanda laughed. "Aaron, put me down. Put me down. I's gettin dizzy."

"Not until you tell me you love me. Tell me you love me. Tell me now."

Amanda squealed. "I does, Aaron. I does. I loves you. Now put me down." Her funny feeling was gone. Certainty returned.

Aaron slowed their swirling, until her feet were on the ground, until she was standing in front of him. He held her to him. He picked up the guitar, took her hand and they walked toward the tree. "I'm going to carry Little Mandy today," he said. "And I don't want any argument."

"You c'n carry it today." she said. Then the ground again demanded her attention. "I's gonna play for you," she said shyly. "Somethin special."

"Play it for me first thing."

"Maybe," Amanda teased, looking at him out of the corner of her eye.

"Promise to play it for me now, or I'll tickle you."

"No, you ain gonna tickle me."

Playfully, he lunged at her.

She adeptly stepped aside.

His momentum carried him past her. He lost his footing, stumbled, came almost upright, lost his footing again, and ended up flat in the grass.

"Aaron, is you all right?" She ran toward his prone body, then bent to see if he was still breathing. "Is you still breathin? Aaron?"

He lay still.

"Aaron, is you all right?"

Like a snake, his arm darted out and grabbed her leg. "Gotcha," he said.

She could not get away. "Aaron!"

With one leap, he was up, tickling her on the stomach. "Play it for me now. You won't get away until you promise."

Amanda squealed and began to laugh, out of control. "Stop it. I plays it for you now. Stop it. Stop it. Aaron, stop it!"

Dropping to the ground, they became a tangle of arms and legs rolling over and over on the grass, laughing. When she got his arms pinned to the ground, the tickling stopped. She sat on his belly, breathing hard.

"Let me go, Amanda."

"Naw, you jus tickles some more. Don let you go till you promises."

"I promise."

"Don believe you."

"Oh, kiss me then."

"Cain kiss you less'n I let go a your arms."

"Then I'll have to kiss you," he said, straining toward her.

The movement freed his arms and he sat up, playfulness gone. His mouth found hers. His kiss was warm and easy. Passion flamed between them.

Aaron became serious. "You have to move, Mandy. Sitting like this makes me want to love you and it isn't time yet. When I love you this afternoon, I want it to be special for your birthday. But not yet."

Amanda got up slowly, savoring her feelings. "I plays my song for you now."

She took her guitar out of its dilapidated case. Sitting on the log, she rested the guitar on her knee. She leaned over it, tuning it, humming each note. Satisfied, she began to play. The guitar sang under her expert touch.

"I's got a man now, with the bluest of blue, blue eyes.

Oh my, I's got a man now, with the bluest of blue, blue eyes.
And when he love me, he make me shiver an cry.
Yeah, Yeah, Yeah. I's got this man now who make my eagle fly.
Tha's right, I's got this man now, who make my eagle fly.
Yeah, Yeah, Yeah, Yeah, Yeah, Yeah, my eagle gone to the sky.

When this man, he love me, I jus lays right down an dies.
Oh, yeah, when this man, he love me, I jus lays right down an dies.
Cause every time he love me, he make me shiver an cry.
Yeah, he make me shiver an cry.
This man with the blue, blue eyes."

The last notes hung in the air. Amanda's eyes again explored the ground. "He don like it," was in her thoughts.

Aaron's hand was on her chin, lifting her head. "Look at me," he said.

Amanda raised her eyes. Fear looked out.

Love looked back. She saw it.

"Aaron," she said, laying the guitar on the grass. "I loves you so." She threw her arms around his neck.

In that moment, their souls reconnected as in centuries before. Finding each other again, to fulfill what had been unfulfilled, to live out the love denied them in lives past. And to face their hostile world, so full of each other that no force could be strong enough to disconnect them.

Aaron reached in his pocket and pulled out a small box wrapped in silver paper and tied with a white ribbon. "This is for our love," he said, as he handed it to her.

Amanda untied the ribbon and released the paper. She pulled the top off the box. There, glinting in the sunlight, were gold earrings in the shape of a teardrop, about two inches long and an inch wide at their widest. She took one out and held it up to the sun. "Oh, Aaron," she said, as her fingers touched the strange writing on the bottom. They travelled to the red rivulets at the top of the earring, a little longer than a half inch, ending in what looked like tiny droplets of blood. The suns rays radiated into it, then seemed to leap out again. She held it to her ear. "Is beautiful," she said, her eyes wide. "I's gonna be the admiration a Papa Jack's wearin these. I wants to put them on." She fumbled for the large silver rings now in her ears.

"Mandy, before you put them on, you've got to know something. You have to know that once you put the earrings on, our souls unite and won't ever be separated again, not only while we live, but for eternity."

"How you know that?" asked Amanda.

You remember my telling you about Iola?"

"Your Nanny you so close to."

"Umhmmm. She told me."

"But how she know bout souls an eternity?"

"I think she knows about everything, Mandy. She told me that these earrings are symbols. Symbols of two souls who are so close they'll never be parted. They can't be parted. They come together because they have no choice. Their lives together are decided before they are even born. And they'll stay together as long as they live and even beyond."

"Once you put them on, Mandy, we'll never be parted again, even after we're dead."

Amanda's eyes became wider and wider as Aaron talked.

"Don know bout these earrings now," she said. "What you's talkin bout be voodoo. I's scared a voodoo." She quickly dropped the earring back in its box.

"Wait, Mandy, put it back in your hand."

"Don wanna touch it."

Aaron retrieved the box and took out the earring. He enclosed it in the palm of his right hand. "Give me your hand, Mandy."

"Ain gonna do it."

"It's all right. Just give me your hand. I'll be sure it won't hurt you."

Reluctantly, she presented her hand.

Aaron covered her hand with his, placing the earring between them.

"Aaron, I feels funny. I's scairt."

"I feel it, too, Mandy."

"Ain you scairt?"

"No."

"I ain gonna be scairt then, neither."

Silence.

Birds twittered. A breeze blew over them. A steamboat blasted its imminent launching.

"Aaron, my hand. Is hot."

"Mine, too."

"Wha's happenin?"

"I don't know."

Amanda closed her eyes. In her vision, a woman appeared. She was a black woman, young and strong-looking. She was wearing only a loin cloth. Her breasts were bare. Her hair was short-cropped all over her head. **And** she was wearing the earrings.

The woman began to talk. "I'm Sabia," she said. "I'm sending you the earrings. Wear them, Amanda Rochelle. And love him. For your love traverses the centuries. Wear them, Amanda. They belong to you and to no one else."

The woman began to fade away.

She was gone.

Amanda opened her eyes. "Aaron, I sees a woman. She say she be Sabia. She say to wear the earrings cause they belong to me. Aaron, what do it mean?"

Aaron's face lit up. "She said her name was Sabia? Oh, Mandy. She was the last woman to wear the earrings. Iola told me Sabia was an African woman who loved a boy named Tacuma. He gave her these earrings before he was stolen by slavers and brought to America. She stayed behind. Their love was never finished; their souls are still together."

"Is we s'posed to finish it?"

"I think so. That's what Iola told me. Iola says she thinks you have Sabia's soul and I have Tacuma's."

"How she know that?"

"Iola just knows. She knew about our love a long time ago, before I even knew it. She said you had to have the earrings. She said that we have no choice. We have to live out what Sabia and Tacuma couldn't."

"You's tellin me that I's African an my name be Sabia; an you's African too, an your name be Tacuma; an I's got to wear them earrings cause our souls already be's together for eternity. And all a this cause Iola tole you?"

"Yes, that's what I'm telling you."

"Iola mus be crazy in the head."

"No, Mandy. Iola just knows everything. She just does. She always has."

"How she git them earrings?"

"From her grandmother, who was Tacuma's child."

"Oh!"

Amanda felt the weight of the earring in her hand. She ran her thumb over the Egyptian writing. Again she felt the red rivulets. She held it up to her ears. "How do it look?"

Aaron grinned widely. "Beautiful. Just like you."

"I's gonna wear em. I reckon it too late anyhow, cause a my soul already belonging to you."

Aaron's grin widened.

Now she did remove the silver rings adorning her ears.

Aaron sat on his knees in front of her. He reached for the earring she'd been holding. He slipped the wire through the hole in her ear. He said, "My soul walks with you now and forever."

He slid the other earring into her ear and said, "As your soul walks with me, now and forever."

"I ain scairt no more, Aaron. I ain scairt. I's all right." She put her hand to her ears to feel the earrings. "Aaron, is you all right?" His face was ashen under his tan.

"Just a little pain in my chest. There. It's going away now. Oh, yes, Mandy. I'm fine." He reached out and touched the earrings as they dangled from her ears.

"We's one now, ain we?"

"We're one now, for forever." His fingers began to explore her face. He touched her forehead, the hollows of her eyes, the fullness of her lips. He gently caressed her cheekbone, the angle of her jaw. Each touch let him know more and more about her. Each touch let her trust him more.

His lips were on her mouth, tasting, exploring, learning its contours, testing the softness, the fullness.

He stopped. He was talking. "I love you more than life itself; I want you to know that. I want you always to remember our love today, a celebration of us and a celebration of our being one. Iola told me to follow my feelings and to know yours. It will be a celebration."

Amanda nodded.

His lips were on her face. They lingered over her closed eyes, brushed her forehead, travelled across her nose to each cheek, exploring her mouth, finding her tongue, entwining, searching, finding each part of her face in a brand new way.

He found the sensitive spots on her neck, along the spaces under her jaw, behind her ear.

Amanda purred as tingling sensations streamed across her face and down her body.

His mouth found her chest between the open buttons of her blouse. Sensations were streaming from her breasts as his mouth came close. She put her arms around his neck, to guide, to direct him toward her waiting breasts. His hands touched them, lifting them toward his face. Through the cloth of her blouse, she felt his lips, touching the nipples, pulling them to him.

She wanted to crush his head to her, to feel the passion of his lips against her bare skin.

His hand unbuttoned her blouse, pulling it loose from her skirt. His lips found her breasts, kissed them and caressed them.

Amanda's breathing deepened. Desire surged through her. Sensations awakened in her loins.

He slipped her blouse off her shoulders. A warm breeze breathed over her body, cooling it. He leaned away from her.

She reached for his shirt, unbuttoning each button, looking into his eyes as she worked. His love for her was there.

Free of his shirt, he pulled her toward him, skin touching skin.

His hands were on her legs, finding the tenderness of her thigh, pushing her skirt up. Amanda moaned, uncontrollably. His hands slid along the outside of her thighs, pulling her skirt with it. It bunched clumsily around her waist. His lips again found her mouth while his hands pulled her skirt up and over her head. They parted briefly as the skirt moved between them.

Naked, she sat before him, passion filling her, heat emanating from her body. She worked the buttons on his pants, wanting to free him. He rolled away from her and removed his pants. She saw him now in his fullness.

He returned to his position on his knees, inviting her to come to him. He pulled her toward him, and she straddled his hips. She felt the tip of him gently nudging her, inviting her, asking her, demanding her to take him.

His hands found her buttocks and pulled her toward him. Dampness aided his entry, slowly, so slowly. Amanda cried out for more.

"We don't need to hurry," he said softly. "I want to feel every bit of you."

Amanda's insides pulsated and quivered, demanding all of him.

He refused, coming into her a little at a time. He felt her. He gently moved through.

She gasped.

She pulled him all the way inside her.

He let her but he held still, not moving.

Amanda felt all of him against her. Her breasts pressing on his chest. Her head on his shoulder. Her belly against his. They breathed in unison. Her soft convolutions around him, holding his hardness into the center of her body. He held her still so she could not demand from him before he was ready.

He stayed very still, not moving, not letting her move, refusing to let them go beyond . . . into the chasm of darkness . . . of unknowingness . . . keeping sensations alive. He held her to him, and began to move again.

Her hands slid up and down his back, pulling him closer, as if closer would quell the fire that was burning inside. Thrusting and pulsations overtook her.

Once more he held her still.

Sensation after sensation spread through her loins, reaching to the very tip of her toes and the ends of her fingers. Her heat spread through her body into his.

"Aaron? Aaron? Aaron!" she said, beginning to struggle.

"Is happening."

He let go of her and let her thrust herself toward him, let the pulsating of her insides carry him over his edge into oblivion of her body and his body, knowing only one body. They went into the place of lightness where soul meets soul. Where unity becomes unable to be separated. Where differences evaporate. Where Amanda and Aaron become eternal.

They stayed.

They separated and let the breeze blow over them, cooling their over-heated bodies. Aaron lay back on the grass, bringing Amanda with him.

A mockingbird sang above them.

The sweetness of her song filled them.

"Happy Birthday, Mandy."

Tears trickled down her cheeks, tears of joy, of passion spent, of love reborn.

They lay soaking in the sun until . . . ..

They knew it was time to part.

They dressed slowly, wanting to hold onto the wonder of the moment.

They parted, holding each other until the last minute, arms around each other, then hands holding hands, until it was only fingers touching fingers.

Amanda finally turned and walked toward the river. Aaron watched her walk away, her body proud and free, earrings glistening in the sun.

Clara was standing at the kitchen stove when Amanda bounced in. The first thing she saw was the earrings.

"Hi, Mama," Amanda said with a lilt in her voice.

"Good lookin earrings you got," Clara said, scowling over the stove.

"They pretty, ain they, Mama? Aaron give em to me for bein sixteen. They special earrings, he say. They got a story to em. I's never to take em off."

"You got them earrings from that white boy? What he doin givin you somethin as spensive as that?"

"We's in love, Mama."

"You's in love? You's in love with a white boy? Whachu doin thinkin you loves a white boy? They's plenty a boys down at Papa Jack's glad to have you. Why you insistin on that white boy?"

"Cause I loves him, Mama. Ain nothin I c'n do bout it."

Clara grumbled as she checked the cake she was baking . . . special for Amanda's birthday.

"What dress you reckon I ought to wear tonight so's to show off these earrings?

"Don rightly know," said Clara, glowering into her soup.

"Reckon I's gonna wear this black one. How's it look, Mama?"

Clara sighed. "You looks right smart in that dress. Won be no one at Papa Jack's c'n miss them earrings with you wearin that black dress."

"Thanks, Mama." Amanda walked to the stove and kissed her on the cheek. "Everythin gonna be all right. You sees."

Clara sighed again. "Everythin ain all right," she thought.

Amanda sang her heart out that night at Papa Jack's, every song a tribute to her love for Aaron . . . the earrings swinging from her ears, shining in the light.

CHAPTER 40

Amanda was in love. She floated through her days; she waited patiently until the moment she could head for the hill; she sang with an excitement that rocked Papa Jack's every night; she radiated happiness. Her exuberance was infectious. Even Clara caught it and stopped nagging.

All true, until six months after the earrings. Clara was in bed when she heard the sound. Amanda was vomiting in the sink.

Clara made her way to the kitchen. When there was a pause in the retching, she said, "You stop bleedin?"

"Yes, Mama, two months now."

"You with child." It was a proclamation, not a question.

"I thinks so. I ain been feelin too good lately."

"Do it belong to that white boy?"

"Yes, Mama."

"Whachu gonna do now?"

"I's gonna have Aaron's chile an I's gonna love it . . . .Aaron's gonna love it, too."

"Do that white boy know bout this chile?"

"I ain tole him yet."

"You ain gonna let his people know bout this chile, is you? Cause if you does, you won be seein no more a that white boy, mark my word."

"Mama, Aaron's people ain gonna stop him lovin me, or lovin this chile neither."

"We sees. We sees."

For the first time in six months, Amanda felt fear. Clara had succeeded in planting the seed of doubt.

She half ran, half stumbled her way to the hill that afternoon to find reassurance in his arms. But even when he was holding her, suddenly it was not enough. "Aaron, love me today. Love me now." His love would tell her the truth.

Without speaking, he lifted her in his arms and carried her to the base of the tree. Today their love was charged with a frenzy unknown before. Her question, "Will you love me now?" underscored her tumult. His love for her answered the question. Somehow through their bodies, she knew. His love was not to be questioned. Her mother was wrong, dead wrong.

Question answered, they both rested on their backs looking at the sky. But Amanda could not stay peaceful long. She knew she had something to do. She knew it was time. She rolled over on her stomach, propped herself on her elbows and tickled his face with a long-stemmed weed. "I's got somethin to tell you," she said.

"What's that?" he said, rather sleepily.

"I's with chile."

Aaron startled out of his sleepy state. "Did I hear right? Did you say you were with child?"

"I is. An tha's what I said. Sides that I already names her. I names her Delia."

Aaron grabbed Amanda, rolling with her over and over on the grass, laughing and shouting at the same time. "Delia. Delia. We're gonna have a Delia. I'm gonna be a Daddy. I'm so happy, Mandy. I'm so happy. I'm gonna be a Daddy."

As quickly as he had started, he stopped. "Amanda," he said, alarm on his face. "This might hurt you. Are you all right?"

Amanda sat up, brushing grass from her dress. "Course I's all right. Ain gonna hurt. Ain nothin gonna hurt Delia neither. She a special chile. She our chile."

"Our child," said Aaron, sobering, his laughter and his exuberance fading.

Amanda's doubts returned. "Why's you so quiet?"

"I'm thinking, Mandy."

"Wha chu thinkin bout?"

"I'm thinking about our plans. Now we'll have to make plans."

"Plans? "

"Umhmmm. Plans to get married."

"Married? You wants to get married?"

"Of course I want to get married. You're going to have my baby. We've got to be together, more than just on this hill."

"But we cain git married, Aaron. You's white."

"What's that got to do with marrying you?"

"White boys don marry up with colored girls," she said, naming the truth.

"But I want to marry you," he said, naming another truth. "Do you want to marry me?"

"I wants you to be papa to our chile. I wants us to love her together. I wants us to stay lovin each other. If tha's what marryin up be all bout, then I reckon I wants it."

"Then it's settled. We'll be married as soon as we can. I'll tell my father tonight. He'll be furious, of course. He'll rage for a while. Then he'll calm down and wink at me and say 'Well, you just go and have your fun with her and forget about this marrying. Having your baby, is she?' Then he'll slap me on the back and chuckle and say, 'So you've been making it with the colored wenches and not telling me. Just like your old Pa. Chip off the old block, after all.'"

"He ain gonna let us marry, then," she said.

Aaron reached for her hands that were icy cold at the moment. "Mandy, it doesn't matter, whether he'll let me or not. We're going to get married no matter what he thinks. He can fuss and fume all he wants. He can disinherit me. He can tell me what a fine son Hal is. He can say or do anything. When he's all through with his ranting, we'll still be married. We'll find a place down in the flats and we'll be happy. You and I and Delia."

"It don make no difference what he say?"

"It doesn't make one bit of difference what he says, Amanda. Our souls are pledged to travel together for all our lives and for eternity. He can't stop that."

They left each other that day with plans in their heads, lightness in their hearts - heading home - to trouble.

Clara was the first trouble. "You's full a smiles tonight," she snapped when Amanda came through the door.

"I's smilin cause I's happy," countered Amanda.

"I's glad you is," snapped Clara again.

"Aaron'n me, we's gonna be married. We's gonna raise this chile together." Amanda patted her stomach happily.

Clara dropped the spoon she'd been using to stir the soup she was cooking. It clattered to the floor. She stared at Amanda, mouth agape. "You ain marryin that white boy!"

"I is," said Amanda, taken aback by the sharpness of her mother's words.

"No, you ain gonna marry up with that white boy."

"Yes, I is."

"I ain gonna allow it."

"Mama, I's sorry, but I's gonna marry Aaron."

"No you ain. I hates white mens an I ain havin one in this family. I ain gonna have no white boy in this family. No, I ain."

"What difference do it make whether Aaron be white or whether he ain?"

"It jus do. I hates white mens. Your papa, he a white man, an I hates him."

The truth hung in the air like a blackened cloud between them.

Clara clapped her hand over her mouth, fast realizing what she had just said.

Amanda stared at her mother. Moments ticked away. Finally, Amanda found her tongue. "Lewis ain white," she said.

Clara didn't answer. She turned her back on her daughter and faced the sink.

"Mama! I say, Lewis ain white. What you mean, my papa a white man?"

"I's sorry, Mandy. I din mean to tell you."

"Tell me what, Mama?"

Now there was no way Clara could avoid the truth. The truth was out there and could not be retracted. Slowly Clara began to speak. "Lewis . . . he . . . he . . . he ain your papa. Your papa be a white man name a Big Eddie. I's comin home from the Jessups one night, an this Big Eddie, he beats me, then he takes me. You comin from him. He your real papa."

Amanda's feet rooted to the floor. Her mind was in turmoil. "Big Eddie. Big Eddie? I members that name from somewheres. Big Eddie."

"He the man Lewis shoot. It were fer shootin Big Eddie that them mens come an ties him to the hangin tree."

Understanding dawned on Amanda. "Tha's why you always worryin bout how black I is. Tha's why you always checkin my head to see if my hair be nappy nuff. Tha's why Sarah talkin like she do bout Lewis an a gun an how him dyin be my fault. Tha's why you sayin what you sayin bout Aaron."

Clara stood at the sink, tears streaming down her face. "I din mean to tell you. I din mean to tell you." She said it over and over again.

Amanda, seeing her mother's distress, became unrooted. She found her feet. Her steps quickly closed the gap between she and her mother and she was hugging her around the waist. In a moment, Clara was sobbing on her daughter's shoulder. Sobbing out the pain of rape. The pain of Amanda's birth. The pain of Lewis' death. The pain of all the rapes of black women by white men through the centuries. Amanda held her shaking mother, daughter becoming mother for this brief moment in their history together . . . until the sobbing ebbed. "Is all right, Mama. Is all right," she said stroking her mother's hair. "Lewis still be my papa. It don matter none that it be Big Eddie what make me. Lewis still my papa. It be Lewis who hold me an rock me. It be Lewis who teached me. It be Lewis who laugh with me an sing to me. That be Lewis, Mama, not Big Eddie. I's colored jus like you'n Papa. I ain never gonna be white."

"Then you don marry up with that white boy?" Clara sniffed.

Amanda led her mother to a chair by the kitchen table. "Mama, sits yourself down. I wants to tell you how it be with me'n Aaron. It ain like with you an Big Eddie. Aaron'n me, we loves each other. We wants to be together always, jus like you'n Papa. Aaron don care what the white folks say. He wanna be with me an be papa to our chile. He gonna tell his papa tonight; then we's gonna be married. Mama! Is all right! I loves Aaron like you loves Lewis. Is all right. I loves Aaron."

Suddenly Clara's concern about Amanda marrying a white boy was gone. Now she had a new worry. "That boy gonna tell his papa?"

"Aaron gonna tell him tonight."

"Don know bout that. I hears terrible things bout that boy's papa."

"Wha chu hear?"

"His name Spellman, ain it?"

"Yes."

"I hear tell they's a Matthew Spellman what be leader to them mens what run roun in them white sheets . . . the same mens what come'n git Lewis. Be hearin em talk over at Truefels."

"Aaron ain gonna let his papa do nothin, Mama. Ain no need for you to worry."

"I shore hopes you's right."

"You all right with my marryin Aaron now, Mama?"

"I ain crazy bout it, no I ain . . . but if'n you thinks this white boy be makin you happy, I be's all right with it."

Amanda threw her arms around her mother. "Thank you, Mama. We's gonna give you the bestest granchile ever. You sees. We names her Delia."

"How you knows you ain havin a boy chile? Cain be namin no boy chile Delia."

"Ain gonna have no boy chile, Mama."

"Harumph," said Clara, looking askance at her naive daughter.

That night, at Papa Jack's an old song rang out.

"My Papa's gone now. My Mama weeps'n cries.
Oh, Yeah, my papa's gone now an my Mama, she weeps'n cries.

Silently, Amanda dedicated the song to her mother . . . for all the pain and the anguish.

CHAPTER 41

Papa Jack was shouting. "Wha's goin on here? Wha's goin on?"

People sitting at a table near the door tried to get out of the way and dumped the table over. Beer was running all over the the floor. There was the sound of breaking glass as several mugs were broken.

Amanda stopped singing, mid-song.

Screaming women flew in all directions.

Everybody else was on their feet, crowding to see what happened.

"Wha's goin on?" repeated Papa Jack, elbowing his way to the door.

A burly white man in police clothes pushed his way through the door. He had the doorman by the scruff of the neck. Seeing Papa Jack, he threw the doorman roughly against the wall. "You the owner of this joint?"

"Yes, Sir, I's the owner."

The policeman pulled out his gun and levelled it at the crowd.

The extent of the crowd noise increased correspondingly. The women's screams could be heard above the general degree of noise.

"Nobody try to get out of here and there won't be any trouble!" the policeman shouted to the room at large. "And you," he said, turning to Papa Jack, "You tell that bitch to stop screeching."

Papa Jack turned to the crowd, raised his hands and yelled, "Quiet!" He was a big man with a booming voice. It had the desired effect. The noise of the crowd diminished to a low hum.

The policeman leaned into Papa Jack and breathed into his face. He was shouting. "I want Amanda Rochelle Blake. She's been charged with theft. You got her here?"

Amanda heard the bellowed words all the way to her corner.

"Oh, my God," she whispered to her brother. "He wants me!"

"Quick, out the back door," he said.

"Cain do that, Curtis. They already sees me an they's comin this way. What does I do?"

"Jus ac like nothin be wrong," advised Curtis. "Jus don let em see you scairt."

"Jus don let em see me scairt," Amanda repeated.

"Yeah. Jus don let em see you scairt."

Suddenly they were upon her. She had to do something. She stepped forward. "I's Amanda Rochelle Blake," she said. "Does you want me?"

The policeman seized her roughly by the arm. "Don't ask no questions, nigger bitch. Just come along with me. Come easy now and there won't be no trouble."

Amanda looked composed and unafraid, a pose belied by the look in her eyes. They pleaded with Papa Jack, then with Curtis. They said, "Do something. Do something."

Both shrugged, feeling helpless.

The policeman had what he wanted. He yanked Amanda toward the door, pulling roughly on her arm. Curtis stared back at a pair of frightened eyes taking one last look over her shoulder as she was dragged out the door.

Mayhem erupted in Papa Jack's. Everybody talked at once. People surrounded Papa Jack, asking, demanding to know: Where was the policeman taking their Mandy?

Papa Jack wiped his brow. White policemen were known to close down places like his for no reason. He wiped his brow again. "Don know," he said feeling decidedly relieved that he still had a place of business. "Man say Mandy wanted for theft. Tha's all he say. Don know nothin more. Quiet now."

He turned to Curtis. "Curtis, play and shuts these niggers up."

Outside there was a second policeman. Together they hauled Amanda toward a waiting carriage. One held her in a vice-like grip while the other opened the door. Together they threw her onto the floor inside. Almost stepping on her they climbed inside and sat down hard onto the leather seat. One shouted at the driver. "Move," he said.

Amanda could see nothing but two pairs of booted feet immediately in front of her eyes. She dared not move for fear that one of the feet would mangle her face. She hardly dared breath for fear of the policeman's wrath. She lay on the dirty floor, not moving, being jounced over rough roads . . . until the carriage reached its destination. When the carriage stopped, she was pulled out of the door with one yank. She lost her footing and fell to the ground. Standing over her, one of the policeman was shouting, "Get up, you nigger bitch!"

Amanda staggered to her feet. She was barely up when one pair of rough hands half-pushed, half-dragged her inside what must have been the police station. Inside, she was immediately blinded by the bright lights. When her vision cleared, she saw a third policeman, ruddy in complexion with red hair and a beard, sitting behind a wide brown desk. Another man stood in the center of the room. Seeing him sent shock waves through her. He was an older version of Aaron. The same broad shoulders and slim waist, the same blue eyes. But in the eyes he deviated from Aaron. These eyes were icy and cruel and glared at her from beneath a scowling brow. His mouth turned down as vindictive words rolled off his tongue. This man was Matthew Spellman.

The policemen shoved her to the center of the room while Mathew Spellman approached, menacing. He stood assessing her from head to foot, his eyes cruel in their intent. Without warning, his hand crashed across her face, spinning her head to the side. A second hand spun it back. Blood spurted from her mouth. Tears welled into her eyes.

"Thief!" he growled, prowling in front of her. "Thief! Thought you could get away with it, didn't you? Thought you could steal the family earrings and get away with it. All right now, I'll just take them. Hand them over."

Amanda hesitated.

The hand cracked again, against her face.

Stunned, she tried to clear her head, shaking it quickly.

Crack! The hand again sent her head spinning.

Her shaking hands removed the earrings. Feeling them hot in her hand, she droppped them in his open hand.

Now in possession of the earrings, Mathew Spellman leaned into her face and sneered. "Thought you could marry my son, did you? Now you ought to know better. No nigger bitch is gonna marry my son."

Again, the sting of his hand on her face. Now blood dripped on the floor.

Amanda was beginning to lose her vision.

"So what do you say to me now, nigger bitch?"

"I's sorry."

His hand again whipped across her face. "I'm sorry, **sir**, for stealing your earrings," he prompted.

"I's sorry, sir, for having your earrings."

Again the stinging hand. "That's not what you say, nigger bitch. Say it right."

"I's sorry, sir, for stealing your earrings."

"That's right. Now you got it right. You've got some brains after all." Matthew Spellman turned away. "Harry . . . Red . . . take care of her." He abruptly turned and walked out of the room, slamming the door behind him.

The two policemen were immediately at her side, dragging her toward a back room.

Red uncoiled a black snake whip from a nail on the wall. He dangled it in front of her face. "Lookee what we got here," he said.

Harry ripped off her dress, sending a shiver of cold through her body. Harry leered at her naked body.

Amanda shrunk away, her eyes wide with terror.

"This is for niggers who don't know their place," Red said, dangling it in front of her.

The first sting across her legs was unbearable. She screamed and bent to protect herself.

Another searing sting fell across her back. Another scream. She fell to the floor, instinctively covering her belly, protecting Delia.

The room filled with screams as the whip came down, again and again. "This is what you get, nigger, for gettin out of your place, for stealing white men's valuables, for cavorting with white boys." The pain burned through her. Blood ran down her back.

"Thinking you were gonna marry one, did you? There won't be a white boy in the world who'll have you when we finish with you."

Each lash of the whip sent her closer and closer to oblivion. Pools of blood were forming on the floor. Every part of her body was burning. One last flame of pain seared through her and she fell into sweet unconsciousness.

"She's out," said Harry, who had been watching the beating.

"Might as well get her into the cell. I'll save the whip for when she comes to again."

"Right."

Now she lay on the cell floor, blood seeping from her body: her back, her buttocks, her legs and trickling from her face. The cold dampness of the floor creeped into her body. Convulsions overtook her.

Blackness consumed her.

She knew only vaguely of the policeman standing in the cell door. "You still out, nigger bitch?" The beady eyes of a rat peering into her from a corner while she stifled a scream; the shivering cold; the burning pain; the fear of more beatings.

And visions. Two women. The faces of two women, one with long black hair and huge eyes, light skin; the other . . . black like herself, short-cropped nappy hair, robust.

"I'm Duanna," said one.

"I'm Sabia," said the other.

"We are the same," they said in chorus.

"You daid?" asked Amanda.

"We're dead," they said.

"I's gonna die, too," said Amanda.

"You're not going to die," said Duanna.

"You're going to live to have your child, a child I wasn't allowed," said Sabia.

"And to wear the earrings in love for Aaron," they said in chorus.

"I ain got the earrings."

"Be strong, Amanda," they said in chorus. "And walk the way of the powerful. Do not let those who pretend to be strong take your power from you."

"How's I gonna be strong, when I's mos daid in this jail cell?"

But there was no answer, for they were gone.

Another vision: strong arms picking her up, carrying her out of the cell; angry voices, "Nigger bitch! Don't know her place;" her body moving, rocking; the sound of horses; wounds being washed; gentle faces hovering over her; white sheets; a soft bed; an easing of the pain; words - "Will she live?" "I think so, Mr. Spellman. She's got a strong body."

Her eyes flew open. Aaron's gentle face was above her. He smiled and touched her hand. She went back to sleep.

Again her eyes opened. This was no vision.

"Aaron!" she said, struggling.

"Shhh, Amanda. Everything is all right."

"Delia?"

"Delia's fine. She's a scrapper. She's fine."

Amanda relaxed. Then more agitation. "The earrings. Aaron, the earrings! He took the earrings!"

"They're back in your ears."

Amanda's hands flew up to the reassurance of the metal and the teardrop shape. She went back to sleep.

The next time she woke there was a cloth cooling her forehead. Aaron was smoothing out the cloth.

"Aaron?"

"Yes, Mandy?"

"Where is I?"

"You're in the Saint Thomas Infirmary."

"Who them ladies lookin so funny in them long white dresses, an all that stuff roun their faces?"

"Those are the sisters of the Saint Thomas Catholic Church. They're nurses. They've been taking care of you."

"How long I been here?"

"About a week."

"A week!" She struggled to sit up. "I's got to git home. I's got to git down to Papa Jack's."

Aaron gently pushed her back onto the pillows. "Lay back down, Mandy. You don't know how sick you've been. You can't go home quite yet."

"I ain goin nowhere," she agreed, as sweat beaded on her forehead from her effort to sit up.

"Lay down. Go back to sleep now."

"You gonna be here when I wakes up?"

"Yes, I'll be here when you wake up."

Amanda slept. White clad bodies came and went. Faces hovered over her: Clara's face with Curtis behind; Earlie Mae's face and the baby; Papa Jack's face; Aaron's face. Words penetrated through the fog. "Get well, we miss you." "Your job is waitin." "Everythin's all right now; jus res."

Aaron never left her side. Nights he slept on a cot near her bed. Days he sat in the chair, keeping cool compresses on her head, seeing that she ate, holding her glass for her to drink, reassuring her of his love.

Little by little, she was able to sit up; she started walking; a smile returned to her face; she laughed again.

One day Aaron brought up what they had been avoiding - her night of horror. "Mandy, my father . . . my father . . . he . . . " His voice broke and he could not talk.

Amanda covered his hand. "Is all right, Aaron. Is all right. You don needs to tell me."

Aaron looked at the floor. "It's not all right, Mandy. My father . . . . He . . . he tricked me . . . I need to tell you. He didn't do any of the things I thought he would do."

"What he do?"

"He acted understanding, Mandy. He was actually understanding. I told him about you, and that we were going to get married. He absolutely amazed me, Mandy. He didn't get mad or anything. He listened and he asked a lot of questions.

When did we plan on getting married? Where did I think we would live? How was I planning on supporting a wife? What were you like? I told him everything."

"Then he said, 'Well, I didn't expect you to get married so young and I didn't expect you to marry a colored girl, but I guess if you love her, everything will be all right.'"

"I couldn't believe it, Mandy. He wasn't doing any of the things I expected him to do. I expected him to be furious and to try to stop me and here he was telling me it was okay. So I relaxed, and I told him about the earrings. I told him the whole story. About Iola, and Iola's grandmother and the slave Tacuma. He just nodded and listened. I even told him that we pledged our love for eternity. I thought I could trust him. He was being so understanding."

"Then all hell broke loose. He got up from his chair. He started to pace back and forth. His face got red and puffy. He was breathing hard. For a few minutes I was afraid he was going to have a heart attack. Then he looked at me and his eyes got all black. Black, Amanda, black. He pulled me from my chair and he shook me. Then he hit me in the mouth. He got his face right up into mine and he said, 'No son of mine is going to marry any nigger bitch. I didn't think you had much sense, but I thought you had more sense than that. I'm going see to it that you don't marry her, and furthermore, I'm going to see to it that she doesn't marry anyone'."

"Then he started to yell. 'Rubin. Rubin! Rubin, get your nigger ass in here! Now!' Rubin must have been just outside the door, listening because he was right there. The next thing I knew my father was bellowing at Rubin. 'Keep this idiot boy of mine right here until I can take care of that nigger bitch. Don't let him out of your sight. Don't go to sleep. Don't even close an eye. Do you hear me?'"

"'Yes, Suh, Mistah Spellman, Suh.'"

"My father stormed out of the room and closed and locked the door. Mandy, he actually locked the door. I looked at Rubin, and he looked at me. I was ready to knock old Rubin unconscious if it meant I could get out."

"He was way ahead of me. He said 'Don you be thinkin bout gittin out that window, there, Mr. Aaron, Suh, or I would needs to knock you out. I won be pleased to do that, Mr. Aaron, Suh, but I gots to do what your papa say.'"

"Rubin is a big man, Mandy. He meant it. And I don't know the first thing about fighting. So we sat there staring at each other. I paced the floor. I sat in the chair. I paced again. I sat and stared at Rubin. My father had outsmarted me. I was terrified for you. I couldn't do anything." Aaron was squeezing her hand so tightly that it hurt. He looked into her eyes, pleading for forgiveness.

She retrieved her hand and rubbed it.

He went on. "In the morning, somebody unlocked the door and Rubin let me out. I couldn't find my father anywhere. I was frantic. I ran to your house. Curtis told me what had happened at Papa Jack's. Then I went to the police station. They laughed in my face when I told them I wanted you released. I saw you there, Mandy." His voice broke again. "I saw you lying there on the floor. Your beautiful body that I have loved so much, they . . . they . . . they had . . . Oh, God . . . Mandy, you didn't have any clothes on, and I saw the blood on your back. Oh, Mandy. I cried. I cried right there in the police station. One of the policemen saw me and I'll never forget his words. He said 'Harry, would you look at this. This boy's cryin over that nigger bitch in there. Would you look at this. This boy's cryin'.''

"I ran out of there. I had never run so fast in my life. I started to run toward my father's office. By now I knew the truth. The truth was that they were going to kill you unless I did something. I decided what I was going to do. I decided I needed to lie, to steal, to tell him anything to save you. I was ready when I walked into his office. He said, 'Well, boy, have you come to your senses?'"

"That's when I started to lie, Mandy. I sat down just as relaxed as could be and I said to him, 'Yes, I've had plenty of time to think about it.' Then I told him I'd been to the police station and I saw you lying in a cell. Oh, Mandy, I can hardly forgive myself for this lie." His voice was choking again. "I told him, I said . . . I said . . . 'I saw her lying there naked, and the sight of her black skin made me sick.' Then I said, 'I know now that you're right, Sir, I don't love her. What I want to do is get as far away from her as possible.' I'm so sorry for that, Mandy. I'm sorry for that. I'm so ashamed to tell you."

"Tha's a lie be all right with me, Aaron. Onliest lie ain all right was when I thinks you lyin to me bout them earrings. Your papa, he say they belong to the family. I's scairt then, thinkin you's lyin to me."

"Do you know the truth now?"

"I knows the truth now."

Aaron picked up her hand from the bed and squeezed it, more gently this time.

"What your papa do then?"

"Well, he leaned back in his chair and lit a cigar and puffed on it for a while. He looked happy as a Tom cat who'd just finished off three pussys. 'Thought you'd see it my way, boy. Thought you would.' Then he reached in his pocket and held up the earrings. 'We can give these back to Iola now, can't we, son. I'll do that myself. Yes, sir, I'll do that myself tonight.'"

"I said, 'Yes, Sir.' Then I took a deep breath. This **had** to work to get you out of jail. I said, 'Sir, you've been wanting me to go to that school in Boston.'"

"My father looked at me intently. 'Yes,' he said."

"'Well, Dad,' I said. 'Now that I'm through with Mandy, I'm ready to go.' Mandy, my father looked proud as a peacock. He said, 'Now you're talking, boy. Get an education.'

"I nodded. Then I said, 'Since I'm going to be gone, Sir, there isn't any reason for that girl to die, just because she made the mistake of being with me, especially now that I see how it really is.'"

"He started to puff on his cigar, blowing smoke all over the room. I was afraid I'd said too much, but I had to get you out of that jail. So I said . . . I said, 'Well.' Then I winked at him and said, 'She's a good lay, Sir. If we take her to a hospital and get her well, maybe you could use her yourself, once I'm gone.' Then I started to cough. I coughed and I coughed. I coughed so hard I was afraid I was going to vomit. Dad gave me his handkerchief. I told him that it was the smoke that was making me cough."

"Then he leaned back again and puffed away on his cigar. He was real quiet for a long time. I was pretty scared then. When he started to talk again he said, 'Well, son, she was a pretty thing, for a nigger bitch. You've got good taste, son. Yes, good taste. Guess you just made the mistake of thinking you wanted to marry some wild young thing. Even did it myself once. Mistakes of youth. Yes, boy. The mistakes of youth. Maybe I could use her myself some day.' Then he went back to puffing on his cigar."

"I was pretty sure I had him then, so I said, 'Why don't we go over to the police station and get her out. I'll take her to Saint Thomas Infirmary. They'll take care of her even if she is a nigger.'"

"Then he looked hard at me and scowled. I really got scared then. I thought I'd pushed too hard. He puffed a few more times on his cigar. Then he said,'No rush about that, boy. Let her stay there a few more hours, learn her lesson. We can do it tonight, or maybe tomorrow.'"

"That was what I wanted, his agreement to get you out. I was worried about your staying any longer than necessary, but I knew I couldn't push him any faster than he would move. So then I winked at him and said, 'Now that I'm not going to be using Mandy any more, have you got any other nigger bitches I could use?' Then he said, 'Now that you've come to your senses, boy, we'll go together. How about that, son?' Then he got up from his chair, came over and slapped me on the back. 'Here, have a cigar,' he said and pushed one into my shirt pocket. 'Now you go home. I've got work to do.'"

Aaron took both her hands in his. "Mandy, I'm so ashamed of what I said to my father but I would have said anything to get you out of that jail, anything that would work. You see - the two women I love most were laying on that floor in that jail."

"Two?"

"You and Delia."

Amanda actually laughed.

But a serious thought followed. "Aaron, do all this mean we ain gittin married?"

"Yes, we're getting married. I intend to be Delia's father and your man for the rest of our lives."

"But your papa . . . ?"

"My papa isn't going to know. I've figured out a way to get around him. What I've going to do is, I'm going to have to go away to school, just like I promised. I'll stay just long enough to convince him I'm there, maybe a couple of months. Then I'll come back and get you, and we'll be married."

With those words, Amanda was able to get well and go home to the love of her family.

Aaron left for Boston in September, as he had agreed. Their love, on the night that he left, was intense: tender and gentle and full of longing . . . intermingled with their tears.

"I'll be back before Christmas," he said. "Take care of Delia until then."

CHAPTER 42

"**Here** she be, folks. Back with us again. Jus back from her trip to Natchez' beloved police station. Cheer her on, folks. Miz Mandy Blake." Papa Jack's infectious introduction had the whole room on its feet, cheering, stomping, whistling, calling her name.

"Miz Amanda, how you be?"

"How the police treatin us niggers these days?"

"You gonna sing fer us tonight, Mandy?"

"Who that peekin out from your belly?"

"Come'n sits here when you finishes, Miz Amanda."

"I shore is glad you's back."

Nothing had changed. She raised her hands for silence. "Ready, Curtis?" she said.

"Sad, so sad, so sad. I's missin my baby so bad.
Sad, so sad, so sad. Oh, you better know it, I's missin my baby so bad."

"I'll cheer ya up, Mandy, baby."

"Missin all that lovin; an the good times we had.
Sad, so sad, so sad, I's missin my baby so bad."

"Come sits on my knee, Mandy, an I makes it better for ya."

"I say I's sad, so sad, so sad. I's missin my baby so bad."

"Don let him do ya that way, Mandy."

"He lef me in the autumn. An I's tellin ya, when he comin home, I's glad.
But for now, I's sad, so sad, so sad. Yes, I's sad, so sad, too bad."

"I gives ya my hanky if'n ya wants it."

No doubt . . . she was back at work. Back where the smoke swirled around her head, where the bottles clinked in her ears, and now there was Delia kicking in her stomach. She was the same Mandy . . . yet she was not the same Mandy. Pain was on her face, in her expressions, in her eyes, in the scars left by the whip and in the memory of Matthew Spellman's brutality to her body. Her voice, always throaty and deep, was deeper.

Every week a letter came. "Boston is cold," he said. "I have to keep my shirt on all the time." Another letter. "I'm studying hard. I want Papa to get good reports." Another letter. "I've met a friend. He's from New Orleans. His name is Eric." And in all the letters. "I love you. I miss you terribly, but it won't be long now. I'll be home by Christmas. Be sure to take care of Delia for me."

Sarah was acting strangly. She was fighting with everybody. She stumbled a lot, and sometimes fell. She forgot things. She dropped things. Her eyes looked glazed. Clara said, "You's got the sickness."

"I ain got no sickness."

"You shore does. You got the sickness all right. Is what you gits for takin all them mens."

"Ain so. Reason I ain feelin so good is causa this chile in my belly."

"Who that chile's papa?" Clara wanted to know.

"Don know."

"Don know. Don know," repeated Clara. "You got the sickness and that chile's got no papa." Clara shook her head.

"Ain got no sickness."

And so it went.

Just before Thanksgiving, a stranger knocked on their door. When Earlie Mae answered, there stood a young white boy about the age of Curtis. "Hi," said the white face. "I'm looking for Amanda Blake. I go to school in Boston with a friend of hers named Aaron Spellman. My name is Eric."

Amanda heard and ran to the door.

They sat on the front porch for two hours while Eric talked of Aaron. "All he talks about is you," Eric said. "I just had to meet you."

Amanda glowed.

Before Eric took the train to New Orleans, Amanda was devouring the letter from Aaron that Eric had carried to her in his pocket.

Curtis came home with news. "We's to play on the riverboa 'Saint Louis' on Saturday. You wants ta do it?"

"I reckon Saint Louis be good as any other place." Amanda was uninterested in anything except the fact that Christmas was coming.

The letter finally arrived.

My Darling Amanda,

Our waiting is almost over. I finish my examinations on Wednesday. I'll board the train Wednesday night and be in Natchez Saturday morning. Meet me at the train station at 10:30 in your best dress and hat. We'll find a minister and get married. My love for you grows stronger every day we're apart. I want to feel you in my arms again, my Mandy.

Until Saturday,

Aaron

"Oh, Mama. I don got no hat," Amanda moaned.

"Don need no hat to get married," Clara said.

"I ain even got no bes dress."

"We makes you one. Got to have a bes dress for marryin up with."

"Oh, Mama."

"Don you cry now. Cain stan for you to cry when you's happy. What kin' a dress you wantin?"

Curtis took her to the station way before 10:30 on that Saturday morning. She was proudly wearing her new dress. It was white cotton patterned with bright yellow flowers. She was even wearing a hat she had managed to borrow from Sarah. The weather was cold and it was misting. They got out of the way of the rain by sitting on a bench just outside the waiting room. Amanda wasn't sure she could wait one more minute for the train to arrive.

They amused themselves by watching the few people bustling about on the platform. Amanda became intrigued by the colored boy in the red cap, pushing a cart from place to place. The cart was variously loaded with luggage, packages and newspapers. "Wonder if one a them suitcases be Aaron's," she wanted to know.

"Naw, he still have it on the train," said the ever-practical Curtis.

As they waited, more and more people climbed the platform and milled around. Christmas anticipation was in the air. A few people even smiled and spoke to the pair on the bench. To Amanda, now big with child, and Curtis, obviously the proud father.

Ten-thirty came . . . and went . . . and there was no train. The crowd was beginning to grumble. A few people walked down the track to see if they could see the engine coming down the tracks. Others were craning their necks, looking eastward. "Wha's wrong with the train?" Amanda wanted to know.

"Don know," said Curtis.

A white woman wanted their seats. Curtis helped Amanda up and they joined the crowd, watching . . . anticipating. Still, there was no train. All they could see was the smoke from the cotton mill just east of the city. The smoke was billowing and belching; the cotton mill working fast and furiously . . . much more furiously than usual.

The belching of the smoke interfered with the people's vision . . . their vigil of waiting for the train. There was no way to see what was coming down the track as long as the smoke was billowing as it was.

The longer the watch, the more the crowd grumbled. There was a growing realization among them. Something was wrong.

There was more milling . . . more grumbling.

One of the men in the crowd finally spoke up, speaking the unspeakable. "That's not the cotton mill smoking. That's something else."

Now the crowd became visibly agitated. "Let's go see what it is," said one of the men. Several of them gathered together and started up the track . . . going to investigate the cause of the smoke.

As the rest of the crowd craned their necks and watched the movement of the more courageous men, there was a commotion on the edge of the platform. "Let me through folks. Let me through," yelled an official looking man elbowing his way through the mass of people and moving toward the ticket office.

Now the crowd had a target for their frustrations. "Hey, you know why that damn train is so late?" someone yelled.

"Yeah, we've been here over an hour now."

"We're tired of waiting."

"Why can't you train people ever tell us the truth? If the train is going to be late like this why can't you tell us instead of making us wait like this out in the rain?"

"Can't trust you train people."

The official ignored everybody. He simply looked at them with displeasure and hurried inside. Amanda could see him through the office window talking with the station master; talking, waving his arms, shaking his head.

The station master looked decidedly worried. He turned to some contraption he had on his desk and tapped on some buttons. Amanda heard some sort of strange tapping coming back. After the tapping the station master looked more worried than before.

"Curtis, what be the matter? Them white folk lookin' mighty worried. Sump'n wrong with the train?"

"Don know, Mandy. Don know nothin more than you does."

As they spoke the station master was slowly making his way to the platform. His manner was clear. He did not want to be there. When he spoke he spoke haltingly and with a voice that Mandy could barely hear. "Might as well go home, folks. There won't be any train by here today. The train you folks are waiting for jumped the tracks about three miles back. Won't be no more trains by here today until they clear the wreckage."

The crowd was immediately agitated. Some of the people murmered among themselves. Others started to shout.

"What's happened to the people on the train?" . . . "My wife's on that train. Is she hurt?" . . . "My son, where's my son. What have you done to my son?" . . . "My whole family's coming for Christmas. What's happened to them?" . . .

The station master was maddeningly slow in his answer. "Tell us what happened," people shouted.

One man went up to the station master and grabbed him by the collar. "You tell us what happened."

"Don't know about what you're asking. All I know is a few cars overturned and a few are burning. There probably are some people hurt, maybe some dead. Don't know about that."

With his words mayhem erupted. A woman screamed. "My baby's on that train." Others babbled incoherently. Men, helping hysterical women, headed for their carriages.

"Curtis, we's got to git up there," Amanda said. "Gots to see if Aaron be hurt."

"Le's go," he said. Curtis grabbed Amanda's hand and they started to run, following the tracks and the sight and smell of the smoke. Big with Delia, running was almost imposible for her . . . but run she did. More than once she stumbled and fell. Curtis caught her, bringing her upright. Her hat was lost in the rush. Her dress caught on the weeds and tore. Her legs were scratched from the brambles. Three miles they ran, rain hitting them in the face.

The sights and sounds that greeted their arrival were worse than Amanda's wildest fears. Two cars were in flames, five more were overturned. Smoke billowed from the boiler of the engine. There were people lying all over the ground, some moaning in pain, some beyond pain. A few people were walking around in a daze. Officials were trying to care for the wounded and get them to the hospital. Many of the carriages coming from the train station were pressed into service.

Amanda stumbled through the crowd, searching for Aaron. The smoke from the fire caught in her lungs; people laying on the ground caught her dress, asking for help; tears mingled with the rain on her face.

"There he is," she yelled. She saw him . . . Aaron . . . lying on the ground flanked by two men who were trying to lift him onto a make-shift litter.

"Aaron," she screamed.

He turned at the sound, unrecognizing. The two men were just lifting the litter as she dashed headlong into one of them.

When he saw her he smiled a weak smile and spoke with difficulty. "It looks like we're gonna have to wait a few more days to get married, Mandy. At least until the doctor takes care of this chest of mine. I . . . I love you." His voice trailed off as he lost consciousness.

"Aaron!" she screamed.

"You've got to get out of the way now, miss," said one of the litter bearers. "We want to get him to the hospital as fast as possible."

Amanda watched as the litter jostled toward a waiting carriage.

"Curtis, we's got to get to that hospital."

"Ain no sense in us goin to that hospital, Mandy. Tha's a white man's hospital. They ain gonna let us in."

"They's got to let us in," Amanda screamed at him.

"They ain gonna, but we goes anyway."

Their walk back was slower, but no less difficult. The rain was coming down harder now, pelting their bodies with huge drops of water. Amanda was shivering uncontrollably by the time they reached the city limits. Curtis wrapped her in his jacket.

At the hospital, Curtis's words proved prophetic. A large nurse was sitting at the front desk when they came in the front door. They were busy shaking rain off their bodies and didn't see her immediately. Her words, however, were immediate. "No niggers allowed in here. Out!"

For three days Amanda waited outside the hospital, entreating each visitor to bring her news of Aaron. Some were helpful. Some refused. Some acknowledged her entreaties with stony silence. Curtis brought her food, warm dry clothes, and kept her company when he could. She didn't care about the food, barely niblling on what Curtis had so carefully packaged and brought to her. Curtis had to insist that she discard her tattered wedding dress and get into something whole and dry. She cried when he threw the dress into the waste. She was alone when the Matthew Spellmans arrived in their carriage, Mrs. Spellman holding a handkerchief to her puffy red eyes. She was quick enough to hide behind the corner of the hospital as they walked toward the door.

The news of Aaron seemed to follow the weather. It was not good. One helpful man told her, "He's hanging onto life by a thread. The doctors don't think he'll make it." The rain pelted down. The next day, a woman said, "He's breathing a little easier and there is hope." The sun peaked through the clouds. On the third day, Amanda saw the Spellmans walk out of the hospital. His mother was crying without shame. The rain came down in sheets.

Amanda ran through the streets, blinded by the rain. She was running, stumbling, falling, getting up to run again, her lungs bursting for air. Still she refused to stop. She ran to the hill, their hill, flinging herself onto the ground at the base of their tree, face to the earth, sobbing, pounding the earth with her fists. Her screams pierced the sky. The rain pounded down.

That was where Curtis found her two hours later. He put his hand on her shoulder. "Come on home, Mandy, fore you kills yourself from freezin."

"Ain goin home. I's stayin here till Aaron come."

"Aaron ain comin, Mandy. Aaron dead."

"He comin," she screamed. "Ain goin home now. He be here any minute."

Curtis pulled her to a sitting position. He put his arms around her shoulder. "Mandy," he said. "You's got to come home now. Let me take you home."

"Ain comin home. Gots to wait for Aaron. He be here. He say he be here, an he be here".

"Mandy," said Curtis, not knowing quite what to do with this. "Aaron be dead. He die at that hospital. He dead. You got to come home fore you dies too, from the rain. Come home now."

"I's got to go home," she said, her eyes glazing over. "Aaron ain comin today?"

"No, Mandy, Aaron ain comin today."

Like a bewildered child she let Curtis help her to her feet.

He took her hand and slowly led her down the hill toward home. She said nothing . . . knew nothing . . . letting her numbness take the pain where it needed to be. He led . . . she followed . . . like a child following its mother.

Once home, she slid down into a spot in the corner of the kitchen, curled into a ball, stuck her fist into her eyes, and stayed. Curtis talked to her. Clara talked to her. Earlie Mae talked to her. She heard nothing. She responded to nothing. She lay immobile. All the family heard were repeated mumblings "Aaron ain comin today. Aaron ain comin today."

Curtis did some fast investigating. He wasn't sure what would bring Amanda out of that devil space she was in, but there was only one way he knew to try. He found out where the funeral would be. Armed with that information he approached Amanda's corner. "Mandy, they's puttin Aaron in the groun day after Christmas, bout 1 o'clock. I takes you if'n you wantin ta go."

Her nod was the first sign of recognition, her first response to anything since she had dropped into that corner.

There was no Christmas for Amanda that year. The celebration took place around her as she refused to move from her corner. Her mumblings about Aaron had stopped. Now, emanating from the corner, was stony silence . . . more frightening than her mutterings.

The day after Christmas, she and Curtis climbed the hill above the cemetery where Aaron was to be buried. As they arrived, carriages were winding slowly down the road past where they were standing. Finally the parade came to a stop and people got out. They watched as the casket was unloaded by six men and placed over the grave. There were about fifteen people who surrounded the casket. They heard sounds as the minister intoned the final internment. Aaron's mother was crying. The men were stoic.

Amanda was as stoic as the men. Not a tear fell from her eyes. She stood, without moving . . . seeing . . . not seeing.

When it was over all the people left, a few dropped flowers on the casket.

Amanda waited until they were all gone. For the first time since leaving home she spoke. "Takes me down to the grave," she said.

Curtis nodded. He took her by the hand and, slowly, they wended their way down the hill.

Once over the casket her feelings, those feelings that had been hidden behind her craziness, came loose. She began to cry. Silently, her waiting tears flowed from her eyes. Unabashed, they streamed down her face. She stood, saying nothing, while her tears dampened her dress. The wind, cold on this day, whipped her dress around her legs. Still there were no words. Curtis sat back, waiting. He knew he must give her all the time she needed to grieve. He knew she needed to do, now, what she had never done for Lewis. Cry . . . until she was finished.

It was a long time before words came. When they did they were clear and without tears. "Aaron, our souls be together always, jus like we say." That was all. Just those simple words. Then she stood quietly, reverently. Finally she picked one of the flowers from a wreath lying at the center of the casket. She tenderly put it over the place of Aaron's head. Only then did she turn away. "I's ready to go now, Curtis. Walk with me to the hill."

Standing under the tree, the tree that had witnessed their everything, she looked out at the river. Now, along with the cold wind, the rain had started again and it mixed with her tears. As though unaware of the elements, she stood, unmoving, for almost an hour. Something was happening. Something important. Curtis didn't know what it was, but he could feel the importance of it. He didn't mind waiting. He didn't mind the cold or the rain. What he wanted was his Amanda back again. His Amanda. Healthy . . . happy . . . singing.

When she turned to go, her tears had stopped. She took Curtis' hand and said, "I's ready to go now. I's ready." Together they walked home, silently, Curtis knowing that no words were needed.

And it was years before she ever went back.

CHAPTER 43

"**Your** baby comin now, Manda. Jus you push one more time. Jus one more time." Speaking was 'Ole Miz Harmon,' biggest woman living in the flats, known for birthing all the babies in the area.

A moan tore through Amanda's throat as her insides convulsed for one last time. Delia Blake Spellman filled the room with her lusty cry, letting the world know she had arrived.

Miz Harmon deftly clipped the cord, handed the baby to Clara for cleaning, then took care of the rest of the details. Clara wrapped the whimpering Delia in a blanket and brought her to Amanda. "She look like Aaron, don she, Mama," Amanda said, bursting with pride.

"She shore do, she ain even got kinky hair."

"She do so," said Amanda. "Lookee." Amanda held a strand of Delia's hair in her hand. There was a whisper of a curl.

"An she got blue eyes," said Miz Harmon.

That was too much for Clara. "Ain no granchile a mine gonna have blue eyes. They turns brown by tomorrow. Ain gonna have no blue eyes in this family."

Amanda laughed. "They be blue if'n they wants, Mama. Ain nothin you c'n do bout it," she said.

Amanda looked down with all the pride of a new mother, at the bundle in her arms. Delia's mouth was working hard. "What she doin now, Miz Harmon?" Amanda asked.

"She jus lookin for somethin to suck. Put her to your breas, chile. Put her to your breas. Ain no milk yet, but she brings it with the suckin," said Miz Harmon, picking up towels, putting them into a pail to soak.

A few minutes later they were both asleep, Delia still at Amanda's breast.

Three months later Amanda was back singing at Papa Jack's.

"Mandy, what happened to that belly a your'n?"

"Hush up, Willis. I's got the cutest little baby you ever did see out a that belly."

"Mandy, you's so pretty, a man c'd jus feast his eyes on you. Ain she pretty, Curtis?"

"Feast all you wants, Jimmy. Feast all you wants."

"Buy you a beer, Mandy, if'n you sings 'Back-O-Town Blues'."

"Don wan no beer, Otis, but I sings it for ya."

"Glad ta see ya, Mandy. Sorry to hear bout your man."

"Tell me, tell me. Tell me how long that train been gone."

"Too long, Mandy."

"Tell me, tell me. Tell me how long that train been gone."

"Yeah, way too long."

"That train done took my baby, he's been gone jus way too long."

"We's sorry bout that."

"So long, baby. I knows you ain never comin back.
Bye, bye, baby. I knows you ain never comin back."

"Naw . . . .Cain come back."

"I knows you gone forever, cause that train done jump it's track."

"Whachu gonna do now, Mandy?"

"Your baby weeps'n cries now, cause you been gone so long."

Your baby weeps'n cries now, cause you been gone so long.
That train be gone forever, I knows you ain never comin home."

"I be comin home if'n I was your man."

"Come back baby, your Mama weepin an a cryin."

"I's cryin, too, Mandy."

"Come back, baby. Your Mama, she weepin an a cryin.
If you comin back, my baby, is in my bed I be lyin."

"If'n I be your man, I be right there, Mandy baby."

"Sam waitin for you when you takes a break," said Papa Jack, bringing them a tall glass of water.

"Thanks," said Curtis. "Tell Sam we talks to him shortly."

"I's got the back-o-town blues, baby, cause you don pay me no min.
Yeah, yeah, yeah, I's got the back-o-town blues, baby, cause you don pay me no min.
You got your milk man an your doctor, an you be doin jus fine."

"Tha's it, Mandy. Who else she got?"

Sam stood as they approached the table. He shook hands with Curtis and put his arm around Amanda's shoulder. "I hear things have been pretty hard for you lately, Amanda. I'm sorry."

"I's all right, Sam. I's got my baby now an ain no bein sad when she roun."

"I'm glad to hear it. Sit down, sit down, both of you. I've got some good news."

"Could use some good news bout now, Sam," said Curtis.

"Whachu got?" said Amanda.

"I've got a good job for you. It's steady and the pay is good."

Curtis sat up straighter. "Whatsa job, Sam?"

"The 'Mississippi Queen' riverboat is looking for a pair of entertainers to make the New Orleans to Saint Louis run. I thought about you two right away, seeing as how you were such a hit when you played the 'Natchez'. It doesn't start until June so you'd have time to wind things up here."

"How much does it pay?" asked the ever-practical Curtis.

"It starts at twenty-five dollars a week and goes up if they like you."

"How long do we be gone, Sam? I's got my baby now an cain be gone too long."

"A normal run last about two weeks, Mandy. From here to New Orleans, then back up to Saint Louis, and back here. About two weeks."

"Two weeks a long time to be gone, Sam. My baby be needin me in two weeks."

"Twenty-five dollars a week would buy her a lot of what she needs, Mandy, and you don't need to start until June. That's three months away. She'll be almost grown up by then."

"Yeah."

"I tells ya, Sam. We thinks bout it," said Curtis. "You comes back tomorrow, an we knows."

"Think hard on it. This could be a really big chance for you two to start making it big. A lot of new folks would hear you. Think really hard about doing it."

"Right, Sam."

"Everybody up now an do the Slow Drag. Everybody! Up on your feet." Amanda sat on her stool, while Curtis' guitar wailed throughout the room. It was the only way she could get the customers to leave her alone. "Don min the teasin, but I's got to think now. Two weeks away from Delia! Two weeks! Don know bout that. But we be makin twenty-five dollars. Needs the money, we does. Needs the money for to get Sarah to the doctor. Somp'n bad wrong with her. Needin a doctor bad. An Sarah's baby don seem right, neither. He don see too good. Needin the doctor for to see him, too. An Delia needin a bed a her own. I's scared one a these nights I crush her tossin an turnin the way I does."

"Two weeks. Suppos'n Delia be all right if'n it only two weeks. Then we be's back at Papa Jack's. Two weeks. I c'n do it."

They next night they met with Sam to tell him they would do it.

Delia was almost six months old when Amanda and Curtis boarded the 'Mississippi Queen' for a two-week gig. Clara and Earlie Mae brought Delia to the boat to say goodbye to her mother. Amanda was in such a state that Curtis had to drag her onto the boat before it pulled away without them. She stood on the deck, crying and waving long after Delia was out of sight.

"What if she don be all right?" Amanda worried to Curtis.

"She be all right. Mama see to that."

"But what if'n she git sick or somp'n?"

"She ain gonna git sick. She ain been sick a day since she be birthed."

"What if she die, Curtis?" Her deepest fear was now out in the open.

"Amanda!" said an exasperated Curtis. "She ain gonna die. She the healthiest baby I ever done see."

"I s'pose," said Amanda, unconvinced. "She ain gonna die till we gits back in two weeks."

But it was more than two weeks before the 'Queen' again tied up at Natchez. It was four weeks. A month of triumph for Curtis and especially for Amanda. Every night Amanda left the stage in tears, not tears that eased her loneliness for Delia, but tears of pride as the audience cheered and applauded . . . crying out for more.

One of the reasons for the delay was that the 'Queen' had tied up in New Orleans for two weeks of repairs. Since they were there they threw down the gang plank every night for the New Orleans folks to come and hear 'Amanda Blake and her brother, Curtis.' After two nights, there wasn't enough room in the lounge to hold all the people so they stood outside on the deck and peered through the windows. Some nights there were so many people, they couldn't even get on the boat.

One night Amanda and Curtis slipped away from the 'Queen' with a roustabout named Lonnie. Lonnie knew the city. "I takes ya to the joints," he promised. And he did. Wonder filled their eyes and ears as they bar-hopped the city from spot to spot.

They heard the blues. "Wha's that thing that man bangin on?" Amanda demanded.

"Tha's a piano, Mandy. Been roun now, four-five years."

"How they gits it roun?" asked Curtis.

They heard a new brand of music. "This ain the blues," said Mandy. "Is funny soundin."

"Naw, ain the blues. They's callin it jazz."

"Jazz?"

They saw sights all new in Natchez. "They's both colored'n whites in this place," said Curtis.

""Ain no problem. This be New Orleans. Place where the black an the white folks meet."

"Yeah?"

They finished their triumphant tour and when they returned to Natchez a triumphant Sam presented them with a contract for thirty dollars a week for a whole year.

"Ain gonna work on this here 'Queen' lessen I gits time off to be with Delia," Amanda announced.

An amended contract stipulated two weeks off out of every eight for Amanda.

They signed the contract.

After a victorious year on the 'Queen' it was six months on the new 'Natchez', then another six months on the 'Lady Belle'. Another year on the 'Queen.' Then eight months on the 'Robert E. Lee'. And so it went for seven years.

Then Sam brought them another contract. They were to play in Chicago . . . a little place on the Southside just off Lake Michigan. They signed. They brought down the house. Now their salary was seventy-five dollars a week. Their life was a combination of weeks in Chicago and weeks on the boats with only a few weeks at home.

Amanda became more and more despondent. She began to drink.

"Curtis, you stays up with me while I has this here drink," she would say to him after work. "You c'n have one, too."

"Don wanna drink, Mandy."

"Stays anyhow."

A drink would turn into two, then three, until Curtis left her for bed. Then she'd buy the bottle and take it to her room. Sometimes the bottle would be accompanied by some man she met. Curtis always knew about those binges, because she would wake up vomiting. He could hear her through the thin partition between their rooms.

One day he made up his mind. Enough was enough. That very day he confronted her as she stood on the deck of the 'Natchez' staring morosely into the river.

"Mandy, we's got to talk."

"Bout what?"

"Bout you an your drinkin."

"What bout my drinkin?"

"I's thinkin you's been drinkin too much lately."

"I's workin sober, ain I? What I does when I ain workin ain none a your business."

"Mandy, sump'n ain right. You ain never been a drinker. You's drinkin causa sump'n. If'n they's a way to fix it, le's fix it. Whatever ain right."

Amanda stared at Curtis. She started to cry. "Is Delia. I wants to be with Delia. She growin up now. She mos eight and gittin to be a big girl. She gittin away from me. Curtis, when I be eight, I be big nuff to be singin with you on the streets. Seems firs I's losin Aaron; now I's losin Delia."

"What bout we ask Sam if'n you c'n go home for a while?"

Amanda buried her head in Curtis' shoulder. "I wants to go home," she said through her sniffles.

It took some talking to get Sam to agree, but Curtis was persuasive and Amanda adamant. Sam finally reluctantly relented.

The train brought Amanda home six days later, while Curtis stayed on . . . working alone.

She had three months.

Her welcome was all that she'd been missing for so many months . . . so many years. "Mama, Mama!" shouted Delia, leaving Sarah's blind boy on the floor where they had been playing.

"I's hearin huggin an a kissin goin on out there. I gits me some, too," said Clara appearing from the back room.

"Mandy's back! Come in here. Mandy's back!" yelled Earlie Mae, rounding up her brood who were all out playing, up and down the street.

"This be better'n all the cheerin an a stompin in the worl," Amanda said hugging one child after another, holding Delia by her side.

"Where Sarah be at? I don see Sarah," Amanda said, looking at her sister's child.

The room was suddenly silent.

It was Earlie Mae who broke the news. "Dead. Sarah be dead."

"She die crazy," explained Clara. "That sickness she git from them mens. Firs she be crazy, then she be dead. Weren't nothin to do bout it. Baby boy, Lewis, he all right, though, ceptin he don see much. He talkin good though an walkin straight as he can be. He jus don see. Don bother him none. He still a bundle a trouble."

Amanda grieved for Sarah.

She cooked for the whole brood.

She laughed with Earlie Mae and Jesse.

She went to bed early and slept late.

But most of her time, she spent with Delia. They were inseparable. One day Amanda took her to the hill.

"Why we comin here, Mama?" Delia asked.

"Cause this here the place I be lovin the mos, chile, an I wants you to see it."

"This jus an ole tree," said Delia.

"This ain jus an ole tree!" said Amanda. "This tree belong to your papa an to me."

Delia's eyes filled with tears. "I's sorry, Mama."

Amanda saw the tears. She gathered Delia into her arms and wiped them away. "I's sorry too. I ain wantin to be mean."

Delia looked around. She could see Natchez below; she could see the flats where she lived, and 200 feet above - the bluffs where the rich folks lived. She could see the river winding toward New Orleans. She took in the weeds and tall grass, the bushes, and the tree her mother set so much store by. "Whachu sayin bout my papa?"

"Your papa'n me, we comes here every day for mos five years."

"You comes here? What you comin here for?"

"I comes here firs cause this your grandpa's hangin tree. Your papa, he comes here when he hears me singin."

"This be Grandpa Lewis' hangin tree?"

"Umhmmm. Your papa an me, we plays on this hill when we ain much bigger'n you. Then when we gits bigger we makes you richere on this hill an then he givin me these here earrings."

"They pretty, Mama. They pretty. I members em hangin from your ears every time you comin home."

"I ain never to take em off. They's magic earrings, Delia. They means your papa an me, we be's together always, even though he be dead."

Amanda told her everything. About Duanna and Sabia, about Tacuma and Iola. About Aaron's father and the night of horror. About Aaron and their love. Everything. Delia was wide-eyed.

"An when I dies, I wants you to take these earrings. You keeps em till you fin's someone who loves each other the way your papa an me do. You knows em when you fin's em. You gives em away then, hear?"

"I hears, Mama." Tears again bubbled up in her eyes. "You ain gonna die, is you, Mama?"

"No, baby, I ain gonna die. What I is gonna do is stop workin on them boats an in them joints an come home an be with you."

"Oh, Mama."

And the sun shone down on the pair, the woman and her child, hugging beneath the old oak tree, scene of so much tragedy and so much love.

But Sam had other plans. "We've got contracts. Contracts, Amanda. You can't quit now."

"It ain gonna work no more, Sam. Delia, she be growin up without me. I ain havin it."

"Just finish the contracts, Amanda. Then you can quit."

"How long that be?"

"About a year."

"A year?"

"A year," Sam said.

"All right, Sam. I works till we finishes them contracts. Then I ain gonna work no more. I ain, Sam. No more contracts."

"I promise, Amanda. Just finish out this year, then you can go home to Delia."

Amanda stopped drinking. Nights, after work, she wrote letters. "Delia, baby. Only one more year an I's comin home for good. We be's together jus like on the hill."

It was just six month later when Sam came to them with a new offer. "How about you two splitting up?"

"We ain gonna split up, Sam," said Curtis.

"Let me finish before you decide."

"We's already decided. We ain splittin up," said Amanda.

"There's a vaudeville show in Saint Louis looking for a colored guitar player. Two men heard you playing, Curtis, and they want you. You go, Curtis, and you can make alone what the two of you've been making together here. Mandy, you can keep your full salary and work with Tiny Lee Terrell. He plays almost as good as Curtis."

"Don need the money that bad, Sam. We ain splittin up," repeated Curtis.

"You two been talking bout moving your mother out of that tiny shack in the flats to something over on Saint Catherine Street. With Amanda quitting in six months, I don't know that I can get that kind of money for you again. And buying new houses takes money."

"We'll talk about it, Sam," said Curtis.

Later on they talked about it. "Don wanna do it, Curtis. I ain never worked with no one but you, an I don wanna start now."

"But Sam be right, Mandy. Workin alone, we could have nuff money for Mama by the time you quittin. Then we both go back to Papa Jack's with nuff money to be okay."

"Curtis, I don wanna do it. What is I gonna do when you ain roun? Firs I loses Aaron, then Delia. I don wanna lose you, too."

"Ain losin me, Mandy. Jus a few months."

"Tha's what Aaron say, too, afore he die."

"Is only for six months, Mandy."

"All right. Six months. Then we goes back to Papa Jack's."

It was only a few weeks before Amanda again was hitting the bottle after she quit work late at night. Her letters to Delia stopped. She became morose and silent. The only time she was herself was when she was singing. It was the only time she was happy.

In six months, Sam had yet another contract. "Just a few more months, Mandy. They want you in Chicago as a regular."

"Sam, I tole you I's quittin."

"This is the best chance you'll ever get. A regular in Chicago. Salary's a hundred a week."

Amanda went to Chicago. She sang to packed houses, blacks and whites together. Every night was like the first night on the 'Natchez' so many years ago. Every night she brought down the house. The few months turned into a year.

For days on end she was alone in her Chicago hotel room, still separated from Curtis. She slept late, waking to her inevitable bottle of gin by the bedside. She drank. She paced. She drank some more. She slept.

Until one day she couldn't stand it any more. She stormed out of her room and down the hall to Sam's. She pounded on the door. "Sam, I ain gonna work no more. I's sick, an I's tired, an I's goin home. You ain gonna stop me this time."

"I don't want to stop you, Amanda. You can go home. You want to go home now, or will you work tonight?"

"I feels sick, Sam. I works tonight, if'n I feels better; then I goes home on the train Sunday."

"Come on in then. I've got something here that will make you feel better. What I got'll fix you up."

Two men were already in the room when Amanda entered. They were lounging, one on the bed, the other on a couch. The room was smoky.

Sam took a lump of something that looked like brown putty out of a drawer. He broke off a little piece. Holding it with a pair of tweezers, he lit a match under it. Then he dropped the putty into a long-stemmed pipe, which he handed to Amanda. "When I tell you, you pull on the pipe and inhale all the smoke into your lungs. I promise you'll feel just fine in a few minutes. You'll work tonight better than you ever have before."

"What do this be?" asked Amanda, ever suspicious.

"It's opium. It will just relax you, and you won't feel sick anymore."

"Do it hurt?"

"No, it doesn't hurt. It'll just make you feel good."

"How come I ain never see'd this here opium afore?"

"It's only been in America a couple of years now. I get it from France and sell it up and down the river. It's okay, Amanda. Try it."

"I tries it."

Amanda inhaled the smoke as Sam put a match to the bowl. The effect was magical. The knot in her stomach untied. Her head stopped throbbing. She didn't want to throw up anymore. Her caged feeling disappeared. Instead, her head felt light and dreamy. She wanted to work, to get back on the stage, to feel the pulse, the adulation of the crowd. "I does feel better, Sam."

"Good. Go back to your room now and rest. I'll come and get you when it's time to go to work."

As Amanda was floating out the door, he said, "You can come back and get some more of this any time you want."

Amanda sang that night like she hadn't sung in a year. The crowd knew it. They cheered and whistled and called her back again and again for just one more song. She forgot about going home.

Less than a week later she was back at Sam's door. "Gots the miseries again tonight, Sam. Got any more a that smoke?"

"Any time you want it, Mandy. Any time."

'Any time' wasn't often until Sam asked her to stay in Chicago another two months.

"You's always sayin jus a little bit longer, Mandy. Jus a little bit longer. An a little bit longer turns into longer'n longer. I's tired of it, Sam. In two months, Sam. In two months, I quits. Min you, I quits."

She came for the pipe more often. Twice a week at first, then every day. Soon she dropped by Sam's in the morning when she got up and then again just before work. Then it was after work, as well. Her eyes became glazed. She forgot what day it was. She forgot how long she'd been working. She didn't write to Delia. She didn't care that Curtis was still working away from her. She lived only for the next pipe.

Her work began to suffer. She forgot words in the middle of a song. Occasionally, she sang off key. Her vibrancy disappeared and her playfulness with the audience diminished. She argued about coming to rehearsals. Sam had to escort her to work every night or she wouldn't show up.

Sam began to worry.

"She's not sounding so good, Sam," said the bartender one night.

The owner was on the next stool. "Yeah, take a week off, Sam. Let her rest. Then we'll see how she sounds."

"I've got to get her clean in a week," Sam decided.

But getting clean in a week was not what Amanda had in mind.

"You say I c'n have it whenever I wants, Sam. An I wants it. I needin it now. I ain feelin so good."

"I haven't got any, Amanda. Go back to your room. I'll see you later."

Back in her room, beads of sweat appeared on her forehead. She ached all over and her nose began to run. Every joint ached when she moved. She tried to sleep. As soon as she closed her eyes she saw Aaron. She saw Lewis hanging from the tree. She saw Curtis playing at Papa Jack's. Aaron was making love to her. Aaron was dead!

The sound of her scream carried out into the corridor. Doors cracked open as she ran down the hall. She pounded on Sam's door. She screamed and pounded. "Sam, you opens this door. Sam! Sam! I cain stan it. Open this door!"

Sam heard the sound and worried about what the management would do to him. He opened the door.

She raced past him. "I knows you got some in here. I knows you does. I c'n smell it. Where it at, Sam? Where it at?" She ran around the room opening drawers, dumping them on the floor, scraping lamps and vases off of the dressers. Finding nothing, she tore at Sam, crying and screaming. "Give it to me. Give it to me, I's sick. I's got to have it." Sam was wrestling with her, trying to pin her arms behind her.

She was strong . . . beyond controlling.

A friend of Sam's sat placidly at a table watching the proceedings. "You'd better give it to her, Sam, or she'll be worth nothing to you."

Sam considered for a minute. He had to clean her up, but right now he had a mad woman on his hand. Just this once wouldn't hurt. He agreed. He pushed her into a chair. "Sit down, Amanda. I'll give it to you. Sit down. I won't give it to you until you sit down."

She sat on the chair, shivering, holding her stomach, rocking, moaning. "Hurry, Sam."

"Better give her a shot, Sam, she's in bad shape."

"Probably right."

"Hurry, Sam, hurry. I's so sick."

Sam pulled a syringe and needle out of his suitcase, along with a piece of the putty. He put the putty in a spoon and added a little water. He heated it with a match until it liquified. He sucked the mixture into the syringe. He took a piece of rubber tubing out of the suitcase and tied it around Amanda's upper arm. "Make a fist," he told her.

"Hurry, Sam!"

The needle went into her vein, liquid seeped into her arm. Her head dropped forward. She relaxed and the pain was over.

Sam cleaned up his paraphernalia and turned back to the conversation with his friend. "I think I'd better take her off much more slowly. I didn't know she was in such bad shape."

"Yeah, you got her hooked, man. That was not too smart."

"I know, I know. I didn't intend to get her hooked, just relaxed enough to work, and to stop telling me she wanted to go home. I needed her. She was my best talent. She was making me a lot of money."

"Yes, but hooked, she won't make you a cent."

"You're right. I sure know that now. Now I've got to deal with her . . . and I didn't know she could be such a mad woman."

"Better check her breathing, Sam. It looks bad."

Sam put his hand on her chest. There was no movement. He checked her pulse. There was none.

Amanda Rochelle Blake was dead at twenty-seven of an overdose of opium.

CHAPTER 44

A young man with a Western Union cap brought it to the door - the telegram from Chicago. It was Clara that answered the knock. "Earlie Mae, read this here for me. Man jus brought it. He say it comin from Chicago."

Earlie Mae tore open the envelope. "Mus be from Amanda," she said, ripping the envelope in her haste. "Maybe she comin home." Earlie Mae read Sam's short message, and her hands trembled. "Amanda dead of congestive heart failure. Stop. Body on 2:30 train Friday. Stop. Sam."

"Is Mandy, Mama. She dead."

And again, as when Big Eddie took her, as when Lewis was taken from her, as when Sarah died, as when the innumerable indignities had been heaped on her small body, the world stopped for Clara. Retreat was what she knew. But retreat was no longer allowed to her. She knew she couldn't stop living. She had tried that. She had to go on . . . go on living with one more piece of grief . . . with one more deep undying pain that would never leave her body . . . that would never leave her mind.

Nonetheless she went with Earlie Mae, Jesse, Curtis and Delia to the train station to pick up the plain box that brought Amanda's body back to Natchez. Jesse and Sam loaded the box onto the carriage Sam rented: the box that would take Amanda on her last trip back to the house on Rosalie Street.

"Put the box in the back room," Clara directed.

Once they had the box in position, Jesse slowly opened the lid. He saw her body . . . peaceful now . . . with only her vibrancy gone. Still was the voice that had entertained thousands of people. But somehow, as Jesse looked at her, it was as if her soul remained, the soul that spoke through her music, the soul that dared to transcend convention and do what no black woman had yet done, and to bear the sometimes terrible consequences. Her body remained the Amanda they knew: tall, full, the long braid lying across her chest, eyes closed now, the face without the expressions they treasured. Yes, her body was theirs but her soul belonged to the crowds.

And crowds came. Some from as far as New Orleans and Saint Louis. They filed through the kitchen of the little house and into the back room to silently say goodbye. Some sang her songs. Some talked to her. Some wept. Some just stared.

For two days they came, standing on the porch, waiting their turn, bringing food, a few coins, leaving gifts for the family, talking to Clara about her daughter whom they loved.

Delia, fourteen now and turning into a lovely young woman, sat in the corner behind the stream of people . . . inconsolable in her grief. She sat on a small stool, never moving, tears streaming down her face, refusing to sleep, refusing to eat, staring at the body of the woman she knew so well, yet, never knew.

It was deep into the night before Delia moved from her stool. The rest of the household was asleep. The visitors had stopped. Trancelike, Delia got up and walked to the side of the box. There she stood over her mother's body. As she stood looking at the still silent form, words came to her, words that assuaged her grief, that gave her purpose. Words that had been spoken on the hill. "When I dies, I wants you to take these earrings. You keeps em till you fin's someone who loves the way your papa an me do."

Clara found her the next morning curled into a small ball beside the casket, the earrings clutched in her hands.

More than two hundred people were at the cemetery the next day. Curtis sang a song for his Mandy, for everybody's Mandy.

"Time will never heal the pain left in my heart.
No, no, no, no, time will never heal this pain left in my heart.
Mandy,'s gone away now. She's gone, gone, gone, gone.

Mandy's gone away now an lef me with nothin but a moan.
Yes, Mandy's gone away now an she lef me with nothin but a moan.
Yes, she's gone an lef me, she's gone , gone, gone, gone.

I weeps an cries now. She lef me with nothin but the blues.
I weeps an cries now, cause she lef me with nothin but the blues.
I hears her tell me, Curtis, I's gone, gone, gone, gone.

Then I hears her tell me, Curtis, don you grieve for me.
Yes, I hears her tell me, Curtis, don you grieve for me.
The blues, they overtakes me, an I's where I wants to be.

Mandy tells you, all you people, don you grieve for me.
Yes, Mandy tells you, all you people, don you weep an cry for me.
Cause I's gone away for good now, but I's where I wants to be.

Yes, I's where I wants to be, right where I wants to be."

During the singing of her mother's song Delia held tight to a pair of gold earrings, earrings implanted with Egyptian writing on the bottom and with red lines running, now, an inch down from the top and ending in what looked like little droplets of blood. She felt at peace.

'AMANDA ROCHELLE'

CHAPTER 45

"You bes wakes up now. Manda's gone to her Lord. She ain gonna be singin no more."

Kate opened her eyes, but even with her eyes open she couldn't see. Quiet tears blurred her vision. She lay still in silent grief at the death of this extraordinary woman; grief for another part of herself. The room was silent . . . reverent. It seemed that all noises had stopped, suspended, while Kate paid her respects.

The first interferences were the sound of the clock ticking on the wall, the heater whirring.

Kate tossed aside the blanket Lena had thrown over her and sat up, knees to her chest. She could see a little now, even through her tears. She could see Lena outlined against the window. She pulled a tissue out of her pocket and wiped away her tears. Now she could see clearly.

"Lena?"

Lena nodded.

"Lena, you're crying," Kate said softly. This caused her to move out of her self-pity and to feel for the old woman. She struggled to get up from her mattress.

"You stays where you is," commanded Lena. "Don be needin your commiseratin. I's jus an ole woman feelin mournful bout Manda dyin."

Kate sat back on the mattress. She knew enough not to go against Lena's force. And, of course, she understood why Lena would cry about Amanda's death, Amanda more than either of the others. Amanda was one of her people. Kate understood.

"I knows Mandy."

Kate couldn't believe her ears. "You knew her, Lena? You really knew her?"

"Shore did. Lives jus down the street from her, I did. It were my Mama who be birthin woman for Manda when she be comin into this worl. An Delia too."

The wheels were turning in Kate's head. She was trying to remember. Then it hit. "Your mother was Miz. Harmon?"

"Tha's my Mama. I sees Manda growin up. I sees her fall in love with that white boy. Then I sees them earrings a your'n swingin from her ears. I watches her singin in Papa Jack's. I even be's there when them po-lice come ta git her and beats her up. I goes to her funeral an hears Curtis singin them blues she lovin so much."

"Now I understand," said Kate. "That is why you were so interested in my earrings on that first day. Now I know why you were so insistent on my knowing myself. Why you said I had to know these other women. You and I have known each other before."

Lena didn't respond. Tears were still trickling down her cheeks. "I's tired of it," she said, pounding her fist on the side table. "I's tired a seein black folks die. I's tired a seein what happens to em when life gits full a the miseries. I's tired a seein em gittin nowhere, bein pushed roun by them white folks wherever they turns. I's tired a seein em give up, an actin jus as good as dead. I's tired of it. Good thing I's mos ready to go to my res or one a these days I be's out in them streets a burnin an a shootin jus like the res."

Kate did not know what to say. She had just lived two lives knowing the suffering in having a black skin. But today her skin was white. Today she was one of those white folks Lena was condemning. She did not know what to say.

"I's born jus ten years after that war," Lena continued. "Jus ten years after that Civil War s'pposed to free us up from slavin. My mama, she know bout slavin cause she pickin cotton for the white mens when she no mor'n able to walk. She be followin her mama up and down them rows a cotton gittin them thorns in her hands. Then comes that war, s'pposed to make us free. We's free all right, free to starve cause they ain no food, free to sit cause they ain no work, free to worry ourselfs to our deaths bout wha's gonna happen to our chillens when they grows up, an free to die when them white mens wearin them white sheets comes roun a sayin they's protectin they white women from the black man what don wan em no how."

"We's jus as good as dead if'n we tries to do somp'n for ourselfs sides survive. Tha's why Manda die. She wantin ta do somp'n for herself. She wantin to go home to Delia where they's love for her. She pinin away for the love she los when Aaron die. She strong an she do what she needin to do, but she still pinin away. She git herself a big hole in her insides where love s'posed to be. Ain no way, even with all them folks cheerin bout her singin, she gonna git that hole filled up. Ain no way, even with that money Sam be givin her, gonna fill up that hole. She needin to go home to her lovin. An Sam, he kills her. Jus as sure as that Cacanja kill Sabia an that Shamash kill Duanna. Jus as sure. An I's tired of it. I's tired a grievin an mournin for folks goin to they deaths cause they don know what else to do. We kills ourselfs, we does, drinkin an shootin all that stuff into our arms. Ain got no spirit lef to fight, we ain. We's been fightin so long ain no spirit lef in us. We knows nothin's gonna git better no how, so we might as well git drunk. Might as well be happy for a few hours fore them folks what give us the credit come and takes away all we owns or them po-lice come an hauls us off to jail. Might as well git ourselfs drunk. Might as well shoot that stuff into our arms. Might as well try to survive any way we can. They kills our spirit, they does. Tha's what they does. They kills our spirit."

Kate felt awful. For years she'd been writing stories about the black people of Chicago, about how they lived, about the criminal and the prostitute, the pimp and the hustler. Sometimes she'd even said 'ain't it awful.' That was before she knew. Now she knew what she had only suspected before. Now she had lived that life, that life of no respect from the powerful majority. Now she knew what kind of a struggle it was to make good. Now she knew about the temptations to give up. To just give up and take money and pleasure wherever it could be found. Now she knew. Now she understood Lena's despair, her despair at the death of the spirit that occurred in her ghetto, at the unmourned death of the spirit.

Then there were the current events, the events that were taking place now: the Black Panthers carrying their guns, H. Rap Brown shouting at every opportunity for Black Power, the Muslims wanting black separatism, and the whites trembling behind their righteous views. Before, she had looked on with horror. Now she understood.

The room remained quiet. The two women sat, lost in their own thoughts. Lena was angrily tapping her walking stick on the floor. Kate, still on the floor on the edge of her mattress, watched her.

Lena broke the silence. "Whachu starin at me for?"

As usual, Kate got flustered at Lena's bluntness. "I . . . I . . . ." she stammered.

"Don talk afore you knows what you's talkin bout."

"Don't yell at me, Lena. I didn't do it. It's not my fault that all of those things are happening. I didn't do it."

"You's white, ain you? Tha's all you needin to be. Tha's enough."

"I haven't always been white, Lena. Remember, when you were young, I was as black as you are."

Lena smiled . . . one of her rare smiles. "You ain as black as me. Your daddy, he be white, an don you forgit it."

The fight was over.

Quiet prevailed. Again, the only sound in the room was the ticking of the clock.

"Lena?"

"Whachu want now?"

"Amanda, did she die for nothing? All those other people, are they dying for nothing? What about all the rhetoric, all the killing and the bombing and the burning? Is that all for nothing or are some things going to change?"

"They shore is a shootin an a carryin on somethin fierce if'n it ain gonna git em no place. I reckon things be better when all the shoutin's done, but is gonna take a long time afore things be good. They's gonna be some black folks what makes sump'n of theyselfs when them white folks got they guard down. They gonna be others what jus gits what they can for theyselfs and runs away laughin. They's some what already thinks they's superman, an they ain goin nowhere. An they's some what's so lazy they ain goin nowhere no time. I knows one thing for sure. Them white folks ain gonna give up nothin they ain forced to give up. An when we learns ta take it, then we gits it. Then Mandy's dyin don be for nothin."

"Thanks, Lena."

"Whachu thankin me for?"

"Telling me how it's going to be. Helping me to know how it was."

"Hmmmmmph," Lena grumbled.

"I suppose I'm through now," said Kate. "I suppose I won't be seeing you any more."

"Whachu talkin bout? You ain through."

"I must be through. There were only three women in my dreams."

"They's a fourth one."

"A fourth one? But I only dreamed about three. Who's the other woman?"

"You is."

"Me! I don't have to relive my life. I already know it."

"Why your daddy be so cruel to you?"

"I don't know, Lena. He was just that way, I guess."

"What bout your mama? Why she so weak?"

"I don't know that either. She was just a weak woman. She couldn't stand up to my father."

"See! You don know so much bout yourself as you thinks you does. We's gonna fin out bout one more woman. The fourth one an she be Kathryn Angela Pritchard Andrews."

"That's me, huh?"

"Tha's right. You comes back nex' week an we fin's out bout the fourth one, Kathryn Angela Pritchard Andrews."

"I can't come next week. I've got . . . ."

"You comes back soons you can, hear? We don gots much time lef."

Kate walked out of Lena's house, flying, on this day. She had something to celebrate now. Lena didn't scare her any more. Now they were friends. That was enough to make her fly.

And the rain had stopped.

Everything was right with the world . . . .that is, everything was right with the world until a young boy on a bicycle, bent on hitting every puddle, splashed her all over with mud. She flipped the bird at his retreating back. "And that for you too," she yelled.

CHAPTER 46

After Amanda, Kate had a hard time. The high she felt after leaving Lena didn't last long. By the time she reached home Amanda had started to haunt her . . . much more than the others. Both Sabia and Duanna had been cooperative and had not bothered her until she was ready to deal with them. Amanda, however, was not cooperative. She refused, yes, refused to go away. She refused to leave Kate's mind . . . or her gut. Kate would be sitting at her typewriter at work, and there would be Amanda . . . standing by her tree on the hill, or standing on stage in front of hundreds of people. Kate would be riding home on the train and there would be Amanda on every corner. On one corner Amanda would be playing her one-string, on another she would be singing with Curtis for pennies. While watching television Amanda would suddenly pop onto the screen, bruised and beaten, with the police standing over her with a cat-o-nine tails. In Kate's dreams she saw Amanda and Aaron . . . she saw Aaron dead . . . she saw Amanda dead. She would wake up crying into her pillow.

At times it seemed that the images would never stop. They were interfering with her work, sometimes causing tears at the most inopportune times. She saw Lewis . . . dead. She saw Clara . . . struggling to keep herself together through tragedy after tragedy. She saw Sarah . . . a prostitute, with her blind boy Lewis . . . her progeny. She saw Matthew Spellman . . . the epitome of bigotry. Again and again, she saw the police . . . as they brutalized her, the nuns . . . who saved her, and Sam . . . who killed her. She felt the hardness of it all and the beauty of the family love that showed through everything.Sometimes she was surprised at the ease in which she understood what Amanda's life meant to her own. Amanda wasn't giving her anywhere near the trouble she'd had understanding what Sabia's life had meant, or Duanna's. As a matter of fact understandings leaped around in her brain with almost as much regularity as did the images; understandings of why she was doing what she was doing in these crazy days of tumult. Understandings of why she had been so touched by Montgomery and the whole black movement. Understandings of why Martin Luther King had moved her to tears. Understandings of why she had to speak out about oppression. And most of all the understanding of the why of Joshua, something she had **never** understood before.

Amanda had taught her, even as Sabia could not, what it was like to be oppressed in America. The pain . . . the tasks made impossible by those in power . . . the punishment for just being, yet the fullness in that being.

It had been weeks after her experience as Amanda and the images were still appearing with regularity. On this day she sat at her typewriter, trying to write her weekly column. Nothing was coming, nothing she was supposed to write about. All she could concentrate on was Amanda's image standing in her brain.

In frustration she began to speak. "Amanda, I'm tired of this. Go away. Just go away. I can't get any work done with you popping into my head any time you please."

"Cain go away," said the image. "I wants to be sure you understands."

Anybody looking into Kate's office for the next few minutes would have been convinced that Kate was going mad, stark raving mad, talking to herself as she was doing. But for Kate, these three-way conversations were getting to be second nature. It was no surprise to **her** that Amanda had answered her plea . . . and again had refused to be cooperative. These conversations no longer made her feel crazy as they once had. Ignoring any possible assumptions from her colleagues, she jumped right in. "But, Amanda, I thought I was understanding. This time I was understanding."

"Well then, you tells me what you's understandin."

"Mostly it's why I'm doing what I'm doing: writing and speaking about oppression . . . Joshua . . . the earrings."

"You waits a minute. What you means, o-pression?"

"Oppression? Well, it's what happened to you when they killed your father. It's how you felt when they arrested you on that trumped-up charge of stealing the earrings. It's how you felt when the police beat you up. It's that whole feeling you had about white people, that feeling that you couldn't trust them, that feeling of being afraid of them, that feeling that they were doing everything they could to keep you from being free. Remember when you told Aaron that he couldn't marry you because he was white? That's oppression."

Amanda was quiet and Kate could almost see the wheels of her mind turning. Finally she said, "I think I sees. Yeah, I sees. So what is you knowin now what you ain knowin afore - bout this **o**-pression. Tha's what I wants ta know. What does you learn bout this **o**-pression when you was me?"

Now Kate had to think. What did she know now that she hadn't known before? The unexpectedness of the question caused her mind to become blank. When her mind was no longer blank, there was nothing but a muddle of thoughts up there. "What do I know? What do I know?"

Suddenly her thoughts cleared and she knew. "I lived it," she said. "Yes, that's what's different. I lived it. In my life now I only watch it. When I was you I **felt** Lewis's death. I **saw** the white-sheeted men come to **my** house and try to burn it down. I saw my mother raped by a white man. I **felt** afraid of white people. I **felt** the distrust. I **knew** what it was to be kicked and beaten. I **knew** what it was to be hated for the color of my skin. I **knew** what it was to be kept away from the bedside of my love . . . as he died."

Kate hadn't been looking at Amanda while she talked. She had been too much into her own thoughts. When she finally looked up she saw tears rolling down Amanda's cheeks.

Kate couldn't hide her surprise.

Amanda nodded. That was all she did. She simply nodded. Neither spoke for some time.

Kate finally broke the silence. "And now that I've felt it, I know I'll never forget it. I'll never forget how it was. And now I have to tell people. Even more than before, I have to tell people. And now I know I can. I can tell them with more eloquence. I can convince more people of the horror of it. I can show the people who perpetrate it the results of what they do. I can help people who have lived under it how to fight it." Now, Amanda was crying harder. "I reckon you understands. I reckon you **does** understand."

"Thanks, Amanda. I think so too, now more than ever. I thought I understood before, but now I really know I do."

"An tha's what you's s'posed to do. **Know** bout it."

"Yes, that's what they tell me."

Kate grinned, and Amanda's face lit up. Amanda spoke. "Guess you ain needin me no more. Guess I's free to go now. Guess I ain needin ta bother you no more. I goes now."

Kate watched as the form of Amanda faded from her mind. Now, she wanted to call her back, not to let her go. A few hours ago she wanted to get rid of her. She would have done anything to get rid of her. Now she was feeling the loss of that vibrant power that was Amanda. Now she was knowing . . . really knowing this time . . . that Amanda would not be back. She sat in silence for a short time, trying to bring herself back to what she had been trying to type on her blank sheet of paper.

All of a sudden, her fingers started to fly over the typewriter as though possessed. The column she was writing leapt onto the sheet. She wasn't sure what she was writing, but she knew she was writing exactly what she was 'supposed' to write. She wrote with new power, new vibrancy and even new purpose.

As her fingers flew over the keys Kate realized that the way she felt now was not unfamiliar. It was a feeling she had felt in a previous time. She had felt it when she was Sabia. She had felt it when she was Amanda. She had even felt it when she was Duanna. But now that feeling was mixed with Kate, the Kate she already knew. She had each of the three women as part of her, and she had herself as well. "A dynamite combination," she thought.

Kate tried to bring the image of Amanda back into her head . . . to thank her. While before, she couldn't get her out, now she couldn't get her in. Amanda was nowhere to be seen.

Kate smiled. "Thanks, Amanda," she said out loud. "And I know you hear me wherever you are."

Chapter 47

Lena had said 'come back soon's you can, we ain got much time lef.' Kate wondered about that. What did Lena mean, we haven't got much time left? What was the hurry? Possibilities raced through her mind. The worst possibility was that Lena wouldn't be alive if they waited. Whatever the reason, Kate felt compelled toward the house on South Damen, compelled to finish the story of her lives, to live through the story of the fourth woman. She had cleared her desk of all assignments. She was free the last weekend in March. Lena was expecting her.

On Friday night she was sitting in her cubicle typing the last of her feature story when she smelled the cigar marching toward her office. "Kate," it bellowed.

"I'm still here, Ed."

It marched into the cubicle, belly and cigar first. The rest of Ed Mahoney followed. "Can't find that damned Shaskowitz anywhere. Johnson says he's gone to some goddamned wedding."

"His own, I believe," said Kate.

"If he's getting married, he's more of a fool than I gave him credit for. You'll have to take this assignment tomorrow."

"Oh, no I don't. I've got plans for this weekend. I'm taking no assignments."

"Listen here, Missy," Ed said, leaning toward her. "You cancel em. If you want this job, you cancel em. This assignment's got to be covered and there's nobody else to do it."

"Then you cover it, Ed," Kate said through gritted teeth. "I told you I am busy. I am not married to this newspaper. I have other plans. And if that means my job, then you can take your job and shove it. Now take that stinking cigar out of my face before I puke."

Ed's glare could have turned anybody to ice. Kate ignored him and went back to her typing. Ed stood as though he had been struck; then he began muttering. "I'll call Berger. Berger still wants to keep his job." He stalked out of the cubicle in a cloud of smoke, still muttering to himself. It took five minutes before Kate's heart stopped pounding.

Saturday dawned beautiful, nippy but sunny. Kate had nothing to do all morning. She stayed in bed reading a novel and drinking coffee. It was noon before she plodded downstairs for food. She was early for the bus. It was coming down the street when she got to the corner. With that good luck, she arrived at the house on Damen ahead of schedule.

"Glad to see you sided to be on time, jus this once."

"Lena! I've only been late once. And that time it was only ten minutes."

"Harumph."

"Don't harumph me. I worked hard to be here today."

"S'pose you did. S'pose you did. Sits yourself down. Sits yourself down. Who's we s'posed to be talkin bout today anyway?" Lena said, her eyes twinkling mischievously.

"Me, Lena. Me. The fourth woman, remember?"

"Now I members. Whachu wanna know bout yourself?"

"What do I want to know about myself? Lena, I don't know. I thought I knew everything I needed to know about myself. You were the one who said I didn't."

"S'pose I said that. S'pose I done said that."

"You're teasing me, aren't you, Lena?"

"Ain never teased nobody in my life," Lena said, the twinkle in her eyes betraying her words. "Whachu members bout your daddy?"

She began to remember her father, Max Pritchard. A perfect name for the Hitler-like German that he was. Short, muscular, balding just a little, and just a touch overweight. The army had been a perfect place for her father . . . as a Colonel . . . yet. That was, until he hurt his leg in a jeep accident. As luck would have it, the leg never healed the way it should and they put him out of the service. He never forgave them. He never stopped wanting to get back in. When he got back home to Minneapolis, he needed someone to order around and to do his dirty work so he married Doris, ten years younger than himself.

"From then on it was all downhill," she told Lena. "I was born, and then he really had someone to pick on. me. I was his whipping girl. And I do mean whipping. Every time I turned around, he was on me for something."

"What bout your mama? Whachu members bout her?"

Doris was easier. Her stomach didn't go 'scrunch' when she thought about Doris. Thin, small, plain, even dowdy, would describe her mother. And she took orders like a private. 'Doris do this. Doris do that.' And Doris did the this and the that.

"She was the perfect wife for the perfect ass, my father," Kate said. "She did everything for him and nothing for me. Except once; she saved my life. I never did understand that. I expected to die."

"You hates your daddy, is I right?"

"Yes. **I hate him.** He gave me nothing but pain and a messed-up life."

"Tha's right. You gots the right to hate him. He a miserable scuse for a man. He thinkin he all man cause he tough. He thinkin he all man cause he know all them rules; an he say everybody gots ta do em his way. That be workin good when he in the army, cause he git hisself obeyed when he there. But he spectin to be obeyed outside the army, too. If'n folks don do it his way, he fix em with his belittlin an with his fists."

"Your mama, she scairt a him. She do all-time obey him. Onliest time she don obey him be when you comin long. You knows bout that?"

"No, I didn't know about that."

"Well, cordin to him, you ain s'posed to be. You was one colossal mistake. Your mama, she don count too good an she git to spectin right off. Your daddy, he be furious. He say he don wan no squallin brat roun. He say he marryin up with your mama so's he gits his food cooked an his house took care of. He don wan no yellin brat in his way. When you comes long, you gits in the way a his comforts. Tha's what you done."

"That's about right. I was always in his way. I never could please him."

"Ain nobody could please him. Even them army folk. Much as they obeys him, they never pleases him. Your mama mos din git to the hospital a havin you, tryin to please him. She be laborin an laborin till them pains be mos one on top a the other. She scairt ta wake him up. He a snorin an a snorin; an she don wake him till she more scairt a havin you in that bed than she be of wakin him up. An he be mad bout the wakin. He tell her, 'wait till mornin'. An he goin back to snorin. She tell him, 'ain gonna wait. You's deliverin this here baby your own self if'n we don go now.' So he gits hisself up, an he goes. An he be drivin crazy, actin the fool, an he be tellin your mama, he say 'I ain havin no girl chile.' He sayin to Doris, 'you havin a boy chile if'n you knows wha's bes for you. Don wan no chile atall, but you actin stupid, you don count them days the way you's s'posed to. Now we's havin a chile. I ain havin no girl chile.' When you comes out a girl, he leavin that hospital an he goin on a three-day drunk."

"I'm not surprised, Lena. He did that a lot. Whenever my mother didn't please him, he'd storm out of the house and slam the door. Then he wouldn't come back until late. Sometimes he'd be gone for days. I was always glad. I didn't have to be afraid when he was gone. I was always afraid when he was home. Hardly a day went by that he didn't hit me for something and when he wasn't hitting me, he was yelling at me. I was always afraid his rages would turn into a beating."

"How old was you when he beatin you?"

"I don't remember any beatings before I was in school. He just hit me maybe once or twice across the face and he was always yelling, but I don't remember any beatings."

Lena looked off into the distance. She was calling up a vision. "He beatin you afore that. He beatin you when you was bout six months old. You be cryin an cryin an Doris, she doin her bes to make you stop. Your daddy, he tryin to read his newspaper. He tellin Doris,'make that chile shut up.' You don shut up. He throwin that paper all over the livin room. He stormin through the house till he findin you. Then he beatin you an beatin you with his fists. He don stop till you quits cryin. Doris, she yellin an fussin an tryin to make him stop. He don stop till you's all bruised up. Then he storm out'n the house."

"Doris, she scairt. She ain findin no way to make you come roun. She shakin you an shakin you some more, an you don come roun. Then she runnin to them neighbors, an they takin you to the hospital. You comes roun then, but the doctor, he say you got one a them concussions. Then Max, he don beat you no more."

"Until I got older, is that right?"

"Umhmmm. When you was older he ain so scairt a killin you no more."

"But he almost did once, Lena. It was the only time my mother stood up against him. I was just ten."

The scene jumped into her vision and played there, just as it had when she was ten. She was standing in the kitchen door, watching him. She had just come home from the park. He was drunk. He was angry. He had a knife in his hand, cutting some meat for a sandwich.

"Where have you been?" he yelled, seeing her. He was still holding the knife.

Kate didn't answer. Between his being drunk and his waving that knife she was too frightened to answer. He scared all the words right out of her.

"Answer me," he said, starting after her, pointing the knife in her direction.

Kate started to run.

He threw the knife on the table and ran after her. When he caught her he grabbed her across her chest and twisted her arm behind her. "You answer me when I talk to you," he said, breathing hard.

Then he turned her around, and she could see the hatred in his eyes. The hatred that seemed to build as he stood there looking at her. She cowered. With his free hand he started to hit her. She could feel the blows now, just as she had then. Blows to her back, her belly, her head, her legs. She fell on the floor, using her arms to try to cover her head. Then he kicked her.

At that moment Doris ran in from the outside. She had her arms full of groceries. She dropped both sacks. She simply dropped them, spilling groceries all over the floor. "Max, stop!" she shrieked. Without thinking she threw her body into him, sending him off balance.

"Goddamn it, Doris, get out of my way. I'll discipline her any goddamned way I want."

Doris backed away. She backed away but there was fury in her eyes. She wasn't through with him yet. She'd seen the knife. She backed up far enough until she could pick it up. Once armed, she went after him with it. "Stop it Max, or I'll kill you."

"He let go of me like a sack of potatoes," Kate said. "I think he believed her. She looked mad enough to be believed."

"For whatever reason he stopped. He started to back away. He kept on backing up until he was right out the door."

"I just laid there, crying, on the floor."

"Mother took me to the doctor right away. I had two broken ribs and multiple contusions, they said."

"My father never came back after that. Two weeks later Japan bombed Pearl Harbor. Roosevelt declared war. My father showed up at the army recruiting office and wangled his way back into the army. I was never so happy about anything in my life. If he hadn't gone, some day I might have killed him. I sure wanted to bad enough."

Kate started to cry. She was rocking in her chair, comforting herself.

Lena produced a huge handkerchief and handed it to her.

Then more scenes infested Kate's mind.

Dinner when he was home: 'Don't play with your food!' 'Eat! Don't spill your milk! Jesus Christ, watch what you're doing!' When she walked through the house: 'Pick up your damned feet! I can't think with all that stomp, stomping going on around here!'

'Stop running! Don't come up on me that way. You're a goddamned shadow. I never know where you are!'

When she talked, which wasn't often, it was: 'Shut up. Doris, can't you shut this brat up! I want to read. Shut her up, will you?'

When she cried, which was often, he would raise his arms ready to hit and say 'Goddamned, sniveling brat! Quit!'

"It was awful, Lena. The only place I did anything right was in school, and even there I didn't do much right."

"Oh, you smart nuff in school. You was jus all-time scairt. An you so scairt you don never answer none a them questions for recitin an stuff. Them teachers, they kepa writin home to Doris sayin somethin be wrong with you. You ain talkin to nobody. An you ain got no friends."

"I was so scared, Lena. The teachers were nice, and they wanted me to talk but every time I tried to open my mouth, I could hear him yell at me or see his hand in the air."

Kate saw herself in school. She remembered the dizzy spells when she thought they wanted her to talk. She remembered how often she thought they were going to hit her for being bad.

Then she remembered how she had saved herself. She remembered what she had done. She wrote. She remembered how she had written and written and written, and how she had saved everything she wrote until pieces of paper were falling out of her drawers. She always got A's in school for writing; F's for not talking.

Her mind had been in constant turmoil. The same thoughts kept going around and around in her brain:

"Everybody hates me."

"They don't want to play with me."

"Those boys are looking at me funny."

"They're going to beat me up after school."

"They don't want me on their team."

"They hate me."

"I never dated, Lena. In high school, I was never part of the fun the other girls were having. I just stayed home and wrote stories."

"An college be jus as bad, is I right?"

"College was worse. In the fall of 1949, I went to Northwestern in Evanston, Illinois, to their Journalism School. I knew I could write. I just couldn't talk . . . so I decided to be a writer."

"You has a roommate, name a Julia. The boys be likin her. Is I right bout that?"

"Oh, yes." Kate laughed, thinking about Julia. "She had so many dates, I don't know how she stayed in school."

"She be trying to teach you, din she?"

Kate saw her beautiful and popular roommate trying to teach her about boys: Showing her how to dress . . . even taking her shopping.

Showing her how to put on make up, which she constantly smeared.

Teaching her to dance, while she had two left feet.

Giving her her first drink, watching her choke on it.

Teaching her the fraternity songs, which she could not remember.

Getting her dates, which she messed up . . . every time.

Giving up and joining a sorority.

"An then you starts havin them crazies," said Lena.

Kate remembered. Her crazies came back to her with full force. It was the thoughts again. Those crazy thoughts that would not leave her alone.

"Everybody thinks I'm dumb because I don't talk."

"The teachers don't like what I write."

"They're going to flunk me."

"They're just like my father."

"If I flunk, I'm going to die."

"I'll have to kill myself."

"I'll take a whole bottle of aspirin."

And the nightmares. Every night, the nightmares.

"I don't remember much about that time, but I remember it was awful," she said.

"I's gonna help you member."

"You're gonna do what?"

"Jus what I's sayin. I's gonna help you member. We's gonna start re-livin your life, bout that time you ain memberin."

"You mean when I was crazy? Oh, Lena! I don't **want** to remember all that."

"Don you be 'Oh, Lenain' me. You gots to member. You don know who you is till you members when you was crazy."

Kate sighed. "You are determined to make this hard, aren't you? I don't suppose I have a choice?"

"No, you ain gots no choice."

"All right Lena, you win. We'll begin when I was crazy."

Lena nodded and pulled a match out of the pocket of her dress, preparing to light her lamp.

Kate knew what to do. She moved to the mattress and made herself comfortable. "Crazy Kate, here I come," she muttered.

"Kakung a runga, Kakang a ranga."

THE FOURTH WOMAN

KATE

(1931 -   )

"We live within a system of fixed and blinded power where a small group have power **over** others. Power misused is oppression maintained by fear and lies."
Daughters of the Moon Tarot p. 21.

CHAPTER 48

The sweet smell of Lena's lamp wafted through the room and into her nostrils. Even before Lena began her incantations, Kate was drifting away. Drifting back to when she was nineteen, back to her second year at Northwestern. Memories darted into her sub-conscious mind, memories of herself: thin, drawn-looking, with sunken eyes that darted about, looking for danger. Memories came back to her of what had been in her mind at the time: the constant danger, her imagination always working overtime.

In her mind she began to see them: all her enemies, all her imagined enemies.

First, there were the group of girls, gossiping and laughing on the steps of Jordan Hall as she walked by. "It's me they're laughing at," she decided. "They've heard about how strange I am; they're laughing at me."

Then it was a boy who happened to glance at her as she walked on campus. "That boy thinks I'm ugly. I can see him looking at me."

When she saw two boys she had met at a party, in the book store, her mind said, "They're whispering about me. They're whispering about how weird I was at that party Julia dragged me to. They're whispering about how miserable my date felt being with me."

Some of the girls on her floor in the dorm came into her mind. They had been a constant source of fantasies back then. They were the ones who saw her. They were the ones who heard her in the night. "They won't come near me. They're afraid of me. They call me crazy Kate. I've heard them. They know I'm crazy."

Finally, it was a teacher from one of her journalism classes who appeared. This one frightened her the most. He was in charge of her grades. "He watches me all the time. Every time I look up, he's watching me. I know he wants to see if I'm listening. He's just waiting to catch me daydreaming. Then he can put a bad mark in his book. He's just waiting to give me a bad mark. He doesn't like me."

And on and on and on.

Just as the scene changed, Lena's words interrupted her mind's meandering. "Whachu seein?"

"Uh . . . I see me . . . uh . . . I'm asleep. I'm asleep in my room at school, at Northwestern. I'm rolling around in bed. The covers are all rumpled. I'm having one of my nightmares."

"Tell me bout them nightmares," said Lena.

"It's starting out like all of my dreams start out. With something that will make me happy, with something that makes me feel safe. This time I'm in a garden. I'm walking down the path among the flowers. They smell so good and I love the colors. I stop and pick some. I see other people over there pulling weeds. They wave and smile at me. They're lulling me into believing that everything is all right. I see a little dog ahead of me. He's wagging his tail. He wants me to pet him. Even he wants me to think there isn't any danger. But there is always danger. I know there's always danger. I have to be alert. I have to watch for it. It will come at me when I least expect it."

"I reach down to pet the dog. As soon as I touch it, it starts to grow bigger. Right in front of my face, it grows bigger. It grows bigger than me. It turns ugly. Fangs grow out of its mouth. Its hair stands straight up. It's angry. Its face gets dark, and it's angry. I start to run. It's chasing me. I look back. It's gaining on me. I run faster . . . as fast as my legs can go but they can't go fast enough. I look back again, and it's just about to catch me. And it's my father."

"I start to scream. I scream and scream and scream. He is pounding on me, pounding on my brain. Then I wake up. Somebody is pounding on my door, yelling at me. 'Shut up. We're trying to sleep around here.'"

I drag myself up through a sea of darkness and terror, and my rumpled covers. I pull my knees to my chest and hold myself tight. I rock, there on the bed, rock and cry in my loneliness and my terror. Nobody comes to comfort me."

"Res now, an leave them dreams be."

Kate was quiet. The pictures of herself, sitting like a waif in her bed, holding and rocking herself, faded away. Her mind emptied.

Lena's voice punctuated the quiet. "You seein somethin now?"

"Yes. I'm seeing me. I'm in a hallway of a building. It's the Speech Building where I have most of my classes. It looks like I'm late to class, because I'm hurrying. Oh, God, Lena. I remember this. This is where it started."

"I knows. You's goin back now. You's gonna live your life all over again. Tell her you's here."

"I'm scared, Lena. I don't want to do this."

"Ain no wors'n bein Duanna an gittin yourself run through with a sword, or bein Manda an gittin beat up by the po-lice. Bein crazy ain no worse. Gits yourself in there."

"I don't want to be crazy again."

"You needs to be crazy now, so's you won never be crazy no more. Tell her you's here."

Kate sighed. She knew the inevitable. "She sees me. She's telling me to hurry up if I'm coming, or we'll be late for class."

"Go on then. Git yourself into her."

"She's running now. I have to hurry."

"You hurries then."

The last thing Kate knew was fading into the body of her nineteen-year-old self, running down the hall to a class she never got to.

Her mind was working over time. "Run, stupid. Run. Run faster. Hurry up. He's already started class. He always starts on time. Never a minute late. Hurry up, legs. He'll see me now, when I come in. He'll see me, and glare at me. He always glares at me. He glares at me, even when I'm not late. Every chance he gets, he glares at me. I won't look at him any more because he glares at me. He wants to fail me. He doesn't want me in his class. I can't fail. Hurry up, legs."

She picked up speed. One of her books started to slip from the pile in her arms. She juggled them to keep it from falling. "Only a little further," she told herself. She rounded a corner.

Crash!

She slammed into another student. They're both on the floor, books scattered all over the place. The young man is yelling.

"What the hell do you think you're doing? Can't you watch where you're going? Look what you've done." He picked himself up and tried to get the dust off his pants.

"I'm terribly sorry. I was late for class."

"Stupid bitch. Now **I'm** late for class!"

Kate was beginning to feel dizzy. Her head was starting to spin. "I'm really sorry. I wasn't looking where I was going. Here, let me help you pick up your books."

"Get away from my books. You've done enough damage. That's my term paper all over the floor. Don't touch it. Get away from me."

Kate backed against the wall and stared at him with her darkened eyes. She was losing her vision. Her stomach was feeling sick. She bent to pick up her own books, but her hands wouldn't hold them.

"My term paper's all wet. Look what you've done? My term paper's all wet."

Kate knew it was coming. She felt it moving up from her lungs into her throat. When it came out of her mouth, it sounded like it was miles away. Her scream penetrated the hall, even advancing into the classrooms. She screamed. Again and again she screamed.

She saw him. He was coming at her. His hand was raised to hit her. He was going to beat her. She cowered. She raised her hands over her head to protect herself. She collapsed against the wall, intermittently sobbing, screaming, and asking for mercy. She had her hands over her head, crying. "Don't hit me! Don't beat me!"

Doors opened and teachers emerged from their rooms, staring at the spectacle of a surprised young man and a screaming girl among a pile of books. Students stopped in their tracks. Others poured out of rooms. They started to whisper among themselves.

Some knew her. Some were on her floor in the dormitory and had heard her screams in the night.

The dean himself emerged from his office. "What's going on here?" he demanded, coming up to the crowd that was gathering around. "She bumped into me and spilled my books all over. Then she just started screaming," said the young man.

Kate's screaming had diminished. Her sobbing had not.

"Somebody take her over to the health service. Have Dr. Acker see her. Does anybody know where her room is?"

"I do," said a tall skinny girl who lived just down the hall from Kate.

"Take her books back to her room for her. Who'll take her to the health service?"

"I can take her," offered one of the secretaries.

Kate felt herself lifted from her spot on the floor and almost dragged out of the building, across the grounds, and into another building. The nurse took one look at her hollow eyes and tear-stained cheeks and ushered her into an inner office. "Dr. Acker will see her right away," she assured the nervous secretary.

By the time Dr. Acker arrived, Kate was almost composed. She had stopped crying and was looking around the room, wondering where she was. When he came in, she felt as though she were out of danger. He was old. Older than her father, with hair greying at the temples. He wore glasses, which kept falling down on his nose, and he smoked a nice-smelling pipe. He sat down behind his desk and looked kindly at her. She felt comfortable as she related her side of the story. He asked her lots of questions, seemed interested in her, wrote down everything she said on a yellow pad and when it was over, he wrote out a prescription. "Here, get this filled and take one in the morning and one at night. They'll make you feel better. And I think it would be a good idea to come in for some counseling, don't you?"

Kate nodded.

"I'll make an appointment with our psychologist, Dr. Froleck, for 4 o'clock Thursday afternoon. I'm sure you'll feel better by then."

Kate did feel better. She had her first dreamless night in months.

On Thursday she arrived for her appointment. As soon as she saw him, she turned icy cold. It was his eyes . . . followed by his inevitable condemnation. He was tall and thin. Almost as thin as he was tall. He was wearing a perfect blue serge suit, with the perfectly-knotted tie and the perfectly shined shoes. His hair was perfectly combed and there was a perfect three-cornered handkerchief in his perfectly pressed suit pocket. The only thing not perfect about him was that he didn't look a bit like her father.

"I'm Dr. Froleck," he said. "Come in and sit down." Even his voice was perfect.

"And you were found screaming on the floor in Jordan Hall, is that not so?"

"Yes, I . . . ."

"And you reportedly are having nightmares, is that correct?"

"Yes, about my father."

He straightened his already-straight tie. "Miss Pritchard," he said. "I must take your history before we can begin. Please don't elaborate until I have your history. Your full name please."

"Kathryn Angela Pritchard but everybody calls me Kate."

She felt dutifully scolded. From then on she carefully answered each of his questions without elaboration.

"Yes, Kathryn. Now, how old are you?"

"I'm nineteen."

"And your birth-date exactly?"

"October 15th, 1931."

And so it went for several sessions. Kate answering the doctor's perfect questions, exactly and with perfection. He wrote down her answers, neatly on his yellow pad, with his perfectly sharpened pencil.

Kate returned to class, diligently did her homework, talked to no one, ate only when hunger forced her to, fantasized about the stares of her classmates, and continued to have nightmares. Her only sign of progress was that she no longer woke up screaming. Fear of the pounding on her door had stifled that.

Finally her therapy began. "You say it's your father who caused your problems, Kathryn. Tell me about your father."

"I was afraid of him, Dr. Froleck. He used to hit me when he thought I was bad."

"And what did you do that was bad."

"I was noisy; I was too messy when I ate and I got in his way sometimes."

"You were too noisy, is that right?"

"Sometimes. I tried not to make noise, but . . . ."

"And you were messy?"

"Yes, I was afraid of him and I kept spilling things."

"And you got in his way?"

"Yes, he liked everything peaceful and I interfered with his peace."

"That doesn't sound so unusual. Most men want some peace and quiet when they come home from work."

"Yes, Sir."

When she left his office, she was sure her father's beatings had been her fault. "If only I hadn't been bad, he wouldn't have had reason to beat me," she thought.

"I assume your mother took good care of you," Dr. Froleck said on another day.

"Yes, she was home all the time. She didn't work or anything but she was so busy she didn't have much time for me."

"Yes, mothers are busy people. Someday when you're a mother, you'll understand."

Leaving that day she was convinced that if only she had been more understanding of her mother, things would have been better.

"You stated that you never date. Is that correct, Katheryn?" he asked her one day.

"No, I get all tongue-tied and awkward when I'm around boys. Sometimes I've had dates, but they never take me out more than once."

"Do you get enough sleep? Your eyes are so dark. You'd be almost pretty, if your eyes weren't so dark. Perhaps then you'd have more dates."

"I have trouble sleeping, Doctor. It's the nightmares."

"Oh, yes, the nightmares about your father. I suggest you get more sleep. I'll have Dr. Acker write you a prescription for sleeping pills. You get more sleep, get rid of those dark circles, and you'll have more dates."

"It isn't my looks, Dr. Froleck. I'm afraid . . . ."

"Yes, well, I suggest you talk to some of the other girls in the dorm. They can teach you about make up, and how to dress . . . perhaps some new clothes."

Now she knew she had to work harder to attract boys.

Week followed week. Month followed month. He asked her questions. He never heard the answers. He wrote everything down on his yellow pad. He straightened his already straight tie. He straightened his already perfect papers on his perfect desk. And Kate left each session, knowing she was supposed to be more perfect than she was.

She hated him.

She didn't feel any better. She didn't want to go back to see him any more. Her thoughts were getting more and more confused. He was supposed to be helping her. She didn't feel any better.

"He hates me," she thought. "He doesn't want me to come and see him any more. He's decided that I'm incurable. That I really am crazy. He's going to tell them I shouldn't be in school any more. He wants to send me back to Minneapolis, to Doris. I've got to get better so he won't tell my teachers I'm crazy."

Her nightmares increased in their intensity. She was having a hard time studying. She couldn't eat. She was losing weight that she had no business losing. She was again thinking about killing herself.

It was spring quarter when it happened. She took her usual seat in the high-backed chair in front of his desk. He took his usual seat behind the huge mahogany desk, yellow pad neatly placed in front of him, yellow pencil exactly parallel alongside. Only today a file folder lay next to the yellow pad. "Let's see now what we have," he said, as he picked up the file and opened it. "You've been coming to see me since October, is that not correct?"

"Yes."

"Is it not now the last week in April?"

"Yes." Her suspicious mind became more suspicious. "He knows what month it is," she thought. "Why is he asking me?"

"Are you feeling any better than you did in October?"

"Not really, I . . . ."

"That's what I thought. It seems to me that you haven't been working at getting better." He looked intently at the folder. "I see that you have all A's in your classes. You must be working better there. Since you're working so well in your classes, perhaps you could tell me why you're not working harder here?"

Kate started to feel dizzy. Her vision was blurring. She wanted to tell him how hard she was trying to get better. He didn't stop talking long enough for her to say anything.

"I'm afraid if you don't start working harder in your therapy, I simply won't be able to take the time to see you any more. There are other students who want to come and are ready to work."

The room started swirling. Kate couldn't see him any more. There was only a blurry outline. Her head started to hurt. The thoughts swirling inside felt crazy. "He's going to tell everybody about me. He's got it all written down on those yellow sheets. He'll let everybody read it. He'll tell everybody about me. Then they'll all know how crazy I am. They'll put me out of school."

He was still talking. "I am just going to have to make room for some of the other students. You see here in the chart. . . ." Suddenly her vision cleared; he got shorter. His head was balding. Instead of tall and thin he was short and stocky. He was her father. He was telling her for the umpteenth time that she wasn't doing it right. That **she** wasn't good enough. Rage raced through her body.

She saw him coming toward her. He had picked up the file and was coming around the desk. He was coming toward her. He was going to beat her again.

Not this time. Her face contorted. Her hands changed to claws. Just as he approached, file in hand, she sprang from her chair. She struck at him, clawing at his face. Immediately she opened a three inch gash on his cheek. Blood dripped on his perfect grey flannel suit. She kicked him in the ankles. The folder flew out of his hands. He tried to grab her. He missed. She hit him in the stomach with her fist. He gasped for breath and doubled over. Using both hands she hit him repeatedly on the back and on top of his head. Finally he crumpled to the floor.

The activity was causing an uproar. The secretary threw open the door. "Oh, my God," she said, running for the phone.

"You little bitch," said Dr. Froleck, trying to get up.

"You're not going to beat me this time. You're not! You're not!" Kate screamed.

Dr. Acker and a nurse in a white uniform raced into the room.

Dr. Acker grabbed Kate from behind, twisting both her arms behind her.

"She's gone off," puffed Dr. Froleck. "We're simply going to have to put her in the hospital." He reached into his breast pocket for his carefully-ironed three-cornered handkerchief. He put it to his cheek. Then he noticed his suit. "Oh, my God," he said. "My suit. Look at what she's done. She's ruined my suit."

Kate was still struggling. With a free foot, she kicked Dr. Acker in the shin.

"Quick, get that shot ready," Dr. Acker ordered.

The nurse was measuring liquid into a syringe.

"Froleck, could you forget your suit for a moment and get a hold of her legs before she maims me for life."

The nurse came at her with the needle.

Kate saw it coming. She saw the needle getting bigger and bigger. It kept coming at her. There was a face behind it. The needle and the face, they kept getting bigger. She started to jerk and to kick. She was almost free. "You're going to kill me," she screamed.

The needle jabbed into her arm.

The dizziness, the swirling room, Dr. Froleck, Dr. Acker, the nurse; they all disappeared in a rush of peace.

The next thing she knew she was lying in a hospital bed. Her head hurt. Her arm was badly bruised. A nurse was standing next to her.

The nurse smiled. "How are you, sweetie?" she said. "Better, I hope. I'm glad you finally came around. I thought you were going to sleep right through my shift. You must have put up quite a fight. I'd sure like to see the other guy. Here's your water. I'll be right back to take your temperature."

Kate's mind was fuzzy. She had to look hard to see what was around her. When her vision cleared a little, she realized she was in a large room with nine other beds. There were three other people occupying the beds; a young girl about her age, and two older women, almost thirty.

The nurse was back with the thermometer. She stuck it under her tongue. "Where am I?" Kate muttered through the thermometer.

"You're in the student infirmary, sweetie. Dr. Froleck wants you to stay here for a week or so. He says you need observation."

Kate immediately started struggling. She had to get out of that bed. "But I can't stay here," she said. "I've got to go to class."

"The doctors have admitted you for a week, sweetie. Dr. Froleck says you're not to go to class. He says it could be dangerous for you to go to class. He'll be by later, if you want to talk to him about it. Now let's see about that temperature."

The nurse who called her sweetie looked at the thermometer, shook it down, and wrote something on the chart.

Kate's mind wouldn't hold still. "I've got to get out of here. I have to go to class. I can't stay here for a week. They're keeping me here because they think I'm crazy. I'm not crazy. I've got to go to class and prove I'm not crazy. I can't stay here."

In spite of her agitation, the effect of the sedative was too strong. She couldn't get up. She fell back to sleep. A dream crept into her unconscious. He was staring at her. Staring at her and analyzing her with those eyes. He was telling everybody. Now everybody knew. He was sending her home; home to Minneapolis; home to Doris. Her eyes flew open.

This time it was no dream. There he was, standing at the end of her bed.

The first thing she saw was the gash on his cheek, now red and raw. Just like in her dream, he was looking at her. Looking at her with those eyes: distant, demanding, without love, analyzing her.

The dizziness started again. Thoughts pounded her brain. "I know what you're up to. You're going to keep me here in this place until I flunk out of school. You're going to keep me here in this place until I die. You're trying to kill me."

She screamed and jumped out of bed, grabbing at him. "I'm not going to let you kill me! I'm not! I'm not!"

This time he was ready for her. He grabbed both her arms and held them above her head. No matter how she twisted and fought, she couldn't get away. Three nurses ran out of the nurses' station. One of them jabbed a needle into her arm. One of the last things she heard was "Now, sweetie, we don't want to start that again, do we?"

One of the last things she saw before the sedative took her away was Dr. Froleck's face. It was contorted with rage. Then she heard, "Put her in restraints and keep her there until I give the orders."

CHAPTER 49

Wham! Wham! Wham! The pain in her head was relentless. Fog permeated her mind. Everything hurt, but most especially her head. She tried to reach for it, to sooth the pain. Then she discovered it. She couldn't move.

Her eyes flew open. Now she saw it. The white canvas cloth that tied her arms to herself. The ties that held her feet to the bed. Light was streaming in through the windows. Two figures in white moved around behind a glass enclosure. The other three women were still sleeping. One of her arms was asleep inside the contraption. She tried to move it, to wake it up. She was almost immobile. "Hey!" she yelled. "Can someone untie me?"

Her nurse of yesterday appeared by her side. "Sweetie, we can't untie you. Dr. Froleck's orders. You'll just have to get used to it. Would you like some water? Here sweetie, I'll hold it for you." She left.

Kate's eyes darted around the room. Escape. How to escape.

She struggled. It made her hurt. She stared at defeat. Defeat. Defeat in the body of Dr. Froleck.

She started to cry. Her nose began to run. She couldn't get to the tissues by the side of her bed. She couldn't blow her nose. Not a nurse was around to help. Her face and chin became a mass of tears and snot. She was miserable. She went back to sleep.

At noon they brought her a try of food. "Sweetie, your face is a mess. Let me wipe you off."

Even clean, she refused the food. They took it away. There were more tears. More snot. Again, sleep relieved her misery.

In her dream a fairy godmother was standing over her, all dressed in filmy white, talking to her, saying "Open you eyes, Kate. Nobody's going to hurt you."

Kate opened her eyes. She had sandy hair and freckles; and she was smiling. Her smile made the corners of her brown eyes crinkle up. She had a row of perfectly-spaced white teeth. But she wasn't wearing filmy white. It was blue. Light blue, like the sky with no clouds. Kate noticed, immediately, that she didn't call her 'sweetie'.

"My goodness, but you're a mess," said the fairy godmother in a soft melodious voice that instantly sent Kate's fears scuttling. "Here, let me clean you up a bit."

As she worked, she kept on talking, asking nothing, just talking. "You have really been through it, haven't you? First you're beaten up by that pompous ass, Froleck; then they tie you up like a common criminal; and now they've let your face get all caked up with snot. What kind of a place is this anyway? Don't move. There's some more over here by your ear. There. That's better."

"Goodness, let's untie you so you'll be more comfortable. That looks awful. Let me just get at those ties, here. There, that's better."

"Oh, I'm sorry. I forgot to tell you who I am. I'm Jenny. I'm replacing Froleck as your therapist. That is, if it's all right with you."

Kate couldn't speak. Relief overwhelmed her. All she could do was produce more tears.

"Hey, I didn't mean to make you cry again. Here, take the tissues. Take the whole box. You're probably going to need them to clean yourself up again, and just after I did such a super job, too."

Kate started to smile.

"Ah, that looks wonderful. Much better than all those tears."

"You mean," said Kate still sniffing, "that I don't have to go back to Dr. Froleck for my therapy any more? Are you sure?"

"Absolutely. He abdicated. This afternoon, as a matter of fact. I told him. I said, 'Froleck,' I said. Of course I didn't call him Froleck. He'd have had a shit fit. 'Dr. Froleck,' I said. 'She might do better with a woman, being as how it was her father that gave her the trouble in the first place. I think she needs a woman. As a matter of fact, I'm sure she needs a woman.' I didn't tell him that it was because he was such a pompous ass. I didn't tell him that. I didn't say to him, 'Froleck, you're a pompous ass.'"

Now Kate started to laugh. Now the tears were tears of laughter.

"My God, here we are wiping away tears again. What did I do this time?"

"Oh, Jenny, he is a pompous ass, isn't he? He made me feel crazy."

"Well, he makes **me** feel crazy. I'm not surprised that you felt crazy being around him every week for all that time. So, is it okay that I be your new therapist?"

"Oh, yes."

"Good, Then let's start right now. You tell me everything you want me to know. I'll just stop flapping my mouth and listen. I won't say a word. If I don't keep my mouth shut, you tell me. Jenny, you say to me, Jenny, shut up. You promised."

And there began one of the nicest afternoons Kate had spent in her life. Kate told her everything. About her nightmares, about her fears and fantasies, about her accident in the hallway of Jordan Hall, about her sessions with Dr. Froleck, about her father, about the similarity between Froleck and her father, about how awful she felt whenever she was around boys, about feeling crazy, even about her thoughts of killing herself.

She finally wound down. It was late afternoon. They were interrupted with "Sweetie, it's time to take your temperature. I've got to go home now."

"My name is Kate."

"Well, Kate, sweetie, it sure is good to see you talking. Here, put this in your mouth."

Jenny started it. Snickering.

Kate couldn't help it. The laughter came from someplace deep inside of her. She wanted to behave properly, but she couldn't. She just couldn't. She was laughing so hard, the thermometer fell out of her mouth.

When the episode was over and the sweetie nurse was gone Jenny stood up to go. "I'll come back tomorrow," she said. "As a matter of fact, I'll see you every day while you're in the hospital. Then, when you leave we'll set up some appointments."

"I . . . uh . . . How long will I be here? I don't want to miss my classes."

"Let's see how you are in a couple of days. Maybe no longer than that. Why don't you give me a couple of names of your classmates. I'll have them drop off their notes."

Kate's relief was infinite. She started to eat after that. She started to heal. She wasn't going to flunk out of school after all.

Kate was shocked when she saw Jenny's office for the first time. There was no over-sized desk and straight-backed chair as there was in Dr. Froleck's office. There was no desk at all, and only two comfortable looking chairs. The whole room was full of pillows, big ones, little ones, middle sized ones, plain ones, multicolored ones, simple ones, complicated ones. Kate wondered what if would be like to pile them all up and fling herself into the middle of their softness.

"How about we start with your father. Let's get rid of him right off," said Jenny, after Kate was comfortable in one of the chairs.

"My father?" said Kate, with some alarm.

"Umhmmm. I'm going to teach you a new game. It's a pillow game. You choose a pillow; and we'll pretend your father is sitting on it. Then you tell him whatever you want him to know."

"I'm going to tell my father?" said Kate, her eyes wide.

"Umhmmm. You're gong to tell him."

"I can't tell my father anything. I can't even ask him whether he had a nice day. If I did he would likely tell me to shut up and stop bothering him, and I'd probably end up being hit. No, I can't talk to my father."

"This time that's not going to happen. This time he's going to listen to you."

"Are you sure?"

"Absolutely."

"Well then I . . . I'll try."

Kate chose a red pillow with jagged black stripes on it to represent her father. Jenny put the pillow in front of her chair.

Immediately Kate felt terror.

Kate peered at the pillow. She could see him. She could really see him on the pillow. He was there. He was berating her. He was yelling at her. He was threatening to hit her.

She jumped up from her chair, and started to circle the pillow, eyeing it with horror.

"Tell him how afraid of him you are," Jenny encouraged.

"No. I can't tell him." Her voice was quavering. "I can't tell him."

"Try."

"I can't tell him. I can't," Kate said.

"Try again. I won't let him hurt you."

Kate returned her attention to the pillow. She really saw him sitting there. But for once in her life, he wasn't saying anything.

She opened her mouth to tell him.

She closed it again.

She went back to circling.

She opened her mouth again.

No words came.

She started to feel dizzy.

She backed away from the pillow.

Back.

Back.

Back.

Terror was in her eyes.

It was only the wall that stopped her.

She pushed herself against the wall, as if enough force would make it give way.

She started to cry.

She slid down the wall to the floor, shoulders hunched, knees to her chest. She started to rock, back and forth, back and forth.

Her crying became hysterical.

Then there were arms around her, gentle, trusting arms; holding her, protecting her, keeping her from her pain.

"It's alright to be afraid," said the owner of the arms.

Kate spoke gibberish between her sobs.

"He can't hurt you now," Jenny said.

Kate buried herself in Jenny's softness. She cried until the crying stopped.

Jenny rocked until no more rocking was needed.

There they sat, in the corner, as far away from the red pillow with the jagged black stripes as the room allowed... one crying, the other holding, rocking, protecting.

For the first time, Kate knew the comfort of somebody's loving arms, extricating her from her lonely terror.

Each week as she returned to Jenny's office, she tried again to tell her father, the red pillow with the jagged black stripes.

Week after week, she confronted him.

Sometimes words would come, sometimes not.

Sometimes she had courage, sometimes she retreated to the safety of her corner, to the safety of Jenny's arms.

It was into the fall of her Junior year, after a summer away, that she was finally able to eliminate the ghost of her father from her life.

Jenny had brought a cardboard box. It had originally contained a four drawer filing cabinet.

"Today, this is your father," Jenny proclaimed.

Today Kate had courage. Out of her throat came a low moan.

The moan turned into a growl. The growl changed into a challenging roar. She attacked the box with all the force of her thin body. She picked up the box and smashed it down on the floor, again and again and again. She smashed it. The box became lopsided. It became flat. She tore at it, ripping pieces from it.

"Tell him. Tell him how you feel," prodded Jenny.

"I hate you. I hate you," screamed Kate. "I was just a baby. I didn't know. How could I know? I hate you. You are the vilest of men."

"Tell him more."

"I'm going to destroy you, piece by piece, like you destroyed me. I'm going to kill you. I've wanted to kill you all my life. Now I'm going to kill you." She ripped the box, piece by piece, into smaller and smaller shreds.

She picked up the pillows and threw them at the shreds.

She overturned chairs in her haste.

She pummelled the shreds into smaller and smaller shreds.

She finally stopped, sinking to her knees, in the middle of the room, in the middle of one shredded box, fifteen pillows thrown every which way, and two upside-down chairs.

Her chest was heaving.

She looked at Jenny.

She smiled.

She started to laugh.

"I did it, Jenny. I did it. He can't hurt me any more. I did it."

"You certainly did," said Jenny, standing to the side of the room, out of the way of the destruction.

Kate was quiet for a moment. Then she jumped up and raced into Jenny's arms. "I did it. I really did it," she said, as Jenny held her.

Two people were celebrating the destruction of one father, who, with his violence, had taken on the proportions of the demon in one small girl's mind.

When the celebrating was finished, Kate moved out of Jenny's arms. Then, for the first time, she saw the devastation in the room. She hung her head and looked at Jenny out of the corner of her eye. "I'll help you clean up," she said.

Jenny took her first complete look. "You know, I think I'll let you."

As Kate left the office that day, Jenny's last words rang in her ear. "Next week we'll start on your mother."

Before the week was out, she had another event to celebrate. She had her first date since her freshman year. He was a young man she had met in one of her journalism classes. He'd been making it a point to sit next to her in class since the beginning of fall quarter. He wrote for the Daily Northwestern. He'd been talking to her about trying out for staff. She'd been resisting.

The next week Kate burst into Jenny's office with the news. She was talking so fast that her words jumbled, one on top of the other. "Then he took me down to the newspaper office and got me to sign up. I've got my first assignment; and then, Jenny, he asked me to go out with him on Saturday. I think he likes me."

"I bet he does," said Jenny. "See, all it took was getting rid of the ghost of your father to make the boys start flocking around."

"Now, Jenny, they're not exactly flocking."

"They will, they will. I'm so proud of you, I feel like a mother sending her daughter on a first date."

"Well, one thing's for sure. You've been a whole lot more mother to me than my mother."

"I think your mother needs to hear that. Why don't you tell her?" Jenny pulled up a bland-looking off-white pillow.

Kate changed so fast she could have been Hyde going back to Jeckle. Her face lost the smile she had come in with. She turned completely serious. A worried frown replaced the smile. She stared at the pillow in silence. A minute. Two minutes. Three minutes. She didn't move a muscle.

"What's happening, Kate?" asked Jenny.

"I can't tell her."

"Why can't you?" Jenny asked gently.

"Because she's not there. I can't see her. She won't come to me. She won't sit on the pillow."

Kate was silent again. Then her face lit up. "That's the way it was, wasn't it Jenny? She really was never there with me. I didn't have a father, and I really didn't have a mother, either."

"Why don't you tell her that?" Jenny prodded. "Why don't you tell your mother, who's not there, how that was for you."

"It . . . it's hard to talk to someone who isn't there," said Kate, still addressing Jenny.

"It is, isn't it?" said Jenny.

"But you want me to try, don't you?"

"Yes, I want you to not only try; I want you to do it."

Kate turned back to the pillow. There were still no words. All her feelings were in her face. At first it was serious, but animated. Then it took on the hollow look of loneliness. Then, what had been loneliness turned to desolation. Tears appeared in her eyes, expressing her sadness for that child, who had a father who beat her and a mother who wasn't there.

Kate moved into what was becoming a characteristic posture for her. She rested her head on her knee caps and rocked. Then the words came.

"I was so lonely, Mom. Why did you abandon me? What did I do that was so bad for you to abandon me like that? Was I bad? I tried not to be bad? I tried always to be good. I did everything you told me to do. and I never got in the way. But I couldn't make you care about me. You just didn't care about me."

"If you'd cared about me, you wouldn't have let him beat me. You would have stopped him." Kate's rocking increased in speed. "I couldn't have stopped him. I was too little. But you could have stopped him. Why didn't you stop him? You let him do it, Mama."

Now tears were streaming down her face. "Where were you? Where were you? Where were you?"

Come and sit over here," Jenny said patting the pillow that was supposed to be her non-existent mother.

Kate unwound herself, moving to the bland pillow.

"Now, I want you to be your mother. I want you to become Doris Pritchard. Tell Kate, tell your daughter, tell her why you couldn't protect her."

Kate again fell silent. The tears dried on her cheeks. Her young face changed. It became old and hard. It put on a mask of protection. Kate turned to Jenny. "I know what she wants to say."

"Then tell Kate. Tell your daughter what you need to tell her. Say it."

Kate turned back to her task. "I had to let him beat you, or otherwise he would have beaten me. I sacrificed you to save myself." The words were barely out of Kate's mouth when she jumped off the pillow. She backed away. She began circling it, as she had the pillow of her father.

"What happened?" Jenny asked.

A look of hardness crossed Kate's face. "She's as bad as my father. I don't love **her**. I don't even like her. I'm never going to sit on her pillow again. You can't make me. No. You can't make me."

"No?"

"No! I hate her. I hate her as much as I do my father. I hate her. I don't ever want to see her again. I hate her."

Then a look of horror crossed Kate's face, hearing her own words. "Oh, Jenny, I'm sorry. I shouldn't have said that."

"Maybe you have a right to hate her," said Jenny.

"I don't have a right," Kate wailed. "Nobody has a right to hate their mother."

"If they deserve it, you do. Did she deserve it?"

Kate's hands clenched into fists. "She deserved it. But Jenny, she was so weak. She couldn't help it."

"Maybe not. Maybe not. But her being weak doesn't stop you from hating her, does it?"

"I guess not. No, I guess not."

True to her word, Kate had nothing to do with her mother in the weeks and months to come. She refused to sit again on the bland pillow; she refused to talk to her in any way, even refusing to write letters home. Jenny pointed out that she was punishing her mother, by being just like her. Kate said she didn't care.

In spite of Kate's struggle over her mother, or maybe because of it, Kate made some remarkable changes. She began to eat. Her sleep was no longer infested with nightmares. She wasn't even having dreams. Now she slept soundly from the time she went to bed until morning. The dark hollows under her eyes all but disappeared. Her face lost its haggard looks. Weight was distributing itself around her body, giving her an attractive, full figure. Success at the Daily Northwestern was a great feather in her cap. She was getting byline after byline for her stories.

It also seemed as though Jenny's words were coming true. Boys were flocking around. Now she was never without dates. The young man from her journalism class had come and gone, as had several others but now, in May of her Junior year, there was a gentle but persistent music student who was awakening her sexual yearnings.

That week in Jenny's office, she brought it up. "He wants to have sex with me. What am I gonna do?"

"Do you want to have sex with him?"

"I don't know. Sometimes yes, and sometimes no, and even when I want to, I know I shouldn't. It's wrong to have sex until I get married. Isn't it Jenny?"

"Who said that?"

"Why, everybody says that?"

"Who specifically told you that?"

"Well, my mother, I guess."

"Did she like sex?"

"I . . . she never told me whether she liked it or not."

"But you know, don't you?"

"Yeah, I guess I know."

"Well?"

"She didn't like it. She couldn't have liked it. There was no way she could have liked it with that brute she was married to."

"Would she have liked it better if she hadn't been married to a brute?"

"I . . . I don't know."

"Yes, you do."

"How do you know what I know?" Kate said, her anger jumping out of her.

Jenny was silent.

"You're right. I do know. She didn't like sex, period. Not with my father. Not with anybody."

"Do you want to end up the same way?"

"I . . . hadn't thought about it. I . . . I guess I don't."

"Maybe then, it would be a good idea to talk to her. Maybe you need to find out who she is. I think she had her reasons for being the way she was. I think she had her reasons for being afraid of sex, and her reasons for being drab and letting your father rule her. I don't think she knew how to do anything else but sacrifice you to protect herself. I think you need to learn about these things from your mother."

"No! I hate my mother! I don't want to know anything more about her."

"Then you'll probably end up just like her."

The look of horror on Kate's face was almost comical. "No!" she said. "I'm not like her. I'm not a bit like her. I'm not weak and scared and afraid of sex."

Jenny's silence permeated the air.

Kate extended a tentative question. "You think I'm like her?"

"Well?" said Jenny.

"Maybe I am a little weak and a little scared."

"And what about sex?"

"I'm afraid of that, too."

"Then you'd better learn the truth," said Jenny softly.

"I . . . I guess you're right. What do you think I should do?"

"Why don't you call your mother?" suggested Jenny.

"You mean really call her . . . like on the telephone?"

"Yes, that's what I mean. Really call her, like on the telephone."

"Ohhh, Jenny. Can't I do it with the pillow?" There was silence in the room. Kate looked across at Jenny only to find her therapist looking back at her, simply looking back at her with that look in her eyes. She had seen that look before. "I can't do it with the pillow, huh?" Kate said.

Kate made the call, immediately after leaving Jenny's office, before she lost her nerve. She couldn't stop her fingers from shaking as she dialed.

Doris's monotone answered the phone.

"Mom?"

Now there was animation. "Kate. I've been worried about you, honey. It's been a long time."

"I know, Mom. I'm sorry. Things have been kind of hard for me lately."

"Oh. I understand. I'm just glad you called now."

"Thanks. I was wondering; could you answer a question? I need your help."

Although answering the question was hard for her, Doris's words, coming over the phone that day, explained it all. "Kate, I loved you more than you ever knew. I was so happy when I knew you were coming along. But your father was not happy. He didn't want a child, so having you was hard for me, harder than I could ever tell you. You see, your father was just an extension of my father. I thought he would be different, but he wasn't. My father was brutal to me, too. You see, I was twelve when my mother died. From then on my father used me for his wife. In all ways he used me for his wife. I took care of the house. I took care of my brothers and sisters. and when he wanted sex, he came to me. I was terrified of him. I cried and I struggled but he didn't care. All he wanted was his satisfaction. Finally, I learned not to struggle, just to lay there and take it. But when I wasn't the perfect wife, when he thought my chores hadn't been done right, then he was mean. He hurt me terribly then, Kate. What I learned was that I had to do what he wanted. Always."

"I married Max, your father, because I thought he was different. He was. Before we were married, he was different. But afterwards, I found out that he was just like my father. All he wanted from me was to take care of his house, cook his food, and lay down and have sex when he wanted. He didn't love me any more than my father had. Kate, honey, he petrified me. I got sick every time he hurt you but I didn't know how to stop him. If I defied him, I knew he would hurt me. He might even kill me; and I was your only protector. I was so afraid of him. I let him hurt you. I'm sorry, honey. I never wanted it that way."

By the end of the phone call, they both were crying.

"I'm sorry, Mama. I'm sorry for all of that. But I do want you to know that I'm getting well. I'll be all right."

When Kate reported her conversation to Jenny, she knew the pain of her mother as she knew her own. and she knew the despair out of which it came.

Jenny became mother to both the child and the adult, both Kate and her mother, the mother that was inside Kate; holding them, comforting them, as the truth emerged in one body.

"I didn't even have a grandfather," Kate sniffed. "Not even a grandfather."

"Not even a grandfather," Jenny repeated.

CHAPTER 50

It was the first quarter of her senior year when Kate bounded into Jenny's office with news. "I'm in love," she said, bursting with her own excitement.

"Well, **all right!**" said Jenny, almost as excited as Kate. "Tell me about this lucky man!"

"Oh, Jenny, he's wonderful. His name is Bryan Andrews and he's in Engineering. He's kind of short, about five foot, ten inches tall, but he's really good looking. He has lots of dark curly hair and dark brown eyes. He's older. He's almost twenty-five. He's super intelligent and he's lots of fun. Everybody likes him. He has lots of friends, and they all like me, too. And he thinks I'm super intelligent, too. Besides, he tells me I'm pretty."

"You are, you know."

"Intelligent?"

"That too . . . but pretty. You're getting prettier and prettier all the time."

Kate blushed.

Over the next months it was hard for Kate to talk bout anything but Bryan. It was: "Bryan took me out to dinner last night."

"Bryan and I went to a weekend party with his fraternity brothers."

"Bryan's taking me to the fall formal next week. I just bought a new dress. You should see it, Jenny. It's white with a huge purple sash. It's got this huge skirt, and it's strapless. I hope I can keep it up."

"Bryan is taking me to all the football games. He knows all about the game. He's teaching me all those complicated plays."

"Jenny, you wouldn't believe where we went. Bryan took me to this place downtown called the 'Blue Note'. I heard the greatest singer. Her name is Sarah Vaughn. Then, coming home, we listened to this all-night disc jockey named Sid McCoy. He has this low, low, sexy voice. If I weren't in love with Bryan, I'd fall in love with him."

"Oh, Jenny, I went to the beauty parlor and had my hair done. It was awful. I came home immediately and washed it out."

By the middle of winter quarter she had his fraternity pin. In the spring she came in wearing a half-carat diamond.

"Now, this we have to celebrate," said Jenny, breaking out a bottle of wine and a cork screw. Together, they toasted Kate's engagement. Alone, Jenny toasted her success at bringing one very sick and very frightened girl out of that desperate place into this vibrant health she was seeing in front of her.

Two weeks later they toasted again. "Jenny, I've got a job. It's at the *Chicago Daily News*. I'm just a copy girl but Jenny, I'll work so hard, they'll think I'm a whirlwind, and then they'll have to let me write. I know they will."

There was only one piece of ill wind blowing on her happiness. It was sex. Kate couldn't have an orgasm. The search for the elusive orgasm began.

"Pretend that you are an orgasm," instructed Jenny.

"What?"

"Just start this way. I am an orgasm, and I . . . and just keep on talking."

"That's crazy," said Kate.

"Probably, but do it anyway."

"I am an orgasm and I . . . uh . . . I give lots of people pleasure. But I'm not going to let Kate have any of my pleasure. She's not supposed to have my pleasure. I'm not going to cooperate with her. I'm only going to cooperate with Bryan."

"Now move over to this chair and talk to the orgasm."

"Jenny, how do you think these things up? Talk to an orgasm, indeed."

"Just do it," Jenny insisted. "Don't argue with me."

"I'm doing it. I'm doing it." Kate stared at the other chair containing her fictional, but all powerful orgasm. Even fictional, it made her cower. "I . . . uh . . . You scare me. You're so big and important. Bryan keeps asking me if I have you, and I have to keep saying no. He's getting impatient with you. Then he gets impatient with me. Remember last time when he got really mad. Remember how he said I wasn't trying, that if I tried, I could have you. He scared me that time. He sounded a lot like my father. Why don't you cooperate? Everything would be a lot nicer if you cooperated."

Jenny worried about this turn of events. She saw future difficulties with the relationship. But, within weeks, it was out of her hands. Kate graduated Summa Cum Laude. With her graduation from Northwestern came her graduation from therapy. A healthy, happy Kate traveled home to Minneapolis for her last summer with Doris. There, she rested, preparing for her new job at the *Chicago Daily News*.

On the night of her last therapy session, Jenny, very privately, toasted herself. A toast to the pain she, herself, had endured and dispatched through long hours of her own therapy, to the hours and hours of training she had gone through to allow herself to ebb and flow to whatever place Kate needed to be, to the tremendous dues she had paid to see the look of happiness on Kate's face that day.

In June, 1954, one year later, Jenny sat in the second row, directly behind Doris Pritchard, at the wedding of Kathryn Angela Pritchard and Bryan Clifford Andrews.

About a year later there was a note. "Congratulate me, Jenny. We need another toast. I've been made reporter. This is the most exciting job in the world and I love it. But sometimes I feel so dumb. Everybody here knows everything, and I'm not sure I know anything. But I'm learning. This office is so busy, people running hither and thither, yelling at each other, typewriters clacking. It's wonderful. Now I'm going to be doing it, too. I will be clacking at my typewriter and running hither and thither. Thank you, Jenny."

In the spring of 1956, Jenny found another envelope on her desk. "Jeffrey Todd Andrews weighed in at eight pounds two ounces." In the fall of 1958 came another one. "Eugene Christopher Andrews hit the scales at seven pounds eleven ounces." There was a different address. They had moved back to Evanston from Chicago.

In January of 1959, Jenny found Kate's name on her appointment book. It had been six years.

Kate looked the part of a successful career woman, dressed in her suit and high heels. But her dress was the only part that had been sacrificed on the alter of the work place. Her hair was still disheveled and windblown. Her face was still without makeup, and she still exhibited that rare ability of straight-forward determination, mixed with honest feelings.

"You look wonderful," Jenny said, as Kate sat down. "I'm so glad to see you."

Kate pushed a lock of hair out of her face. "I'm so glad to be here," she said. "I feel like I've just come home."

"Then welcome home, Kate. How are you?"

"I'm tired, Jenny. I've been working hard. I think I've been on the inside of every court room, hospital, prison, government office, concert hall, and auditorium in this city. I've covered them all. And I love it."

"I bet you have. I see your byline in the paper all the time. I read it from cover to cover just to find your articles. That series you did on Montgomery was the best ever."

"Thanks."

"Well, now, what brings you to see me after all this time?"

"It's Bryan. Well, it's Bryan and me. I've decided to go back to school and he's furious. After all this time, he tells me he wants me to stay home and be wife and mother. I worked all the time I was pregnant with Jeff, and he didn't object. Then I worked all the time I was pregnant with Gene, and he didn't mind. But now I'm getting well-known, Jenny. I'm even a little bit famous. I'm finding my nitch. My trip to Montgomery made me see some things I've never known before. I feel strong inside, Jenny, and he doesn't like it. So now he's telling me to quit work. He says we don't need the money any more and he thinks I should stay home. And the longer I resist, the more he criticizes me. Jenny, I don't want to give up my work. I love it. But he's making it very hard."

"Mmmmmmmmmm. It sounds like he's getting more and more like your father."

"You know, you're right! I hadn't thought about that, but you're right. I'm not afraid of him like I was my father. I know he won't beat me but he's getting more and more critical and unfair."

"Umhmmmmm. Now, tell me what's happening in the bedroom."

Kate's eyes widened, and she stared at Jenny. "How did you know?"

"Just a guess. Just an educated guess."

"I should have know you'd get right to the heart of the matter. The bedroom is a pretty unhappy place. I'm still not having orgasms. I thought once we got married, I wouldn't have any more trouble. But I haven't had one, not one, since we've been married. There's got to be something still wrong with me, Jenny. Something terribly wrong."

"You think it's all your fault?"

"Well, isn't it? I mean I'm the one that can't. I don't even want sex any more. I don't even want him to touch me. What am I going to do?"

"Close your eyes and remember the last time you and Bryan made love."

"All right."

"Do you see Bryan?"

"Yes."

"Do you see yourself?"

"Yes."

"Watch what happens and tell me."

"We are standing in the kitchen. I've just finished the dishes, and Bryan has been in the living room watching television. I'm feeling frustrated because he left all the dishes to me. I work as hard as he does and I would like some help with the house work, but he seems to think it's his prerogative to have me do it all. I'm especially mad, because I had talked to him about it just the night before. He'd been grouchy about it, but he had agreed to help me. Then when it came down to really helping me he waltzed off into the living room to watch television."

"I'm pushing my hair out of my eyes, and straightening up from putting the last dish in the dishwasher. When I'm upright, I know he's behind me."

"Yes, then what do you see?" said Jenny.

"Then he puts his arms around my waist and nuzzles against my hair. I know what that means. It doesn't mean he wants to touch me, or that he wants to be close to me. That's his signal. That's his 'Let's go screw' signal. I'm tired and I don't want to, besides being mad at him. I'm saying 'Bryan,' but he's interrupting me."

"'Katie?' he's saying. He always calls me Katie when he wants to screw. 'Katie, you smell so good.'"

"'I smell like dishwasher soap,' I'm saying."

"Then he puts his hands on my breasts and rubs up against me. I can feel his erection sticking into my rear. 'Let's go upstairs,' he says."

"I don't want a row with him, which is what I'll get if I argue so I go. I'm thinking, all the way upstairs, that maybe we can get this over with quick. I get undressed, and he gets undressed. I lay down on the bed and he lays down next to me. He kisses me on the mouth and puts his hand on my breast. I just lay there. Then he puts his hand down in my crotch and starts to rub. I feel a little bit of excitement, but not much. Then he quits. He kneels over me, and starts to come into me. I'm pretty dry, so it hurts. But he just keeps pushing. Then he pushes hard and he's inside. I feel a little more excitement and I try to respond. I don't want to just lay there."

"Then he's saying, 'Do you feel it, Katie? Do you feel me?'"

"I'm saying, 'Yes.' How can I help but feel him? He's so big. He's so big that sometimes he hurts me."

"Now he's starting to move fast. I'm taking a deep breath, because I know it won't be long."

"Then he starts to pump hard. He probably pumps like that for two or three minutes. I'm thinking, 'Hurry up and get this over with. I'm not going to feel anything anyway.'"

"Now his face is getting all contorted and he's coming. He's breathing hard and smashing into me."

"Now he's finished. He's collapsing on top of me. He's saying, 'Did you come?' I'm saying, 'No, not this time.' He's looking angry. Now he's rolling off of me and going into the bathroom. I'm laying there feeling awful."

"Now he's coming back. He's patting me on the shoulder and turning his back to me and going to sleep. I'm getting up and heading for the bathroom. Now, I'm going downstairs to stare at the T.V. and get over being upset. I'm trying to figure out what's wrong with me."

"The picture is fading."

"Oh, Jenny, it's so awful .I didn't think I'd be having this kind of trouble after all our therapy. It's just ruining our marriage."

"You remember our pillows, don't you?" said Jenny.

"How could I forget?"

"All right, let's start out with a conversation with yourself. Pick a pillow that you want to be you."

To a rather plain looking pillow with one awful-looking flower on it, she started to address herself. "Kate," she said. "You're going to ruin your marriage if you can't figure out what's wrong with you. Bryan may already be having an affair. He's been coming home pretty late in the last four or five months, and remember that strange handkerchief you found in his pocket, the one with the perfume smell that he claimed belonged to one of the secretaries in the office. Remember how he said that he'd found it on the floor and meant to return it. Remember how you thought that that was a'likely story' if you'd ever heard one."

"But he wouldn't even be thinking about an affair if you were doing better in bed. He's certainly not pleased with your performance. And that's causing him to be critical of you about other things. It's all your fault. If you could just get over your problem about having an orgasm, you'd be all right."

"Now come and sit on yourself, and answer," directed Jenny.

Once sitting on the ugly flower, Kate was silent. She turned to Jenny. "I don't know what to say to her. She's so pathetic."

"Tell her that," directed Jenny.

"You look so pathetic. I don't know what to say to you. A fine pickle you've gotten yourself into. You're sitting over there accusing me of ruining your marriage. Maybe it's Bryan that's ruining your marriage."

Suddenly a whole new expression came over her face. Without being directed, she moved back to the original pillow. "Bryan? He hasn't done anything. He'd be fine if I weren't such a lousy bed partner."

Back on the ugly flower, Kate said, "Bryan is a lousy bed partner. He doesn't try to make it good for you. He comes at you when you're already upset. He moves in on you out of the blue, without prior communication. His foreplay does nothing for you. Then he enters you and pumps away until he has his pleasure. He doesn't even have the courtesy to hold you after he's through. He simply checks to see if you've had an orgasm; when you tell him 'no;' he acts mad at you, then goes off in a huff. Who's fault is this anyway?"

Kate directed herself back to Jenny. "Jesus, Jenny, I hadn't thought of it like that before. Maybe it isn't all my fault."

"Why don't you tell Bryan that. Here, let's put a pillow over here that belongs to Bryan. Now tell him."

"Goddamn it, Bryan. You've been blaming me all these years. Maybe you're not such a hot-shot lover either. Maybe if you didn't try to have sex just after you've made me mad; just after you've told me what a terrible wife I am . . . maybe I'd be more responsive. Maybe if you'd touch me once in a while without it meaning let's go to bed, maybe I'd like it better. Whenever you kiss me, or hug me I know what it means. It doesn't mean you want to touch me. It doesn't mean you want to kiss me; it means let's go to bed. It means you want sex, and you don't care what I want. And then, maybe if you'd take me to bed and touch me in a loving way instead of grabbing my breasts, or biting me after shooting me full of your stuff, I'd be able to have an orgasm. I can't have an orgasm because you're a lousy lover!" By now she was shouting.

Then she turned to Jenny and said, "And that's the truth."

"So what are you going to do about school?" said Jenny. "What do you want to do?"

Kate entered the University of Chicago in the fall of 1959, majoring in Urban Studies. She arranged to work part time at the paper. Bryan took to sulking.

CHAPTER 51

Leaving Jenny's office, Kate began musing about the past few years, remembering the events that had brought her to this place, to the decision to go back to school. It had started with her resolve to go to Montgomery; with her interest in the bus boycott. She remembered her foray into Ed's office prepared to wage war.

"Yeah. Whadayawant?"

"I want to go to Montgomery."

"You want to do what?"

At least now, she had his attention. "I said, I want to go to Montgomery. I want to cover the bus boycott. I want to interview the people on both sides and find out what's really going on."

"Out of the question." He returned his attention to the papers on his desk.

"Ed, this bus boycott is a big thing. Those Negroes down there have been walking or car pooling it to work now for four months now."

"I read the wire services. You're not giving me any big news."

"Listen, Ed, those people are being harassed. Not just by the people, but by the police, and thc government. Some of their houses have been bombed and some people think the police have been behind it. Almost 100 of their leaders were arrested on some trumped-up charge. And they're still not riding the buses. It's a big story, Ed, and it's getting bigger."

"Maybe it is but you still can't go."

"If I go, I could scoop the Trib on this one, Ed. I want to interview both sides and find out what they're saying. It could be a hell of a story."

"You've got more damn-fool ideas," said Ed, his face looking thundercloud dark. I don't know why I keep you around."

"Because I'm cute," she said. "Besides being talented and bright, and the best reporter you've got."

"You can go."

"What?"

"I said okay. You can go. Isn't that what you want? Go Saturday. Be back in a week."

Kate leaned across the desk and planted a kiss on his forehead. "Ed, you're just an old softy at heart." she said.

"Don't do that! Don't slobber on me! Go make your plane reservations."

Kate flew into the Montgomery Airport on the last Saturday of March, 1956. Her first task was to rent a car. The girl behind the desk was cute, accommodating, and had the prettiest southern accent. While she was making out the contract, Kate asked for information. "I want to stay in a Negro-owned motel," she said. "Could you recommend one?"

"Ah don't know anything about tha'et," she said. "Tha'et ma'en ovah the'ah could maybe help y'all." She was pointing at a colored porter.

"Why ma'am, you don wanna stay in no colored place. There's plenty of motels nice fer white folks. Here, let me show you on this here board we got over here."

"No! No, I don't want to do that. I want to stay in a motel that's owned by somebody colored."

"Is you sure, Ma'am?"

"Absolutely."

Reluctantly he gave her a name and directions.

The Negro man behind the desk wasn't exactly glad to see her when she walked in. If she wanted to be honest, he seemed down right surly.

She found her room clean, neat, and comfortable. It felt right. She unpacked, then headed back to the motel office. The man behind the desk was to be her first interview.

He barely looked up when she walked in. "Excuse me," she said.

The man didn't answer. He didn't even acknowledge her presence. His full attention was on the papers in front of him. "Sir?" she persisted.

He threw his pencil against the wall, and looked up, exasperation on his face. "Look, lady. I don't know what you want, but I don't want no trouble in my motel. This is a respectable motel, and I don't need your kind bringing it in."

Kate literally backed away from the force of his words. "I . . . uh . . . I don't mean to cause trouble."

"Then why aren't you in one of your own motels?"

"Because I want to be here. I can move if you want but I want to be here. I've come from Chicago; I'm a reporter, and I'm trying to get the real story about your bus boycott. It seemed I'd get closer to the truth if I lived here."

The ice around the man thawed a little. "Ah," he said. "You want to know what it's like to be colored, is that right? And then you want to write about it?"

"Well . . . Yes. Something like that. They say, don't judge a man until you've walked in his shoes. I didn't think I could write a very good story until I'd been in your shoes for a while. This is the closest I could get."

"I see," he said, still with some ice, but the thaw had set in.

"Thanks. I'm glad you do. Now, could you tell me a little about what's been going on?"

"No, I don't mind. Harassment! That's what's been going on. It ain't nothing new, though. That's what's been going on all our lives. Only now it's worse because we're fighting back. Not a week goes by that some city official isn't out here with a new harassment. 'Fill out this form. Clean that up. Repair this. Fill out another form.' And right now, Miss Newspaper Woman, I'm going to say 'Yes Sir', and fill out their fuckin forms, and clean the this and the that. And then I'm going to fight with everything I've got for the right to ride on those buses. Then I'm going to fight some more for the right to take my kids to the park when I want. And then I've going to fight some more to make those sons a bitches let my kids get a good education. I'm willing to fight until I'm dead if necessary; until I'm dead or free. Are you writing this down, Miss Newspaper woman?"

"No . . . I . . . ."

"Well, write it down, because if you want to understand what it's like here in Montgomery, that's what it's like. It's like a prison without walls. And people have been too scared to break out of prison. But we're not scared any more. We'll walk. And we'll wait in the cold for our car pools, and we'll go to jail, and we're gonna let them know that we're not taking their shit lying down any more. And that's what you should write down. Write it all down, word for word."

Kate was writing as fast as she could.

"Have you got what you came for?"

"Yes, I have. Now, do you still want me to leave?"

"No! You can stay," he glowered at her. "But if you get into trouble, you're on your own."

"I don't plan on being in trouble." said Kate, completely unaware of the possible trouble she **could** get into.

"Nobody plans on it." Then his glower softened. "I'm here most of the time and if I'm not I'm in unit number three if you need me. Now, go interview someone else. I've got to fill out yet another form for yet another city official." He almost smiled as Kate left the office.

She headed downtown to start asking more questions.

She found what looked like a main street and parked the car.

She walked around for while getting her bearings. An almost empty coffee shop caught her eye and she went in. "I'll start with the waitress," she thought. She sat at the counter and ordered coffee.

The waitress surprised her by starting the conversation. "You're a yankee, ain't ya?

"Yes, I'm from Chicago."

"That's 'damnyankee' you know. One word."

Kate laughed. "Are we that bad?"

"Worse," said the girl. "You seem all right, but you should see some a them uppity ones comin in here. Swaggerin around with their noses in the air, wantin me to run faster'n my legs can carry me. Always in a hurry. 'Damnyankees' is always in a hurry."

Kate laughed. "Sounds like a pretty accurate description if you ask me."

"I knowed it. I knowed it," she said, grinning from ear to ear. "What are you doing here anyway?"

"I'm trying to find out what people think about this bus boycott."

"How come you want to know about that?"

"I work for a newspaper and I'm writing a story."

Suddenly the friendly atmosphere disappeared. A decided freeze set in. "You ain't gonna write about me. I ain't got nothin to say to you. Why don't you yankees leave us alone. Got to all the time be stirrin up trouble. All the time. Damnyankees, anyhow."

"It looks like I'm getting what I came for," Kate thought.

"So far, nothing but abuse." She finished her coffee and went outside before taking out her notebook to write.

She continued her ambling, watched the people walking by, heard the car horns honking, heard the piercing screech of the policeman's whistle as he directed traffic. She was only a few doors along when she was stopped by a young black boy who was bobbing and bouncing in front of her. He couldn't have been more than nine or ten. He had a shoe shine box in his hand. He was directly in her path.

"Shine, Ma'am?" he said.

"I don't think I need one," she said.

"Only twenty-five cents. Twenty-five cents, Ma'am."

"No, I just shined them before I left home."

"I betcha I know sump'n bout you that'd be worth mor'n twenty-five cents."

Kate decided to play along. "What do you know about me that I don't know."

"Double or nothing. Fifty cents says I can tell you where you got them shoes." The boy looked up at her with pure innocence.

"All right. Double or nothing. Where did I get these shoes?"

"You gots them shoes right on your feets. That's where you gots em."

Kate doubled over laughing. Tears came to her eyes. She couldn't stop. The boy stood, looking at her, a completely serious expression on his face. He was holding out his hand.

"All right, double it is. If you'll answer a questions for me."

"Yeah. I answers any questions you got."

"Are you walking now or are you still riding the bus when you come downtown to shine shoes?"

"Ain takin no buses. Mama say don ride them buses no more till she say so. I's walkin now. But that don make me no never min. I's been walkin' all my life. Gets where I wants to go with them shoes I's got on my feets. Makes me some money, too, walkin. Finds more folks with dirty shoes."

"And gullible minds, too," thought Kate as she handed him his fifty cents. "Thanks," she said. "You were worth it."

She watched him bobbing and bending, almost like a dancer, whistling his way down the street, now fifty cents richer. Before half a block he had stopped another unsuspecting victim. "A con man at nine," she thought. "Wouldn't surprise me if he grew up to be a millionaire."

She wandered into a department store and interviewed one of the white clerks. "If y'all are askin me, the'ah all crazy. Ah just don't know what all this fussin is about. We all ride the same bus and we all get to whe'ah we're goin. I just don't understand. All this fussin about ridin' the buses. I just don't understand."

As he came off duty, she asked the white policemen, whose whistle had been piercing her ears for the last hour. "You want to know how I feel about the bus boycott? Is that what you want to know? Let em walk. Let the damn niggers walk."

After this piece of nastiness Kate decided she had had enough. She located her car and headed back to the motel. On the way she stopped at MacDonalds and picked up a hamburger and some fries. "I'm ready for a nice quiet evening in front of the T.V.," she thought.

Sunday dawned bright and sunny. She opened her eyes to the sound of church bells. "That's what I'll do today," she thought. "I'll go to church."

She found a small Baptist church near her motel. The congregation was well into the service by the time she walked in. She was relatively unnoticed except by the ushers and a few people in the back. She was surprised at how comfortable she felt. Never before had she been the only white person in a sea of black faces. Not only was she comfortable, she felt absolutely exhilarated.

The room was exhilarating. The people were standing and singing, not the way they stood and sang in the churches she knew; they were singing with their whole bodies, "with their whole souls," she thought. At first she was afraid to sing, but the singing was infectious. Before long she was singing as lustily as the rest, clapping and swaying to the beat.

A minister dressed in a long black robe, was standing in front of the people, leading them on. "Everybody praise the Lord," he shouted above the music.

And the music; it was coming from a piano, not from an organ. It was pouring forth an incessant beat, more like the jazz she heard in Chicago, than the Sunday morning church music she was used to.

"Everybody praise the Lord," shouted the minister

"Everybody praise the Lord," they all shouted.

"Ain gonna never stop praising him."

"Ain gonna never stop praising him."

Ain't gonna never stop praising him.

"Ain gonna never stop praising the Lord."

The whole congregation; men, women, young, and old, boys and girls . . . all were on their feet, clapping and stomping, swaying and bending to the music. The voices were rich and strong, full of feeling for their Lord.

"Hallelujah," shouted the minister.

"Help me, help me, help me Lord.
Help me, Lord, today.
Help me wake up in the mornin'.
Help me wake up in the sunshine.
Help me wake up to praise the Lord."

"Thank you Jesus, praise God," said the minister.

"Praise God," the congregation responded.

"Get on your feet, all you sinners."

"Yes, get up on your feet to praise."

"Everybody on your feet for the singing."

"Everybody praise the Lord."

"Yes, everybody praise the Lord."

"Everybody! Praise the Lord."

And everybody was praising the Lord; on their feet, clapping, hands above their heads, using their bodies as drums, swinging and swaying. Enjoying their church. Kate felt carried away.

"Yes, everybody praise the Lord," shouted the minister. "Praise him **every** day. And you shall praise him with your deeds. How shall we praise him, brothers and sisters?"

"With our deeds," they responded.

"And your deeds are to **love,** brothers and sisters," the minister continued. "Then you shall not transgress the Lord. And what are your deeds?"

"Not to transgress the Lord," they responded.

"Now, let us pray." he said.

They stayed on their feet, continuing to sway, as if the music were still playing. And from their hearts, they prayed.

"Our father, who art in heaven, we're in need of you now," said the minister.

"Yes, Lord, we're in need," responded the congregation.

"Come down to us."

"Yes, Lord, keep on a comin."

"We want to do your will, your will be done."

"We want to, Lord. We want to do your will."

"We want to love

"Yes, Lord, we want to love."

"But somehow we fall short. We transgress, Lord."

"Yes, sometimes we transgress."

"And sometimes we are transgressed against."

"Yes, Lord, we are transgressed against."

"Forgive us our transgressions as we forgive thosee who transgress against us. And for our sermon today, we are going to ask the Lord's forgivencss for all the transgressions that are going on in Montgomery today. And we are going to ask him to give us strength, yes strength, to stand tall even when we're transgressed against. That's what we're going to do brothes and sisters. Stand tall, against all transgressions."

"Yes, Lord, we are going to stand tall." For the first time the congregation sat down, standing as tall while sitting as they had while they were standing tall.

"Yes, Lord, in this city of Montgomery we have been transgressed. We have been down-trodden, brothers and sisters. We have been cast out. Just like Jesus, who was born in a stable. He was cast out. We have been cast out. Cast out of restaurants, cast out of churches, cast out of schools, we've even been cast out of our own homes."

"Yeah. We've been cast out."

"And all manner of evil has been committed against us by our transgressors. First they threatened us, brothers and sisters. They threatened to take away our jobs. They threatened to take away our livelihood, brothers and sisters. They threatened to take away the bread with which we feed our babies."

"Yes, Lord, they threatened us."

"But we are strong. We are stronger than the walls of Jericho. We do not fall down. We do not give in to the threats of our transgressors. No, brothers and sisters. We are too strong for that. We do not fall down in the face of evil. Even when they take away our jobs. Even when they take away our livelihood. Even when they do **all manner** of evil against us."

"Yes, Lord. We are strong."

"Even when they wear white robes. Even when they burn their crosses on our front lawns. Even when they put us in jail for no reason. **Even**, brothers and sisters, when they bomb our homes. We have suffered all manner of transgressions, and still we are strong."

"Yes, Lord. We are strong."

"Yes, brothers and sisters. We are strong in the face of the evil massing against us. We are strong in the face of hate. We are strong in the faces of the enemies who cast us out. We don't fall to the temptation of the devil. The temptation of the sin of evil and hate. The temptation to do evil . . . to do violence. We are too strong, brothers and sisters . . . "

"Yes, Lord, we don't fall to the temptation of the devil."

"Our deeds are clear. Brothers and sisters, our deeds are clear. Our deeds are to suffer burning feet, from walking. To suffer the abuse of our enemies. Our deeds are clear. Our deeds are to **stay off the buses."**

The congregation was on its feet.

The piano player started the beat.

"Hallelujah," said the minister.

"Hallelujah," shouted the congregation. **"Hallelujah, to the Lord."**

"No matter what you're going through," said the minister, "Shout Hallelujah. Hallelujah to the Lord."

And again the church rocked with the wonderful energies of the people. Their rich voices raised in praise to the Lord who was leading them through the hardship and suffering of their everyday lives, made only a little bit more difficult by having to find other transportation to work, but also made easier by hope.

Then they discovered her. The last 'Amen' was said, and the service was over. Then they discovered her. The excitement of the service had carried her away and she had forgotten that she was an alien in an unknown territory. She had forgotten. But they had not. Their shocked looks brought Kate back to the reality of her whiteness.

Then they all welcomed her. Shock over, they welcomed her. They actually welcomed her; with the same exuberance that they praised the Lord, they welcomed her. She found herself swept into the basement, cups of coffee pressed into her hands, delicious cakes popped into her mouth, and all the information she needed at her disposal. They gave her an invitation to one of their mass meetings the following Tuesday night.

Kate wondered if she weren't in her own private heaven when she left the church that day... She was leaving with so many well wishes from her new-found friends. She was so full of her success, she decided to keep going. She found another Negro Baptist Church not far from the first. This congregation was just letting out. People were standing around outside, enjoying the sunshine and each other. Kate parked her car across the street and waited. She had a jolt of envy as she watched their easy comradarie.

When the last family was piling into their car, Kate crossed the street and caught the minister as he was about to re-enter the church.

"You've come to the right man, Miss," he said. "Come on in. Come on in. Have a cup of coffee while we talk. Yes, Ma'am, I've been working with the boycott since just after Rosa Parks was arrested. Yes, Ma'am, I have. It was forty of us, got this thing going, right in the basement of the Dexter Avenue Church, that's Dr. King's church. Forty of us, right there in the basement; we worked it out. Decided that the time was right, we did and we called the boycott. I'll tell you, we were scared. We reckoned the people were with us, but then again, you never know. I'll tell you, when I woke up Monday morning and looked at those empty buses, I cheered. Yes, Ma'am, I stood right in my living room and I cheered. Empty bus after empty bus went by."

"And they're still goin by. Empty. Yes, Ma'am. Empty. Lots of people tempted to get back on those buses, but they ain't gonna do it. No, Ma'am, they ain't gonna do it. We have meetings, we do. Twice a week we have meetings to keep em cheered up. And now we've got station wagons, all we can find, to use in our car pools. We're gettin our people to work, yes, Lord. And I'm here to tell you, Ma'am, we're gonna keep at it, until we get what we want. And what we want ain't all that much. Just a beginning, that's all we're asking. Just a beginning. We want fair treatment on those buses, that's what we want. We don't want to pay in the front and then have to get back out and get on in the back, while that bus, half the time, goes off without us. And we want to take our seats and keep em. We don't want to have to get up half way home and give our seats to the white folks. No Ma'am, we don't. And we want our own Negro drivers, out here in the colored section. Now, I know we're gonna keep on walkin till we get it. Yes, Ma'am, we are."

Success number two. So different than yesterday. Kate started to believe she couldn't fail. Flush with those two experiences, she decided to try a white Baptist Church. She drove toward the outskirts of town, finding a pretty white church with a tall spiral. It was nestled among stately homes on a quiet dignified street. Church was obviously over but the house next door was marked "Rectory." She rang the bell.

A slim, young, colored woman answered the door. To Kate's inquiry, she said, "Just a minute. I'll call him."

A tall, thin, rather wiry man came to the door. He heard her question, then left her standing on the porch while he answered.

"Well, Miss, I'd say all those nigras are just plain crazy. They're just stirring up trouble; that's all they're doing. They're going to bring violence to this city, mark my word. We've done everything we could to stop it. We've told them that we've always treated them fairly. They get seats just like we do. And now they're saying they want to sit just anywhere on that bus. Why, we just can't have that. The Lord decreed that the whites and the nigras are meant to sit separate and that's the way it's going to be. Now, if y'all will excuse me, I was right in the middle of my dinner."

The next moment Kate was staring at a closed door. Stunned, she descended from the porch, wondering about the legendary hospitality of the southern people.

Undaunted, she continued her tour. Several blocks away she found a Methodist Church, red brick, set among the budding of some beautiful flowers and several magnolia trees. She rang the bell of the rectory. This time she was greeted by the rector, himself, a portly slightly greying, kindly-looking man.

"Well, come on in. Come on in. The misses and I were just having our dessert in the living room. Join us for some good old southern apple pie and chicory coffee. What is it you're wanting to know, now? Oh, yes, the boycott. What do I think of it?"

"Now you're a yankee, aren't you? Well, I was born right here in Montgomery. Yes, Ma'am. Right here in this city. I've been here all my life. I've always gotten along with the nigras. I just don't know what's gotten into em now. Gittin down right uppity if you're asking me. But then, you being a yankee and all, you wouldn't understand. You let your nigras ride your buses and sit wherever they like. And you even let em sit in the same restaurants as you. That's why you've got all this intermarrying up there. Same schools, same seats on those buses, even the same toilets. Got to be careful about those toilets. Those nigras got diseases, you know."

"But I hear tell you don't let em in your neighborhoods. Now, we let em in our neighborhoods all the time. They come in our neighborhoods to work every mornin. They're in our houses all day. We know em. We understand em. We know what they want. I tell you, they don't want to be intermixin with us. They've got things good, just the way it is. It's their leaders that's doing it. It's the leaders all right. The nigras don't have minds of their own. Everybody knows that. So when somebody says jump, they jump. Somebody says don't ride the buses, they don't ride the buses. You want to know the truth? It's the communists that's got em all stirred up. That's the truth if you ask me. Would you like a little more sugar for your coffee?"

Kate's good feelings were diminishing rapidly. Now she was beginning to realize how strong was the force of resistance faced by those who were refusing to ride the buses. If this was the attitude of the white ministers, the leaders of morality, no wonder the frustration, no wonder the despair of people like her landlord.

After leaving the rectory she made a decision. "I'll try one more." She found a phone booth and looked up the address of a Catholic Church. "Might as well be ecumenical," she thought, as she headed her car north.

A handsome young man, no more than thirty, with dark hair and a turned around collar invited her in. He had been reading in a book-lined room complete with fireplace. His warm fire took the chill off the March air and invited an easy congeniality. Kate sensed he appreciated the company.

"You're interested in the boycott," he said. "I am too. I think what they're doing is taking a great deal of courage. I admire them, every one. They're putting everything on the line: their jobs, and even their lives. They're putting everything on the line just for the right to ride those buses in freedom. I admire them."

"But I've got to admit, my congregation doesn't agree with me. If they heard me talking like this, I'd be out of a job. I've tried to help them see but they believe that integration is the worst kind of evil, a worse evil than the inhuman treatment of other human beings. They've been taught that from babyhood."

The man was shaking his head. "I can't make a dent in their belief so I've quit trying. If I said to them what I'm saying to you, I'd be out on my ear so fast. There aren't many Catholics here in Montgomery. Those we have don't want to be stirred up into thinking something different than they already believe. Consequently, I have to keep my views to myself."

"I wish I had the courage of those Negroes out there who are willing to put their jobs on the line. But I don't. And I pray to God every day to forgive me the sin of my guilt."

Back in her motel room, Kate wrote one hell of a story to call in to Ed the next day.

Chapter 52

Kate was barely able to stand still. Excitement was racing through her veins. Hundreds of dark faces were coming toward her from all directions, pouring into the basement of the Holt Avenue Baptist Church. Those faces touched her: determined faces, tired faces, friendly faces, sad faces, dejected faces, elated faces, all coalescing around the rightness of what they were doing. She stood under a street light, watching, fascinated by all the activity. They laughed with each other, joked back and forth and greeted each other with hugs and good-natured punches. Their kinship was awesome. Kate was caught up in it; outside of it, yet caught up in it.

When the droves filtered down to a trickle, she went in. She hesitantly stood at the door, seeing almost no empty chairs. From one side of the room she heard, "Pssssst. Come sit over here." It was Martha, waving and gesturing. It was Martha, the woman who had been so warm and welcoming during her first foray into the black Baptist Church on Sunday, the woman who had been the instigator of her being here in the first place.

The crowd settled into the program . . . the singing, the prayers, the reading of the scriptures, the committee reports. Finally, came the high-light of the night. A man stepped to the front of the room, a man Kate did not recognize.

"That's Dr. King," Martha whispered in her ear.

"That's Dr. King?" Kate said. "He's so short. A lot shorter than I thought he would be. But he's sure got broad shoulders."

"He needs them broad shoulders, the work he's been doin," whispered Martha. "He's the one keepin us together. When we gits tired and ready to give up, he comes right along and inspires us again. And then we don't give up. Listen."

Kate could do nothing but listen. It was his voice. His deep melodious voice. Right away, it touched her, touched her in some profound place where God resided, where the rightness of herself resided, where rightness itself resided. He wasn't saying anything important. He was simply greeting the people in the room. He was chatting with them. He was asking them how things were going. As they spilled out their worries and their frustrations, as they discharged their angers and their woes, he simply listened. Then he commended them for their courage. It was simple; yet it was one of the most profound interchanges Kate had ever heard. She was stunned by the feelings stirring inside of herself.

Martha was, again, whispering in her ear. "Sometimes that's all he does. He just talks to us like that. Sometimes that's all he needs to do. Just some talkin. Sometimes he gives us a speech. I reckon we'll get a speech tonight."

Martha was right. Shortly, this impelling man made himself comfortable, half sitting, half standing against a table at the front of the room.

He began. "I'm glad to see so many of you here tonight, especially those of you with tired feet and sore bodies. I'm glad to see you here to continue with our fight, our struggle, yes, our struggle for our human dignity. I want to commend you for your courage and your commitment to this, our struggle for freedom. I want to commend you for being here, those of you who are tired from hours of hard work, coming here for more hours of hard work, struggling for our justice."

The crowd was surprisingly quiet.

Kate's confusion of feelings finally settled on one. It was envy. She was envious of the people in this room, envious of their fight, envious of the solidarity it brought to them, envious of the commendation he was giving them.

"We know, yes, we know it is God's will that we be free. That we break the chains of the segregation that has imprisoned us. We have a right, my brethren; yes, we have a right to struggle. To struggle until exhaustion. To take no rest. To give those who imprisoned us in the chains of segregation no peace, until our freedom is won."

Now voices were being heard throughout the crowd. "We have a right." "We will struggle." "No more prisons."

Freedom! Their voices caused Kate to think about freedom. The freedom that was entitled to her by her birthright. The freedom denied to the others in this room, as surely as it was entitled to her.

Dr. King went on talking. "In spite of the difficulties and the frustration of the moment, we will show our white brothers and sisters that there is no turning away from the force of our struggle for this freedom. No matter what injustices we are made to suffer, no matter how wronged we have been, we will continue in our struggle for this freedom. We will continue, but we will continue without violence. Our struggle is non-violent; for you know and I know that we cannot win with violence. Our enemies would crush us with their superior strength and shame us for our efforts. Many of us would die. We do not want to die for our efforts. Nor do we want to kill, maim, or destroy. But we will let the nation know, even though we do not wish to destroy, we will have our freedom, the freedom promised us in the constitution, in the emancipation proclamation, and by the laws of this great land."

"Amen, Martin."

"Tell em like it is, Martin."

"Yeah, tell em, Martin."

Kate was swept away by his words, by the feelings in the room, by the dignity of the crowd; a dignity that did not come from their entitlement, as did hers, but came from their inner beings, from their very souls. They knew who they were, not because they were told, but just because they knew. "Freedom!" she thought.

He was continuing. "No longer will we be ignored. No longer will our enemies make the mistake of believing in our contentment. We are not content! We will no longer allow those who perpetuated our chains of segregation to believe we are content. Our voices will ring out. Our feet will march. Our injustices will be heard. And we will not stop, my brethren, until we win. Until we win, my brethren."

"Until we win," came the response.

"And we will win. We will win, not through violence, but through love. The love I see on your faces tonight, the love we have for each other, and even the love we have for our oppressors. It is through our love that we will win. In spite of our tired feet and tired bodies, our spirits are not tired. Our spirits will struggle on, until we have the right to be free! And we will be free! We have the right to be free! And we will be free! Hallelujah to the Lord! We will be free!"

Everybody in the room was on their feet. Chairs crashed to the floor. "Hallelujah, Martin!"

"Amen. Amen!"

"We will be free!"

Kate couldn't hold back her tears.

Amidst the shouting and the clapping, Kate made a vow to the spirit within every human being. "I vow that I will do everything according to my talents, to free the spirit of myself and as many others as possible, as it is within my power."

Then the piano pounded out and the room vibrated with song.

"Hallelujah, anyhow.
Hallelujah, anyhow.
Hallelujah, anyhow.
No matter what our trials,
Hallelujah, anyhow.

Hallelujah, anyhow.
Hallelujah, anyhow.
You taught me, Lord,
Hallelujah, anyhow.

It was love that you taught me, Lord.
Hallelujah, anyhow.
No matter what my tribulations
Hallelujah, anyhow.

When I wake up in the morning,
Hallelujah, anyhow.
No matter what my day brings,
Hallelujah, anyhow.

Hallelujah, anyhow.
Hallelujah, anyhow.
With your love, I can make it,
Hallelujah, anyhow."

Kate was singing and clapping with the best. Her body was bending and swaying as the feelings overwhelmed her.

Meeting over, Martha steered her to the front of the room. "You got to meet Dr. King," she insisted. But the front of the room as a hubbub of activity, all of it around Dr. King. Kate prepared to wait.

But he saw her. She was hard to hide. He smiled at her and very quickly made his way through the throng of people, hand out-stretched. "Welcome," he said. "Welcome to the Holt Baptist Church. I am very glad you're here."

"Thank you," she said, feeling a wonderful warmth from his hand. "Thank you. I . . . "Kate was struggling with her feelings. Tears kept pushing their way forward.

"I . . . I . . . . " Finally she was able to blurt it out. "Thank you for not treating me as an enemy."

"You are a friend," he said, his smile completely reassuring.

"I . . . I . . . ," she said, still flustered. Then she found her tongue. "Yes, I am your friend and I want you to know I will do everything I can to help your struggle."

"She writes for one of them newspapers up north," interrupted Martha.

"Ah," he said. "Then you can be a great help to us. Our story needs to be told. We want people to know of our work here in Montgomery. We will be forever grateful to you for letting the world know. God bless you for your work."

He took her hand in both of his and squeezed it warmly.

Kate wondered why she didn't melt on the spot.

The next morning a remarkable story was called in to Ed in Chicago.

After the phone call Kate sailed out of the motel capable of challenging anything . . . she thought. Today she was going to high schools, both black and white, to talk to the students. She was in high spirits. She wasn't looking for trouble. She didn't know that trouble was looking for her.

She started at the Negro High School near her motel. She got directions from her reluctant landlord.

She was appalled when she drove up to the building. It was a falling-down ramshackled frame building that would have been put to shame by the worst of the northern country schools.

The outside was made of grey weather-beaten boards, some nailed over with more grey weather-beaten boards. Holes marked the lower levels and it appeared that animals came and went through these holes with impunity. Several windows were broken and covered over from the inside with pieces of sheets and other ragged cloth. The steps to the front door were non-existent. They consisted of a pile of rocks that at one time had pretended to be concrete steps. Inside was an incredible array of rooms and half rooms serving as classrooms.

Kate was greet warmly by a slightly bent, grey-haired man in glasses, who was toiling over some papers on his desk. "Good morning, Ma'am. Can I help you. You want to talk to the students about the boycott. Why, yes, Ma'am. Why don't you just go down to one of the classrooms and ask them. Why, no, they wouldn't mind a bit. Probably enjoy the diversion."

Within five minutes, Kate was facing a classroom of maybe thirty students, all looking quizzically at her. To her question, "What do you think about the bus boycott?" she heard:

"Well, Ma'am, I hadn't thought much about it. I don't go nowhere no ways so ridin them buses don't make no never mind to me."

"Bout time my Daddy did something bout what he believes. He's been yellin bout the whites this and the whites that for years. Now he's doing something bout it."

"I rides them buses cause I goes to work after I finishes school. Is hard to be walking now. I's tired fore I even gits to work."

"My Mama, she lost her job cause she say she ain't takin no buses. Ain't no other way for her to git there, so she ain't workin no more. Good thing, too, cause she shore be tired a workin. I likes her better, now, I does."

"My Daddy drives one a those car pools. Now we got ourselves one of those station wagons and he picks up people all over and takes them to work. Maybellene, why didn't you tell me your Mama didn't have a ride to work? My Daddy'd see to it that she got to work."

To her question; "What do you think about the schools being desegregated," they said: "I likes it here."

"We've got our own basketball team here, and we can beat any team in the city. In the white schools they wouldn't even let us play."

"I'd go if we could keep our teachers."

"Well, Ma'am, I want to go to college. I think I'd be better prepared if I went to the white school."

"I thinks they ought to come here to go to school. I don't see no reason why I needs to go off to one a their schools."

"Ain't gonna happen no how. Ain't no need to be thinkin' on it."

Kate got instructions from the grey-haired principal on how to get to the white High School. She drove with her windows down, taking in the smell of spring that was definitely in the Montgomery air.

It was close to 2 o'clock when she drove up to a large brick building with a well kept playground and lawn. The principal sat behind a well-windowed office positioned behind a flank of four secretaries. At first he was reluctant. "Well, I don't know about tha'et," he said. When she explained that she had already been to the black high school and wanted both sides, he became more interested. "In tha'et case, I suppose it would be all ra'ht." He peered out of his window. "Yes, Miz Andrews. A numbah of ou'ah students are out on the playground now; why don't ya'all go out the'ah. Ahm sure ya'all'l get the answers you ah aftah."

Kate was unprepared for the amount of hostility in those so young.

"What's it to ya, yankee?"

"I ain't sittin' next to no nigger, no way!"

"You one a them nigger-lovin yankees?"

"Ah don't ca'ah whe'ah they rahd. Just so it's not next to me."

"My papa says that they can walk till hell freezes over. Nobody's givin them niggers nothin. And my papa ought to know. He works in the mayor's office."

"You better watch who y'all are askin questions to, Miz Yankee, Ma'am."

"I don't have to tell you nothin."

And to her question about integrating the schools: "My papa says I'm not going to school with niggers. He says he'll take me out of school first."

"My church is settin up a private school. I'm gonna go there."

"Any nigger gets in my face, I'll beat him bloody."

"Never!"

"You one a them nigger lovin yankees?"

"Yeah, tell us about the integration up there in Chicago, Miz Yankee, Ma'am."

"My papa says not to worry. There aren't going to be any niggers in our school. And he knows all about it. He has friends on the school board."

"What's it to ya, anyhow?"

Kate had to sit quietly in her car for a long time, calming her confused emotions. One thought kept recurring. "Where I am one of the enemy, I am accepted as a friend . . . even welcomed. Where I should be a friend, I'm treated like the enemy." It was more than an hour before she got herself together enough to drive.

Her frazzled nerves dictated that she drive only a short distance. As she drove down the street she noticed a small coffee shop on the right hand side of the road. Her body wanted something, just something, after her ordeal. It seemed as if the car turned automatically into the parking space in front of the place. "I'll just go in for a cup of coffee and try to try to sort out my day." she thought. "I'll write my story while I'm there. Then I'll go on to the motel."

The restaurant was almost empty when she went in. She found a booth and went to work. Little by little the booths filled, noises increased, dishes rattled, blenders mixed shakes and malts, waitresses yelled out orders and voice levels increased with greetings, shouts, curses, laughter.

Kate, absorbed in her writing, ignored it all. She was slightly aware of an increasing level of activity at a large table toward the front, but not enough to disrupt her activity. Then it seemed as though bedlam erupted at that table. It was so loud that she could no longer ignore it.

A stab of fear went through her when she saw the occupants of the table. Two of them had been among the nastiest of her afternoon interviewees. And they were all turned towards her.

"That's the lady nigger-lover."

"Yeah?"

"Yankee nigger-lover?"

"Yeah."

"Askin all them questions that ain't none a her business."

"Yeah."

"Maybe we should take care of her nigger-lovin ass."

"Yeah."

Kate quickly gathered her papers and paid the bill. She walked out into the dark.

She was followed outside by five boys and two girls.

She was afraid to run, and afraid not to.

Her wobbly legs did manage to carry her to the car and safely inside. "God, please let this car start," she prayed as she watched the group pouring into their two cars.

It did, and she was out of the lot in a shot but they peeled rubber and were out of the parking lot right behind her.

They were leaning out of the car windows, spewing verbal abuse. "Nigger-lover."

"See the nigger-lovin bitch."

"Yankee nigger-lover."

"White nigger-lovin bitch."

"Bitch loves nigger ass."

One car had pulled alongside, while the other was directly behind, blinding her by alternating bright and low beams.

Approaching an open parkway, they started to crowd her. One car was pushing from behind, edging her over toward the grass. The side of her car was brushing perilously close to the trees.

"The only thing I can say for myself now," she thought ruefully, "is that I'm not lost." Then she looked at the road ahead. "Oh, my God, there's a bridge ahead. If I stay where I am, I'll ram the abutment."

Adrenalin soured through her veins. 'Move!' was the command. She gunned the motor. No time to be scared. No time to be timid. Outrun them. She caught them with their reflexes down. Momentarily they dropped behind, long enough for her to cross the bridge. She sailed around the next corner and careened around the next. They were on her tail. The motel was just ahead. She hit the parking lot at full speed, squealing to a stop under the canopy to the office. They either had to hit her in the rear or turn to the outside of the canopy. They elected not to hit her.

They squealed to a stop just as she dashed for the office door. Her sometime antagonist was inside. She didn't need to tell him. He saw the trouble.

He pulled two guns from under the counter. "Get down Miss Andrews. I'll take care of this. Ralph, get in here." He tossed one of the guns to a second man as he appeared from the back room. "Come on," he said.

Almost before the two men were outside, there was a screeching of tires. Both cars had taken off.

When the owner came back into the office, he was shaking his head. "Knew there'd be trouble with you around. I knew it. I just knew it."

Kate had nothing to say. She couldn't stop her legs from shaking, and words were unavailable. There was only one word she needed anyway. She finally forced it out of her hoarse throat.

"Thanks." She almost managed a weak smile.

His smile was broad. "Well, Miss Andrews. You're a piece of trouble, just like I said but I can deal with it. I approve of what you've been writing about us."

Kate looked perplexed. "How do you know what I've been writing?"

"I listen from the switchboard when you call your newspaper."

Kate started to laugh. She couldn't stop herself. Suddenly her weak legs and misplaced voice were forgotten. When she finally gained control of herself, she wiped the tears from her eyes and said "So you've been snooping on my conversations, have you?"

"Yup."

"Now that you approve of what I write, are we friends?"

"Well, I'm not sure I'd go so far as to say that. I'm not sure I'd go that far."

"But you're willing to save my life, right?"

"Yup. I'd go that far."

Back in her room, Kate added to her story for tomorrow's paper.

The next day Kate visited various members of the city government: the Mayor, the Police Chief, the Fire Chief, the Health Commissioner, the Superintendent of Education, etc. It was a repeat of the afternoon with the students, without the adolescent violence. They used their own adult violence, their official power . . . that portended no danger.

"Vermin. Nothing but black vermin."

"Trouble makers. They'll get all the trouble they're asking for."

"Communist agitators."

"We'll see to it that those nigras aah taken ca'ah of."

"Give in? Negotiate? Never."

"Integrate the schools? Nevah!"

"No stinking nigger buck'll sit next to me on any bus."

"Well, they might have a point."

"They can damn well walk forever. I'm not budging one inch."

"I didn't hear about anybody's home being bombed."

"Damn niggers. Don't know their place any more."

"What? You mean the police have been implicated? Preposterous."

Kate didn't try for dinner that night. Instead, she went home and threw up the lunch so hospitably bought for her by the City Commissioner. No story was written that night. She fell weakly into bed before eight and slept around the clock. The story was called in just in time for deadline the next morning. Then, she got back into bed and stayed for the rest of the day.

The next morning was Saturday. She returned the car to the rental agency and caught the plane for Chicago. As the plane gained altitude, Kate watched out the window as the peaceful scene of Montgomery faded below her. "Deceiving. Deceiving. All that peace," she thought. "Seething would be closer to the truth. Peaceful on the outside, seething on the inside."

She tried to go back to watching the scenery, but her mind wouldn't give her that kind of peace. A message kept flashing through her brain. "There's a meaning to all of this. A meaning, a meaning you need to **know**."

The 'no smoking' sign went off and she leaned back and closed her eyes. Images started parading across her visual field: the contorted faces of the city officials she had interviewed, the hostility of the students, the excitement of her foray into a Negro church, Martin Luther King speaking, Martha's friendship, her narrow escape from injury at the hands of adolescents, the gun in the hands of the motel owner, the little black shoeshine boy, the anger and hate on one side, the frustration and determination on the other.

A new set of images: her father beating her, Dr. Froleck rejecting her, Bryan criticizing her, Ed making her feel small, little Jeff and little Gene growing up to be just like her father, just like Froleck and Bryan.

Her mother, weak and ineffectual. . . Jenny! Fighting back . . . Martin Luther King! Fighting back . . . Jenny. Insisting on love . . . Dr. King. Insisting on love.

What did it all mean?

She looked at the clouds billowing and reshaping beneath her. She looked at the sun illuminating the tops of the clouds and glinting off the metal of the plane. Then, suddenly she knew!

She immediately took out her notepad and started to write.

'A Woman's Eye View.'

It was the title of her new column.

CHAPTER 53

"Ed, I want to know if I can reduce my work load?"

"Two kids are too much, huh?"

"No, I still have Lucia to look after the boys, but I want to go back to school."

"What?"

"I said I want to go back to school."

"I heard you. You've got two boys, a husband at home, and a job and now you want to go back to school. That's the damndest fool idea I've ever heard."

"Will you reduce my work load so I can go back to school?"

"And just what school is it you want to go back to?"

"The University of Chicago. I want to go for my Master's degree in Urban Studies. I want to know more about what's going on in this city."

"Thought you knew enough about this city. You want I should have you cover more of it, so you can know more?"

"No, Ed. That's not what I want. I want my work load reduced so I can go back to school. Will you do it?"

"No."

"Then you'll have my resignation this afternoon."

"Wait just a minute here. I didn't mean for you to resign."

"No, Ed, what you meant to say was, 'No, you won't reduce my work load.' I can not work full-time here and go to school full time, too. And I **am** going to school."

"Determined broad, aren't you?"

"Yes. And don't call me a broad!"

"And what hours would suit you?"

"I think I could manage one-quarter time and still go to school. Since I'm going to be there, I could cover the University and the south side. Actually, I could take over Horowitz's beat. Then he could have mine. He's always wanted my beat."

"Horowitz isn't competent to cover your beat."

"Well, thank you, Ed. I'm more competent than Horowitz?"

"Harumph. I didn't say that."

"Well . . . whatever. Is one-quarter time all right?"

"Suppose there's nothing I can do about it. When do you want to start?"

"In September. I want to go back to school fall quarter."

"So start in September, then."

"Thanks, Ed." Kate started toward the door. She paused and turned back. "Oh, by the way, Ed. When are you going to start printing my columns? My 'Woman's Eye View.'"

"Never. You stick to reporting and let the columnists write the columns. If you want to write about a woman's eye view, I'll transfer you to the woman's page."

"Ed . . . ."

"Go back to work. I'm not going to print them. Damned fool idea anyway."

"I'm going to keep writing them."

"Get out of here."

Back in her cubicle she turned her thoughts to the next step in getting back to school . . . telling Bryan. Her conversation with Ed was a piece of cake in comparison to what she expected from Bryan. He did not disappoint her.

She waited until that night after dinner. "Bryan, I've decided to go back to school in September. I've applied, and I've been accepted. Ed has agreed to reduce my hours."

Bryan had just picked up the newspaper and was looking for the sports page. "I've already told you I don't want you going back to school."

"And that is that, am I right?"

"That's right." Bryan was now absorbed in the Cub's second loss of the season.

"And I'm telling you something else that's right, Bryan. I'm going anyway."

"No, you're not."

"How do you plan to stop me?"

Bryan jammed the paper together, managing to drop some of the pages on the floor in the process. He glared at her. "I said you're not going. You're never here as it is. I never see you. What about the boys? Do you forget you have two boys? You can't go." He began to piece the paper together again.

"Bryan, I'm going. This is important to me, and I'm going."

From behind his paper Bryan said, "And where do you think you're going to get the money? I'll not give you a red cent."

"Too bad, Bryan. I don't need your money. I've got a scholarship. The rest I'll get from my own earnings. And I wish you'd come out from behind that newspaper if we're going to discuss this."

"We're not going to discuss it. My decision is made."

"So is mine, Bryan. So is mine."

Bryan was right. There was no more discussion. In September Kate enrolled in the University of Chicago in Urban Studies, signed up for her classes and bought her books . . . while Bryan sulked.

On the day of her first class she was putting the last touches on an article for the paper. She was frantically typing, working in her cubicle, just a half hour before she was to be in class. Unfortunately class was held sixty-five blocks south of where she was. After a pell-mell race down Lake Shore Drive she arrived late and breathless.

"You must be Kate," said the man at the head of the room.

She liked him immediately. He was in his late thirties, had slightly greying hair and a boyish face. His tall, lanky body acted as though it had no bones. "I'm Dr. Tim Russell. You can call me Tim. Just find yourself a seat. We've already started introducing ourselves."

It wasn't hard to find a seat. There were only six students in a room large enough for thirty. A tall, black-eyed girl with equally black hair had been talking when Kate came in. "I'm Jackie Marinelli," she said directly to Kate as she pushed some of her long hair out of her face. "I'm from Brooklyn, and I'm Italian." She then returned her attention to the rest of the group. "I'm here because I've been in trouble all my life. Now I want out of the trouble, and so I'm going to school."

Kate liked her immediately. She was so vibrant and alive. Her face was especially fascinating. It was a face that was anything but naive, as though she had fully experienced life's reality and it had not always been a pleasant reality.

The next to speak was a beautiful Negro girl with a French accent. She looked young . . . in her early twenties . . . no more. "My name is Ella Benodin," she said so softly that Kate could hardly hear her. "I lived in Haiti when I was a little girl but my papa, he fought in the revolution against Papa Doc . . . when my papa was wounded, we came here. I've lived in Chicago since I was ten. Now I want to fight a revolution of my own. An American revolution for kids who need and don't have. So I'm here to learn how." She sat down quickly.

"Such different people," thought Kate. "Jackie, so outgoing, and Ella, so shy."

A shaggy-looking young man about thirty with long hair and a beard was the next to stand up. His accent was distinctly New York, Jewish and superior. He was holding an unlit pipe in his hand. "My name is Leonard Shapiro. I'm from New York, too," he said, looking at Jackie out of the corner of his eye. "My father is the most prejudiced man I know. He wants me to be a Rabbi, so I came here to learn about cities. I'm not going to be a Rabbi. I don't know what I want to be, but I'm not going to be a Rabbi."

"I wonder what learning about cities has to do with not wanting to be a Rabbi," thought Kate. "He certainly is an interesting-looking man. I hope he gets the snob out of him."

Next was a short, wiry-looking boy who looked as if he was just about drinking age. His hair was dark and cut just above his ears. He seemed to be in a great hurry to say what he wanted to say. "I'm Nathan Rabinowitz," he said. "But everybody calls me Nat. You can call me Nat. I just graduated from Northwestern University last year. I wrote for the Northwestern Daily and I was good, too. I live in Wilmette where the rich folks live. My folks are rich. That's why I live there. I don't know why I'm here. I guess I just don't want to work yet."

"Hmmm. Another writer," thought Kate.

After Nat sat down there was silence in the classroom. Nobody made any move to get up. Dr. Russell began to stir at the front of the room.

"Oh, I guess I can be next," said Kate. "My name is Kate Andrews and I'm a writer. I work at *The Chicago Daily News*. Even though I write a lot about urban Chicago, I don't think I understand what's really going on. I want to understand more about this city, and then, maybe, I can write better."

Nat was unable to contain himself when she finished. "You're Kate Andrews! You're name used to be Pritchard, right? I've read your articles in the Northwestern Daily and for the Daily News. You wrote that whole series about Montgomery, right?"

"Right."

"Can you get me a job at *The Daily News?*"

Kate grinned. "Probably not."

Nat went right on as if he hadn't heard. "I'll give you some of my columns. You can take them down there."

"I'll tell you what, Nat. I'll give you the name of my editor. Then you can take your columns to him and get yourself a job."

"Right," he said.

Suddenly both of them realized what they were doing and felt embarrassed. Dr. Russell didn't seem a bit annoyed at the disruption. On the contrary, he seemed quite amused. "And who would like to be next?" he asked.

A medium-tall Negro man with the body of a football player stood up. He looked as if he might be close to thirty. "I'm Joshua Thomas," he said, and sat down.

Dr. Russell looked surprised, and said "Would you like to tell us anything else about yourself, Mr. Thomas?"

"No," he said.

"All right, who's next?"

A tall gangling blond young man stood up next looking as if he would like to crawl into the woodwork; as if he would rather do anything that do what he was now doing. "Uh . . . I . . . uh . . . my name is Dana. Dana Swanson. Uh . . . I'm from North Dakota. Minot, North Dakota. I don't think I belong here. I . . . uh . . . think I'll just mosey on back to where I came from. Maybe take up wheat farming." Then, he quickly sat down.

Everybody laughed.

Introductions over, Kate looked again around the group. "Two Negroes, two Jews, one militant Italian, a Swede from North Dakota, and me, a midwestern hybrid. I think I'm going to like it here."

After class she was hailed by both Jackie and Nat. "Come for coffee at the union," Jackie said. "We're all going."

Nat fell in beside her as they walked, talking nonstop. Ostensibly he wanted to know everything about her, but what he really wanted to do was to tell her all about himself.

At the cafeteria they found a table big enough for the whole group and started in on what would be a pattern for them for the rest of their time in school together. Leonard pulled out his pipe and leaned back to watch. Nat and Jackie were arguing before the others were hardly seated. Ella and Dana looked as if they wanted to hide. Joshua leaned his elbows on the table and was digging into the cream and sugar to put in his coffee. Kate was simply enjoying herself.

And that was the way it was. Diverse as they were, they became a group that day. For the next two years they went to classes together, studied together, ate together, talked together, laughed together, and fought together. They fought about everything.

They fought over music: "Did you see Elvis on T.V. last night?" asked Jackie. "It's about time the boob tube showed up with some decent entertainment."

"I thought he was indecent," said Ella. " My parents made me turn it off."

"Turn it off?" said Leonard. "You still let your parents tell you what to do?"

"Well, he was indecent," said Ella. "All that swiveling and gyrating."

"I agree," said Kate. "It was like he was having sex right there on the screen."

"And what's the matter with sex?" muttered Joshua.

They argued about teenage values: "I saw a movie on T.V. last night and I don't understand it," said Dana.

"What was the movie?" said Nat.

"Rebel Without a Cause," said Dana.

"What do you mean, you don't understand it?" said Jackie.

"I just didn't understand why that boy was rebelling. He had everything, and his parents weren't doing anything to him. He just wasn't very nice."

"His parents were like dictators, Dana," said Jackie. "They were trying to make him be nicey, nicey. And that's full of crap."

"What's wrong with being nice?" said Ella.

"Because nice gets you nowhere," said Leonard. "I tried to be nice at home, and what that got me was under my father's thumb. And when I tried to get away from him he put me out of the house with no money. That's what nice got me. Nothing but trouble."

"I thought the movie was dumb," said Nat. "I don't understand why that kid had to rebel. He should have done what I do. I get to do what I want all the time. If my parents object I just fight with them. That's what I do. I always get what I want."

"Yeah, but what you want is exactly what they want, you dumbhead," said Jackie. "Perfect grades, perfect achievements, and lots of money in the end. You're gonna end up just like em, just you wait and see."

"Wait a minute, Jackie. I'm not so perfect."

"Bullshit. Look at your grades. Best in the class," said Jackie.

"You just don't like it because I'm smarter than you," Nat said.

"You're not so smart. Spend one week on the street, and we'll see how smart you are!" said Jackie.

"What do you mean, 'on the street', Jackie?" asked Dana.

"On the streets. On the streets. That's where I lived when I was growing up, Dana. On the streets of Brooklyn.

"But didn't you live at home?" said Dana.

"Home! I didn't have a home. My old man was a drunk and my Mama was in church all the time when she wasn't working. Home was the worst possible place to be. I hated it. So I lived on the streets. My brother and I, we lived on the streets. And let me tell you, those streets were tough and mean. And I was the toughest and the meanest. We had our territory and nobody, but nobody, violated it. My brother's in jail now because somebody violated our territory. They tried to take it over and my brother pulled his knife. Cut the son-of-a-bitch's up pretty bad. And then the son's-of-bitch's sucked the police on him and he went to jail. That's when I left. When he went to jail, I couldn't take it anymore. I just left. I lived in Manhattan, then, sleeping wherever I could and eating what I could steal. Then one day I decided. 'Fuck this', I said. I'm going to get revenge for my brother and I know how to do it. I'm going to school. I'm not going to tell you how I got the money, but I did and I enrolled in City College of New York. Right now, even, there isn't anything but revenge in my heart. I'm going back there when I'm done with this place. And I'm gonna work with those kids who live on the street like I did. And then I'm gonna get those lousy institutions that got my brother. And they won't be able to do anything to me because I'll get them from inside the law. Because then I'll know how to do it."

For the first time ever, there were seven closed mouths at the table. Nobody knew quite what to say.

It was Kate who finally broke the silence. "I don't know how you could do all of that, Jackie. I never could. I'd never be tough enough to live like that. I would have died somewhere along the way."

"You'd be tough enough if that's all you knew," said Jackie.

"The streets, at least, are honest," said Joshua. "Not full of bullshit, like here."

They talked about drugs: "Have you ever used drugs, Jackie?" asked Dana.

"Sure, lots of times."

"You have?" Dana's eyes opened wide. "What's it like?"

"Like lots of other things. I felt better for a while. Then I felt the same. Then I took more drugs."

"What drugs did you take?" asked Ella.

"I smoked weed. I shot some smack when I could get it."

"What's weed?" asked Dana.

"Marijuana, Dana. Marijuana. Haven't you ever heard of marijuana?" said Nat.

"No. What does it do?"

"It just makes you feel good, like easy," said Jackie.

"And sexy," said Leonard.

"What's smack?" said Kate.

"Heroin," said Jackie.

"You used heroin?" said Kate.

"Whenever I could get it. It cost too much to get it often, but then I owned the world. When I was loaded on smack I owned the world."

"But isn't it dangerous?" asked Ella.

"Sure, but not if you don't get addicted. And I wasn't getting addicted. Getting addicted wasn't part of the scene."

"That's dumb, Jackie. People get addicted even though they don't plan on it," said Leonard.

"It wasn't dumb. It was available and we all were doing it. Getting loaded was the scene. Nothing could have stopped me."

"Whew, my father would have killed me if I used heroin," said Ella.

"Your father wouldn't have needed to know. My old man didn't know. And if he'd known, he wouldn't have cared."

"Is that why you did it, Jackie? Because nobody cared?" asked Kate.

"Naw. I did it because it was fun. And everybody else was doing it. I don't do it any more because now the scene is here. I can't use smack and go to school, too. So now I only smoke weed."

"You still smoke marijuana," said Ella, alarmed.

"Sure. It's better'n pouring all that beer into me, like everybody else around here. I wouldn't put that shit in my body."

"I'd put all that shit in my body," said Joshua. "And then I wouldn't have to put up with all of this shit."

Civil rights was bound to come up: "Hey, did you read about the sit-ins down in North Carolina. Greensboro, I think," said Nat. "Four Negroes just sat down at this lunch counter in Woolworths and refused to leave unless they were served."

"Did they get served?" asked Leonard.

"Hell, no," said Joshua. "The only thing that will get them served is the National Guard."

"Why are you so cynical, Joshua?" said Ella. "Don't you have any faith?"

"Faith, hell! It's going to take the atomic bomb before the niggers down there get anywhere. Those honkys aren't gonna give away anything without a fight. Civil disobedience; turning the other cheek; trying to torment their conscience. Bullshit. All bullshit."

"But Joshua, it can work. It's beginning to work. I see it," said Kate.

"White people are noticing now, Joshua. It is bothering their consciences," said Leonard.

"Consciences ain't worth shit," said Joshua. "Eating in some restaurant with those bastards won't get them any richer. They're talking about equality. Who needs it. Give me money. That's all I want."

"Be reasonable, Joshua," said Leonard. "They've got to take one step at a time. Be patient."

"Patient, man. Patient. Is that what you're telling me to be? That's what you Jews did at Auschwitz and Bugenvield, and Dachau and look what happened to you. Patience gets you dead. I ain't gonna be dead. That's not where it's at for me."

"But Joshua, things are getting better," said Kate. "Life is a lot better for Negroes up here than it is in the south. Schools and living and freedom. It's all better."

"Things are no better here," said Joshua.

"What do you mean, things are no better here?" said Kate.

"Just what I said. Things are no better here."

"But blacks can sit on buses where they want to here. Blacks can use the same bathrooms and drinking fountains here. The schools aren't segregated here. It's a lot better."

"Do you want to see how things really are here. Right here in Chicago?"

"Sure. Show me. How are things right here in Chicago?"

"Yeah, I'll show you. When do you want to go?"

He was bluffing, she knew. She decided to call his bluff. "We don't have class Tuesday. How about Tuesday?"

"Tuesday it is."

CHAPTER 54

He wasn't bluffing. Joshua met her in their prearranged place on Tuesday and it was clear they were going somewhere.

"Where are you taking me?" asked Kate, as Joshua turned his car north on Lake Shore Drive.

"Forty-seventh and South Park. Ever been there?"

"No. Not really. I've driven through there, and I read about it all the time on the police blotter. That's the highest crime area in the city, right?"

"Depends on what you call crime. If you call prostitutes and drug dealers criminals, then it's a high crime area."

"Well, aren't they?" asked Kate. "From what I read there's also a lot of muggings, robberies, shootings, cuttings, burglaries, and just a bit of gang violence. That sounds like high crime to me."

"Yeah. Well, there, it's a way of life. Different rules and different goals, that's all."

For the first time, Kate thought he sounded defensive.

At Forty-seventh Street Joshua turned left, leaving the integrated Hyde Park behind, moving into an area of mostly black faces. The stores were less well-kept, and the streets were littered. Even though it was only mid-afternoon, neon lights flashed from most of the stores announcing 'Liquor', 'Rooms for Rent', 'Pawn Shop', 'Pool Hall', 'Chicken', 'Sandwiches'.

Joshua parked his ten-year-old Chevrolet convertible on a side street. "Lock it up," he said. "Hand me that box on the floor. I'll put it in the trunk. No sense in letting them slash my top to get at this box."

Waiting for Joshua to lock the trunk, Kate couldn't help but stare. An old man in a long black coat, torn at the sleeves, weaved drunkenly down the street. A woman slouched in a doorway, holding a sleeping baby. Three school-aged children raced down the street and into the same doorway, oblivious of her presence. The sound of a man and a woman fighting came from an upstairs window. Music blared from a juke box in the bar on the corner. The 'El' thundered overhead, making its Forty-seventh Street stop, discharging new hordes to be absorbed into the already crowded streets. The wail of police cars added to the street noises.

Finished with his car, Joshua steered Kate into the stream of people. "Where are we going?" she asked.

"There's a clinic just down the street. A clinic that treats drug addicts."

"You mean heroin?"

"Mostly."

"I don't know anybody who uses heroin."

"Then you should have an interesting time. Turn here. It's right down this block."

They walked about a half a block, coming to what looked like just another store. It was different from the other stores only in that it was spilling over with people. They were everywhere: some sitting on the stoop, some sitting against the building, some standing, one sitting on a garbage can next to the curb. Some were smoking, staring into space, eyes vacant. Others had watchful eyes, looking for danger in all corners. Some were silent. Others talked animatedly. Their dress varied from expensive and immaculate to poor and shabby.

All talking stopped when Joshua ushered Kate to the door.

"Joshua, where you been so long?"

"Man, I been wonderin where you been."

"That university keepin' you too busy to come by?"

"Say, who's that lady witchya. A new piece?"

Joshua smiled and nodded, but kept on walking, steering Kate through the melee. "Keep going. Inside," Joshua instructed.

"Hey, Joshua," hailed a tall slim man with a thick mustache who was standing behind the front desk. "Been by your place. Where you been, man? This lady keepin you too busy to see your friends?"

"Yeah, well. You know how it is, man. School's kept me gone most nights. At the library and shit."

"Yeah. I bet," said the man, eyeing Kate openly.

"Tony, this is Kate," said Joshua. "Tony is director of this place."

"Well now, Kate. Welcome," said Tony, winking at her.

"She wants to see the center," said Joshua. "Can you show her around?"

"Can't right now, man. You see how it is. They're all here at once. You show her around. You ought to know the place by now."

Kate was decidedly uncomfortable. Here, she was truly an alien. Not only that but an alien in a house of aliens. She was afraid to stare. She was afraid not to. Inside, were almost as many people as had been outside. Three women lounged on a couch, doing nothing, looking into the room, seeing nothing. Another woman leafed lazily through a magazine, seeing it, but not seeing it. A few people sat on the floor, leaning against the wall. All other space was taken by men and women of varying colors and hues of blackness interspersed with a few whites, standing, slouching, talking, laughing, cursing, complaining, or staring at Kate in astonishment.

"Joshua," hailed an extremely tall man, long hair in disarray, with a pock-marked face. He slouched into his more than six-foot frame leaning against the wall, cigarette hanging from his mouth.

"There's a man you should meet, Kate. He's the black bard of the clinic. He's had at least two books of poems published."

"Him?" she said, sounding surprised that such a specimen could, or would, write poetry.

"Yeah, him," Joshua said, looking amused at her surprise.

"And he's addicted to heroin?"

"Yeah. Been addicted for more than ten years." He steered Kate toward the man. "Eldridge, I want you to meet Kate."

At seeing Kate, the man's expression turned icy cold. He faced Joshua. "Hey, man, wha chu doin bringin this straight white bitch in here. You crazy? You fuckin her?"

"No, man. It ain't like that."

"Then what the fuck is she doin here?"

"She wants to see the center. Why don't you talk to her, man, show her around."

"Fuck you. I don't do tours. That university must be fuckin over your mind."

"Just talk to her, man. You might like it."

Kate felt the man's icy eyes on her. Her insides turned to stone. She had never known such open hostility. "What the fuck are you doin here?" he asked.

"I . . . I . . . " stammered Kate. "I don't know. I just came to learn."

"And to look down your privileged nose at us junkies, the scum of the earth, is that it?"

"No, I . . . ."

"Then it must be that you want to help. Just bring your white ass down here so you can help. Help us poor black bastards who can't help ourselves. That's it, isn't it? You think you're a fuckin Good Samaritan, don't you?"

His accusation hurt. Confusion took over her brain. "I do want to help," she thought. "Is that wrong? He acts like it's wrong. He's acting like I'm a downright criminal for wanting to help." She couldn't stop her voice from quivering. "Yes, maybe I could help," she said.

"The only help I want from you is to stay out of my face and let me live my life."

"Addicted to heroin? You call that living?"

"You're Goddamned right! If that's what I want. It's what you want, isn't it?"

"No! Why should I want that," said Kate.

"So I won't get all agitated and upset," he said sarcastically. "So I won't tell you honky bastards what I really think of you in words you can hear instead of in poetry you never read. So I won't kill every fuckin one of you for what you've done to me."

"But I didn't do anything to you."

"Oh, yeah, you did. You holed me up in this ghetto where I got nowhere to turn, where I couldn't get a job no matter how hard I tried, where I couldn't feed my kids or hold my head up in front of my family. Oh, yeah, you did it all right. Yeah. No nigger's gonna marry my sister. Yeah. Well, let me tell you something, Miss Lily White, I wouldn't marry you if my life depended on it but I would fuck you and try to drill your ass through the mattress, but I wouldn't marry you. Your white ass ain't worth marrying. Tell that to your brother."

Now she hurt. His words cut like a knife. "And you think heroin is the solution?" she said as bravely as she could muster.

"Lady, there ain't no solution, but when I'm loaded, it's the only time I can get far enough away from the shit you lay on me. Nothing else is far enough."

Now he was really enjoying his role: keeping the knife inserted and then twisting it.

She eyed the door. She wished she could get out. She wished she'd never come. He told a truth, a truth she didn't want to hear. She wanted to justify her presence here. She wanted to deny her guilt. She didn't want to face his truths.

She looked at his face, ugly to begin with, now contorted in anger, eyes still like stones. "What do I do now," she thought. "He's got me."

Then suddenly, anger filled her. "Oh, no he hasn't. No he hasn't." She held out her hand and smiled sweetly. "Thanks," she said. "I won't need that tour now. I've heard it all, straight from the head horse's ass."

He hesitated, his mouth half open, staring at her hand, his shield of ice still thick around him. Then his eyes softened. He almost smiled as his ice melted, then disappeared. He took her hand and held it for a moment. Then he turned to Joshua. "Hey, man. You struck oil this time. Bring her back any time."

"Cool! I'll do that."

They threaded their way out the door. Kate's legs felt like rubber. Now she knew what it was like to be the enemy. To be hated as an enemy. Not like in Montgomery where even as an enemy she was welcomed. Here she was hated.

"Joshua, what happened to make him thaw?" she asked.

"You heard him. You heard him, and he knew it. He's full of anger and hate. His poems, too. But first you heard him, and then you stood up to his shit. He thinks nobody hears him, especially nobody white, but you earned his respect."

"Ummmmm," she said. "Is everybody here as angry as he is?"

"A lot are."

"It's going to be an interesting day," she thought. She took a deep breath and tried to make her rubbery legs move faster to keep up with Joshua's broader steps. "Where now?"

"Ever been to a numbers joint?"

"No."

"Would you like to see one."

At this point, Kate was game for anything. "Sure."

"It's across the street," he said, taking her elbow and steering her through the crowd just coming off the 'El.'

They walked to a small building with a sign in front labeling it 'Variety Store.' It differed from the other stores by an entry, where their progress was stopped by a 250-pound man standing in her way. The man was ugly. The man was big. And the man had a mean scowl on his face.

The scowl lifted when he saw Joshua. "Hey, my man. Where you been? Ain't seen you around lately."

"Didn't I tell you? I'm going to school. The University."

"University? My ass! No university should keep you so busy you can't stop by to see old friends."

"Yeah. You're right. I'll be by more often now. Nick around?"

"Yeah, man, he's inside. He'll be glad to see ya. He was askin bout ya, just yesterday."

"Later then," said Joshua. "Stay cool."

The man stepped aside to let them pass.

Inside were two rooms, a front room with people mingling about, and a back room with two lines waiting to get to the counter. Two men stood behind the counter writing numbers on slips of papers or handing out small tabs already filled with numbers. Two women sat behind a counter to the side taking the money. While waiting in line, Joshua explained the system. Kate nodded, understanding very little. Joshua gave four numbers to a man named Nick behind the counter.

"You missed my party Saturday. Where were you?" growled Nick, completely ignoring Kate's existence.

"Haven't been getting out much lately, Nick, but I'll make it next time."

"Better had, better had."

Joshua tucked four tickets into his pocket, paid his money, and steered her toward the door. Now Kate know what it was like to be invisible. Everybody saw her. Everybody dissected her but nobody saw her. They all branded her an alien, without branding her an alien. She was the most visible person in the room, but nobody acknowledged her existence. She remembered the book, *The Invisible Man* by Ralph Ellison. She had read it for class. Now she knew about invisibility.

A sign on the wall caught her eye. "Don't legalize it. That takes away all the fun." She wondered if the people were really having fun.

Back on the street, Kate stuck her hands in the pockets of her coat and took a deep breath. Now she could watch the people.

They had branded her invisible, so she was free to watch, free to know the energy.

The energy! She suddenly realized she was walking in the middle of an incendiary energy, so different than what she felt from the crowds in downtown Chicago, or walking from class to class at school. She felt strange. "What is it?" she thought. "Intense, yes, intense. Primitive, too. And creative. But something else. What? What? What?"

"Crazy! That's it. Crazy! Anything can happen here. And everything does."

She looked around. A man in a dark brown tattered coat, who a minute ago had been standing quietly on the corner, suddenly started yelling and cursing at the people walking by. A doorway burst open. Two teenage boys darted out followed immediately by a screaming woman. A wild-looking man in a long black coat, hair in small braids extending from his head in all directions, was accosting everyone, telling them about the Lord. A vacant-eyed man slouched against the wall, little by little dropping toward the cement. A beautiful girl with cleavage to her waist, leaned over an open car window talking to an expectant trick, while a richly-dressed black man hovered in an immaculate Cadillac. Passers-by ignored it all.

The energy - it frightened her. Yet it invited her. It was so raw. She was drawn by the invitation to join it, to be as free as these people, to indulge herself, even to the point of craziness if she wished. To be as angry, as direct, as uninhibited by politeness as these people if she wished.

But no. All of that had to be contained inside of herself. It was too frightening if she didn't contain it. "Maybe it isn't even in me," she thought. "But, of course it's in me. I remember my ravings in Jenny's office."

Then she noticed the series of Chicago City Police cars prowling the streets. "There's the containment," she thought

She stopped her ruminations when Joshua ushered her into the door of a bar. Count Basie's band blared from the juke box. The place was crowded. Smoke hung in the air like a black cloud. Everybody was talking; yelling actually, to be heard above everybody else. It was a small room with a long bar on the right side. Almost every stool was taken. A handsome young man in an immaculate white shirt and shiny pants stood behind the bar enchanting the customers. His adam's apple bobbed above a perfectly-tied black bow tie. There were about ten tables scattered about the rest of the room, most of them filled with people. Pool balls clicked from a table at the far end of the room and four men lounged against the walls, heckling.

Joshua leaned toward her. "There's two seats at the bar."

Kate found herself squashed between Joshua and a four-hundred-pound giant of a man who was loquaciously talking to the woman next to him. "And I said to him, I said. See that window over there. He said,'Yeah.' I said, if you don't get off my ass you're gonna take a trip right through it."

Kate heard the throatiness of the woman's laughter.

"I'd stay off your ass for sure," Kate thought. She looked up to see the handsome bartender smiling at her. "Well, Joshua, who have you here? Is this the pretty who's been keeping you away so long?"

"Naw. I'm in school now, Eddie. This is Kate. She's a friend."

"Well, Kate. I'd like a friend like you."

"Watch out for him Kate. He's dangerous," said Joshua.

"I'll watch out," she said, smiling her most winning smile. It was nice to be seen, even welcomed.

"What'll it be?" he asked.

"You know what I want, man. Make it a double. Kate?"

"Scotch," she said. "Scotch and water."

"One double vodka martini, very dry, with extra olives, and one scotch and water comin up."

Kate amused herself by looking around the room. An old man, grey-haired and bent, sat alone at one of the tables, half asleep. Two women, more than twice their natural weight, gossiped at the table next to him. A well-dressed man in a beige hat and brown leather coat lounged at another table, smoke curling from the cigarette dangling from his mouth. He looked asleep, but Kate knew he wasn't. He was watching her through those lowered lids.

Joshua's voice interrupted her observations. "That's the Prince. Biggest dope dealer on the street. That one keeps most of the junkies around here supplied."

The man raised his fist. "Joshua," he said.

"Prince." Joshua returned the salute.

Loud voices near the door diverted her attention. Two men sitting at the table nearest the door were talking, their volume increasing with every statement. The waitress seemed to be the object of the argument.

"Man, I think I'll just take her home and have a piece of that pussy."

"LeRoy, you could take her home, but you wouldn't get any pussy. You wouldn't know what to do with a prime piece like that. The last pussy you had walked on four feet and chased mice."

"Fuck you, fat ass! I'd hump her till she hollered. When was the last time you made a woman holler, fat ass?"

"Watch this," Joshua whispered in her ear. "The game's been called."

"Are they gonna fight?" said Kate, looking a little nervous.

"No. Just watch."

"I got your fat ass swingin, cocksucker. I'll tell you who I made holler. Your mama. She squealed like a stuck pig when I rammed my dick into her."

"Your dick ain't big enough to make a woman holler, especially my mama. All you could do for my mama is show her which way my daddy went."

"Your daddy goes anywhere, motherfucker."

"Who you callin a motherfucker? You been peepin into your mama's window?"

By now the two men were half out of their chairs, leaning over the table into each other's faces.

Somewhere, out of nowhere, a third man appeared. He grabbed both men by the collars and pulled them apart.

"That's Jake, our local social worker," whispered Joshua. "So educated he doesn't even know that's just a game they're playing."

Argument forgotten, both men stood to their fullest heights and turned toward the intruder. The one called LeRoy threw two punches, one to the chin and the other to the belly.

The man named Jake lay on the floor curled into a ball gasping for breath. He was in pain.

"Black meddlin motherfucker! Stickin your face in where it ain't none a your business."

Jake clawed his way to a standing position, weaving slightly. He tried to brush the dirt off his immaculate brown pants, without much success. He glared at both men. "You bastards are gonna kill each other one of these days." He tentatively stepped toward the door.

"What's it to ya, ass hole?" said the two men in unison.

Briefly, the fight had captured everyone's attention. Then it was back to business as usual. The two women resumed gossiping. The old man went back to sleep. Prince got up and left. Muddy Waters sang out of the juke box.

On his way out the door, Prince brushed against one of the most beautiful women Kate had ever seen. She had long hair that waved instead of curled. It reached below her shoulders. Her honey-colored face was hardening around the edges, but was perfect in its beauty. Her body curved in all the right places; while her short skirt and skin-tight shirt showed off every curve. She paused at the door inspecting the occupants of the room.

Then she saw Joshua. "Joshua! Baby!" She flew across the room and into his arms. He held her to him. She rubbed her body seductively against his. "Oh, baby, you feel so good. Where you been? Why haven't you been to see your Deetra?"

"School, baby. School."

"Ain't no school big enough to keep you away. You come by the crib, baby, an I'll give you somethin you can't get at school. I've been missin your lovin somethin awful."

"Mmmmmmmmmmmm. I've missed you too, baby, but I really have been hitting the books."

Over Joshua's shoulder she spotted Kate. She pulled away. "Who the fuck is this white bitch you got with you?"

"This is Kate, Deetra. This is Kate."

Kate didn't know when she'd felt so much hate. Even Eldridge's ice was nothing compared to this.

"You fuckin this bitch?" she said, her eyes burning into Joshua.

"No, Deetra. It isn't like that. We're taking some classes together. I invited her down here to see what it's like."

The hate deepened. "You brought this white bitch down here to see what it's like? Have you lost what's left of your mind? We don't need no white college bitch lookin down her nose at us. Where you gettin at bein such a fool?"

"Let it go, Deetra. I'm not fucking her and I'm not going to. Leave it alone. Sit here while I go to the john. I'll buy you a drink. Eddie, get Deetra what she wants."

With Joshua gone, Deetra faced Kate with all her hate. "What the fuck are you doin here? Are you one of them do-gooders tryin to help?"

"Maybe I can help, I don't know," said Kate, knowing as she said it that now she was in deeper trouble.

"We don't need your help. Thank you very much, Miss Anne. And just what would you do? Clean the place up? Get rid of the junkies? Throw the pimps and the women like me into jail? Move us all into high rises? Is that what you'd do?"

"No . . . I . . . "

"Well, Miss Anne, let me tell you. We ain't gonna be gotten rid of. Not while them white bastards downtown see to it that we get our stuff. You can put us in jail but we ain't stayin. You put me in jail and before your ass could shit, I'd be back on the streets. My man could buy and sell any narc who'd care to put my ass in jail where I couldn't make no money." Venom dripped from Deetra's mouth.

The poison struck home. Kate had nothing she could say.

"And just what do you do, Miss Anne, when you ain't visitin us poor bastards in the ghetto?"

"My name is Kate. My name is not Anne."

"Your name is Miss Anne. And you didn't answer my question. Just what do you do when you ain't visitin us poor bastards down here in the ghetto?"

Kate's fury started to get the better of her. "I write about poor bastards like you down here in the ghetto who are making it just fine, and certainly don't need any help."

"That's the first truth your lyin ass has said yet."

"That's the first truth your mouth has let me say," countered Kate.

"Well, any time you don't like my mouth you can get your ass out of here. It wouldn't be too soon for me."

"Look, Deetra, yell if you want, but if you're yelling because you think I want Joshua, you're wrong. He just brought me here to help me understand. And now I understand. So get off my back."

Joshua reappeared and wisely stood between them. "I see you haven't quit running your mouth, Deetra. Shut it up now. Just shut it up."

"Shut it up. Yeah. You and your hot-shot white woman. And you can just forget about comin round." Before he could protect himself she was beating on his chest with her fists.

He caught her by the wrists. She struggled. He held fast. She finally gave up and glared at him. Hostility leapt from her eyes. He twisted her hands behind her back and held until she stopped struggling. His eyes held hers. Slowly and deliberately he leaned down and kissed her, deeply on the mouth.

"I'm comin round," he said. "And it will always be all right between us. Now be sweet, baby, and stay cool for me."

"Damn. You still know how to do it to me. Okay, I'm cool. And I'm gettin back to work. Thanks for the drink, baby."

"Later, Deetra, but for sure."

"Goodbye, Miss Anne."

Kate nodded her goodbye. Even she knew they'd played to a stand-off. But she had held her own.

Later over dinner, Joshua explained to Kate what she had seen. "Those are the streets, Kate. The streets are mean. It's the same every day, day in and day out. Mean. We learn to live in them. They're our means of survival. It they weren't mean, we'd grow up weak and then we wouldn't survive."

"It's your white man who dictates the conditions. He has forced us into the ghetto, by exclusion, by seeing to it that we stay in poverty, by seeing to it that we never get a decent education. We had to survive, Kate. Some of us had to win. So we win in the streets. It's our way of being free. We're free on those streets. No white man can get us there. They belong to us. We can cuss and yell and play our music, and drink our gin and shoot stuff into our veins, and have our women and no white man can touch us. The streets are the way they are because we couldn't have it any other way. Now a lot of us don't want it any other way."

"But it's so . . . so . . . d . . .."

"Dirty?"

"Well, yes."

"If your white men would leave us alone to be who we are, we wouldn't be doing all that shit. We wouldn't be living in the dirt he forced us into. We didn't live like that in Africa. We took care of business in Africa. Your white man won't let us do that here. He wanted to civilize us."

"Civilize you?" Kate repeated. "I'd say he failed."

"Or maybe he succeeded. Think about the crime and corruption at City Hall, Kate. We're just doing our own brand of that."

"I'll have to think about that, Joshua. Because right now I'm not sure that what I saw today is better."

"It's better because it's honest."

"I'll have to think about that, too."

CHAPTER 55

Kate sat on a stool watching the party swirl around her. It was April; it was Jackie's apartment; it was Hyde Park; it was late; it was a celebration for the end of midterms. It was fun.

She'd come with Nathan, Bryan having impolitely declined.

She'd expected a quiet little get-together. She'd been greeted by somewhere near fifty people and the sound of 'Little Richard' blaring from the hi fi. Already she'd met the 'Night Preacher' of Rush Street, a bass player having a night off from a basement club called 'The Cloisters', and one of Mayor Daley's government hacks. She'd damn near done a feature story on the spot of 'The Night Preacher', felt the bass player playing bass on her back as they danced, and been bored to death by the government official. She wondered where Jackie had found all these people.

The music was loud, the party jumping, and she was exploring her feelings of the moment. Here she was sitting alone in the midst of so many intense conversations, with nobody paying her the slightest attention, and she wasn't lonely. "It's the music," she thought. "It's got to be the music. There's no way I can be lonely with all of that noise in my head."

She picked up her glass and wandered off. She almost stumbled over Jackie in the hall. Jackie was in high spirits to say the least. "Hey, where have you been? I've been looking all over for you. Come into the smoking room with me. It's time you learned how to smoke. I'll teach you."

"You want me to do what?"

"Come into the smoking room. You know. Grass? Weed?"

"You mean marijuana?" Kate said. "I can't do that."

"Sure. Why not? It's better than what you're drinking there."

Kate went.

Only one dim light, covered with a multicolored shade, lit the room. A pungent sweet smell greeted her nostrils as she entered and she saw everything through a blue haze of smoke. Vaguely, through the haze, she could pick out figures: some sitting on the floor, some lounging on cushions and huge pillows, some leaning against the wall. A couple in the corner were into uproarious laughter. Another trio, sitting on the floor, was engaged in a very serious and world-changing discussion about the relative merits of nearly everything. The wall leaners just looked 'out of it', simply 'out of it.'

Jackie steered her to an open space on the edge of a single bed. Somebody passed her a smoking pipe. "Here," said Jackie. "Put your finger over this hole, draw the smoke into your mouth, and then inhale, simple as that."

Kate tried it. Immediately she was lost in paroxysms of coughing. "Simple as that, huh?" she said, when she finally could talk again.

"Here, try it again. And don't take quite as much smoke this time."

It took six tries before Kate could inhale without coughing.

By then it didn't matter whether she coughed or not, she was comfortably stoned. She got up and wandered back to the party. It was amazing. Everybody looked wonderful. Everybody liked her. She liked everybody. There wasn't an enemy in the room. Even Mayor Daley's hack looked benign. Even so she decided she had better sit on a chair for a while, unsure as she was of her ability to walk at the moment . . . unsure also of what might happen to her words if she tried to talk. The party flowed around her. The music became part of her.

Through a wonderful fog, she heard a voice. "Want to dance?" it said. Through the same wonderful fog, she looked up to see who was talking. It was Joshua.

She tried out her voice. It surprised her. It was the very same voice she'd heard before. "Yes, I would. I haven't seen you all evening."

"That's because I haven't been here all evening."

"I see," nodded Kate, not sure that she saw at all.

She stood up and tried out walking. She discovered she could still get from here to there on the ground. Even though, of course, she was really floating.

Harry Belafonte was singing out of the hi fi; slow and easy . . . and sexy.

She slipped into his arms.

She couldn't believe it. He was shaking. His body was shaking. She, however, had never been more graceful, following every step without the slightest hint of the two left feet she was used to.

She had never felt more safe.

She noticed people were leaving. The front door was opening and closing with regularity. Joshua didn't let go of her. Fast tunes, slow tunes, they never left the floor. Nathan waved to her as he walked out the door. "I've got a ride home," he said.

She barely noticed.

It wasn't long before almost everybody was gone. She murmured something about going home. "Are you tired?" Joshua asked.

"Not really."

"Then come with me. I have a tree I want you to see."

"A what?"

"A tree."

"That's what I thought you said."

Joshua lead her toward the kitchen and onto a back porch. There, indeed, growing three stories tall, was a tree, its branches protruding over the porch railing. "See, I told you it was a tree," he said. "Want a drink?"

"Sure."

Joshua produced, from under his jacket, an open bottle of wine and two glasses. "Here, hold this while I pour."

Kate started to giggle, then to laugh. "Where did you get that?"

"Oh, you don't know the beginnings of my talents," he said.

"Let's see now. As a further example of my abilities, I bet I can find an elephant in your ear." He began a minute examination of her ear, probing every crevice. "Ah, here it is," he said, holding up a tiny plastic elephant. "It was there all the time. Had any trouble hearing lately?"

"Why, yes, as a matter of fact I have."

"Well, you have just submitted to Dr. Thomas's unfailing cure for any and all diseases due to elephant ear."

"Have I had it long, Dr. Thomas?"

"Probably all your life from the size of this elephant. You'd better take him home and watch him carefully so he doesn't infect you with the collywobbles, a malady peculiar to this sized elephant." He put the elephant into her hand.

"I'll do it. I'll put him in a cage and watch him every day."

"You'll have to watch his diet, though. He's on a special diet."

"And what is that, Doctor, Sir?"

"He eats nothing but old anteaters and cow dung."

"No problem. I have a life-time supply of old anteaters in my closet, and plenty of cow dung in my basement."

"Exactly. That should take care of him fine."

And so it went. Kate shivered. He gave her his coat. She finished her glass of wine. He poured more. The moon rose above the tree. They talked of the man residing within. The inside of the apartment became silent. They ignored it.

Kate looked at her watch. It was too late to ignore. "Joshua, it's 2:30. I've got to get home. Bryan will be wondering where I am."

"Let's see if I can find a telephone in your ear here. You can call him to let him know you're all right."

"Joshua," she laughed. "Don't you dare look. You'll probably find one, and I don't want to wake him in case he's asleep. I'll just drive fast."

"Drive carefully," he admonished. "There are lots of crazies out there on a Saturday night and the police are everywhere."

"I'll be careful."

Then his arms were around her. His lips were on hers. They were warm and soft and ever so gentle, belying the toughness of his body and the rawness of his life experiences.

She was sure she was being bewitched.

The tree, the moon, the night, all had hypnotized her.

She floated away, encased in the gentleness of his body.

When he released her, everything was out of order.

"I love you, you know," he said quietly.

"You're crazy," she said.

"I'm not crazy. I love you."

"Well, we can't do anything about that," she said.

"I know, but you will drive carefully."

"I will."

She lied. She didn't drive. She flew. From Hyde Park to Evanston, she flew. All the other cars didn't exist. A policeman . . . he wouldn't dare!

Home, she shut out the car lights before they hit the bedroom window. She inched the garage door up, keeping down the sound. She edged the side door open and tiptoed upstairs.

The boys were sleeping peacefully.

Bryan was snoring on his side of the bed.

She slipped into her side.

An hour later, she slipped out again, to pace the downstairs floor.

"We have nothing in common."

"We could never get along."

"He's a womanizer. Dates a prostitute, yet."

"I know nothing of his kind of life."

"He knows nothing about love."

"I cannot feel this way. I'm a married woman."

"My life is Bryan and the boys."

"I'm not going to run away from my marriage, just because we have a few difficulties. This is a good marriage."

"Why do I feel this way????????"

She slipped back into bed, only to stare at the ceiling until the light began to filter through the window. Then she was up, sipping coffee, immersed in the Sunday paper.

She hoped she was nonchalant when Bryan asked her about the party.

On Monday, Joshua acted as though the conversation had never taken place. She, however, couldn't stop her heart from racing.

CHAPTER 56

By the time the summer of 1960 arrived, events of the nation were heating up. There were more and more Negro students 'sitting in' at lunch counters in the South. Stokely Charmichael was organizing the Student Non-Violent Coordinating Committee to implement even stronger action. There was talk of freedom-riding to integrate bus terminals and interstate public transportation. Some of the South's resistance was cracking; most of the South's resistance was solidifying.

Jackie went back to New York for the summer and Dana to Minot. Kate took the summer off to get in a little vacation with Bryan and the boys and to earn enough money for fall term.

Back at work, her first project was to resume her sadly neglected column 'A Woman's Eye View', yet to see the light of newsprint, yet to get through Ed's encrusted authority.

"America", she wrote:

> **"America, the espoused leader of the free world, who built its strength and leadership on human rights, on human dignity. America, who professes to be the leader of the free world, the proponent of the underdog. America, who has proved its righteousness over and over again by encouraging the development of all nations, lending its expertise to that end,**

even to the degree of building up the strength of its enemies from World War II. Now this America is showing a different face. A face of shame.

By its adamant refusal to allow its Negro citizens to sit in the same restaurants with its white citizens, it shows its face of shame. By its adamant refusal to allow its Negro citizens to ride in a bus or sit in a terminal with its white citizens, it shows its face of shame. By its adamant refusal to seat its Negro citizens in schools with its white citizens, it shows its face of shame. And by its refusal to protect its Negro citizens who are fighting for the same constitutional rights as its white citizens, it shows its face of shame.

What kind of leadership is this for a country that tells other countries 'Communism is the greatest threat to the freedom of the world.' For a country that tells other countries 'Dictatorship is wrong, give the people the right to choose'. For a country that tells other countries 'Talk it over at the bargaining table'?

When we will not give all of our own citizens freedom. When we allow this kind of dictatorship in our own country. When no amount of bargaining has given our Negro citizens bargaining power. What kind of a country are we anyway?"

She finished it. She carried it into Ed's office and laid it on his desk. Then she waited for the explosion.

She didn't have long to wait. The cigar burst into her cubicle within minutes. He waved the column under her nose.

"This is inflammatory! We can't print this! I've told you before, and I'm telling you now: stop writing these abominations. Do the work you're assigned to do."

"Maybe we need to be inflammatory, Ed. And I'm not going to stop. You can expect more of my columns on your desk."

"The Male Authority", she wrote:

"The male authority. An established fact. What is it doing to the women of this nation? To the women who are intelligent, women who are articulate, women with ideas, women who simply want to work to support their children.

What is it that the male authority does to these women? The male authority says, 'A woman's place is in the home, not in the marketplace.' Then he says 'A woman's place is to bear her husband's children, and then spend the rest of her life raising them, probably alone. If she should happen to find her way into the marketplace HE designates her the work of the lowest rank where she cannot use her skills and attributes in ways that fits her ability.

Never mind that her brain is equal to his, that her education is as good as his, that her skills, albeit more undeveloped, are as applicable as his; she is relegated to the lowest position, and he is doing the relegating."

"What the hell are you doing?" said the cigar, holding this latest product of her typewriter.

"I'm stating the truth, Ed. You don't have to like it, and you don't have to print it but I'm going to keep on producing these columns and putting them on your desk."

"Write them on your own Goddamned time then. Not on mine."

"You get your time out of me, Ed. You get your time. And remember that Horowitz, whom you once told me was not as competent as I, makes at least once and a half more money. Isn't that right?"

"I don't want to see any more of your columns."

"The only way you won't see any more of my columns, Ed, is if you don't read them. They'll be on your desk."

"Inflexible, short-sighted bosses," she wrote:

> **"Inflexible, short-sighted bosses, can't see the truth because of the holes in their heads. Holes where eyes ought to be and where intelligence begins. Eyes to see the truth and intelligence enough to name it. Inflexible short-sighted bosses don't think beyond their noses.**
>
> **Inflexible short-sighted bosses say, 'For God's sake, don't offend anyone'; except, of course your own women employees. Inflexible short-sighted bosses protect the vested interests of everyone; except, of course, their hardest working reporter. Inflexible short-sighted bosses spew venom at everybody under their command. Inflexible short-sighted bosses are the worst of the male authorities.**
>
> **I wouldn't print my columns, either, if I were an inflexible short-sighted boss. I might read them and learn something."**

Kate sat at her desk holding the column gingerly by the corner. "If I put this on his desk, he might really fire me. What to do? What to do? She put it in her desk drawer. She went back to working on her assignment. She took it out again and looked at it. She put it back in her drawer. She removed it, marched down the hall to his office, and put it on his desk.

The silence from the smoke-filled room was odious.

Kate could hardly wait to get back to classes in the fall.

Ed had grumbled and growled throughout the whole summer.

Bryan had been argumentative and moody and nothing made him happy, including their vacation to Duluth's North Shore. He didn't catch enough fish. It was too cold. There were too many mosquitoes. She was glad when it was over.

She missed the conversation of the magnificent seven.

Secretly, she wanted to see Joshua.

The first day, over coffee, it was Ella who proposed their first outing of the season: a Haitian club on South Division Street, the first Saturday night of school. The return of the seven, they called it.

The place was dark and very Caribbean, the music positively un-American and the atmosphere spoke of people having fun. The seven added their own liveliness. Everybody danced with everybody: in pairs, in threes, in fours, and sometimes all at once.

Toward the end of the evening, when the music slowed, Joshua asked her for a slow dance . . . alone. There he was, holding her for the first time since their memorable night. She leaned her head against his shoulder, giving into his tenderness, giving up her need to hold herself away from him. Then she felt it. Distinctly, she felt it. He was hard against her.

She looked at him quizzically.

He nodded. "I still love you, you know."

"I guess I do know," she said quietly.

They walked back to the table and sat down.

Again, it was as if the conversation and the experience had never happened. They resumed playing with the group as though the room wasn't simply swirling around her head.

A little over a week later she picked up the telephone at work. It was Joshua. "I know a little place that has 'out-of-sight' ribs," he said. "Would you have some with me on Friday night?"

Kate didn't answer. "I need to say no," she thought. "I shouldn't be with him alone. It's dangerous to be with him alone."

"Kate, are you still there?"

"Yes, I'm here."

"Would you like to have ribs with me on Friday night?"

"Yes, I'd like that very much."

"Six-thirty, all right?"

"Yes, fine."

"I'll meet you at the cafeteria. We'll drive out together."

The place was her idea of a romantic getaway, the kind Bryan abhorred. It was a basement room, lit almost completely by candles placed in the center of each table. Each table was covered with a red and white-checkered tablecloth. The smell of ribs was irresistible and the juke box played nothing but blues and jazz. Joshua ordered a bottle of Chianti, then retreated to the juke box. He pushed six tunes, all by Billie Holiday.

Billie sang:

> ***"More than you know, more than you know.***
> ***Man of my heart, I love you so.***
> ***Lately I find, you're on my mind,***
> ***More than you know."***

They drank wine. They laughed a lot.

They ordered ribs, mild for her and medium for him. Her first taste sent her for her water glass. He laughed at the face she made and told her she just hadn't grown up in the right neighborhood.

They ordered Italian ice cream for desert. "Italian?" she said.

Billie sang:

> ***"Mandy is two, you ought to see how many things she can do."***
> ***"If you could see, her majesty, with braids in her hair.***
> ***Miss Amanda, she's as proud as can be.***
> ***"Cause she's a big girl now."***

As the words to the song filled the room Kate realized that she felt strange. "I like that song," she said, having no idea what it was about that song that was touching her so deeply.

For desert, after their Italian desert, they drank cognac and danced among the tables.

Over the cognac, she tried to be serious. "Joshua, we can't do this."

"We're already doing it," he said.

"I know. I don't understand it."

"Do you have to?" he said. "All I know is that we can be together or not be together; it isn't going to make any difference. I still love you."

"But why, Joshua? We don't have anything in common. We're as different as . . . as . . .."

"Black and white?" he said.

"Yes, as black and white," she laughed.

He stopped teasing her and got serious. "Kate, I know we can't do this. I've told myself that over and over again. But somehow, I can't not do this, either. No amount of argument with myself has made any difference. I have argued myself silly about this, but nothing works."

"But I promise you, Kate. I won't disrespect you or your marriage. We can go on being friends, just like we've been and I'll still love you. Or we could see each other once in a while. No strings attached. Either way I'll love you."

Kate tried to deal with the tumult that was going on inside her head. It was as if fate were drawing her here to this place, into the arms of this diverse black man.

His kisses that night were warm and gentle; there was no demand. There never was any demand. She felt extraordinarily safe.

They worked it out. They saw each other now and then. Kate justified it by saying, "As long as we don't have sex, I won't be violating Bryan." She looked forward to their time together with uncommon anticipation. She refused to realize that she was violating Bryan in spirit, if not in body.

Eventually it had to end. Joshua graduated and took a job at Howard University in Washington D.C. Kate stayed in school to get her Doctorate degree.

On their last day together, as they walked by the lake listening to the pounding surf and viewing the skyline of Chicago, he said, "I would like to make love to you before I leave."

Kate didn't answer. Everything in her screamed, "Yes."

But when she finally spoke, it was "No."

For the next week, she cried tears that wouldn't stop. People asked her, "Do you have a cold?"

"Are you all right?"

"Hay fever bothering you?"

Would that any of those reasons were true. Even Bryan asked, "What's wrong with you?"

All she seemed to be able to do was to mope. She moped around the house. She moped around the office. She didn't want to study. She was so depressed that it seemed as though she had almost stopped trying. One day right after class she bought a copy of *The News*. She leafed through it absently. Then she saw it. It was right there on the third page. Right there in the space where Jack Mabley's column usually was. "A Woman's Eye View" by Kate Andrews. She raced for her car and tore up Lake Shore Drive to her office.

She rushed into Ed's office waving the paper. "You printed it!" she yelled. "You printed it. After two years, you printed it. I can't believe it! Why?"

Ed peered at her without looking up from what he was doing.

Clouds of smoke emitted from his cigar. "Thought it was timely, that's all. Thought it was timely. But don't get your hopes up. It's just a filler until Mabely gets back."

"What's the matter with Jack?"

"Flu or something. Goddamn it, why can't this staff stay healthy?"

"Because we're working ourselves to death, that's why, Ed. Anyway, thanks. I'm going right to my desk and write more columns."

"I'm not going to print any more of them," he shouted at her retreating back.

The cycle of pain was broken.

Letters poured in from readers all over the city and suburbs in support of her stand. Women applauded the title. Even some men applauded the title.

Ed reluctantly gave in to pressure and printed another one. "Just one a week, mind you. Just one a week," he said. Kate retrieved her column on 'Inflexible Short-sighted Bosses' and threw it away.

Life's high points now were seeing her column in print once a week, and the nights she heard Joshua's voice on the phone. And his all too infrequent and brief vacations in Chicago.

It was his spring vacation in 1963 when it happened. It was his last night before returning to Howard. They were sitting in a bar on the Near North Side, drinking wine. He reached out and took her hand. Unfortunately the gossip columnist from the Tribune was sitting at a hidden table in the corner.

The next morning the Trib contained a juicy piece of news.

> **"Kate Andrews, mighty female columnist for the Daily News and fierce warrior against the oppression of women and Negroes, was seen last night in the Rathskeller Bar holding hands with one of those very same Negroes."**

Kate didn't see the column. Bryan, however, was not allowed that luxury. He found three copies of it on his desk when he arrived at work that day.

He barely contained his explosion until he got home. Paper in hand, he marched into the kitchen and threw it on the table.

Through clenched teeth he said, "Explain this, will you."

Kate read what he was pointing to and felt the blush of 'guilty as charged.'

She tried to stall for time. She tried to look innocent as she said, "What do you want to know?"

"I want you to explain this to me. Just explain it to me. What is this all about?"

"Well, Joshua was home for spring vacation," she said, "and he invited me out for a drink; that's all."

"And what is this about you holding hands?"

"Our group does that a lot. It doesn't mean a thing."

"Liar!" he said, raising his voice. "You've been fucking this Joshua, haven't you? And that's why you haven't been fucking me."

"I haven't been fucking Joshua," Kate yelled back. "I haven't been fucking anybody."

"You have to be; you certainly aren't fucking me."

"Joshua and I are just friends, Bryan. That's all we are."

"Well, I'm sorry but that's one friendship you'll have to give up. I'm not having a wife of mine going around town holding hands with a nigger."

"I'll be friends with anybody I want. And don't call him a nigger."

"Offends you, huh?" said Bryan. "Miss nicey nice is offended by 'nigger'. Miss nicey nice, so busy defending all the underdogs, defending the scum of society. All those welfare mothers. All those criminals. All those niggers. The scum of society."

"I'll defend whom I please and if that's what you think about the people I write about, we have nothing more to talk about."

"You get that nigger out of your life, or we won't have a marriage to talk about."

"What are you saying?"

"I'll repeat it, just in case you didn't hear. Get that nigger out of your life or we don't have a marriage."

Shock took over her face. "Are you threatening divorce if I don't do what you say?

"Yes! No wife of mine is going to go around fucking niggers and stay married to me."

"I told you, I haven't been fucking him. But if you think you're going to dictate to me who my friends will be, you're right. We have no marriage to talk about."

A week later Kate filed for divorce.

In a week and two days there was another juicy piece of news for the gossip columnist of *The Tribune.*

> **"Kate Andrews, noted columnist for *The Daily News,* is leaving her husband of nine years to be with the Negro man with whom she was seen in the Rathskeller a few days ago. In a telephone conversation, Mrs. Andrews confirmed the impending divorce but refused comment on the relationship with said Negro man."**

CHAPTER 57

On June 23rd, 1963, Kate became a free woman. Bryan kept the house and the children. Kate got a cash settlement and a lot of pain from leaving the boys. She used the money for a down payment on a two-story brownstone at Seventy-fourth and South Shore Drive. It was big, and it was old but it was exactly what she wanted. She could hear the lake smashing against the shore and it had three fireplaces. She immediately turned the whole upstairs into a bedroom-study where she was up to her ears writing her dissertation on the oppression of women. She kept her bedroom fireplace fueled most nights.

She didn't tell Joshua. It was worth holding the secret until she could see his face. She had to wait longer than she expected. She expected him home in June, but he wrote instead:

"Kate,

I don't know how I did it, but I've been coerced into working on the committee for the March on Washington scheduled for August. I have to stay here and work my ass off, when I'd rather be in Chicago seeing you. Get yourself an assignment and come here. I miss you.

Joshua"

Ed had not taken kindly to the items in the Tribune. The second item had brought him storming into her cubicle. "What is the meaning of this?" he said, waving *The Tribune* under her nose.

"The meaning is just what it says, Ed. Bryan and I are separating."

"Irreconcilable differences, right?"

"Right."

"And fornication with a black man, right?"

"Wrong."

"Just who is this 'said Negro man', then?"

"He's one of the students from school. He's a friend."

"You're getting divorced over a friend?"

"No, Ed, we're getting divorced because of irreconcilable difference mostly over what I write in this newspaper."

"Smart man, that Bryan, smart man," he said while he took his fumes and his cigar out of Kate's office.

"Ed, I want to cover the March on Washington."

"Why?"

"Because I've been covering civil rights issues since Montgomery. I want to cover this one, too."

"It doesn't have anything to do with 'said Negro man' does it? I understand he's in Washington."

Kate blushed. There was no way to hide the truth.

"For chrissake, be discreet, will ya?"

"I can go?"

"Is there any way I can stop you?"

"Not really."

"Then you can go."

Joshua met her at the airport. They had two days before the march. Two wonderful days to be together. "Baby, baby, baby, it's so good to see you," he said, as he enveloped her in his powerful arms. "Oh, you feel so good."

All the strain left Kate's body as he held her. All discord, all the pain, all the struggles of the past months disappeared. Here was her safety. Here was her peace. Maybe, here was all the love she ever needed

"I've got a soul lunch waiting for us at m apartment. And I have the rest of the day free. Nothing to do until tomorrow. Come on."

Back in his apartment, free from the Washington traffic, and from the stares of those who objected to their being together, they dropped her luggage, and she was once again in his arms. His kiss was passionate. It sent sparks through her body.

"I'd like to make love to you," he said.

"All right," she said.

His look of surprise was worth the wait.

"You're sure?"

"I'm sure."

There were no more words. He picked her up and carried her to the bedroom, laying her carefully on the bed. He sat next to her and removed his shoes. Then he lay down beside her and gathered her into his arms. Kate was surprised. She expected him to undress her. Bryan would have been half finished by now.

Instead he started to talk.

"Baby, it's good to see you. It's good to feel you. You wouldn't believe how lonely I've been. Even when I've been with a woman, I've been lonely for you. I don't know what's happening to me. I can't make love to a woman anymore without wishing she were you. You don't know how often I've imagined you here with me, just like this. Holding you like this."

Twinges of jealousy. More than twinges. Gigantic pangs. He had other women. Of course he had other women. "What did you expect, dummy? Celibacy?"

"You made me know I belong with you, Kate. Even miles apart, I belong with you. I feel so good when I'm with you, Kate. I want to be with you forever. I want to love you forever. If you can't love me, I don't care. It doesn't change a thing."

Kate was about to tell him. She even had her mouth open. But she couldn't. His lips were in the way. Instead of talking, she let his body touch her. There, for the first time, she let her guard down and she knew her own loneliness. She knew her own yearnings. She remembered how much she had wanted from Bryan and how little she got. Now it was here. It was in the peace and happiness in Joshua's arms. It was in his love.

Her guard came back up again. Fear hit the pit of her stomach. "He won't like making love to me." she thought. "I don't know anything about it. He's known so many women, all like Deetra. All hot. I'll disappoint him."

But now there was no time to be afraid. He was there again, with a kiss, his soft, gentle kiss, now burning into her. His hands were touching her. Touching her face. Touching her body through her clothes. Turning her body to heat.

It was his hands. It was as if his whole sexuality was, for this moment, in his hands. They excited her until she couldn't remember ever being afraid. She knew only her love for him, and the sensations from those hands.

Now his hands were undressing her. She knew every movement, the release of every button, the discarding of every piece, yet she knew none of it. Something wonderful was happening to her body.

She knew he had discarded his shirt. She felt skin against skin. She felt breasts against his chest. A sound was coming from her throat, a sound she'd never heard before. She began to know the meaning of ecstasy.

Then he was gone, standing next to the bed, removing the rest of his clothes. His eyes looked at her nude body. "My God, but you're beautiful," he said. His face was almost reverent.

Somehow her fear disappeared. It was gone, simply gone. She held out her arms. He slipped into them.

Now his hands, those hands that seemed to contain the sensual universe, started to touch the rest of her body. Her shoulders, her arms, her breasts, her legs, the insides of her thighs. Each new touch brought new sensations . . . sensations she had never known before. "Sex is good," people had told her. She hadn't believed it until now.

Her body started to do things it had never known. It arched as though to devour him, to take him into herself, to hold him, to cover him entirely with herself. He held himself away.

He knelt between her legs, to tantalize her, to tantalize her more . . . with his hands . . . those electric hands. He touched the insides of her thighs . . . until she lost herself . . . until she knew only feelings . . . until she lost her knowing.

She felt his hardness against her. She saw his face above her through a veil of wonder. She lost everything but her feeling of wanting him. Wanting him inside her, where there was only one of them, not two. He stayed outside.

He moved his hardness against her, until wave after wave of sensation seared through her, until convulsions started to overtake her, until her whole body spasmed against his . . . in a feeling so new, she thought she didn't exist.

"Oh, yes," she said, hearing her voice as though it were echoing from a cave . . . so far away was she.

"Oh, yes, Joshua. Oh, yes."

His kiss was again on her lips as he rolled with her, until chest touched chest, thigh touched thigh, and belly touched belly. Until she caught her breath, until she again knew where she was.

Thoughts re-entered her body. "Joshua, you didn't . . .. "

"Shhhhhh," he said, putting his finger to her lips. "I will. And you will again. I wanted to watch you. I loved watching you. You have never been more beautiful."

Kate could hardly stand it. Something extraordinary had just happened. He wanted her ultimate pleasure more than he wanted his own. And part of his pleasure was to watch her in hers. No man before had even cared. Bryan hadn't cared. He only wanted his own pleasure. He didn't know anything about hers. No wonder they parted with irreconcilable differences.

No wonder she had gone thirty-two years and never known the fulfillment of an orgasm with a man. Tears of happiness filled her eyes and rolled freely down her cheeks. His hands gently wiped them away. More took their place.

Then he was over her again. This time he slid inside of her. It was as though nothing had happened a few minutes ago. The feelings were brand new again. This time she knew the fullness of having him inside her. She thought she was going crazy. Her head wasn't staying on her neck. Her body was floating away. She had it all. The fullness of this man who loved her completely and would never leave her. "Why did I wait so long?"

"You're almost there, aren't you baby?" she heard from somewhere out in space.

"Yes," she said. "Yes. Yes!"

"Now?"

"Yes."

His thrusts were deep. She stopped knowing herself. She stopped knowing him. She only knew one.

"Oh! Oh, baby!" he said. His thrusts diminished, then stopped. The sensations stopped. All she knew was satisfaction. "I love you so," he said. "I love you so."

Curled into each others arms, they fell asleep. There was nothing but each other. All knowledge of the world outside had vanished, all remembrances of the hatred they would have to face was gone. All memories of past pain had disappeared. All hunger for anything but each other was no more.

When they woke, the sun was trying to set. The streets outside were packed with government workers wending their way home, oblivious of the two people, ecstatically happy, inside.

He played with her hair. He ran his finger down her nose.

She laughed. It tickled.

"Oh, I almost forgot," he said. I have a bottle of Chenin Blanc in the refrigerator. I'll get it." He was back with the bottle, a corkscrew and two glasses.

"To us," he said, after pouring the wine, propping up pillows and settling himself beside her.

"To us. For today and forever," she said, letting the warmth of the wine fill her to overflowing.

There was no sound in the room. Only their breathing. The time was now. "Joshua, I have something to tell you."

"What is it?" he said, almost indifferently.

"Bryan and I are divorced."

He was in the middle of sipping his wine. He coughed and almost dropped his glass. "Did I hear you right? Say it again."

"Bryan and I are divorced. It's final. I'm a free woman."

"I can't believe what you just said. I don't know what to say."

"Just say you're happy."

"Yes. Yes. I'm happy."

Then he was quiet.

"Joshua?"

"I didn't want my love for you to ruin your marriage. I didn't want to hurt you in any way."

"You didn't ruin our marriage, Joshua. It hadn't been good for a long time, even before I met you. Bryan didn't like me much in the last few years. And the stronger I got, the less he liked me. He wanted to run my life, and I couldn't let him, so he stopped liking me. And then, I didn't like him much either."

"In that case, I'm the happiest man in the world."

Nothing could go wrong after their beautiful afternoon. Joshua sailed through the last minute organizing duties for the march. Kate met thousands of marchers as they poured into the city, interviewing as many as possible. The march itself touched every caring cord in her body, seeing the 50,000 plus people, black and white, marching together from the Washington Monument to the Lincoln. Martin Luther King's speech made her cry. When it was over, they returned to Chicago, together, for a vacation. They spent the next week in bed, making love, drinking wine, eating crackers and cheese, and marveling at the miracle of their being together. Kate was sure it was she who was on the mountain, standing at its peak, seeing all the majesty below.

CHAPTER 58

Kate found ways to be in Washington, stories that just had to be covered. Joshua came home to Chicago as often as possible. Their summer of '64 was to be their first long time span together. Then she got the letter.

"My Darling Kate,

I think I've lost my mind, or else Birmingham blew me away more than I thought. You know SNCC has been registering black voters in Mississippi for a few years, and getting their heads knocked in for their efforts. Now they have got the damndest notion. They want to form a separate political party down there that they say will represent the true black vote. And even more ridiculous they're going to ask white kids to help. They're going to train them, they say. In what , I asked? In getting their heads knocked in like us? They told me they want me to head one of their centers. I said I'd do it.

You've affected my sanity, baby. It's got to be you. You and your idealism. Otherwise why would I have agreed to do this, when all I want out of life right now is to be with you for one whole summer? Besides that, I don't even believe in this non-violent shit. If those white bastards down there give me trouble, I'll hit them upside their heads. I'm not going to turn the other cheek. Not me.

I hate to miss our summer, baby, but it looks like I've got to do this. Can you talk 'Dirty Harry' or Ed, or whatever his name is, into sending you down to Mississippi for the summer to write about some freedom fighters?

I'll call you Friday. I love you.

Joshua"

Kate was disappointed, but not surprised. Somehow it was right for him to do this. He was more idealistic than he realized.

Later he told her on the phone, "Can you believe it, Kate? They want me to train those kids. They really want me to teach a bunch of white kids how to be black. I have to go to this God-forsaken town in Ohio to do it. You can write me in Oxford for two weeks."

Later there was another letter:

"Kate darling,

I miss you so. They've managed to do it to me all right. I never knew Ohio could be so bleak. And so lonely. I'm here trying to teach 300 idealistic white kids and a few dumb blacks what to do when some of those rednecks down in Mississippi give them trouble. Would you believe I'm trying to teach them about non-violence, for Christ's sake? And they're so naive. Full of ideals and no sense. No sense at all. You should see them playing at police harassment, at being in jail, and at living inter-racially. If we can get a little reality knocked into their heads, most of them will be all right. I should take them all on a trip to Forty-seventh Street, right? We sent 280 of them down there last week. I hope they make it. I know one thing for sure; it'll be full of surprises.

I miss you terribly. Why don't you get old Ed to send you out here to cover this mess. I could love you every night for a week, before I go into combat. Surely Ed would understand that.

All my love,

Joshua

P.S. We got word that three of our people are missing down in Neshoba County: two of our white staff and a black volunteer. People here are pretty upset. I knew it would be dangerous, but I didn't think they'd start killing us right off."

"My Darling Kate,

I thought Oxford was God-forsaken. You should see this town. But I'm here; I'm settled, and already I'm up to my ass in rednecks. None of us can walk down the street without the locals making a scene.

I'm not sure my mind is my own any more. I'm sitting in this office trying to write this letter and so far, I haven't been able to write a full sentence without interruptions. People keep coming in and out. 'I want for to read.

Where the teacher at?' 'This here boy here for the freedom school. Where I takes him?' 'You want I should register for this votin y'all's talkin bout?' 'Don know nothin bout this here Mississippi Freedom Party y'all's havin, but I's willin to come.' How do I explain to him, Kate, that it's a political party and he has to vote for it?

Besides that, two kids are scuffling in the back room. Albert just came in and said his car wouldn't start and did I think they'd put sugar in the gas tank. We just had a call from the FBI saying that they didn't have the authority to protect us if we insisted on allowing black and white freedom workers to walk down the street together. Julie told me that she needs a typewriter to type a report, and this is the only one that's working. Now two neighborhood people just came in with a pot of beans and hamhocks. I've got to find some plates and forks. And I thought Forty- seventh Street was a zoo.

Come down here, baby, and save my sanity. I need some of your loving. I'm off to find plates and forks.

I love you,

Joshua"

"To my favorite woman, Kate,

You won't believe it. I'm in jail. For picketing yet. For picketing a damned white-owned store that sits in a colored area. They charge twice as much as the other stores, all those stores downtown that the colored can't get to anyway because they don't have cars, and there aren't any buses. I'm not mad though . . . not a bit.

This place is worse than the Cook County Jail. There are forty of us packed into four tiny cells. I slept on concrete last night because the mattresses stink like old urine and vomit. Albert snored in my ear all night. The food is like gruel and we've decided not to eat. I'll be a shadow of my former self when you see me again.

I can't believe I'm here. For picketing yet. For smashing some damned cop in the nose, maybe. For beating up a whole army of those white punks that patrol past our office day and night, perhaps. But for picketing?

But I'm here, baby. I'm here. Don't worry about me though. We've got lawyers to get us out. We'll be back, ready for the local officials to start harassing again in a few days. They've got more ways to stop us from doing what we came here for than Carter has little liver pills. They're ingenious. But ingenious or not, we're still succeeding. People are registering in droves. And the locals can't stand it.

Right now I wish I'd never heard of Mississippi. I want to be in Chicago with you. I want to hold you. I want to feel you against me. Now, all I feel is cold cement. Except in my dreams.

Loving you always,

Joshua"

"Baby,

I've got news. And I've got a present for you. A very special present. I was in Natchez last weekend. God knows I needed the rest. I found this street right on the river, and it was like being back on Forty-seventh Street. They call it 'down under', like down under the bluff where all the rich folks live in these houses that look like they're right out of GONE WITH THE WIND. But 'down under' was alive. It's got jazz and blues and soul food and lots of pretty asses.

I stumbled into this little bar called Papa Jacks. It had the best blues in town. I practically lived there for three days. It not only had blues, but it had this old woman, so light that she could pass and her name was Delia. She felt like my grandmother or something. I don't know. I just liked her. She was the one that gave me your present. But I'm not going to tell you what it is. You're just going to have to come down here and find out.

When can you come down? Take a vacation. Forget 'Dirty Harry.' Forget that damned paper. Get down here where I can see you, and hold you, and forget all this crap that's going on down here. I'll take you to Natchez, and you can see Delia. Get here soon. I love you.

Joshua"

It was ringing and ringing. She was swimming under water. She had to swim up and up to find out why there was such a ringing in her ears.

It was the phone. It was 3 A.M. Her voice was raspy. "Hello."

Then she was awake. Wide awake. It was Mississippi.

"Is this Kate?"

"Yes."

"This is Albert. From Mississippi, you know."

"Yes."

"I'm sorry to have to wake you, but I thought you should know. Joshua's been hurt. He's pretty bad. His car was bombed. He's in the hospital."

"Oh, my God, Albert. Is he going to die?"

"All they'd tell me is that he is in stable condition."

"I'll be there on the next plane."

She had time only to pack and get to O'Hare. There was a plane at 7 o'clock that would take her to Jackson. There she rented a car. Harried and scared, she presented herself at the Freedom Office about 1 P.M. They sent her up the street to the Negro hospital. Their worried faces were hardly reassuring.

The nurse behind the desk was not glad to see her. "We don't want no trouble here," she said.

"Oh, no. I'm not here to cause trouble. Please, just tell me where he is."

"Room 203. Upstairs and to your right."

Kate didn't wait for an elevator. She took the steps two at a time . . . in spite of her skirt and high heels. She found him in a ward with seven other beds. His leg was raised in a cast and his head was bandaged. Tubes were connected to his arms and in his nose. His eyes were closed, and looked sunken.

She stood by the bed a few moments looking at him, then she closed her eyes and prayed. "Please, Joshua, be all right. Please be all right." The tears she had been bravely holding back, gave way and streamed down her cheeks.

When she could see again she noticed a nurse's aide standing by the end of the bed. "He's lucky to be alive, Miss. They was fixin to kill him, shore nuff. Them po-lice knows tha's the onliest way they was gonna git him. He's been stirrin em up something fierce ever since he's been here. Helpin us black folks an telling them white folks. An they don like it none."

"What happened to him?" Kate said anxiously.

"He jus drivin along in his car with Miz Julia an they pulls up along side him a yellin for him to stop. An then another car pulls up on the other side. An one a them cars throws a bomb an it explodes. Miz Julia, she almos dead. Mr. Joshua, he lucky. That bomb jus threw him out from the car an he lan with his leg under him an his head on a rock. He lucky. He jus got a concussion an a broken leg. He be all right though. Miz Julia, she ain't so lucky. She may not live to tell bout it. He gonna live though, shore nuff."

"He'll be all right?" said Kate, releasing some of the panic she had been holding since the phone call. "Thank you. Thank you. I didn't know."

"Yeah. He be all right. He too ornery to die."

Relief flooded over her now that she realized her worst fears were not going to come true. He was going to live. That's all she needed to know. Now she could begin to get information. "Who did it; do they know?"

"No, an they ain gonna know neither. Ain none a them white po-lice gonna try an find out. An them FBI, they pleads no jurisdiction so they ain gonna fin out neither. Wouldn't surprise me none if it were the po-lice themselfs."

"Is he conscious?"

"Off and on. That rock hit him pretty hard. He wake up soon." Then she looked quizzically at Kate. "You surprise me, bein here, you bein white an all."

"I . . . I'm his wife."

"Ohhhhhh! Well, is good to know you, Miz Thomas. Any kin a his, be a friend a mine, cause he done a lot for me. He done a lot for all us colored folks. He's a fine man, Miz Thomas. He be all right, don you worry none."

"Thanks for that. I have been worried."

"He be all right."

The nurse left the room just as Joshua opened his eyes. He smiled as much of a smile as he could manage. "Kate," he said, reaching for her hand. "I knew I'd find a way to get you here."

"There must have been an easier way, Josh. How do you feel?"

"Now that you are here, on top of the world." And his eyes closed again.

It was like that for two days. He slept. He woke up just long enough to know she was there. He slept again. The nurse threw her out every night at eight and wouldn't let her back in again until eight the next morning.

The first night at eight she went directly to the police station. There, a surly deputy took pride in his rudeness. He even used his southern charm to do it. She, however, used her best northern assurance and her newspaper credentials to try to get as much information as possible.

"I'm sorry, ma'am, we just have no information on the accident you are talking about. No information at all. Yes, I'm sure you would write a fair and non-judgmental piece, given as how you're a yankee and all, but we just have no information."

"Are you looking for any?"

"Why of course we are. You don't think we countenance bombings, now do you? No matter how low the scoundrel, we don't countenance bombings, no ma'am, we don't."

"Well, I'm sure that when Mr. Thomas wakes up, he'll have some information. And I assure you I will send that information along with this report from you to the wire services. Good night, sir."

"Now you don't have to get nasty about it, Miz. Andrews. You don't have to get nasty." But she was already out the door.

Back in her room her fingers couldn't write fast enough. The story, she titled: *The Police of Mississippi do their Dirty Work.*

Even exhausted, she dreamed of white-sheeted policemen in southern drawls, nicely, so very nicely, blowing up the freedom office.

It was three days before Joshua opened his eyes and kept them open. "Baby, what are you doing here?" he said.

"What am I doing here? I've been here for three days, don't you remember?"

"Three days. I've only been here a couple of hours."

"Four days, Joshua. You've been here four days."

"Four days! With my leg up in the air like this?" He lifted his head to look. "Owwwwww," he said, falling back on his pillow. "Owwwww."

"Be careful. You head took quite a bump."

"Yeah. It doesn't feel too swell."

The frown, that had furrowed her forehead since coming to Mississippi, lifted. Now she knew he would be all right.

The next day she began to interview. First, it was the students he had been working with at the freedom office, the students who had given up their summer to be in this place.

The young man named Albert: "He was in trouble from the moment he got here. He says what he believes, and he isn't careful about who he says it to. We love him for it, but the white officialdom doesn't. They don't appreciate it at all."

A young woman named Rosella: "I'm so tired. There's never any rest from the danger. We can't do anything without being afraid. Afraid of those roving cars outside, afraid to walk down the street because of what they'll throw at us, afraid to sleep in our beds because we might be bombed, afraid to call on the phone because they're tapped, afraid to talk to the colored people because of white retaliation, afraid **not** to talk to the colored people because they're the only friends we've got. Right now, I'm just afraid to live."

Another young woman named Sarah: "I'm so mad I could explode. Be non-violent they say. How can I be non-violent in the face of all this violence? Believe me, now I know what it feels like to live in a black skin. To be so mad you want to kill somebody and at the same time so afraid that you're frozen. And what's left is just to survive. No wonder they shut the door in our faces when we want them to register to vote. It's like we're trying to kill them."

A young man named Harry: "They told us what it would be like and I didn't believe them. It couldn't be as bad as they said. People aren't made that way, I thought. Mississippians aren't cruel, I said to myself. They're just misguided. But

Miss Andrews, it's worse. Worse than they told us. Worse than I could ever have imagined."

She interviewed people on the streets:

"Communist instigators."

"Them white girls ought to have their asses whipped. Sashayin around here with niggers on their arms. Maybe whippin's too good for em. Lock em up. That's what I say."

"What's it to you, yankee? Stay out of our business."

"I done gone to some a them rallies they been havin. Then I done lost my job. Now, I ain got no way to feeds my kids. I ain goin to no more a them rallies."

"I think they're right, Miss Andrews. I think those kids are doing exactly what needs to be done. But don't quote me. For God's sake, don't quote me, or my house will be the next one bombed. I wish I had their courage."

"All my time on this earth, I been prayin to God to save me from bein poor. An he don never save me. These kids, they comin long an they sees that we gits food on our table. An now I's got me a job. Them kids is better'n God if you's askin me."

"Why can't you northerners leave well enough alone? Everybody was happy before you came along stirring things up."

"Naw, I ain't talking to the likes of you. Get out of my face."

She interviewed city officials:

"Niggers was happy before them Communists came here to stir up trouble."

"It doesn't matter what you do, Miss Andrews. It doesn't matter what those kids do. Things are going to stay exactly the way they are, Miss Andrews."

"Get out of my office." Slam! ! ! !

"You know we have a White Citizen's Council he'ah to deal with these problems, now don't you, Mz Andrews? We don't need a bunch of nawthawnahs comin in he'ah telling us how to deal with these things. Ou'ah council has things very well undah control, thank you, Miz Andrews, thank you."

"Why don't you clean up things in your own back yard, Miss Andrews. Tell the nation how it is in Chicago. Tell them how your Mayor Daley runs Chicago, Miss Andrews. Tell them how benevolent your mayor is, Miss Andrews, to the Negroes in your city. Tell them that."

"We will run ou'ah police depahtment as we see fit, Miss Andrews. And I will thank you not to come in he'ah insulting ou'ah deputies."

She went back to her motel to write, muttering under her breath. "You think you can win, sitting there in your stinking offices, dictating your policies of oppression. You think you can win because you've got the power. Well, you shall soon see. I've got some power, too."

A WOMAN'S EYE VIEW
What's happening in Mississippi in this summer of 1964? Does this nation know? Three kids, who were part of a drive to register Negro voters were found missing in June. Everybody knew about that. It was on the wire services and in every paper. 'Time' and 'Newsweek' covered it thoroughly. But since then, what have you heard? What have you read? What have you found? Are they alive? Are they dead? Do you know? Do you care?

A war is being waged here in Mississippi, in the swamps and cotton fields. A war as savage as any war ever fought by this country. This time there are no well-equipped United States troops fighting for the high moral principle of democracy for all. This time, ostensibly, there is no savage foe trying to undermine the rights of human beings. Then what is this fight all about? And who are the troops doing the fighting? On one side are a group of idealistic white and black college kids who believe that America should practice what it preaches and give all of its citizens equal rights. On the other side are the Mississippi government officials, the White Citizen's Council, the Ku Klux Klan, and the white population in general who are saying, 'We are the only ones deserving equal rights. And right now we have the power to see to it that we are the only ones who have them.'

On one side is a commitment to see that Negro citizens get the right to vote, the right to an equal education, and the right to a place to play

away from the middle of the street. Non-violence is their tactic.

On the other side are bombings, fires, mental and physical harassment, economic sanctions, legal shenanigans, and a law that is stretched to unbelievable limits. All in the name of moral righteousness.

What is happening in Mississippi? Do you know? Do you care? Do you care to know? Because it is in the sleepy Mississippi towns that a true fight is being waged for the right to democratic ideals."

She made three copies. The first she sent to Ed in Chicago. The second went to the mayor, and the third to the chief of police . . . here in Mississippi . . . the two men who had so nicely told her to mind her own business.

When he was released, Kate picked up Joshua from the hospital, and together they drove out of town. As though he hadn't a worry in the world, he immediately fell asleep. She, however, felt totally paranoid. Every car looked as if it was coming down the road just to harass them, just to run them off, just to do them harm.

Back in Chicago, Joshua suffered his own paranoia. Every night he tossed and turned in the bed, waking at all hours yelling or cursing. Nightmares plagued him. His fever returned, calling for further doses of antibiotics. Kate spent sleepless nights wiping the sweat from his body, holding him in his terror, knowing his anger, his frustration, even his hatred. One night she found him throwing up in the bathroom. "I dreamed I was white," he said.

Fear hit the pit of her stomach. "You hate them?" she said.

"I hate them, yes." Then he was quiet for a moment. "You know, Kate, I didn't used to hate anybody. I just lived my life. If somebody got in my way I stopped him, black or white. If they didn't get in my way they were okay with me. But I think those people in Mississippi, they twisted my mind. They taught me how to hate. Now, when I see a white facc I know what's behind it, and I hate them for it."

Suddenly Kate's mind was full of pictures. What she saw was all the white people in Mississippi walking down the street. Joshua stood on the outside hating them all. And when she looked carefully at the faces, she was among them. She needed to say it. She didn't want to say it. She finally said it. "You haven't forgotten, have you? I'm white."

Joshua studied her for a moment. Then he grinned. "You're not white. You're my woman."

The pictures in her head disappeared. Her stomach unknotted. Now she could joke about it. "You're calling me colorless," she said, laughing.

"No. I think I just awarded you the prize of honorary Negro."

"I think I like that. Right now, I'm not too proud of my race. I don't mind trying on another one."

"Sometimes I'm not proud of mine, either, but maybe together we can . . ."

"Look out now, you might get idealistic."

"Get back in bed before I spank you."

By early September the worst was over. He had talked about it until he had it all out. He had kept secret what he had to keep secret. His night terrors were over. He had seen the results of the Democratic Convention as it was taking place in Atlantic City. He had seen the convention refuse to seat the alternate delegates from Mississippi they had worked so hard to send. He had seen his friends on television picketing and demonstrating. Watching them, he cursed his luck. When it was over he settled down to being home and loving Kate.

Kate took a week's vacation after Labor Day. They rented a cottage on Lake Michigan just south of Saugatuck. They spent the week sitting in the sun, cooking gourmet meals, sleeping on the beach, swimming in the cold waters of the lake, building fires to warm themselves and forgetting about the cruelties and absurdities of the world.

It was Friday night, September 8th, 1964. Kate would never forget it. She swam that day until she was blue from the cold. Joshua, still in his cast, stumped around on the beach searching for firewood. For dinner they roasted wieners on sticks, burnt marshmallows over the flames and consumed a whole bottle of wine. The moon was full, the breeze warm and their contentment was rampant. It was a perfect night.

They dragged an old log up to the fire. Joshua was leaning against it, and Kate snuggled into his arms. "I have something for you," he said.

"Ummm," she said sleepily.

"I got them for you in Natchez."

"What did you get for me in Natchez?" she said, vaguely remembering his letter.

"I got you these," he said, pulling an envelope out of his jacket pocket, then holding up a pair of gold earrings, about two inches long in the shape of a teardrop. They had some foreign carvings on them along with some long red lines. They sparkled as he held them up to the firelight.

"Oh, Joshua. Those are beautiful. Did you come into a fortune, or something?"

"No. They were a gift. Remember the woman I told you about in my letter, the woman, Delia? The one who owned that bar, Papa Jacks?"

"Yes."

"She gave them to me to give to you. Then she said something very strange. She said we were marked to have the earrings."

"What did she mean by that, Joshua?"

"I don't know for sure, but something strange happened to me when I met her, Kate. I felt as if I'd known her before. And like I'd seen these earrings before. I found myself feeling love for her, and yet I hurt when I was around her. I didn't understand it. I hurt and I felt peace at the same time."

Kate frowned. "That is strange, Joshua."

"She had to have some kind of vision I didn't know about. She even knew about you."

"She knew about me?"

"Yes, one night she said, 'You's got a lady you's lovin a lot, ain you? An she bein a white lady.' I said, yes, and then I told her about you."

"Then she said 'You takes these earrings an you give em to her. You tells her never to be takin em off. An if'n she needin to take em off, she be givin em to someone else who got a love as good as the one tween you'n her.' Then she told me the most extraordinary story. She said, 'You takes em. They was Mama's when she be alive an singin them blues richere in this place. She mos git herself killed over em, too. My papa, he a white boy, he givin em to her an he sayin they magic. He say they got a history all the way back to Africa an maybe more. He sayin they mean that they pledgin their love for eternity.' Then she said, 'You gives em to Kate an you haves yourself some magic, too.'"

"Kate, I cried when I took them. Something happened to me inside. And that very night I started to have dreams. And they were all about you. But then you would change into somebody else. And you kept getting away from me. I would chase after you and you'd be gone. One time I was chasing you in one of those old clipper sailing ships. You disappeared into a palace of some kind. Some ugly man stood at the door and laughed at me. It was an ugly cruel laugh. Then, on the next night, I dreamed I was a slave and my master wouldn't let me be with you. But we found ways to be together anyway. Then he found out and he killed us both. He burned us in a fire. Then, on another night, I dreamed I was on a hill with you and you ran away. You ran across a railroad tracks, and the train was coming. When the train was gone, so were you. And the strange thing about the dreams, Kate, was that in each dream your face changed, but you were wearing these earrings."

"Strange."

"I thought so."

"Maybe there was a message in those dreams, Joshua. Maybe Delia was right. Maybe I am marked to have the earrings!"

"Are you willing, Kate? It means that once you put them on, you will wear them forever. You can't take them off. And it means our souls unite forever. Is that what you want? It's what I want."

"Yes, Joshua. For now and forever. That's what I want if you want it."

"Good, then come to me. I'll put them in your ears."

Kate knelt in the sand in front of him. She reached up and unscrewed the little round pearls she was wearing.

He pushed the wire of the earring through her right ear. He said "Kate, I love you. I give you myself for now and for forever , such as I am."

Kate was startled. She felt him. She felt him come into her as surely as if he were making love to her.

Then he pushed the wire of the second earring through her left ear. He said, "Give me you, your love and yourself, for now and for forever."

"I will," she said.

She snuggled back into his arms. They were quiet, contemplative, studying the fire.

Kate broke the silence. "Joshua, you're right. They are magical earrings. I feel strange, and I feel wonderful. I feel like we are walking up there in the stars, looking down at two people lying on a beach in Michigan, who are very much in love."

Joshua loved her that night as never before, there in front of the fire, with the waves of Lake Michigan washing against the sandy beach. As the sound of the surf vibrated in her ears, she felt herself lifted away, back in time, to another place, to another life, a younger person, wearing these same earrings, feeling these same passions, loving this same man.

CHAPTER 59

A week later, Joshua went back to Howard and Kate back to Ed at *The News*. Kate's sadness was mitigated by the feeling of the earrings swinging from her ears; the knowing it was for eternity.

"Kate, pack your bags and go out to Berkeley. Some Goddamned kids are trying to close down the campus out there. Find out what's happening."

"I know what's happening, Ed. The students out there think the university administration is being unfair. They say their right to free speech is being violated. Basically, it's over a patch of sidewalk just outside the University. The administration has told them that they can't use it any more for displaying their literature and recruiting for their causes."

"Don't tell me what's happening. Just go out there and find out. Goddamned rich kids, anyway. Don't know what's good for them. Don't know the value of education. They'd know if they had to work for it, like I did. Stupid kids. Out there causing nothing but trouble."

"Ed, if you were out there, you'd be up to your eyeballs in nothing but trouble."

"Just hold your tongue, woman. Just hold your tongue. Go home and pack. You can be there in the morning."

Kate flew into San Francisco on Thursday morning, a week after Thanksgiving in the fall of 1964. It was almost noon by the time she got to campus. She had to elbow her way through a milling crowd of somewhere around two thousand kids to see what was happening. What was happening was that she saw a constant parade of police who were escorting student after student out of the administration building, and loading them into paddy wagons.

"What's happening?" she asked of anybody who would answer.

An unkempt-looking young man with a beard explained, with a politeness that belied his appearance, "It's because of the administration. They betrayed us. They promised there'd be no disciplinary action against our leaders and then they went and betrayed their word. They called four of them up. Mario Salvo, that's him over there, called this protest. There were about 800 of us camped out in there overnight. They're taking them out now."

"Where are they going to put 800 people?"

"I heard they were taking them to Santa Rita Rehabilitation Center. That's where they took the Japanese Americans in World War II."

Kate wandered around listening to the conversations and comments. Anger was everywhere. Betrayal was what they felt. Righteous indignation ran high. "We'll stay here until this administration gives in," was their battle cry. "Those God-damned men in their ivory towers aren't going to tell us what we can and can't do."

Kate began asking questions. She started with a beautiful girl with long, black hair and at least ten strings of bead around her neck. "This place is a factory," she said. "And we are the products. And we'll be damned if we're going to be what they want us to be."

Smelling publicity, a crowd gathered around her, all wanting to be heard.

"They're trying to manipulate us," said a blond girl in faded jeans.

"Yeah, they think they're our parents," said a boy with long hair and a scraggly beard.

"They don't want us to grow up," said a tiny child of a woman.

"There's no room for disagreement. If we don't like somebody's policies, and we say so, they punish us. This country is supposed to have free speech. They won't let us have free speech." He had to be an engineering student. Short hair and neat.

"They're intractable. As long as we do it their way, we're okay. But if we do it our way, we're in trouble. According to them, there's only one way. Theirs!" This from a smooth-shaven Negro boy with a colorful African shirt.

"See, we were trying to do something about civil rights, so we picketed this hotel and charged them with discrimination. The university didn't like it," said an oversized girl with a strong voice.

"You feel powerless to change anything, is that it?" asked Kate.

"Yeah, that's it. We can't change anything unless we take things into our own hands."

"And it takes a lot of you to get the administration's attention, is that it?" said Kate.

"It takes at least this many. We have to force them to listen."

"Yeah, and they pretend to listen until we quiet down. Then they betray us."

"Yeah."

"That's what they do all right."

"What is it you really want?" asked Kate.

"We want the right to do our thing, without somebody who doesn't know what they're talking about trying to stop us."

That answer brought nods all around.

"What if you hurt someone by what you do?" persisted Kate.

"They are the one's hurting people by doing nothing, by refusing to see the wrongs they are perpetrating."

"Ummmmm hmmmm. I can understand that."

There was a commotion at the edge of the circle. "Hey! Hey! Kate!" A pretty blond girl pushed her way to the center."It's Sarah. From Mississippi. Remember?"

"Sarah! Yes! The last time I saw you, you were shouting obscenities at some FBI man over the phone."

"Yeah. He deserved it, too. Hey, everybody. This is Kate Andrews. She writes for a newspaper in Chicago. She can help us. We can talk to her."

It wasn't long before Kate was spirited off to the cafeteria by Sarah and her entourage. She spent the rest of the day listening to their complaints, their philosophies, their concerns, their frustrations and their tactics.

On Friday, she was up early and back on campus. She went directly to the office of the President. There, she was met by a fussy little grey-haired secretary. "Dr. Kerr and Dr. Strong are both out to a meeting," she said.

"It's important that I see them. I'll wait," Kate said.

"You may have a long wait," said the secretary, with impaticnce. "They aren't expected back this morning."

"That's all right. I'll wait. I need to see them."

Around noon, two men emerged from the inner office, obviously going to lunch.

"Who are they?" Kate asked a young man sitting across from her.

"Don't you know? That was Dr. Kerr, with the bald head and the other man was Dr. Strong."

Kate took one moment to glare at Miss Fussy before she raced after the two men. The elevator door was just closing behind them. She hunted for the exit sign and ran down the stairs. She was outmaneuvered again. Their waiting car was just driving away.

She marched back into the office of the secretary. "You lied to me. I don't know who decided that Dr. Kerr and Dr. Strong were 'not in' this morning but you can take a message for them. Write this down. Tell Dr. Kerr that Miss Kate Andrews from the Chicago Daily News cooled her heels in his office for three hours this morning, while he was ostensibly 'out'. Since she saw him leaving his office at noon, she wonders about his definition of 'out'. Now she has only one side of the controversy to report, which she will do forthwith. Have you got that?"

"Yes, I have," said Miss Fussy, singing her words ever so nicely.

Kate took the next plane back to Chicago, writing furiously as she crossed the mountains of Colorado, the plains of Nebraska, and the farm lands of Iowa.

A WOMAN'S EYE VIEW
Events on the Berkeley Campus

**"The only thing I saw of them were their re-
treating backs. For three hours, I cooled my heels
in the office of the president and that of his assistant.
I had a simple request. Five minutes of their time to
get the other side. The students told me theirs in great
detail. But there is another side and I couldn't get it.**

**The students charged intransigence and betrayal.
Inflexibility and authoritarianism. A refusal to hear.
They say they are being treated like unruly children
with no rights by a parent who is turning out to be
repressive. They say their requests are not unreasonable. The right to free speech, the right to do what the
see fit in order to right the wrongs they see in society,
to work for the underdog, and to act with benevolence
toward those they see as being unfairly treated by society.
All they really want is a patch of, otherwise unused,
sidewalk on which to advertise their concerns.
These and a few others are the allegations and
complaints of the Berkeley students, now thousands
strong, demonstrating against what they consider to
be a restrictive and unfair policy by their administration.**

**I don't know the truth of the situation. Perhaps the
students ARE unruly children who need parental**

authority. Perhaps they are disruptive and need to be stopped. I don't know the full truth.

What I do know is what it was like to wait in the office of the administration for three hours and then be greeted by two retreating backs. It was there that I learned about intransigence. It was there that I learned about betrayal. It was there that I learned about what it was like not to be heard. After all, my request was only for five minutes of their time. Not an unreasonable request.

The students say they are being labeled unruly children when they respond to this intransigence by shouting louder . . . by disrupting and demonstrating. My simple request from the very same administration was met by a refusal to hear. I reacted like an unruly child.

I don't know the truth of the story. I could only get one side."

"Goddamn it, what is this?" said the cigar, pouring forth more smoke than usual and delicately holding her story by the corner of the page as if it were poisonous.

"Why, Ed, that's the story you sent me to California to get."

"I told you to get a story, not the ravings of a bunch of misbehaved adolescents."

"The story is the ravings of those misbehaved adolescents, as you call them. Their ravings were proved by the very behavior of that administration toward me."

"That administration has a reputation for fairness."

"I can't help their reputation, Ed They wouldn't see me to show me how fair they were. They had three hours of chance."

"Goddamned women reporters," he muttered, as he headed for the door. "Can't just get the facts. Can't just get the facts."

Kate decided to write her next column on hypocritical practices in the newsroom. About Editorial Directors who send a woman, with an avowed reputation for defending the underdog, to get that kind of a story, and then objecting to her point of view. Then she grinned. "You know what he is, Kate? He's really all bluff. He just has too much masculine ego to let you know he likes what you write."

A letter from Joshua was waiting for her when she got home. She tore it open.

"Kate,

I just had to write. I just met him, Kate. I just met the man who's going to lead the movement now. Malcolm X. He says it like it is, Kate, and he knows it like it is. He knows the games, the cons, the hustles, the drugs. He's done it all. Just like me. And he knows it's the white man who's forced us into the ghettos and onto the streets. He's my man, Kate. He says we won't be turning the other cheek ANY MORE. He says, if we want our freedom, take it. If we get shot at while taking it, shoot back. Now we've got somebody talking for us. Now that he's given up that religious crap, I can hear him. 'Right on!' I say. I'm going with him to New York next week to help him give a speech in Harlem. This is my chance, baby.

Did I tell you I love you? I do, you know. Christmas isn't very far away. We'll spend the whole day in bed.

Forever,
Joshua"

There is was. That familiar knot in the pit of her stomach. He'd met Malcolm X. Angry, experienced, awe-inspiring in his knowledge, fanatical in his teachings. Malcolm X: speaking the rage of the northern ghettos, throwing history at white superiority, advocating black separatism.

The knot in her stomach tightened. "If it comes to a fight, Joshua will be in the middle of it. God, I hope it doesn't come to that."

Christmas did come that year. When Joshua came home, all was forgotten: black separatism, the possibility of guns, the possibility of violence. They all took a back seat to two people in love.

It was music that took center stage. Chicago was full of it, just for them. Oscar Peterson's piano glorified the London House. They stumbled onto a little bar near Rush Street and found a singer with a soul, Ernie Harper. For weeks, he sang love songs just for them. Josh White was in Old Town. Kate fell in love with his eyes. Joshua refused to go back.

"Jealous?" she said.

They cooked dinner together, they ate by candlelight, they toasted each other with wine, they laughed, they cried, they made love. And there was no black separation. There was no white superiority. Only two happy people in love.

Joshua went back to Howard and Kate's fears eased.

In the late spring there came a letter that proved her fears well-founded.

"Kate, my love,

I have been in anguish for months now, over what I have to tell you. I have finally made my decision and there isn't any use in discussing it. Even though it causes me great pain, I cannot change my mind. I have decided I must live my blackness. I have decided to work with Stokely to promote Black Power. Now that Malcolm is dead, they need me.

I have decided that this is something I must do without you by my side. I ache to think of you not being with me in this fight, but it is one I must fight alone. My soul will always be with you, but now my body needs to be elsewhere.

I will be going to Africa this summer, probably to Ghana. Something is drawing me to Nigeria. I may go there also. If things go as I believe they might, some people will be killed. I may be one of them. If so, I want you to know my love will be with you even then. Take care of yourself.

Joshua"

Life stopped. Pain descended like a cancerous sword. She wandered her bedroom in a daze, reading and re-reading the letter, as if in one of the readings, the message might be different. She spent the night, sleepless, staring into the blackness. She went to work. Ed sent her home. She collapsed on her bed with a fever. She refused to eat. Her nightmares returned.

Every night it was the same. Joshua came to her, arms outstretched. Just as he was about to enfold her in his arms, his face turned into her father. She ran, screaming, into the night, the figure chasing her. Every night, she woke up screaming. Every night, she feared for her precious sanity.

Finally, in desperation, she called Jenny and pleaded for a house call. "I'll leave the front door unlocked," she said.

Jenny let herself into the house and found Kate asleep. She waited. She didn't have long to wait. First, Kate began to toss and turn in the bed. Then she began to whimper. This was followed by a blood-curdling scream exploding into the room.

The scream went on and on and on. Kate tore at her bed clothes, at her nightgown, at her face, at anything she could get her fingernails on.

Jenny jumped onto the bed and tried to grab Kate's hands. This only heightened her terror. The struggle escalated. Kate began to tear at Jenny, to scratch at her, to try to get at her eyes. Jenny began to know the strength that comes to one who is about to die. She knew Kate would kill her if she could. She had all she could do to dodge thrashing arms, at the same time, grabbing at flailing limbs. They tumbled over the bed. Jenny felt a tear on her face, and blood dripping down her cheek. With one final lunge she got a hold of Kate's arms and pinned her to the bed.

Kate twisted and contorted on the bed under Jenny's weight. She used all of her strength to get away. Screams exploded from her throat, one after another after another.

Finally the sound of the screams dropped in intensity and the contortions diminished. Tears took their place. Jenny picked up the limp Kate and held her. Now it was the tears that escalated until they had turned to sobs. Jenny was holding a much quieter Kate, who was now sobbing in her arms.

Jenny didn't move for fifteen minutes, for twenty minutes, for almost a half an hour, until the tears were becoming a trickle . . . until Kate slept from exhaustion.

Jenny settled herself against the backboard of the bed with Kate in her arms. She was in the same position when they both awoke in the morning. Jenny tried to move her paralyzed legs, deciding she had lost them forever.

Kate was demanding to know what happened. "Your face looks awful," she said.

"You're getting pretty uppity for someone as sick as you are," Jenny said.

"Sick," said Kate. "I'm not sick. See. I'm on my way downstairs for coffee." Kate hopped out of bed and immediately crumpled to the floor.

"You're sick," said Jenny, trying to stand herself up on her paralyzed legs. "Get back in bed."

"You're right. I'm sick. I'm sick," said Kate.

"I'm going to take your temperature," Jenny said, heading for the bathroom. "Don't try that again."

"Ah ha!" Jenny crowed. "A normal temperature. You've probably been faking all this time."

Kate smiled.

"I am going to give you a prescription. I want you to use this phone and call Ed," Jenny said, handing her the phone.

"Yes, ma'am. And what do you want me to tell him?"

"I want you to tell him that you won't be back to work until September."

"Oh, Jenny," Kate said, dropping the phone on the bed. "I can't do that. Ed's got this feature he wants me to write on . . . "

"You're not going to do anything else," Jenny said, retrieving the phone and handing it back. "You have no business working right now. Call Ed, and tell him you'll be back in September."

"You really think I need to do that?"

"Yes, you need to do that. I'm not going to let you do anything else."

"Well, in that case, aye aye, ma'am."

Ed was his usual furious self, ranting and raving, fuming and fussing He finally gave his okay, only after talking to Jenny and finding out that his favorite reporter was in more serious condition than he had been willing to believe.

Then Kate made a second call. It was to the owner of the cottage near Saugatuck. Eureka! The owner would be in Europe all summer and she would be able to rent it uninterrupted.

Healing happened slowly, but her days spent lying in the warmth of the sun, swimming in the cold waves, sailing a little boat she rented in Saugatuck, and just simply walking up and down the beach feeling the wind on her body, helped it along. She didn't read a newspaper. She didn't turn on a radio. She didn't watch television. She didn't want to know. She even missed the eruption of violence in Watts. When a neighbor told her about it, she didn't even care.

The summer was almost over before she went back to her typewriter for anything. Then, it was only to revise her dissertation on the oppression of women. There was a publisher who wanted to print it in book form.

In the fall, she went back to work, still with the ache in her soul, but the summer had given her back her healthy body. Again, she could bend her mind to the events of the nation.

Those events happened so fast she could hardly keep up with them. After the Watt's explosion, there were other ghettos that followed. The war in Vietnam accelerated. The death toll rose, followed by the draft toll. Johnson tried to fool the nation with "Guns and Butter" as his slogan. Students erupted against the war, against Johnson, against university administrations, against almost anything they didn't like. There was Black Power, Stokely Carmicheal, H. Rap Brown, the Black Panthers, the P. Stone Rangers, and the white backlash. Martin Luther King won the Nobel Peace Prize for his non-violent efforts toward racial integration. Martin Luther King was shot; the ghettos were burned. Eugene McCarthy ran for president. Robert Kennedy ran for president. Robert Kennedy was shot. The nation was shocked. The hippies flourished. Haight-Ashbury happened. Kids were stoned out of their minds, first on 'pot', then on 'speed', then on heroin. Mayor Daley ordered police to shoot to kill when Chicago's ghettos erupted. Black Panther Fred Hampton was killed in his Chicago apartment. Black Panthers served breakfast to kids in the ghettos. Chicago was smothered under twenty-seven inches of snow, paralyzing the city. Women's liberation became an issue. Chicago was assaulted at the Democratic National Convention of 1968 by Hippies, Yippies, and what have you. Daley ordered a force of 25,000 police and national guardsmen to maintain order. Order was not maintained. Humphrey was nominated in a hollow victory. He ran against Nixon, and Nixon won on a promise to put the nation back together again. Weathermen appeared and destroyed and destroyed and destroyed. Oscar Brown Jr. wrote "Brother, Where Are You?"

Kate was everywhere. Her interviewing style gained her the reputation for getting at the truth. Her columns and books gave her broader and broader exposure. She worked night and day and weekends. When she wasn't working at the paper, she was working on her next book. Her book on the oppression of women was published in 1966, and a book of her best columns in 1968. As if a woman obsessed, she started on another one. Between times, she spoke at universities, women's conventions and to any organization that wanted to hear her views.

Occasionally she dated. Men from the paper, men in politics, men she met on her travels: students, demonstrators, businessmen. They never stayed. One or two dates, and they were gone. At every meeting, T.V. interview and speech, the same earrings swung from her ears.

Sometimes people gave her news of Joshua. She heard he had left Howard. She heard he was working with Stokely. She heard he had joined the Black Panthers. She heard he was making speeches: in Harlem, in Boston, in Detroit, in Los Angeles. She heard he was in Chicago. Her heart stopped beating.

One night toward the end of 1969, she began to have dreams. Dreams of women she didn't know, yet somehow knew she did know. There were three of them. They named themselves. "Amanda," said one. "Duanna," said another. "Sabia," said a third.

They came and they went. They revealed themselves, they hid themselves. They darted at her from all sides. They stood solemnly in front of her. They talked in voluminous words. They were silent. She knew them, one from the other. She knew them not.

She learned about a woman named Lena, a psychic who would help her. She lay on a mattress under the spell of Lena's hypnotic powers and the heady incense of a lamp.

She started to wake up.

'Kate'

CHAPTER 60

Kate opened her eyes. It was dark in the room. A candle that was burning on the mantle illuminated Lena's form. The sweet smell of the lamp still pervaded.

Today there was no grief. Today she felt alive in every pore of her body, as though years and years of burdens had been lifted from her shoulders. She swung herself into a sitting position, pulling her legs up to her chin . . . resting . . . with her arms wrapped around them. "What time is it, Lena?" she asked.

"Mos 6 o'clock."

"What day is it?"

"Is Sunday mornin fore folks be goin to them churches."

"MMMmmmmmm," said Kate. She had never felt so peaceful. She felt as if she was floating on a cloud of peace and all she wanted was for her cloud of peace to stay. Lena's clock was ticking. Somebody outside started a car and she heard the whir of its motor. She thought she heard rain on the roof.

She closed her eyes to soak in the peace. Then she felt their presence. She knew they were not through with her.

When she opened her eyes, Lena was still illuminated by the candle, but the other one was there - in the shadows. Not standing - floating. Not real - a dream. She was dark of skin and short of hair. Sabia.

"Kate, you have lived your life well. You have learned much in your living, and in your reliving. Now it is time to decide."

"Decide what?" said Kate.

But she was gone.

To be replaced by another, still dark of skin, but longer of hair . . . Amanda Rochelle. "It is time, Kate. What will you do?"

"I don't know," said Kate.

And Amanda faded from sight.

To make room for a small figure in white with a purple sash. It was Duanna. "Your destiny," she said. "Have you decided?"

"Don't go," said Kate. "I don't understand what my destiny is supposed to be."

"To take your power as a woman. The power of knowing **all** that you are. Will you take it?"

"If that is my destiny, I can take it. Now I can take it. I have lived your pain, all three. I have no more fear of it. I have lived your joy, all three, which is sometimes more fearful than the pain and I have lost my fear of laughter and fun and playfulness. Now I know that I can live and I can die, and live and die again and each time I live I can fight for what I believe. I can be strong or I can be weak, and each is all right. I can be brave, and I can be scared. I can be angry and give in to despair or I can be angry and I can act. I have all of that in me and what I know now that I didn't know before is that **that** is my place of power: to feel everything, and therefore to **know** everything and from there to act."

"Yes," said Duanna, beginning to fade. "To know is to give up fear. To give up the fear of knowing is to take your power. To be powerful is to act."

And she was gone. To be replaced by another. Sabia. "Are you ready to take your spirit?"

"My spirit?"

"Yes. Are you ready to know what you can never know, to go where you can never go, and to be who you can never be?"

"Yes. Now I know that you do not speak in absurdities, but in truths. Now I know what was senseless makes perfect sense. Now I am open to all possibilities."

"Then take your spirit into you. To be open to all possibilities will give you your spirit." And Sabia was gone.

"And what about love?" said Amanda, now floating where Sabia had been. "Are you ready to suffer the pain of love? To suffer the pain of saying all of your truth in order to love?"

"Yes. I have learned that to truly love I must always speak the truth. What I now know that I didn't know before is: sometimes, to truly love means to give up what I love. If I speak the truth . . . I take the chance of giving up what I love. If I accept without malice . . . I love. and then to fulfill love, I must walk away . . . to let the truth grow or die . . . without me."

"Yes," said Amanda. "To love is often to give up love."

And she was joined by her sisters. But now there were four. A fourth woman stood with them. She was the hope of their fulfillment. Kate of the shadows stood with her sisters.

"I give you my talent . . . to finish my life," said Amanda.

"I give you my magic . . . to finish my life," said Sabia.

"I give you the holy love of a child . . . to finish my life," said Duanna.

"And I give you yourself," said Kate of the shadow.

"I will not disappoint you," said Kate. "I am ready to tell the world. I am ready to finish what was never finished."

"It is time," said they all.

"You will live," said Kate of the shadow, "and you will finish what your sisters could not."

"And I will love," said Kate.

And they were gone . . . never to populate her life in their shadowy selves again.

As they left, a breath of Lake Michigan air wafted through the closed window, lifting away the last scent of the lamp.

"Lena?"

"Whachu wantin now?"

"I know what I'm going to do."

"I ain likin what you's thinkin."

"I'm going to write a book about all this. You're going to be in my book."

"Ain gonna be in no book. I tole you afore we starts I don wan you writin nothin bout me."

"But Lena . . .."

"Don you 'but Lena' me. Ain gonna be in no book. You forgits bout that."

"I can't forget it, Lena. It's part of me now, and I've got to be who I am. I've got to tell the world about what I know. That's my talent. That's where my power lies. That's how I express my spirit. Now that I know, I have to do."

"Din reckon you was gonna write no book. You spresses yourself any way you wants but you ain gonna write bout me in no book."

And so it was that Kate left the house on South Damen as she had come, fighting with Lena. This was as it should be. Their love was not forever . . . and it was time for Kate to leave it . . . as she had left so much else . . . to make room for the new.

That night, the four came one more time . . . to tell her one more time. "Well done," they said. One by one, they told her, "Well done." And they left, for the last time, to make room for the new. To make room for her final destiny.

CHAPTER 61

For Kate, 1970 was a wonderful year. For America, it was a year that reached the pinnacle of the bizarre. Disruption of anything came almost to be expected. Riots proliferated. Buildings exploded, killing innocents. Rock music blared from everywhere. Concerts turned into melees, reversing the spirit of Woodstock. Clothes were so bizarre, they were beyond description. Sex, drugs, and radical social behavior became the norm among the young. What had been called love was turning ugly, selfish, and squalid. Kate covered it all with increasing dismay, wondering what had happened to the high ideals with which it had begun.

Then in May came a phenomena. It was Kent State. Four white students were killed in a demonstration against whatever.

Uprisings erupted on campuses across the nation.

Kent State, for all its despair, turned out to be the knife that severed the cord of discord. The nation was spent. The violence untenable. By fall, it was over. The draft was ended, and the flame went out. America, for whatever reason, settled down to search for a different kind of power, a different sort of equality, a new kind of wisdom.

Everything went back to normal. Nothing would be normal again. There was a new freedom that could not be denied. A new disdain for the power of the authority, a new recognition of hypocrisy in high places. A new impatience for waiting. A new sense of freedom for the individual.

For Kate, each day was alive with newness. She lived life to its fullest, with a vibrancy that was infectious. Each night she labored at her typewriter, determined to tell the story, her story of love and internal power, and the power of the spirit, her story of four women. Each night the earrings swung from her ears, illuminated by the light of her desk lamp, a symbol of what was missing.

It was May of 1971, more than a year after she had last seen Lena, when the doorbell rang. "Damn," she said. "One thing I don't need tonight is company."

She padded down the stairs in her bare feet, dressed in her writing costume: her faded blue jeans with the frayed knees and her oversized floppy shirt. She had managed to get ink smudged on her nose. She was planning to throw the intruder out.

She opened the door.

"My God," she said. "Joshua."

"I've been watching you through the window for over an hour now. I've been across the street trying to get up enough courage to ring this bell. I'll leave if you want, but I had to see you this one more time."

"No. Don't leave. Please don't leave. Just hold me."

She was in his arms. She was smelling his manhood. She was crying. "Have you come back?"

"I've come back, if you'll have me. I know now what I want. No matter what life is, it's nothing without you. But if you want nothing to do with me, I don't blame you."

"I've never wanted anyone but you, Joshua. Then, or now, or anytime in between. Just keep holding me, so I'll really know you're here. Just keep holding me."

"I'll hold you forever, if you'll have me. I'll never let you go again. Never again. How long I have wanted to feel you against me like this."

His kiss was everything she'd never forgotten.

He grabbed her hand and led her upstairs to the bedroom. He pulled her onto the bed with him. "I want more than anything to know, again, our bodies together. I want to be one with your soul like we were. I thought during all those years, that it was my soul I was looking for, my black soul. But no matter how hard I searched, and no matter what fight I fought, and no matter what part of my soul I thought I had, it was empty without you."

And as they loved that night, two tormented souls that had been lost in search of themselves, were found. Two bodies came together with passion - the passion of six years of longing, of yearning, of unfulfillment. His hands, those hands that contained it all, touched her in all the lonely spots, in all the places of pent-up pain, in all the places that only he knew, in all the sources of her ecstasy.

She touched him, again, with the newness of herself. The newness that was the same in its love for him. To reawaken her passion. To reawaken her sensuality. To be everything that was herself.

He came into her that night as never before. Out of his own pain. The pain of searching and not finding. For ending his search where he had started, in the whiteness of her body. In the blackness of his.

She took him into herself on that night as never before. As a completeness of herself. As she had taken three other women. To be separate, yet apart.

When they came to the fullness of themselves, he exploded into her softness losing the hardness that was man, while she took in his power, losing the fragility that was woman. They merged. Man and woman. Woman and man. One soul. To take their lives and live them to the fullest . . . together. To face whatever came their way with the strength of love, each with their own power, each with their own self, to give and to take, to fight and to harmonize, in two to become one, and in one to become two.

The earrings swung in the night, shining from the rays of the moon that streamed through her window. A pair of earrings in the shape of a tear drop. Two inches long, and one inch wide at their widest. A name was written in Egyptian hieroglyphics, the name Amon. But now there were no little red rivulets that had ended in what looked like little droplets of blood. The rivulets were no more. Death was outwitted that night. Life prevailed.

When their bodies again lay spent and satisfied, and he held her in his arms, she had to tell him. "Joshua, while you were gone, the most incredible thing happened. I was having these terrible dreams about women I didn't know. Yet, somehow I knew I did know. I went to see this old, old woman named Lena who lived on South Damen and she . . .. "

ABOUT THE AUTHOR:

What can I say about myself? I can talk about the usual: married for twenty-five years, currently divorced, mother of two grown girls, in private practice as a Gestalt Therapist. I was educated through the Ph.D. level at Northwestern University, took a recent sabatical of three years traveling to Europe, India and Africa, am living in a log cabin in the woods in southern Indiana, etc. etc. etc. But none of these say much about the essence of me. I believe the essence of me is written in the theme of this book: a search for myself . . . a search for **my** destiny. I believe that my whole life has been a search for myself. Who is this woman named Audrey Savage? I have looked everywhere. I have hunted in the area of relationships . .this has taken me all the way from warmth and wonderfulness to the horror of a rapist. I have searched in the area of the intellect . . . this has taken me through three degrees and (briefly) into the ivory tower. I have searched in the area of my career. . . this has taken me through three professions: one as a speech and language therapist and university instructor, one as a psychotherapist and now as a writer. I have searched in the area of my emotions . . . this has taken me into spaces inside myself that were beyond my wildest dreams. But writing this book has taken me on my most meaningful search yet . . . my search into my spirituality and my womanness. (And, glory be, they are one and the same). The women who populate this book came to my mind, I believe, to teach me this lesson. They clearly were not randomly chosen. They came to me in various ways - to tell me I must write about them. They came to me in various ways to tell me I must write **this** book . . .this story. Through all of the rejections from established publishers . . . and even from publishers of women's books, I often wondered why I was driven to write this particular story. But none the less, through one lonely year in an unheated summer cabin in Wisconsin - with no electricity, no running water, and no interruptions - write it I did. It was the most peaceful and one of the most powerful experiences of my life. And through that experience I believe I found my spritual path . . . and myself. And now that I've found myself, I know my destiny. . . as Kate knows hers. I've always lived it, but now I **know** it. I hope that by knowing Kate and her search for **her** destiny, you will either be encouraged to begin your journey into destiny or validated in your already-established path.

ORDER FORM

______WORD WEAVER PUBLISHING CO.
______P.O. BOX 30072 - B
______INDIANAPOLIS, IN. 46230
______(317) 253 - 5160

Please send me___ copies of THE FOURTH WOMAN by Audrey Savage

NAME:____

ADDRESS: ______________________________________

__________________________Zip______________

Enclosed $9.95 for each book.
Indiana residents, please add
$.50 sales tax.
Shipping: $1 for the first book and $.50
for each additional book

Books: $ ______

Sales Tax:$

Shipping:$ ______

Total Enclosd:$______

I understand that I may return the book for a full refund if not totally satisfied.

I am interested in your lectures and workshops. Please send me a free brochure.

Word Weaver Publishing Co.
P.O Box 30072 - S
Indianapolis, Indiana 46230

ORDER FORM

WORD WEAVER PUBLISHING CO.
P.O. BOX 30072 - B
INDIANAPOLIS, IN. 46230
(317) 253 - 5160

Please send me___ copies of THE FOURTH WOMAN by Audrey Savage

NAME:____

ADDRESS:______________________________________

______________________________Zip_______________

Enclosed $9.95 for each book.
Indiana residents, please add
$.50 sales tax.
Shipping: $1 for the first book and $.50
for each additional book

Books: $ ______

Sales Tax:$

Shipping:$ ______

Total Enclosd:$______

I understand that I may return the book for a full refund if not totally satisfied.

I am interested in your lectures and workshops. Please send me a free brochure.

Word Weaver Publishing Co.
P.O Box 30072 - S
Indianapolis, Indiana 46230